The
Big Knockover

The
Big Knockover

Selected Stories and Short Novels of

DASHIELL HAMMETT

Edited and with an Introduction by
LILLIAN HELLMAN

VINTAGE BOOKS

A Division of Random House
NEW YORK

VINTAGE BOOKS EDITION, October 1972

Copyright © 1962, 1965, 1966, by Lillian Hellman
Copyright 1924, 1925, 1926, 1927, 1929, by Pro-Distributors
Company, Inc.
Copyright renewed, 1951, 1952, 1953, 1954, 1956, by Popular
Publications, Inc., assigned to Lillian Hellman as successor to
Dashiell Hammett

Library of Congress Cataloging in Publication Data

Hammett, Dashiell, 1894–1961.
The big knockover.

I. Title.
[PZ3.H1884Bi 6] [PS3515.A4347]   813'.5'2   72–1750
ISBN 0–394–71829–1

Manufactured in the United States of America

INTRODUCTION
by Lillian Hellman

For years we made jokes about the day I would write about him. In the early years, I would say, "Tell me more about the girl in San Francisco. The silly one who lived across the hall in Pine Street." And he would laugh and say, "She lived across the hall in Pine Street and was silly." "Tell more than that. How much did you like her, and—?" He would yawn. "Finish your drink and go to sleep." But days later, maybe even that night, if I was on the find-out kick, and I was, most of the years, I would say, "Okay, be stubborn about the girls. So tell me about your grandmother and what you looked like as a baby." "I was a very fat baby. My grandmother went to the movies every afternoon. She was very fond of a movie star called Wallace Reid and I've told you all this before." I would say I wanted to get everything straight for the days after his death when I would write his biography and he would say that I was not to bother writing his biography because it would turn out to be the history of Lillian Hellman with an occasional reference to a friend called Hammett.

The day of his death came almost five years ago, on January 10, 1961. I will never write that biography because I cannot write about my closest, my most beloved friend. And maybe, too, because all those questions through all the thirty-one on and off years, and the sometime answers, got muddled, and life changed for both of us and the questions and answers became one in the end, flowing together from the days when I was young to the days when I was middle-aged. And so this will be no attempt at a biography of Samuel Dashiell Hammett, born in St. Mary's County, Maryland on May 27, 1894. Nor will it be a critical appraisal of the stories in this book. There was a day when I thought all of them very good. But all of them are not good, though most of them, I think, are very good. It is only right to say immediately that, by publishing them at all, I have done what Hammett did not want to do: he turned down offers to republish the stories, although I never knew the reason and never asked. I did know, from what he said about "Tulip," the unfinished novel that is included in this book, that he meant to start a new literary life and maybe didn't want the old work to get in the way. But sometimes I think he was just too ill to care, too worn out to listen to plans or read contracts. The fact of breathing, just breathing, took up all the days and nights.

In the First World War, in camp, influenza led to tuberculosis and Hammett was to spend years after in army hospitals. He came out of the Second World War with emphysema, but how he ever got into the Second World War, at the age of forty-eight, still bewilders me. He telephoned me the day the army accepted him to say it was the happiest day of his life and before I could finish saying it wasn't the happiest day of mine and what about the old scars on his lungs, he laughed and hung up. His death was caused by cancer of the lungs, discovered only two months before he died. It was not operable—I doubt that he would have agreed to an operation even if it had been—and so I decided not to tell him about the cancer. The doctor said that when the pain came it would come in the right chest and arm, but that the pain might never come. The doctor was wrong: only a few hours after he told me the pain did come. Hammett had had self-diagnosed rheumatism in the right arm and had always said that was why he had given up hunting. On the day I heard about the cancer, he said his gun shoulder hurt him again, would I rub it for him. I remember sitting behind him, rubbing the shoulder and hoping he would always think it was rheumatism and remember only the autumn hunting days. But the pain never came again, or if it did he never mentioned it, or maybe death was so close that the shoulder pain faded into other pains.

He did not wish to die and I like to think he didn't know he was dying. But I keep from myself even now the possible meaning of a night, very late, a short time before his death. I came into his room and for the only time in the years I knew him, there were tears in his eyes and the book was lying unread. I sat down beside him and waited a long time before I could say, "Do you want to talk about it?" He said, almost with anger, "No. My only chance is not to talk about it." And he never did. His patience, his courage, his dignity in those suffering months were very great. It was as if all that makes a man's life had come together to prove itself: suffering was a private matter and there was to be no invasion of it. He would seldom even ask for anything he needed, and so the most we did—my secretary and my cook who were devoted to him, as most women always had been—was to carry up the meals he barely touched, the books he now could hardly read, the afternoon coffee, and the martini that I insisted upon before the dinner that wasn't eaten. One night of that last year, a bad night, I said, "Have another martini. It will make you feel better." "No," he said, "I don't want it." I said, "Okay, but I bet you never thought I'd urge you to have another drink." He laughed for the first time that day. "Nope. And I never thought I'd turn it down."

Because on the night we had first met he was getting over a five-day drunk and he was to drink very heavily for the next eighteen years, and then one day, warned by a doctor, he said he would never have another drink and he kept his word except for the last year of the one martini, and that was my idea.

We met when I was twenty-four years old and he was

thirty-six in a restaurant in Hollywood. The five-day drunk had left the wonderful face looking rumpled, and the very tall thin figure was tired and sagged. We talked of T. S. Eliot, although I no longer remember what we said, and then went and sat in his car and talked at each other and over each other until it was daylight. We were to meet again a few weeks later and, after that, on and sometimes off again for the rest of his life and thirty years of mine.

Thirty years is a long time, I guess, and yet as I come now to write about them the memories skip about and make no pattern and I know only certain of them are to be trusted. I know about that first meeting and the next, and there are many other pictures and sounds, but they are out of order and out of time, and I don't seem to want to put them into place. (I could have done a research job, I have on other people, but I didn't want to do one on Hammett, or to be a bookkeeper of my own life.) I don't want modesty for either of us, but I ask myself now if it can mean much to anybody but me that my second sharpest memory is of a day when we were living on a small island off the coast of Connecticut. It was six years after we had first met: six happy, unhappy years during which I had, with help from Hammett, written my first play. I was returning from the mainland in a catboat filled with marketing and Hammett had come down to the dock to tie me up. He had been sick that summer—the first of the sicknesses—and he was even thinner than usual. The white hair, the white pants, the white shirt made a straight, flat surface in the late sun. I thought maybe that's the handsomest sight I ever saw, that line of a man, the knife for a nose, and the sheet went out of my hand and the wind went out of the sail. Hammett laughed as I struggled to get back the sail. I don't know why, but I yelled angrily, "So you're a Dostoyevsky sinner-saint. So you are." The laughter stopped, and when I finally came into the dock we didn't speak as we carried up the packages and didn't speak through dinner. Later that night he said, "What did you say that for? What does it mean?" I said I didn't know why I had said it and I didn't know what it meant.

Years later, when his life had changed, I did know what I had meant that day: I had seen the sinner—whatever is a sinner—and sensed the change before it came. When I told him that, Hammett said he didn't know what I was talking about, it was all too religious for him. But he did know what I was talking about and he was pleased.

But the fat, loose, wild years were over by the time we talked that way. When I first met Dash he had written four of the five novels and was the hottest thing in Hollywood and New York. It is not remarkable to be the hottest thing in either city—the hottest kid changes for each winter season—but in his case it was of extra interest to those who collect people that the ex-detective, who had bad cuts on his legs and an indentation in his head from being scrappy with criminals, was gentle in manner, well-educated, elegant to look at, born of early settlers, was eccentric, witty and spent so much money on women that they would have liked him even if he had been none of the good things. But as the years passed from 1930 to 1948, he wrote only one novel and a few short stories. By 1945, the drinking was no longer gay, the drinking bouts were longer and the moods darker. I was there, off and on for most of those years, but in 1948 I didn't want to see the drinking any more. I hadn't seen or spoken to Hammett for two months until the day when his devoted cleaning lady called to say she thought I had better come down to his apartment. I said I wouldn't, and then I did. She and I dressed a man who could barely lift an arm or a leg and brought him to my house, and that night I watched delirium tremens, although I didn't know what I was watching until the doctor told me the next day at the hospital. The doctor was an old friend. He said, "I'm going to tell Hammett that if he goes on drinking he'll be dead in a few months. It's my duty to say it, but it won't do any good." In a few minutes he came out of Dash's room and said, "I told him. Dash said okay, he'd go on the wagon forever, but he can't and he won't." But he could and he did. Five or six years later, I told Hammett that the doctor had said he wouldn't stay on the wagon. Dash looked puzzled: "But I gave my word that day." I said, "Have you always kept your word?" "Most of the time," he said, "maybe because I've so seldom given it."

He had made up honor early in his life and stuck with his rules, fierce in the protection of them. In 1951 he went to jail because he and two other trustees of the bail bond fund of the Civil Rights Congress refused to reveal the names of the contributors to the fund. The truth was that Hammett had never been in the office of the Committee and did not know the name of a single contributor. The night before he was to appear in court, I said, "Why don't you say that you don't know the names?" "No," he said, "I can't say that." "Why?" "I don't know why." After we had a nervous silence, he said, "I guess it has something to do with keeping my word, but I don't want to talk about that. Nothing much will happen, although I think we'll go to jail for a while, but you're not to worry because—" and then suddenly I couldn't understand him because the voice had dropped and the words were coming in a most untypical nervous rush. I said I couldn't hear him, and he raised his voice and dropped his head. "I hate this damn kind of talk, but maybe I better tell you that if it were more than jail, if it were my life, I would give it for what I think democracy is and I don't let cops or judges tell me what I think democracy is." Then he went home to bed, and the next day he went to jail.

July 14, 1965

It is a lovely summer day. Fourteen years ago on another lovely summer day the lawyer Hammett said he didn't need, didn't want, but finally agreed to talk to because it might make me feel better, came back from West Street jail with a message from Hammett that the lawyer had written on the back of an old envelope. "Tell

Lily to go away. Tell her I don't need proof she loves me and don't want it." And so I went to Europe, and wrote a letter almost every day, not knowing that about one letter in ten was given to him, and never getting a letter from him because he wasn't allowed to write to anybody who wasn't related to him. (Hammett had, by this time, been moved to a federal penitentiary in West Virginia.) I had only one message that summer: that his prison job was cleaning bathrooms, and he was cleaning them better than I had ever done.

I came back to New York to meet Hammett the night he came out of jail. Jail had made a thin man thinner, a sick man sicker. The invalid figure was trying to walk proud but, coming down the ramp from the plane, he was holding tight to the railing and before he saw me he stumbled and stopped to rest. I guess that was the first time I knew he would now always be sick. I felt too bad to say hello, and so I ran back into the airport and we lost each other for a few minutes. But in a week, when he had slept and was able to eat small amounts of food, an irritating farce began and was to last for the rest of his life: jail wasn't bad at all. True, the food was awful and sometimes even rotted, but you could always have milk; the moon-shiners and car thieves were dopes but their conversation was no sillier than a New York cocktail party; nobody liked cleaning toilets, but in time you came to take a certain pride in the work and an interest in the different cleaning materials; jail homosexuals were nasty tempered, but no worse than the ones in any bar, and so on. Hammett's form of boasting—and of humor, as well—was always to make fun of trouble or pain. We had once met Howard Fast on the street and he told us about his to-be-served jail sentence. As we moved away, Hammett said, "It will be easier for you, Howard, if you first take off the crown of thorns." And so I should have guessed that Hammett would talk about his own time in jail the way many of us talk about college.

I do not wish to avoid the subject of Hammett's political beliefs, but the truth is that I do not know if he was a member of the Communist Party and I never asked him. If that seems an odd evasion between two people we did not mean it as an evasion; it was, probably, the product of the time we lived through and a certain unspoken agreement about privacy. Now, in looking back, I think we had rather odd rules about privacy, unlike other people's rules. We never, for example, asked each other about money, how much something cost or how much something earned, although each of us gave to the other as, through the years, each of us needed it. It does not matter much to me that I don't know if Hammett was a Communist Party member: most certainly he was a Marxist. But he was a very critical Marxist, often contemptuous of the Soviet Union in the same hick sense that many Americans are contemptuous of foreigners. He was often witty and bitingly sharp about the American Communist Party, but he was, in the end, loyal to them. Once, in an argument with me, he said that of course a great deal about Communism worried him and always had and that when he found something better he intended to change his opinions. And then he said, "Now please don't let's ever argue about it again because we're doing each other harm." And so we did not argue again, and I suppose that itself does a kind of harm or leaves a moat too large for crossing, but it was better than the arguments we had been having—they had started in the 1940's—when he knew that I could not go his way. I think that must have pained him, but he never said so. It pained me, too, but I knew that, unlike many radicals, whatever he believed in, whatever he had arrived at, came from reading and thinking. He took time to find out what he thought, and he had an open mind and a tolerant nature.

Hammett came from a generation of talented writers. The ones I knew were romantic about being writers, it was a good thing to be, a writer, maybe the best, and you made sacrifices for it. I guess they wanted money and praise as much as writers do today, but I don't think the diseased need was as great, nor the poison as strong. You wanted to have money, of course, but you weren't in competition with merchants or bankers, and if you threw your talents around you didn't throw them to the Establishment for catching. When I first met Dash he was throwing himself away on Hollywood parties and New York bars: the throwing away was probably no less damaging but a little more forgivable because those who were there to catch could have stepped from *The Day of the Locust*. But he knew what was happening to him, and after 1948 it was not to happen again. It would be good to say that as his life changed the productivity increased, but it didn't. Perhaps the vigor and the force had been dissipated. But, good as it is, productivity is not the only proof of a serious life, and now, more than ever, he sat down to read. He read everything and anything. He didn't like writers very much, he didn't like or dislike most people, but he was without envy of good writers and was tender about all writers, probably because he remembered his own early struggles.

I don't know when Hammett first decided to write, but I know that he started writing after he left army hospitals in the 1920's, settling with his wife and daughter—there was to be another daughter—in San Francisco. (He went back to work for Pinkerton for a while, although I am not sure if it was this period or later.) Once, when I asked him why he never wanted to go to Europe, why he never wanted to see another country, he said he had wanted to go to Australia, maybe to stay, but on the day he decided to leave Pinkerton forever he decided to give up the idea of Australia forever. An Australian boat, out of Sidney for San Francisco, carrying two hundred thousand dollars in gold, notified its San Francisco insurance broker that the gold was missing. The insurance company was a client of Pinkerton's, and so Hammett and another operative met the boat as it docked, examined all sailors and officers, searched the boat, but couldn't find the gold. They knew the gold had to be on the boat, and so the agency decided that when the boat sailed home Hammett should sail with it. A very happy man, going free where he had always dreamed of going, packed his bags. A few hours before sailing time, the head of the agency suggested they give a last, hopeless search. Hammett climbed a smoke stack he had examined several times before, looked down and shouted, "They moved it. It's here." He said that as the words came out of his mouth, he said to himself, "You haven't sense enough to be a detective. Why couldn't you have discovered the gold one day out to sea?" He fished out the gold, took it back to the Pinkerton office, and resigned that afternoon.

With the resignation came a series of jobs, but I don't remember what he said they were. In a year or so, the tuberculosis started to cut up again and hemorrhages began. He was determined not to go back to army hospitals and, since he thought he had a limited amount of time to live, he decided to spend it on something he wanted to do. He moved away from his wife and children, lived on soup, and began to write. One day the hemorrhages stopped, never to reappear, and sometime in this period he began to earn a small living from pulp magazines and squibs and even poems sold to Mencken's *Smart Set*. I am not clear about this time of Hammett's life, but it always sounded rather nice and free and 1920's Bohemian: the girl on Pine Street and the other on Grant Street, and good San Francisco food in cheap restaurants, and dago red wine, and fame in the pulp magazine field, then and maybe now a world of its own.

July 18, 1965

This memory of Hammett is being written in the summer. Maybe that's why most of what I remember about him has to do with summer, although like all people who live in the country, we were more closely thrown together in winter. Winter was the time of work for me and I worked better if Hammett was in the room. There he was, is, as I close my eyes and see another house, reading *The Autumn Garden*. I was, of course, nervous as I watched him. He had always been critical, I was used to that and wanted it, but now I sensed something new and was worried. He finished the play, came across the room, put the manuscript in my lap, went back to his chair and began to talk. It was not the usual criticism: it was sharp and angry, snarling. He spoke as if I had betrayed him. I was so shocked, so pained that I would not now remember the scene if it weren't for a diary that I've kept for each play. He said that day, "You started as a serious writer. That's what I liked, that's what I worked for. I don't know what's happened, but tear this up and throw it away. It's worse than bad—it's half good." He sat glaring at me and I ran from the room and went down to New York and didn't come back for a week. When I did come back I had torn up the play, put the scraps in a brief case, put the brief case outside his door. We never mentioned the play again until seven months later when I had rewritten it. I was no longer nervous as he read it; I was too tired to care and I went to sleep on the couch. I woke up because Hammett was sitting beside me, patting my hair, grinning at me and nodding. After he had nodded for a long time, I said, "What's the matter with you?" And he said, "Nice things. Because it's the best play anybody's written in a long time. Maybe longer. It's a good day. A good day." I was so shocked with the kind of praise I had never heard before that I started out of the door to take a walk. He said, "Nix. Come on back. There's a speech in the last act went sour. Do it again." I said I wasn't going to do it again. He said okay, he'd do it, and he did, working all through the night.

When *The Autumn Garden* was in rehearsal Dash came almost every day, even more disturbed than I was that something was happening to the play, life was going out of it, which can and does happen on the stage and once started can seldom be changed.

Yesterday I read three letters he wrote to a friend

about his hopes for the play, the rehearsals and the opening. His concern for me and the play was very great, but in time I came to learn that he was good to all writers who came to him for help, and that perhaps the generosity had less to do with the writer than with the writing and the pains of writing. I knew, of course, about the generosity long before, but generosity and profligacy can intertwine and it took me a long time to tell them apart.

A few years after I met Dash the large Hollywood money was gone, given away, spent on me who didn't want it and on others who did. I think Hammett was the only person I ever met who really didn't care about money, made no complaints and had no regrets when it was gone. Maybe money is unreal for most of us, easier to give away than things we want. (But I didn't know that then, maybe confused it with profligacy or showing off.) Once, years later, Hammett bought himself an expensive crossbow at a time when it meant giving up other things to have it. It had just arrived that day and he was testing it, fiddling with it, liking it very much, when friends arrived with their ten-year-old boy. Dash and the boy spent the afternoon with the crossbow and the child's face was awful when he had to leave it. Hammett opened the back door of the car, put in the crossbow, went hurriedly into the house, refusing all cries of "No, no" and such. When our friends had gone, I said, "Was that necessary? You wanted it so much." Hammett said, "The kid wanted it more. Things belong to people who want them most." And thus it was, certainly, with money, and thus the troubles came, and suddenly there were days of no dinners, rent unpaid and so on; but there they were, the lean times, no worse than many other people have had, but the contrast of no dinner on Monday and a wine-feast on Tuesday made me a kind of irritable he never understood.

When we were very broke, those first years in New York, Hammett got a modest advance from Knopf and began to write *The Thin Man*. He moved to what was jokingly called the Diplomat's Suite in a hotel run by our

friend Nathanael West. It was a new hotel, but Pep West
and the depression had managed to run it down immediately. Certainly Hammett's suite had never seen a diplomat because even the smallest Oriental could not have
functioned well in the space. But the rent was cheap, the
awful food could be charged, and some part of my idle
time could be spent with Pep snooping around the lives of
the other rather strange guests. I had known Dash when
he was writing short stories, but I had never been around
for a long piece of work. Life changed: the drinking
stopped, the parties were over. The locking-in time had
come and nothing was allowed to disturb it until the book
was finished. I had never seen anybody work that way: the
care for every word, the pride in the neatness of the typed
page itself, the refusal for ten days or two weeks to go out
even for a walk for fear something would be lost. It was a
good year for me and I learned from it and was, perhaps, a
little frightened by a man who now did not need me. So it
was a happy day when I was given half the manuscript to
read and was told that I was Nora. It was nice to be Nora,
married to Nick Charles, maybe one of the few marriages
in modern literature where the man and woman like each
other and have a fine time together. But I was soon put
back in place—Hammett said I was also the silly girl in
the book and the villainess. I don't know now if he was
joking, but in those days it worried me, I was very anxious
that he think well of me. Most people wanted that from
him. Years later, Richard Wilbur said that as you came
toward Hammett to shake his hand in the first meeting,
you wanted him to approve of you. I don't know what
makes this quality in certain men—something floating all
around them that hasn't much to do with what they've
done—but maybe has to do with reserve so deep that we
all know we cannot touch it with charm or jokes or favors.
It comes out as something more than dignity and shows on
the face. In jail the guards called Hammett "sir" and out of
jail other people came close to it. One night in the last
years of his life, we walked into a restaurant, passing a

group of young writers I knew but he didn't. We stopped and I introduced him: those hip young men suddenly turned into charming, deferential schoolboys and their faces became what they must have been at ten years old. It took me years of teasing to force out of Hammett that he knew what effect he had on many people. Then he told me that when he was fourteen years old and had his first job working for the Baltimore and Ohio Railroad, he had come late to work each day for a week. His employer told him he was fired. Hammett said he nodded, walked to the door, and was called back by a puzzled man who said, "If you give me your word it won't happen again, you can keep the job." Hammett said, "Thank you, but I can't do that." After a silence the man said, "Okay, keep the job anyway." Dash said that he didn't know what was right about what he had done, but he did know that it would always be useful.

When *The Thin Man* was sold to a magazine—most of the big slick magazines had turned it down for being too daring, although what they meant by daring was hard to understand—we got out of New York fast. We got drunk for a few weeks in Miami, then moved on to a primitive fishing camp in the Keys where we stayed through the spring and summer, fishing every day, reading every night. It was a fine year: we found out that we got along best without people and in the country. Hammett, like many Southerners, had a deep feeling for isolated places where there were animals, birds, bugs and sounds. He was easy in the woods, a fine shot, and later when I bought a farm, he would spend the autumn days in the woods, coming back with birds or rabbits, and then, when the shooting season was over, would spend many winter days sitting on a stool in the woods watching squirrels or beavers or deer, or ice-fishing in the lake. (He was, as are most sportsmen, obsessively neat with instruments, and obsessively messy with rooms.) The interests of the day would go into the nights when he would read *Bees, Their Vision and Language* or *German Gun Makers of the 18th Century* or something on how to tie knots, or inland birds, and then leave such a book for another book on whatever he had decided to learn. It would be impossible now for me to remember all that he wanted to learn, but I remember a long year of study on the retina of the eye; how to play chess in your head; the Icelandic sagas; the history of the snapping turtle; Hegel; would a hearing aid—he bought a very good one—help in detecting bird sounds; then from Hegel, of course, to Marx and Engels straight through; to the shore life of the Atlantic; and finally, and for the rest of his life, mathematics. He was more interested in mathematics than in any other subject except baseball; listening to television or the radio, he would mutter about the plays and the players to me who didn't know the difference between a ball and a bat. Often I would ask him to stop it, and then he would shake his head and say, "All I ever wanted was a docile woman and look what I got," and we would talk about docility, how little for a man to want, and he would claim that only vain or neurotic men needed to have "types" in women—all other men took what they could get.

The hit-and-miss reading, the picking up of any book, made for a remarkable mind, neat, accurate, respectful of fact. He took a strong and lasting dislike to a man who insisted mackerel were related to herring, and once he left my living room when a famous writer talked without much knowledge of existentialism, refusing to come down to dinner with the writer because he said, "He's the greatest waste of time since the parcheesi board. Liars are bores." A neighbor once rang up to ask him how to stop a leak in a swimming pool, and he knew; my farmer's son asked him how to make a trap for snapping turtles, and he knew; born a Maryland Catholic (but having long ago left the Church), he knew more about Judaism than I did, and more about New Orleans music, food and architecture than my father who had grown up there. Once I wanted to know about early glassmaking for windows and was headed for the encyclopedia, but Hammett told me before

I got there; he knew the varieties of seaweed, and for a month he studied the cross-pollination of corn, and for many, many months tried plasma physics. It was more than reading: it was a man at work. Any book would do, or almost any—he was narrowly impatient when I read letters or criticism and would refer to them as my "carrying" books, good only for balancing yourself as you climbed the stairs to go to bed. It was always strange to me that he liked books so much and had so little interest in the men who wrote them. (There were, of course, exceptions: he liked Faulkner, and we had fine drinking nights together during Faulkner's New York visits in the thirties.) Or it is more accurate to say that he had a good time with writers when they talked about books, and would leave them when they didn't. But he was deeply moved by painting—he himself tried to paint until the summer when he could no longer stand at an easel, and the last walk we ever took was down the block to the Metropolitan Museum—and by music. But I never remember his liking a painter or a musician although I do remember his saying that he thought most of them peacocks. He was never uncharitable toward simple people, he was often too impatient with famous people.

There are, of course, many men who are happy in an army but I had never known any and didn't want to. I was, therefore, shocked, in 1942, to find that Hammett was one of them. I do not know why an eccentric man who lived more than most Americans by his own standards found the restrictions, the disciplines, and the hard work of an army enlisted man so pleasant and amusing. Maybe a life ruled over by other people solved some of the problems, allowed a place for a man who by himself could not seek out people, maybe gave him a sense of pride that a man of forty-eight could stand up with those half his age; maybe all that and maybe simply that he liked his country and felt that the war had to be fought. Whatever Hammett's reasons, the miseries of the Aleutian Islands were not miseries to him. I have many letters describing their beauty, and for years he talked of going back to see them again. He conducted a training program there for a while and edited a good army newspaper; the copy was clean, the news was accurate, the jokes were funny. He became a kind of legend in the Alaska-Aleutian army. I have talked to many men who served with him, and have a letter from one of them:

> I was a kid then. We all were. The place was awful but there was Hammett, by the time I got there called Pop by some and Grandpop by others, editor of the paper with far more influence on us, scaring us more in a way than the Colonel although I think he also scared the Colonel . . . I remember best that we'd come into the hut screaming or complaining and he'd be lying on his bunk reading. He'd look up and smile and we'd all shut up. Nobody would go near the bed or disturb him. When money was needed or help he'd hear about it and there he was. He paid for the leave and marriage of one kid. When another of us ran up a scarey bar bill in Nome, he gave the guy who cleaned the Nome toilets money to pay it and say it was his bill if anybody in the Army asked him . . . A lot of kids did more than complain—they went half to nuts. And why not? We had the worst weather in the most desolate hole, no fighting, constant williwaws when you had to crawl to the latrines because if you stood up the wind would take you to Siberia, and an entertainment program which got mixed up between Olivia De Havilland and recordings of W. H. Auden. But the main worry was women. When you'd been there a year all kinds of rumors went around about what happened to you without them. I remember nightly bull sessions in our hut about the dangers of celibacy. Hammett would listen for a while, smile, go back to reading or when the talk got too loud he'd

sigh and go to sleep. (Because of the newspaper his work hours started around two A.M.) One night when the session was extra loud crazy and one kid was yelling, Hammett got off his bunk to go to work. The kid yelled, "What do you think, Pop? *Say something.*" Hammett said, "O.K. A woman would be nice, but not getting any doesn't cause your teeth or hair to fall out and if you go nuts you'd have gone anyway and if you kiddies don't stop this stuff I'm going to move into another hut and under my bed is a bottle of Scotch so drink it and go to sleep." Then he walked out to go to work. We got so scared about losing him that we never said another word like that in front of him.

But as I have said, the years after the war, from 1945 to 1948, were not good years; the drinking grew wilder and there was a lost, thoughtless quality I had never seen before. I knew then that I had to go my own way. I do not mean that we were separated, I mean only that we saw less of each other, were less close to each other. But even in those years there still were wonderful days on the farm of autumn hunting and squirrel pies and sausage making and all the books he read as I tried to write a play. I can see him now, getting up to put a log on the fire and coming over to shake me. He swore that I would always say, "I haven't been sleeping. I've been thinking." He would laugh and say, "Sure. You've been asleep for an hour, but lots of people think best when they're asleep and you're one of them."

In 1952 I had to sell the farm. I moved to New York and Dash rented a small house in Katonah. I went once a week to see him, he came once a week to New York, and we talked on the phone every day. But he wanted to be alone—or so I thought then, but am now not so sure because I have learned that proud men who can ask for nothing may be fine characters in life and novels, but they are difficult to live with or to understand. In any case, as the years went on he became a hermit, and the ugly little country cottage grew uglier with books piled on every chair and no place to sit, the desk a foot high with unanswered mail. The signs of sickness were all around: now the phonograph was unplayed, the typewriter untouched, the beloved, foolish gadgets unopened in their packages. When I went for my weekly visits we didn't talk much, and when he came for his weekly visits to me he was worn out from the short journey.

Perhaps it took me too long to realize that he couldn't live alone any more, and even after I realized it I didn't know how to say it. One day, immediately after he had made me promise to stop reading "L'il Abner," and I was laughing at his vehemence about it, he suddenly looked embarrassed—he always looked embarrassed when he had something emotional to say—and he said, "I can't live alone any more. I've been falling. I'm going to a veterans' hospital. It will be okay, we'll see each other all the time, and I don't want any tears from you." But there were tears from me, two days of tears, and finally he consented to come and live in my apartment. (Even now, as I write this, I am still angry and amused that he always had to have things on his own terms: a few minutes ago I got up from the typewriter and railed against him for it, as if he could still hear me. I know as little about the nature of romantic love as I knew when I was eighteen, but I do know about the deep pleasure of continuing interest, the excitement of wanting to know what somebody else thinks, will do, will not do, the tricks played and unplayed, the short cord that the years make into rope and, in my case, is there, hanging loose, long after death. I am not sure what Hammett would feel about the rest of these notes about him, but I am sure that, in his mischief, he would be pleased that I am angry with him today.) And so he lived with me for the last four years of his life. Not all of that time was easy, and some of it was very bad, but it was an unspoken pleasure that having come together so many years before, ruined so much, and repaired a little, we had endured. Sometimes I would resent the understated, or seldom stated side of us and, guessing death wasn't too far away, I would try for something to have afterwards. One day I said, "We've done fine, haven't we?" He said, "Fine's too big a word for me. Why don't we just say we've done better than most people?"

On New Year's Eve, 1960, I left Hammett in the care of a pleasant practical nurse and went to spend a few hours with friends. I left their house at twelve-thirty, not knowing that the nurse began telephoning for me a few minutes later. As I came into Hammett's room, he was sitting at his desk, his face as eager and excited as it had been in the drinking days. In his lap was a heavy book of Japanese prints that he had bought and liked many years before. He was pointing to a print and saying to the nurse, "Look at it, darling, it's wonderful." As I came toward him, the nurse moved away, but he caught her hand and kissed it, in the same charming, flirtatious way of the early days, looking up to wink at me. The book was lying upside down, and so the nurse didn't need to mumble the word "irrational." From then on—we took him to the hospital the next morning—I never knew and will now not ever know what irrational means. Hammett refused all medication, all aid from nurses and doctors in some kind of determined, mysterious wariness. Before the night of the upside-down book our plan had been to move to Cambridge because I was under contract to teach at Harvard. An upside-down book should have told me the end had come, but I didn't want to think that way, and so I flew to Cambridge, found a nursing home for Dash and flew back that night to tell him about it. He said, "But how are we going to get to Boston?" I said we'd take an ambulance and I guess for the first time in his life he said, "That will cost too much." I said, "If it does then we'll take a covered wagon." He smiled and said, "Maybe that's the way we should have gone places anyway." And so I felt better that night, sure of a postponement. I was wrong. Before six o'clock the next morning the hospital called me. Hammett had gone into a coma. As I ran across the room toward his bed there was a last sign of life: his eyes opened in shocked surprise and he tried to raise his head. But he was never to think again and he died two days later.

CONTENTS

The
Big Knockover

THE GUTTING OF COUFFIGNAL

Wedge-shaped Couffignal is not a large island, and not far from the mainland, to which it is linked by a wooden bridge. Its western shore is a high, straight cliff that jumps abruptly up out of San Pablo Bay. From the top of this cliff the island slopes eastward, down to a smooth pebble beach that runs into the water again, where there are piers and a clubhouse and moored pleasure boats.

Couffignal's main street, paralleling the beach, has the usual bank, hotel, moving-picture theater, and stores. But it differs from most main streets of its size in that it is more carefully arranged and preserved. There are trees and hedges and strips of lawn on it, and no glaring signs. The buildings seem to belong beside one another, as if they had been designed by the same architect, and in the stores you will find goods of a quality to match the best city stores.

The intersecting streets—running between rows of neat cottages near the foot of the slope—become winding hedged roads as they climb toward the cliff. The higher these roads get, the farther apart and larger are the houses they lead to. The occupants of these higher houses are the owners and rulers of the island. Most of them are well-fed old gentlemen who, the profits they took from the world with both hands in their younger days now stowed away at safe percentages, have bought into the island colony so they may spend what is left of their lives nursing their livers and improving their golf among their kind. They admit to the island only as many storekeepers, working people, and similar riffraff as are needed to keep them comfortably served.

That is Couffignal.

It was some time after midnight. I was sitting in a second-story room in Couffignal's largest house, surrounded by wedding presents whose value would add up to something between fifty and a hundred thousand dollars.

Of all the work that comes to a private detective (except divorce work, which the Continental Detective Agency doesn't handle) I like weddings as little as any. Usually I manage to avoid them, but this time I hadn't been able to. Dick Foley, who had been slated for the job, had been handed a black eye by an unfriendly pickpocket the day before. That let Dick out and me in. I had come up to Couffignal—a two-hour ride from San Francisco by ferry and auto stage—that morning, and would return the next.

This had been neither better nor worse than the usual wedding detail. The ceremony had been performed in a little stone church down the hill. Then the house had begun to fill with reception guests. They had kept it filled to overflowing until some time after the bride and groom had sneaked off to their eastern train.

The world had been well represented. There had been an admiral and an earl or two from England; an ex-president of a South American country; a Danish baron; a tall young Russian princess surrounded by lesser titles, including a fat, bald, jovial and black-bearded Russian general, who had talked to me for a solid hour about prize fights, in which he had a lot of interest, but not so much knowledge as was possible; an ambassador from one of the Central European countries; a justice of the Supreme Court; and a mob of people whose prominence and near-prominence didn't carry labels.

In theory, a detective guarding wedding presents is supposed to make himself indistinguishable from the other guests. In practice, it never works out that way. He has to spend most of his time within sight of the booty, so he's easily spotted. Besides that, eight or ten people I recognized among the guests were clients or former clients of the Agency, and so knew me. However, being known doesn't make so much difference as you might think, and everything had gone off smoothly.

A couple of the groom's friends, warmed by wine and the necessity of maintaining their reputations as cutups, had tried to smuggle some of the gifts out of the room where they were displayed and hide them in the piano. But I had been expecting that familiar trick, and blocked it before it had gone far enough to embarrass anybody.

Shortly after dark a wind smelling of rain began to pile storm clouds up over the bay. Those guests who lived at a distance, especially those who had water to cross, hurried off for their homes. Those who lived on the island stayed until the first raindrops began to patter down. Then they left.

The Hendrixson house quieted down. Musicians and extra servants left. The weary house servants began to disappear in the direction of their bedrooms. I found some sandwiches, a couple of books and a comfortable armchair, and took them up to the room where the presents were now hidden under gray-white sheeting.

Keith Hendrixson, the bride's grandfather—she was an orphan—put his head in at the door. "Have you everything you need for your comfort?" he asked.

"Yes, thanks."

He said good night and went off to bed—a tall old man, slim as a boy.

The wind and the rain were hard at it when I went downstairs to give the lower windows and doors the up-and-down. Everything on the first floor was tight and secure, everything in the cellar. I went upstairs again.

Pulling my chair over by a floor lamp, I put sandwiches, books, ashtray, gun and flashlight on a small table beside it. Then I switched off the other lights, set fire to a Fatima, sat down, wriggled my spine comfortably into the chair's padding, picked up one of the books, and prepared to make a night of it.

The book was called *The Lord of the Sea*, and had to do with a strong, tough and violent fellow named Hogarth, whose modest plan was to hold the world in one hand. There were plots and counterplots, kidnapings, murders, prisonbreakings, forgeries and burglaries, diamonds large as hats and floating forts larger than Couffignal. It sounds dizzy here, but in the book it was as real as a dime.

Hogarth was still going strong when the lights went out.

In the dark, I got rid of the glowing end of my cigarette by grinding it in one of the sandwiches. Putting the book down, I picked up gun and flashlight, and moved away from the chair.

Listening for noises was no good. The storm was making hundreds of them. What I needed to know was why the lights had gone off. All the other lights in the house had been turned off some time ago. So the darkness of the hall told me nothing.

I waited. My job was to watch the presents. Nobody had touched them yet. There was nothing to get excited about.

Minutes went by, perhaps ten of them.

The floor swayed under my feet. The windows rattled with a violence beyond the strength of the storm. The dull boom of a heavy explosion blotted out the sounds of wind and falling water. The blast was not close at hand, but not far enough away to be off the island.

Crossing to the window, peering through the wet glass, I could see nothing. I should have seen a few misty lights far down the hill. Not being able to see them settled one point. The lights had gone out all over Couffignal, not only in the Hendrixson house.

That was better. The storm could have put the lighting system out of whack, could have been responsible for the explosion—maybe.

Staring through the black window, I had an impression of great excitement down the hill, of movement in the night. But all was too far away for me to have seen or heard even had there been lights, and all too vague to say what was moving. The impression was strong but worthless. It didn't lead anywhere. I told myself I was getting feeble-minded, and turned away from the window.

Another blast spun me back to it. This explosion sounded nearer than the first, maybe because it was stronger. Peering through the glass again, I still saw nothing. And still had the impression of things that were big moving down there.

Bare feet pattered in the hall. A voice was anxiously calling my name. Turning from the window again, I pocketed my gun and snapped on the flashlight. Keith Hendrixson, in pajamas and bathrobe, looking thinner and older than anybody could be, came into the room.

"Is it—"

"I don't think it's an earthquake," I said, since that is Rifle-shots, but of the sort that only the heaviest of rifles went off a little while ago. There have been a couple of explosions down the hill since the—"

I stopped. Three shots, close together, had sounded. Rifle-shots, but of the sort that only the heaviest of rifles could make. Then, sharp and small in the storm, came the report of a far-away pistol.

"What is it?" Hendrixson demanded.

"Shooting."

More feet were pattering in the halls, some bare, some shod. Excited voices whispered questions and exclamations. The butler, a solemn, solid block of a man, partly dressed and carrying a lighted five-pronged candlestick, came in.

"Very good, Brophy," Hendrixson said as the butler

put the candlestick on the table beside my sandwiches. "Will you try to learn what is the matter?"

"I have tried, sir. The telephone seems to be out of order, sir. Shall I send Oliver down to the village?"

"No-o. I don't suppose it's that serious. Do you think it is anything serious?" he asked me.

I said I didn't think so, but I was paying more attention to the outside than to him. I had heard a thin screaming that could have come from a distant woman, and a volley of small-arms shots. The rocket of the storm muffled these shots, but when the heavier firing we had heard before broke out again, it was clear enough.

To have opened the window would have been to let in gallons of water without helping us to hear much clearer. I stood with an ear tilted to the pane, trying to arrive at some idea of what was happening outside.

Another sound took my attention from the window— the ringing of the bell-pull at the front door. It rang loudly and persistently.

Hendrixson looked at me. I nodded. "See who it is, Brophy," he said.

The butler went solemnly away, and came back even more solemnly. "Princess Zhukovski," he announced.

She came running into the room—the tall Russian girl I had seen at the reception. Her eyes were wide and dark with excitement. Her face was very white and wet. Water ran in streams down her blue waterproof cape, the hood of which covered her dark hair.

"Oh, Mr. Hendrixson!" She had caught one of his hands in both of hers. Her voice, with nothing foreign in its accents, was the voice of one who is excited over a delightful surprise. "The bank is being robbed and the— what do you call him?—marshal of police has been killed!"

"What's that?" the old man exclaimed, jumping awkwardly because water from her cape had dripped down on one of his bare feet. "Weegan killed? And the bank robbed?"

"Yes! Isn't it terrible?" She said it as if she were saying wonderful. "When the first explosion woke us, the general sent Ignati down to find out what was the matter, and he got down there just in time to see the bank blow up. Listen!"

We listened, and heard a wild outbreak of mixed gunfire.

"That will be the general arriving!" she said. "He'll enjoy himself most wonderfully. As soon as Ignati returned with the news, the general armed every male in the household from Aleksandr Sergyeevich to Ivan the cook, and led them out happier than he's been since he took his division to East Prussia in 1914."

"And the duchess?" Hendrixson asked.

"He left her at home with me, of course, and I furtively crept out and away from her while she was trying for the first time in her life to put water in a samovar. This is not the night for one to stay at home!"

"H-m-m," Hendrixson said, his mind obviously not on her words. "And the bank!"

He looked at me. I said nothing. The racket of another volley came to us.

"Could you do anything down there?" he asked.

"Maybe, but—" I nodded at the presents under their covers.

"Oh, those!" the old man said. "I'm as much interested in the bank as in them; and besides, we will be here."

"All right!" I was willing enough to carry my curiosity down the hill. "I'll go down. You'd better have the butler stay in here, and plant the chauffeur inside the front door. Better give them guns if you have any. Is there a raincoat I can borrow? I brought only a light overcoat with me."

Brophy found a yellow slicker that fit me. I put it on, stowed gun and flashlight conveniently under it, and found my hat while Brophy was getting and loading an automatic pistol for himself and a rifle for Oliver, the mulatto chauffeur.

Hendrixson and the princess followed me downstairs. At the door I found she wasn't exactly following me—she was going with me.

"But, Sonya!" the old man protested.

"I'm not going to be foolish, though I'd like to," she promised him. "But I'm going back to my Irinia Androvna, who will perhaps have the samovar watered by now."

"That's a sensible girl!" Hendrixson said, and let us out into the rain and the wind.

It wasn't weather to talk in. In silence we turned downhill between two rows of hedging, with the storm driving at our backs. At the first break in the hedge I stopped, nodding toward the black blot a house made. "That is your—"

Her laugh cut me short. She caught my arm and began to urge me down the road again. "I only told Mr. Hendrixson that so he would not worry," she explained. "You do not think I am not going down to see the sights."

She was tall, I am short and thick. I had to look up to see her face—to see as much of it as the rain-gray night would let me see. "You'll be soaked to the hide, running around in this rain," I objected.

"What of that? I am dressed for it." She raised a foot to show me a heavy waterproof boot and a woolen-stockinged leg.

"There's no telling what we'll run into down there, and I've got work to do," I insisted. "I can't be looking out for you."

"I can look out for myself." She pushed her cape aside to show me a square automatic pistol in one hand.

"You'll be in my way."

"I will not," she retorted. "You'll probably find I can help you. I'm as strong as you, and quicker, and I can shoot."

The reports of scattered shooting had punctuated our argument, but now the sound of heavier firing silenced the dozen objections to her company that I could still think of. After all, I could slip away from her in the dark if she became too much of a nuisance.

"Have it your own way," I growled, "but don't expect anything from me."

"You're so kind," she murmured as we got under way

again, hurrying now, with the wind at our backs speeding us along.

Occasionally dark figures moved on the road ahead of us, but too far away to be recognizable. Presently a man passed us, running uphill—a tall man whose nightshirt hung out of his trousers, down below his coat, identifying him as a resident.

"They've finished the bank and are at Medcraft's!" he yelled as he went by.

"Medcraft is the jeweler," the girl informed me.

The sloping under our feet grew less sharp. The houses—dark but with faces vaguely visible here and there at windows—came closer together. Below, the flash of a gun could be seen now and then—orange streaks in the rain.

Our road put us into the lower end of the main street just as a staccato rat-tat-tat broke out.

I pushed the girl into the nearest doorway, and jumped in after her.

Bullets ripped through walls with the sound of hail tapping on leaves.

That was the thing I had taken for an exceptionally heavy rifle—a machine gun.

The girl had fallen back in a corner, all tangled up with something. I helped her up. The something was a boy of seventeen or so, with one leg and a crutch.

"It's the boy who delivers papers," Princess Zhukovski said, "and you've hurt him with your clumsiness."

The boy shook his head, grinning as he got up. "No'm, I ain't hurt none, but you kind of scared me, jumping on me like that."

She had to stop and explain that she hadn't jumped on him, that she had been pushed into him by me, and that she was sorry and so was I.

"What's happening?" I asked the newsboy when I could get a word in.

"Everything," he boasted, as if some of the credit were his. "There must be a hundred of them, and they've blowed the bank wide open, and now some of 'em is in Medcraft's, and I guess they'll blow that up, too. And they killed Tom Weegan. They got a machine gun on a car in the middle of the street. That's it shooting now."

"Where's everybody—all the merry villagers?"

"Most of 'em are up behind the Hall. They can't do nothing, though, because the machine gun won't let 'em get near enough to see what they're shooting at, and that smart Bill Vincent told me to clear out, 'cause I've only got one leg, as if I couldn't shoot as good as the next one, if I only had something to shoot with!"

"That wasn't right of them," I sympathized. "But you can do something for me. You can stick here and keep your eye on this end of the street, so I'll know if they leave in this direction."

"You're not just saying that so I'll stay here out of the way, are you?"

"No," I lied. "I need somebody to watch. I was going to leave the princess here, but you'll do better."

"Yes," she backed me up, catching the idea. "This gentleman is a detective, and if you do what he asks you'll be helping more than if you were up with the others."

The machine gun was still firing, but not in our direction now.

"I'm going across the street," I told the girl. "If you—"

"Aren't you going to join the others?"

"No. If I can get around behind the bandits while they're busy with the others, maybe I can turn a trick."

"Watch sharp now!" I ordered the boy, and the princess and I made a dash for the opposite sidewalk.

We reached it without drawing lead, sidled along a building for a few yards, and turned into an alley. From the alley's other end came the smell and wash and the dull blackness of the bay.

While we moved down this alley I composed a scheme by which I hoped to get rid of my companion, sending her off on a safe wild-goose chase. But I didn't get a chance to try it out.

The big figure of a man loomed ahead of us.

Stepping in front of the girl, I went on toward him. Under my slicker I held my gun on the middle of him.

He stood still. He was larger than he had looked at first. A big, slope-shouldered, barrel-bodied husky. His hands were empty. I spotted the flashlight on his face for a split second. A flat-cheeked, thick-featured face, with high cheekbones and a lot of ruggedness in it.

"Ignati!" the girl exclaimed over my shoulder.

He began to talk what I suppose was Russian to the girl. She laughed and replied. He shook his big head stubbornly, insisting on something. She stamped her foot and spoke sharply. He shook his head again and addressed me. "General Pleshskev, he tell me bring Princess Sonya to home."

His English was almost as hard to understand as his Russian. His tone puzzled me. It was as if he was explaining some absolutely necessary thing that he didn't want to be blamed for, but that nevertheless he was going to do.

While the girl was speaking to him again, I guessed the answer. This big Ignati had been sent out by the general to bring the girl home, and he was going to obey his orders if he had to carry her. He was trying to avoid trouble with me by explaining the situation.

"Take her," I said, stepping aside.

The girl scowled at me, laughed. "Very well, Ignati," she said in English, "I shall go home," and she turned on her heel and went back up the alley, the big man close behind her.

Glad to be alone, I wasted no time in moving in the opposite direction until the pebbles of the beach were under my feet. The pebbles ground harshly under my heels. I moved back to more silent ground and began to work my way as swiftly as I could up the shore toward the center of action. The machine gun barked on. Smaller guns snapped. Three concussions, close together—bombs, hand grenades, my ears and my memory told me.

The stormy sky glared pink over a roof ahead of me

and to the left. The boom of the blast beat my eardrums. Fragments I couldn't see fell around me. That, I thought, would be the jeweler's safe blowing apart.

I crept on up the shore line. The machine gun went silent. Lighter guns snapped, snapped. Another grenade went off. A man's voice shrieked pure terror.

Risking the crunch of pebbles, I turned down to the water's edge again. I had seen no dark shape on the water that could have been a boat. There had been boats moored along this beach in the afternoon. With my feet in the water of the bay I still saw no boat. The storm could have scattered them, but I didn't think it had. The island's western height shielded this shore. The wind was strong here, but not violent.

My feet sometimes on the edge of the pebbles, sometimes in the water, I went on up the shore line. Now I saw a boat. A gently bobbing black shape ahead. No light was on it. Nothing I could see moved on it. It was the only boat on that shore. That made it important.

Foot by foot, I approached.

A shadow moved between me and the dark rear of a building. I froze. The shadow, man-size, moved again, in the direction from which I was coming.

Waiting, I didn't know how nearly invisible, or how plain, I might be against my background. I couldn't risk giving myself away by trying to improve my position.

Twenty feet from me the shadow suddenly stopped.

I was seen. My gun was on the shadow.

"Come on," I called softly. "Keep coming. Let's see who you are."

The shadow hesitated, left the shelter of the building, drew nearer. I couldn't risk the flashlight. I made out dimly a handsome face, boyishly reckless, one cheek dark-stained.

"Oh, how d'you do?" the face's owner said in a musical baritone voice. "You were at the reception this afternoon."

"Yes."

"Have you seen Princess Zhukovski? You know her?"

"She went home with Ignati ten minutes or so ago."

"Excellent!" He wiped his stained cheek with a stained handkerchief, and turned to look at the boat. "That's Hendrixson's boat," he whispered. "They've got it and they've cast the others off."

"That would mean they are going to leave by water."

"Yes," he agreed, "unless— Shall we have a try at it?"

"You mean jump it?"

"Why not?" he asked. "There can't be very many aboard. God knows there are enough of them ashore. You're armed. I've a pistol."

"We'll size it up first," I decided, "so we'll know what we're jumping."

"That is wisdom," he said, and led the way back to the shelter of the buildings.

Hugging the rear walls of the buildings, we stole toward the boat.

The boat grew clearer in the night. A craft perhaps forty-five feet long, its stern to the shore, rising and falling beside a small pier. Across the stern something protruded. Something I couldn't quite make out. Leather soles scuffled now and then on the wooden deck. Presently a dark hood and shoulders showed over the puzzling thing in the stern.

The Russian lad's eyes were better than mine.

"Masked," he breathed in my ear. "Something like a stocking over his head and face."

The masked man was motionless where he stood. We were motionless where we stood.

"Could you hit him from here?" the lad asked.

"Maybe, but night and rain aren't a good combination for sharpshooting. Our best bet is to sneak as close as we can, and start shooting when he spots us."

"That is wisdom," he agreed.

Discovery came with our first step forward. The man in the boat grunted. The lad at my side jumped forward. I recognized the thing in the boat's stern just in time to throw out a leg and trip the young Russian. He tumbled down, all sprawled out on the pebbles. I dropped behind him.

The machine gun in the boat's stern poured metal over our heads.

"No good rushing that!" I said. "Roll out of it!"

I set the example by revolving toward the back of the building we had just left.

The man at the gun sprinkled the beach, but sprinkled it at random, his eyes no doubt spoiled for night-seeing by the flash of his gun.

Around the corner of the building, we sat up.

"You saved my life by tripping me," the lad said coolly.

"Yes. I wonder if they've moved the machine gun from the street, or if—"

The answer to that came immediately. The machine gun in the street mingled its vicious voice with the drumming of the one in the boat.

"A pair of them!" I complained. "Know anything about the layout?"

"I don't think there are more than ten or twelve of them," he said, "although it is not easy to count in the dark. The few I have seen are completely masked—like the man in the boat. They seem to have disconnected the telephone and light lines first and then to have destroyed the bridge. We attacked them while they were looting the bank, but in front they had a machine gun mounted in an automobile, and we were not equipped to combat on equal terms."

"Where are the islanders now?"

"Scattered, and most of them in hiding, I fancy, unless General Pleshskev has succeeded in rallying them again."

I frowned and beat my brains together. You can't fight machine guns and hand grenades with peaceful villagers and retired capitalists. No matter how well led and armed they are, you can't do anything with them. For that matter, how could anybody do much against a game of that toughness?

"Suppose you stick here and keep your eye on the boat," I suggested. "I'll scout around and see what's doing farther up, and if I can get a few good men together, I'll try to jump the boat again, probably from the other side. But we can't count on that. The getaway will be by boat. We can count on that, and try to block it. If you lie down you can watch the boat around the corner of the building without making much of a target of yourself. I wouldn't do anything to attract attention until the break for the boat comes. Then you can do all the shooting you want."

"Excellent!" he said. "You'll probably find most of the islanders up behind the church. You can get to it by going straight up the hill until you come to an iron fence, and then follow that to the right."

"Right."

I moved off in the direction he had indicated.

At the main street I stopped to look around before venturing across. Everything was quiet there. The only man I could see was spread out face-down on the sidewalk near me.

On hands and knees I crawled to his side. He was dead. I didn't stop to examine him further, but sprang up and streaked for the other side of the street.

Nothing tried to stop me. In a doorway, flat against a wall, I peeped out. The wind had stopped. The rain was no longer a driving deluge, but a steady down-pouring of small drops. Couffignal's main street, to my senses, was a deserted street.

I wondered if the retreat to the boat had already started. On the sidewalk, walking swiftly toward the bank, I heard the answer to that guess.

High up on the slope, almost up to the edge of the cliff, by the sound, a machine gun began to hurl out its stream of bullets.

Mixed with the racket of the machine gun were the sounds of smaller arms, and a grenade or two.

At the first crossing, I left the main street and began to run up the hill. Men were running toward me. Two of them passed, paying no attention to my shouted, "What's up now?"

The third man stopped because I grabbed him—a fat

man whose breath bubbled, and whose face was fish-belly white.

"They've moved the car with the machine gun on it up behind us," he gasped when I had shouted my question into his ear again.

"What are you doing without a gun?" I asked.

"I—I dropped it."

"Where's General Pleshskev?"

"Back there somewhere. He's trying to capture the car, but he'll never do it. It's suicide! Why don't help come?"

Other men had passed us, running downhill, as we talked. I let the white-faced man go, and stopped four men who weren't running so fast as the others.

"What's happening now?" I questioned them.

"They're going through the houses up the hill," a sharp-featured man with a small mustache and a rifle said.

"Has anybody got word off the island yet?" I asked.

"Can't," another informed me. "They blew up the bridge first thing."

"Can't anybody swim?"

"Not in that wind. Young Catlan tried it and was lucky to get out again with a couple of broken ribs."

"The wind's gone down," I pointed out.

The sharp-featured man gave his rifle to one of the others and took off his coat. "I'll try it," he promised.

"Good! Wake up the whole country, and get word through to the San Francisco police boat and to the Mare Island Navy Yard. They'll lend a hand if you tell 'em the bandits have machine guns. Tell 'em the bandits have an armed boat waiting to leave in. It's Hendrixson's."

The volunteer swimmer left.

"A boat?" two of the men asked together.

"Yes. With a machine gun on it. If we're going to do anything, it'll have to be now, while we're between them and their get-away. Get every man and every gun you can find down there. Tackle the boat from the roofs if you can. When the bandits' car comes down there, pour it into it. You'll do better from the buildings than from the street."

The three men went on downhill. I went uphill, toward the crackling of firearms ahead. The machine gun was working irregularly. It would pour out its rat-tat-tat for a second or so, and then stop for a couple of seconds. The answering fire was thin, ragged.

I met more men, learned from them the general, with less than a dozen men, was still fighting the car. I repeated the advice I had given the other men. My informants went down to join them. I went on up.

A hundred yards farther along, what was left of the general's dozen broke out of the night, around and past me, flying downhill, with bullets hailing after them.

The road was no place for mortal man. I stumbled over two bodies, scratched myself in a dozen places getting over a hedge. On soft, wet sod I continued my uphill journey.

The machine gun on the hill stopped its clattering. The one in the boat was still at work.

The one ahead opened again, firing too high for anything near at hand to be its target. It was helping its fellow below, spraying the main street.

Before I could get closer it had stopped. I heard the car's motor racing. The car moved toward me.

Rolling into the hedge, I lay there, straining my eyes through the spaces between the stems. I had six bullets in a gun that hadn't yet been fired on this night that had seen tons of powder burned.

When I saw wheels on the lighter face of the road, I emptied my gun, holding it low.

The car went on.

I sprang out of my hiding-place.

The car was suddenly gone from the empty road.

There was a grinding sound. A crash. The noise of metal folding on itself. The tinkle of glass.

I raced toward those sounds.

Out of a black pile where an engine sputtered, a black figure leaped—to dash off across the soggy lawn. I cut after it, hoping that the others in the wreck were down for keeps.

I was less than fifteen feet behind the fleeing man when he cleared a hedge. I'm no sprinter, but neither was he. The wet grass made slippery going.

He stumbled while I was vaulting the hedge. When we straightened out again I was not more than ten feet behind him.

Once I clicked my gun at him, forgetting I had emptied it. Six cartridges were wrapped in a piece of paper in my vest pocket, but this was no time for loading.

I was tempted to chuck the empty gun at his head. But that was too chancy.

A building loomed ahead. My fugitive bore off to the right, to clear the corner.

To the left a heavy shotgun went off.

The running man disappeared around the house-corner.

"Sweet God!" General Pleshskev's mellow voice complained. "That with a shotgun I should miss all of a man at the distance!"

"Go round the other way!" I yelled, plunging around the corner after my quarry.

His feet thudded ahead. I could not see him. The general puffed around from the other side of the house.

"You have him?"

"No."

In front of us was a stone-faced bank, on top of which ran a path. On either side of us was a high and solid hedge.

"But, my friend," the general protested. "How could he have—?"

A pale triangle showed on the path above—a triangle that could have been a bit of shirt showing above the opening of a vest.

"Stay here and talk!" I whispered to the general, and crept forward.

"It must be that he has gone the other way," the

general carried out my instructions, rambling on as if I were standing beside him, "because if he had come my way I should have seen him, and if he had raised himself over either of the hedges or the embankment, one of us would surely have seen him against . . ."

He talked on and on while I gained the shelter of the bank on which the path sat, while I found places for my toes in the rough stone facing.

The man on the road, trying to make himself small with his back in a bush, was looking at the talking general. He saw me when I had my feet on the path.

He jumped, and one hand went up.

I jumped, with both hands out.

A stone, turning under my foot, threw me sidewise, twisting my ankle, but saving my head from the bullet he sent at it.

My outflung left arm caught his legs as I spilled down. He came over on top of me. I kicked him once, caught his gun-arm, and had just decided to bite it when the general puffed up over the edge of the path and prodded the man off me with the muzzle of the shotgun.

When it came my turn to stand up, I found it not so good. My twisted ankle didn't like to support its share of my hundred-and-eighty-some pounds. Putting most of my weight on the other leg, I turned my flashlight on the prisoner.

"Hello, Flippo!" I exclaimed.

"Hello!" he said without joy in the recognition.

He was a roly-poly Italian youth of twenty-three or -four. I had helped send him to San Quentin four years ago for his part in a payroll stick-up. He had been out on parole for several months now.

"The prison board isn't going to like this," I told him.

"You got me wrong," he pleaded. "I ain't been doing a thing. I was up here to see some friends. And when this thing busted loose I had to hide, because I got a record, and if I'm picked up I'll be railroaded for it. And now you got me, and you think I'm in on it!"

"You're a mind reader," I assured him, and asked the general, "Where can we pack this bird away for a while, under lock and key?"

"In my house there is a lumber-room with a strong door and not a window."

"That'll do it. March, Flippo!"

General Pleshskev collared the youth, while I limped along behind them, examining Flippo's gun, which was loaded except for the one shot he had fired at me, and reloading my own.

We had caught our prisoner on the Russian's grounds, so we didn't have far to go.

The general knocked on the door and called out something in his language. Bolts clicked and grated, and the door was swung open by a heavily mustached Russian servant. Behind him the princess and a stalwart older woman stood.

We went in while the general was telling his household about the capture, and took the captive up to the lumber-room. I frisked him for his pocketknife and matches—he had nothing else that could help him get out—locked him in and braced the door solidly with a length of board. Then we went downstairs again.

"You are injured!" the princess cried, seeing me limp across the floor.

"Only a twisted ankle," I said. "But it does bother me some. Is there any adhesive tape around?"

"Yes," and she spoke to the mustached servant, who went out of the room and presently returned, carrying rolls of gauze and tape and a basin of steaming water.

"If you'll sit down," the princess said, taking these things from the servant.

But I shook my head and reached for the adhesive tape.

"I want cold water, because I've got to go out in the wet again. If you'll show me the bathroom, I can fix myself up in no time."

We had to argue about that, but I finally got to the

bathroom, where I ran cold water on my foot and ankle, and strapped it with adhesive tape, as tight as I could without stopping the circulation altogether. Getting my wet shoe on again was a job, but when I was through I had two firm legs under me, even if one of them did hurt some.

When I rejoined the others I noticed that sounds of firing no longer came up the hill, and that the patter of rain was lighter, and a gray streak of coming daylight showed under a drawn blind.

I was buttoning my slicker when the knocker rang on the front door. Russian words came through, and the young Russian I had met on the beach came in.

"Aleksander, you're—" The stalwart older woman screamed, when she saw the blood on his cheek, and fainted.

He paid no attention to her at all, as if he was used to having her faint.

"They've gone in the boat," he told me while the girl and two men-servants gathered up the woman and laid her on an ottoman.

"How many?" I asked.

"I counted ten, and I don't think I missed more than one or two, if any."

"The men I sent down there couldn't stop them?"

He shrugged. "What would you? It takes a strong stomach to face a machine gun. Your men had been cleared out of the buildings almost before they arrived."

The woman who had fainted had revived by now and was pouring anxious questions in Russian at the lad. The princess was getting into her blue cape. The woman stopped questioning the lad and asked her something.

"It's all over," the princess said. "I am going to view the ruins."

That suggestion appealed to everybody. Five minutes later all of us, including the servants, were on our way downhill. Behind us, around us, in front of us, were other people going downhill, hurrying along in the drizzle that was very gentle now, their faces tired and excited in the bleak morning light.

Halfway down, a woman ran out of a cross-path and began to tell me something. I recognized her as one of Hendrixson's maids.

I caught some of her words.

"Presents   gone . . . Mr.   Brophy   murdered . . . Oliver . . ."

"I'll be down later," I told the others, and set out after the maid.

She was running back to the Hendrixson house. I couldn't run, couldn't even walk fast. She and Hendrixson and more of his servants were standing on the front porch when I arrived.

"They killed Oliver and Brophy," the old man said.

"How?"

"We were in the back of the house, the rear second story, watching the flashes of the shooting down in the village. Oliver was down here, just inside the front door, and Brophy in the room with the presents. We heard a shot in there, and immediately a man appeared in the doorway of our room, threatening us with two pistols, making us stay there for perhaps ten minutes. Then he shut and locked the door and went away. We broke the door down—and found Brophy and Oliver dead."

"Let's look at them."

The chauffeur was just inside the front door. He lay on his back, with his brown throat cut straight across the front, almost back to the vertebrae. His rifle was under him. I pulled it out and examined it. It had not been fired.

Upstairs, the butler Brophy was huddled against a leg of one of the tables on which the presents had been spread. His gun was gone. I turned him over, straightened him out, and found a bullet-hole in his chest. Around the hole his coat was charred in a large area.

Most of the presents were still there. But the most valuable pieces were gone. The others were in disorder, lying around any which way, their covers pulled off.

"What did the one you saw look like?" I asked.

"I didn't see him very well," Hendrixson said. "There was no light in our room. He was simply a dark figure against the candle burning in the hall. A large man in a black rubber raincoat, with some sort of black mask that covered his whole head and face, with small eyeholes."

"No hat?"

"No, just the mask over his entire face and head."

As we went downstairs again I gave Hendrixson a brief account of what I had seen and heard and done since I had left him. There wasn't enough of it to make a long tale.

"Do you think you can get information about the others from the one you caught?" he asked, as I prepared to go out.

"No. But I expect to bag them just the same."

Couffignal's main street was jammed with people when I limped into it again. A detachment of Marines from Mare Island was there, and men from a San Francisco police boat. Excited citizens in all degrees of partial nakedness boiled around them. A hundred voices were talking at once, recounting their personal adventures and braveries and losses and what they had seen. Such words as machine gun, bomb, bandit, car, shot, dynamite, and killed sounded again and again, in every variety of voice and tone.

The bank had been completely wrecked by the charge that had blown the vault. The jewelry store was another ruin. A grocer's across the street was serving as a field hospital. Two doctors were toiling there, patching up damaged villagers.

I recognized a familiar face under a uniform cap—Sergeant Roche of the harbor police—and pushed through the crowd to him.

"Just get here?" he asked as we shook hands. "Or were you in on it?"

"In on it."

"What do you know?"

"Everything."

"Who ever heard of a private detective that didn't," he joshed as I led him out of the mob.

"Did you people run into an empty boat out in the bay?" I asked when we were away from audiences.

"Empty boats have been floating around the bay all night," he said.

I hadn't thought of that.

"Where's your boat now?" I asked him.

"Out trying to pick up the bandits. I stayed with a couple of men to lend a hand here."

"You're in luck," I told him. "Now sneak a look across the street. See the stout old boy with the black whiskers, standing in front of the druggist's?"

General Pleshskev stood there, with the woman who had fainted, the young Russian whose bloody cheek had made her faint, and a pale, plump man of forty-something who had been with them at the reception. A little to one side stood big Ignati, the two men-servants I had seen at the house, and another who was obviously one of them. They were chatting together and watching the excited antics of a red-faced property-owner who was telling a curt lieutenant of Marines that it was his own personal private automobile that the bandits had stolen to mount their machine gun on, and what he thought should be done about it.

"Yes," said Roche, "I see your fellow with the whiskers."

"Well, he's your meat. The woman and two men with him are also your meat. And those four Russians standing to the left are some more of it. There's another missing, but I'll take care of that one. Pass the word to the lieutenant, and you can round up those babies without giving them a chance to fight back. They think they're safe as angels."

"Sure, are you?" the sergeant asked.

"Don't be silly!" I growled, as if I had never made a mistake in my life.

I had been standing on my one good prop. When I put my weight on the other to turn away from the sergeant, it stung me all the way to the hip. I pushed my back teeth together and began to work painfully through the crowd to the other side of the street.

The princess didn't seem to be among those present. My idea was that, next to the general, she was the most important member of the push. If she was at their house, and not yet suspicious, I figured I could get close enough to yank her in without a riot.

Walking was hell. My temperature rose. Sweat rolled out on me.

"Mister, they didn't none of 'em come down that way."

The one-legged newsboy was standing at my elbow. I greeted him as if he were my pay-check.

"Come on with me," I said, taking his arm. "You did fine down there, and now I want you to do something else for me."

Half a block from the main street I led him up on the porch of a small yellow cottage. The front door stood open, left that way when the occupants ran down to welcome police and Marines, no doubt. Just inside the door, beside a hall rack, was a wicker porch chair. I committed unlawful entry to the extent of dragging that chair out on the porch.

"Sit down, son," I urged the boy.

He sat, looking up at me with puzzled freckled face. I took a firm grip on his crutch and pulled it out of his hand.

"Here's five bucks for rental," I said, "and if I lose it I'll buy you one of ivory and gold."

And I put the crutch under my arm and began to propel myself up the hill.

It was my first experience with a crutch. I didn't break any records. But it was a lot better than tottering along on an unassisted bum ankle.

The hill was longer and steeper than some mountains I've seen, but the gravel walk to the Russians' house was finally under my feet.

I was still some dozen feet from the porch when Princess Zhukovski opened the door.

"Oh!" she exclaimed, and then, recovering from her

surprise, "your ankle is worse!" She ran down the steps to help me climb them. As she came I noticed that something heavy was sagging and swinging in the right-hand pocket of her gray flannel jacket.

With one hand under my elbow, the other arm across my back, she helped me up the steps and across the porch. That assured me she didn't think I had tumbled to the game. If she had, she wouldn't have trusted herself within reach of my hands. Why, I wondered, had she come back to the house after starting downhill with the others?

While I was wondering we went into the house, where she planted me in a large and soft leather chair.

"You must certainly be starving after your strenuous night," she said. "I will see if—"

"No, sit down." I nodded at a chair facing mine. "I want to talk to you."

She sat down, clasping her slender white hands in her lap. In neither face nor pose was there any sign of nervousness, not even of curiosity. And that was overdoing it.

"Where have you cached the plunder?" I asked.

The whiteness of her face was nothing to go by. It had been white as marble since I had first seen her. The darkness of her eyes was as natural. Nothing happened to her other features. Her voice was smoothly cool.

"I am sorry," she said. "The question doesn't convey anything to me."

"Here's the point," I explained. "I'm charging you with complicity in the gutting of Couffignal, and in the murders that went with it. And I'm asking you where the loot has been hidden."

Slowly she stood up, raised her chin, and looked at least a mile down at me.

"How dare you? How dare you speak so to me, a Zhukovski!"

"I don't care if you're one of the Smith Brothers!" Leaning forward, I had pushed my twisted ankle against a leg of the chair, and the resulting agony didn't improve my disposition. "For the purpose of this talk you are a thief and a murderer."

Her strong slender body became the body of a lean crouching animal. Her white face became the face of an enraged animal. One hand—claw now—swept to the heavy pocket of her jacket.

Then, before I could have batted an eye—though my life seemed to depend on my not batting it—the wild animal had vanished. Out of it—and now I know where the writers of the old fairy stories got their ideas—rose the princess again, cool and straight and tall.

She sat down, crossed her ankles, put an elbow on an arm of her chair, propped her chin on the back of that hand, and looked curiously into my face.

"How ever," she murmured, "did you chance to arrive at so strange and fanciful a theory?"

"It wasn't chance, and it's neither strange nor fanciful," I said. "Maybe it'll save time and trouble if I show you part of the score against you. Then you'll know how you stand and won't waste your brains pleading innocence."

"I shall be grateful," she smiled, "very!"

I tucked my crutch in between one knee and the arm of my chair, so my hands would be free to check off my points on my fingers.

"First—whoever planned the job knew the island—not fairly well, but every inch of it. There's no need to argue about that. Second—the car on which the machine gun was mounted was local property, stolen from the owner here. So was the boat in which the bandits were supposed to have escaped. Bandits from the outside would have needed a car or a boat to bring their machine guns, explosives, and grenades here, and there doesn't seem to be any reason why they shouldn't have used that car or boat instead of stealing a fresh one. Third—there wasn't the least hint of the professional bandit touch on this job. If you ask me, it was a military job from beginning to end. And the worst safe-burglar in the world could have got into both the bank vault and the jeweler's safe without wrecking the buildings. Fourth—bandits from the outside wouldn't have destroyed the bridge. They might have blocked it, but they wouldn't have destroyed it. They'd have saved it in case they had to make their getaway in that direction. Fifth—bandits figuring on a getaway by boat would have cut the job short, wouldn't have spread it over the whole night. Enough racket was made here to wake up California all the way from Sacramento to Los Angeles. What you people did was to send one man out in the boat, shooting, and he didn't go far. As soon as he was at a safe distance, he went overboard, and swam back to the island. Big Ignati could have done it without turning a hair."

That exhausted my right hand. I switched over, counting on my left.

"Sixth—I met one of your party, the lad, down on the beach, and he was coming from the boat. He suggested that we jump it. We were shot at, but the man behind the gun was playing with us. He could have wiped us out in a second if he had been in earnest, but he shot over our heads. Seventh—that same lad is the only man on the island, so far as I know, who saw the departing bandits. Eight—all of your people that I ran into were especially nice to me, the general even spending an hour talking to me at the reception this afternoon. That's a distinctive amateur crook trait. Ninth—after the machine gun car had been wrecked I chased its occupant. I lost him around this house. The Italian boy I picked up wasn't him. He couldn't have climbed up on the path without my seeing him. But he could have run around to the general's side of the house and vanished indoors there. The general liked him, and would have helped him. I know that, because the general performed a downright miracle by missing him at some six feet with a shotgun. Tenth—you called at Hendrixson's house for no other purpose than to get me away from there."

That finished the left hand. I went back to the right.

"Eleventh—Hendrixson's two servants were killed by someone they knew and trusted. Both were killed at close quarters and without firing a shot. I'd say you got Oliver to let you into the house, and were talking to him when one of your men cut his throat from behind. Then you went upstairs and probably shot the unsuspecting Brophy yourself. He wouldn't have been on his guard against you. Twelfth—but that ought to be enough, and I'm getting a sore throat from listing them."

She took her chin off her hand, took a fat white cigarette out of a thin black case, and held it in her mouth while I put a match to the end of it. She took a long pull at it—a draw that accounted for a third of its length—and blew the smoke down at her knees.

"That would be enough," she said when all these things had been done, "if it were not that you yourself know it was impossible for us to have been so engaged. Did you not see us—did not everyone see us—time and time again?"

"That's easy!" I argued. "With a couple of machine guns, a trunkful of grenades, knowing the island from top to bottom, in the darkness and in a storm, against bewildered civilians—it was duck soup. There are nine of you that I know of, including two women. Any five of you could have carried on the work, once it was started, while the others took turns appearing here and there, establishing alibis. And that is what you did. You took turns slipping out to alibi yourselves. Everywhere I went I ran into one of you. And the general! That whiskered old joker running around leading the simple citizens to battle! I'll bet he led 'em plenty! They're lucky there are any of 'em alive this morning!"

She finished her cigarette with another inhalation, dropped the stub on the rug, ground out the light with one foot, sighed wearily, put her hands on her hips, and asked, "And now what?"

"Now I want to know where you have stowed the plunder."

The readiness of her answer surprised me.

"Under the garage, in a cellar we secretly dug there some months ago."

I didn't believe that, of course, but it turned out to be the truth.

I didn't have anything else to say. When I fumbled with my borrowed crutch, preparing to get up, she raised a hand and spoke gently. "Wait a moment, please. I have something to suggest."

Half standing, I leaned toward her, stretching out one hand until it was close to her side.

"I want the gun," I said.

She nodded, and sat still while I plucked it from her pocket, put it in one of my own, and sat down again.

"You said a little while ago that you didn't care who I was," she began immediately. "But I want you to know. There are so many of us Russians who once were some-bodies and who now are nobodies that I won't bore you with the repetition of a tale the world has grown tired of hearing. But you must remember that this weary tale is real to us who are its subjects. However, we fled from Russia with what we could carry of our property, which fortunately was enough to keep us in bearable comfort for a few years.

"In London we opened a Russian restaurant, but London was suddenly full of Russian restaurants, and ours became, instead of a means of livelihood, a source of loss. We tried teaching music and languages, and so on. In short, we hit on all the means of earning our living that other Russian exiles hit upon, and so always found our-selves in overcrowded, and thus unprofitable, fields. But what else did we know—could we do?

"I promised not to bore you. Well, always our capital shrank, and always the day approached on which we should be shabby and hungry, the day when we should become familiar to readers of your Sunday papers—char-women who had been princesses, dukes who now were butlers. There was no place for us in the world. Outcasts easily became outlaws. Why not? Could it be said that we owed the world any fealty? Had not the world sat idly by and seen us despoiled of place and property and country?

"We planned it before we had heard of Couffignal. We could find a small settlement of the wealthy, sufficiently isolated, and, after establishing ourselves there, we would plunder it. Couffignal, when we found it, seemed to be the ideal place. We leased this house for six months, having just enough capital remaining to do that and to live properly here while our plans matured. Here we spent four months establishing ourselves, collecting our arms and our explosives, mapping our offensive, waiting for a favorable night. Last night seemed to be that night, and we had provided, we thought, against every eventuality. But we had not, of course, provided against your presence and your genius. They were simply others of the unforeseen misfortunes to which we seem eternally condemned."

She stopped, and fell to studying me with mournful large eyes that made me feel like fidgeting.

"It's no good calling me a genius," I objected. "The truth is you people botched your job from beginning to end. Your general would get a big laugh out of a man without military training who tried to lead an army. But here are you people with absolutely no criminal experience trying to swing a trick that needed the highest sort of criminal skill. Look at how you all played around with me! Amateur stuff! A professional crook with any intelligence would have either let me alone or knocked me off. No wonder you flopped! As for the rest of it—your troubles—I can't do anything about them."

"Why?" very softly. "Why can't you?"

"Why should I?" I made it blunt.

"No one else knows what you know." She bent forward to put a white hand on my knee. "There is wealth in that cellar beneath the garage. You may have whatever you ask."

I shook my head.

"You aren't a fool!" she protested. "You know—"

"Let me straighten this out for you," I interrupted. "We'll disregard whatever honesty I happen to have, sense of loyalty to employers, and so on. You might doubt them, so we'll throw them out. Now I'm a detective because I happen to like the work. It pays me a fair salary, but I could find other jobs that would pay more. Even a hundred dollars more a month would be twelve hundred a year. Say twenty-five or thirty thousand dollars in the years between now and my sixtieth birthday.

"Now I pass up about twenty-five or thirty thousand of honest gain because I like being a detective, like the work. And liking work makes you want to do it as well as you can. Otherwise there'd be no sense to it. That's the fix I am in. I don't know anything else, don't enjoy anything else, don't want to know or enjoy anything else. You can't weigh that against any sum of money. Money is good stuff. I haven't anything against it. But in the past eighteen years I've been getting my fun out of chasing crooks and tackling puzzles, my satisfaction out of catching crooks and solving riddles. It's the only kind of sport I know anything about, and I can't imagine a pleasanter future than twenty-some years more of it. I'm not going to blow that up!"

She shook her head slowly, lowering it, so that now her dark eyes looked up at me under the thin arcs of her brows.

"You speak only of money," she said. "I said you may have whatever you ask."

That was out. I don't know where these women get their ideas.

"You're still all twisted up," I said brusquely, standing now and adjusting my borrowed crutch. "You think I'm a man and you're a woman. That's wrong. I'm a manhunter and you're something that has been running in front of me. There's nothing human about it. You might just as well expect a hound to play tiddly-winks with the fox he's caught. We're wasting time anyway. I've been thinking the police or Marines might come up here and save me a walk. You've been waiting for your mob to come back and grab me. I could have told you they were being arrested when I left them."

That shook her. She had stood up. Now she fell back a step, putting a hand behind her for steadiness, on her chair. An exclamation I didn't understand popped out of her mouth. Russian, I thought, but the next moment I knew it had been Italian.

"Put your hands up." It was Flippo's husky voice. Flippo stood in the doorway, holding an automatic.

I raised my hands as high as I could without dropping my supporting crutch, meanwhile cursing myself for having been too careless, or too vain, to keep a gun in my hand while I talked to the girl.

So this was why she had come back to the house. If she freed the Italian, she had thought, we would have no reason for suspecting that he hadn't been in on the robbery, and so we would look for the bandits among his friends. A prisoner, of course, he might have persuaded us of his innocence. She had given him the gun so he could either shoot his way clear, or, what would help her as much, get himself killed trying.

While I was arranging those thoughts in my head, Flippo had come up behind me. His empty hand passed over my body, taking away my own gun, his, and the one I had taken from the girl.

"A bargain, Flippo," I said when he had moved away from me, a little to one side, where he made one corner of a triangle whose other corners were the girl and I. "You're out on parole, with some years still to be served. I picked you up with a gun on you. That's plenty to send you back to the big house. I know you weren't in on this job. My idea is that you were up here on a smaller one of your own, but I can't prove that and don't want to. Walk out of here, alone and neutral, and I'll forget I saw you."

Little thoughtful lines grooved the boy's round, dark face.

The princess took a step toward him.

"You heard the offer I just now made him?" she asked. "Well, I make that offer to you, if you will kill him."

The thoughtful lines in the boy's face deepened.

"There's your choice, Flippo," I summed up for him. "All I can give you is freedom from San Quentin. The princess can give you a fat cut of the profits in a busted caper, with a good chance to get yourself hanged."

The girl, remembering her advantage over me, went at him hot and heavy in Italian, a language in which I know only four words. Two of them are profane and the other two obscene. I said all four.

The boy was weakening. If he had been ten years older, he'd have taken my offer and thanked me for it. But he was young and she—now that I thought of it—was beautiful. The answer wasn't hard to guess.

"But not to bump him off," he said to her in English, for my benefit. "We'll lock him up in there where I was at."

I suspected Flippo hadn't any great prejudice against murder. It was just that he thought this one unnecessary, unless he was kidding me to make the killing easier.

The girl wasn't satisfied with his suggestion. She poured more hot Italian at him. Her game looked surefire, but it had a flaw. She couldn't persuade him that his chances of getting any of the loot away were good. She had to depend on her charms to swing him. And that meant she had to hold his eye.

He wasn't far from me.

She came close to him. She was singing, chanting, crooning Italian syllables into his round face.

She had him.

She shrugged. His whole face said yes. He turned—

I knocked him on the noodle with my borrowed crutch.

The crutch splintered apart. Flippo's knees bent. He stretched up to his full height. He fell on his face on the floor. He lay there, dead-still, except for a thin worm of blood that crawled out of his hair to the rug.

A step, a tumble, a foot or so of hand-and-knee scrambling put me within reach of Flippo's gun.

The girl, jumping out of my path, was halfway to the door when I sat up with the gun in my hand.

"Stop!" I ordered.

"I shan't," she said, but she did, for the time at least. "I am going out."

"You are going out when I take you."

She laughed, a pleasant laugh, low and confident.

"I'm going out before that," she insisted good-naturedly. I shook my head.

"How do you propose stopping me?" she asked.

"I don't think I'll have to," I told her. "You've got too much sense to try to run while I'm holding a gun on you."

She laughed again, an amused ripple.

"I've got too much sense to stay," she corrected me. "Your crutch is broken, and you're lame. You can't catch me by running after me, then. You pretend you'll shoot me, but I don't believe you. You'd shoot me if I attacked you, of course, but I shan't do that. I shall simply walk out, and you know you won't shoot me for that. You'll wish you could, but you won't. You'll see."

Her face turned over her shoulder, her dark eyes twinkling at me, she took a step toward the door.

"Better not count on that!" I threatened.

For answer to that she gave me a cooing laugh. And took another step.

"Stop, you idiot!" I bawled at her.

Her face laughed over her shoulder at me. She walked without haste to the door, her short skirt of gray flannel shaping itself to the calf of each gray wool-stockinged leg as its mate stepped forward.

Sweat greased the gun in my hand.

When her right foot was on the doorsill, a little chuckling sound came from her throat.

"Adieu!" she said softly.

And I put a bullet in the calf of her left leg.

She sat down—plump! Utter surprise stretched her white face. It was too soon for pain.

I had never shot a woman before. I felt queer about it.

"You ought to have known I'd do it!" My voice sounded harsh and savage and like a stranger's in my ears. "Didn't I steal a crutch from a cripple?"

FLY PAPER

It was a wandering daughter job.

The Hambletons had been for several generations a wealthy and decently prominent New York family. There was nothing in the Hambleton history to account for Sue, the youngest member of the clan. She grew out of childhood with a kink that made her dislike the polished side of life, like the rough. By the time she was twenty-one, in 1926, she definitely preferred Tenth Avenue to Fifth, grifters to bankers, and Hymie the Riveter to the Honorable Cecil Windown, who had asked her to marry him.

The Hambletons tried to make Sue behave, but it was too late for that. She was legally of age. When she finally told them to go to hell and walked out on them there wasn't much they could do about it. Her father, Major Waldo Hambleton, had given up all the hopes he ever had of salvaging her, but he didn't want her to run into any grief that could be avoided. So he came into the Continental Detective Agency's New York office and asked to have an eye kept on her.

Hymie the Riveter was a Philadelphia racketeer who had moved north to the big city, carrying a Thompson submachine gun wrapped in blue-checkered oil cloth, after a disagreement with his partners. New York wasn't so good a field as Philadelphia for machine gun work. The Thompson lay idle for a year or so while Hymie made expenses with an automatic, preying on small-time crap games in Harlem.

Three or four months after Sue went to live with Hymie he made what looked like a promising connection with the first of the crew that came into New York from Chicago to organize the city on the western scale. But the boys from Chi didn't want Hymie; they wanted the Thompson. When he showed it to them, as the big item in his application for employment, they shot holes in the top of Hymie's head and went away with the gun.

Sue Hambleton buried Hymie, had a couple of lonely weeks in which she hocked a ring to eat, and then got a job as hostess in a speakeasy run by a Greek named Vassos.

One of Vassos' customers was Babe McCloor, two hundred and fifty pounds of hard Scotch-Irish-Indian bone and muscle, a black-haired, blue-eyed, swarthy giant who was resting up after doing a fifteen-year hitch in Leavenworth for ruining most of the smaller post offices between New Orleans and Omaha. Babe was keeping himself in drinking money while he rested by playing with pedestrians in dark streets.

Babe liked Sue. Vassos liked Sue. Sue liked Babe. Vassos didn't like that. Jealousy spoiled the Greek's judgment. He kept the speakeasy door locked one night when Babe wanted to come in. Babe came in, bringing pieces of the door with him. Vassos got his gun out, but couldn't shake Sue off his arm. He stopped trying when Babe hit him with the part of the door that had the brass knob on it. Babe and Sue went away from Vassos' together.

Up to that time the New York office had managed to keep in touch with Sue. She hadn't been kept under constant surveillance. Her father hadn't wanted that. It was simply a matter of sending a man around every week or so to see that she was still alive, to pick up whatever information he could from her friends and neighbors, without, of course, letting her know she was being tabbed. All that had been easy enough, but when she and Babe went away after wrecking the gin mill, they dropped completely out of sight.

After turning the city upside-down, the New York office sent a journal on the job to the other Continental branches throughout the country, giving the information above and enclosing photographs and descriptions of Sue and her new playmate. That was late in 1927.

We had enough copies of the photographs to go around, and for the next month or so whoever had a little idle time on his hands spent it looking through San Francisco and Oakland for the missing pair. We didn't find them. Operatives in other cities, doing the same thing, had the same luck.

Then, nearly a year later, a telegram came to us from the New York office. Decoded, it read:

> Major Hambleton today received telegram from daughter in San Francisco quote Please wire me thousand dollars care apartment two hundred six number six hundred one Eddis Street stop I will come home if you will let me stop Please tell me if I can come but please please wire money anyway unquote Hambleton authorizes payment of money to her immediately stop Detail competent operative to call on her with money and to arrange for her return home stop If possible have man and woman operative accompany her here stop Hambleton wiring her stop Report immediately by wire.

The Old Man gave me the telegram and a check, saying, "You know the situation. You'll know how to handle it."

I pretended I agreed with him, went down to the bank,

swapped the check for a bundle of bills of several sizes, caught a streetcar, and went up to 601 Eddis Street, a fairly large apartment building on the corner of Larkin.

The name on Apartment 206's vestibule mail box was J. M. Wales.

I pushed 206's button. When the locked door buzzed off I went into the building, past the elevator to the stairs, and up a flight. 206 was just around the corner from the stairs.

The apartment door was opened by a tall, slim man of thirty-something in neat dark clothes. He had narrow dark eyes set in a long pale face. There was some gray in the dark hair brushed flat to his scalp.

"Miss Hambleton," I said.

"Uh—what about her?" His voice was smooth, but not too smooth to be agreeable.

"I'd like to see her."

His upper eyelids came down a little and the brows over them came a little closer together. He asked, "Is it—?" and stopped, watching me steadily.

I didn't say anything. Presently he finished his question, "Something to do with a telegram?"

"Yeah."

His long face brightened immediately. He asked, "You're from her father?"

"Yeah."

He stepped back and swung the door wide open, saying, "Come in. Major Hambleton's wire came to her only a few minutes ago. He said someone would call."

We went through a small passageway into a sunny living room that was cheaply furnished, but neat and clean enough.

"Sit down," the man said, pointing at a brown rocking chair.

I sat down. He sat on the burlap-covered sofa facing me. I looked around the room. I didn't see anything to show that a woman was living there.

He rubbed the long bridge of his nose with a longer forefinger and asked slowly, "You brought the money?"

I said I'd feel more like talking with her there.

He looked at the finger with which he had been rubbing his nose, and then up at me, saying softly, "But I'm her friend."

I said, "Yeah?" to that.

"Yes," he repeated. He frowned slightly, drawing back the corners of his thin-lipped mouth. "I've only asked whether you've brought the money."

I didn't say anything.

"The point is," he said quite reasonably, "that if you brought the money she doesn't expect you to hand it over to anybody except her. If you didn't bring it she doesn't want to see you. I don't think her mind can be changed about that. That's why I asked if you had brought it."

"I brought it."

He looked doubtfully at me. I showed him the money I had got from the bank. He jumped up briskly from the sofa.

"I'll have her here in a minute or two," he said over his shoulder as his long legs moved him toward the door. At the door he stopped to ask, "Do you know her? Or shall I have her bring means of identifying herself?"

"That would be best," I told him.

He went out, leaving the corridor door open.

In five minutes he was back with a slender blonde girl of twenty-three in pale green silk. The looseness of her small mouth and the puffiness around her blue eyes weren't yet pronounced enough to spoil her prettiness.

I stood up.

"This is Miss Hambleton," he said.

She gave me a swift glance and then lowered her eyes again, nervously playing with the strap of a handbag she held.

"You can identify yourself?" I asked.

"Sure," the man said. "Show them to him, Sue."

She opened the bag, brought out some papers and things, and held them up for me to take.

"Sit down, sit down," the man said as I took them.

They sat on the sofa. I sat in the rocking chair again and examined the things she had given me. There were two letters addressed to Sue Hambleton here, her father's telegram welcoming her home, a couple of receipted department store bills, an automobile driver's license, and a savings account pass book that showed a balance of less than ten dollars.

By the time I had finished my examination the girl's embarrassment was gone. She looked levelly at me, as did the man beside her. I felt in my pocket, found my copy of the photograph New York had sent us at the beginning of the hunt, and looked from it to her.

"Your mouth could have shrunk, maybe," I said, "but how could your nose have got that much longer?"

"If you don't like my nose," she said, "how'd you like to go to hell?" Her face had turned red.

"That's not the point. It's a swell nose, but it's not Sue's." I held the photograph out to her. "See for yourself."

She glared at the photograph and then at the man.

"What a smart guy you are," she told him.

He was watching me with dark eyes that had a brittle shine to them between narrow-drawn eyelids. He kept on watching me while he spoke to her out the side of his mouth, crisply. "Pipe down."

She piped down. He sat and watched me. I sat and watched him. A clock ticked seconds away behind me. His eyes began shifting their focus from one of my eyes to the other. The girl sighed.

He said in a low voice, "Well?"

I said, "You're in a hole."

"What can you make out of it?" he asked casually.

"Conspiracy to defraud."

The girl jumped up and hit one of his shoulders angrily with the back of a hand, crying, "What a smart guy you are, to get me in a jam like this. It was going to be duck soup—yeh! Eggs in the coffee—yeh! Now look at you. You haven't even got guts enough to tell this guy to go chase himself." She spun around to face me, pushing her red face down at me—I was still sitting in the rocker—snarling, "Well, what are you waiting for? Waiting to be kissed goodbye? We don't owe you anything, do we? We didn't get any of your lousy money, did we? Outside, then. Take the air. Dangle."

"Stop it, sister," I growled. "You'll bust something."

The man said, "For God's sake stop that bawling, Peggy, and give somebody else a chance." He addressed me, "Well, what do you want?"

"How'd you get into this?" I asked.

He spoke quickly, eagerly, "A fellow named Kenny gave me that stuff and told me about this Sue Hambleton, and her old man having plenty. I thought I'd give it a whirl. I figured the old man would either wire the dough right off the reel or wouldn't send it at all. I didn't figure on this send-a-man stuff. Then when his wire came, saying he was sending a man to see her, I ought to have dropped it.

"But hell! Here was a man coming with a grand in cash. That was too good to let go of without a try. It looked like there still might be a chance of copping, so I got Peggy to do Sue for me. If the man was coming today, it was a cinch he belonged out here on the Coast, and it was an even bet he wouldn't know Sue, would only have a description of her. From what Kenny had told me about her, I knew Peggy would come pretty close to fitting her description. I still don't see how you got that photograph. I only wired the old man yesterday. I mailed a couple of letters to Sue, here, yesterday, so we'd have them with the other identification stuff to get the money from the telegraph company on."

"Kenny gave you the old man's address?"

"Sure he did."

"Did he give you Sue's?"

"No."

"How'd Kenny get hold of the stuff?"

"He didn't say."

"Where's Kenny now?"

"I don't know. He was on his way east, with something else on the fire, and couldn't fool with this. That's why he passed it on to me."

"Big-hearted Kenny," I said. "You know Sue Hambleton?"

"No," emphatically. "I'd never even heard of her till Kenny told me."

"I don't like this Kenny," I said, "though without him your story's got some good points. Could you tell it leaving him out?"

He shook his head slowly from side to side, saying, "It wouldn't be the way it happened."

"That's too bad. Conspiracies to defraud don't mean as much to me as finding Sue. I might have made a deal with you."

He shook his head again, but his eyes were thoughtful, and his lower lip moved up to overlap the upper a little.

The girl had stepped back so she could see both of us as we talked, turning her face, which showed she didn't like us, from one to the other as we spoke our pieces. Now she fastened her gaze on the man, and her eyes were growing angry again.

I got up on my feet, telling him, "Suit yourself. But if you want to play it that way I'll have to take you both in."

He smiled with indrawn lips and stood up.

The girl thrust herself in between us, facing him.

"This is a swell time to be dummying up," she spit at him. "Pop off, you lightweight, or I will. You're crazy if you think I'm going to take the fall with you."

"Shut up," he said in his throat.

"Shut me up," she cried.

He tried to, with both hands. I reached over her shoulders and caught one of his wrists, knocked the other hand up.

She slid out from between us and ran around behind me, screaming, "Joe does know her. He got the things from her. She's at the St. Martin on O'Farrell Street—her and Babe McCloor."

While I listened to this I had to pull my head aside to let Joe's right hook miss me, had got his left arm twisted behind him, had turned my hip to catch his knee, and had got the palm of my left hand under his chin. I was ready to give his chin the Japanese tilt when he stopped wrestling and grunted, "Let me tell it."

"Hop to it," I consented, taking my hands away from him and stepping back.

He rubbed the wrist I had wrenched, scowling past me at the girl. He called her four unlovely names, the mildest of which was "a dumb twist," and told her, "He was bluffing about throwing us in the can. You don't think old man Hambleton's hunting for newspaper space, do you?" That wasn't a bad guess.

He sat on the sofa again, still rubbing his wrist. The girl stayed on the other side of the room, laughing at him through her teeth.

I said, "All right, roll it out, one of you."

"You've got it all," he muttered. "I glaumed that stuff last week when I was visiting Babe, knowing the story and hating to see a promising layout like that go to waste."

"What's Babe doing now?" I asked.

"I don't know."

"Is he still puffing them?"

"I don't know."

"Like hell you don't."

"I don't," he insisted. "If you know Babe you know you can't get anything out of him about what he's doing."

"How long have he and Sue been here?"

"About six months that I know of."

"Who's he mobbed up with?"

"I don't know. Any time Babe works with a mob he picks them up on the road and leaves them on the road."

"How's he fixed?"

"I don't know. There's always enough grub and liquor in the joint."

Half an hour of this convinced me that I wasn't going to get much information about my people here.

I went to the phone in the passageway and called the Agency. The boy on the switchboard told me MacMan was in the operative's room. I asked to have him sent up to me, and went back to the living room. Joe and Peggy took their heads apart when I came in.

MacMan arrived in less than ten minutes. I let him in and told him, "This fellow says his name's Joe Wales, and the girl's supposed to be Peggy Carroll who lives upstairs in 421. We've got them cold for conspiracy to defraud, but I've made a deal with them. I'm going out to look at it now. Stay here with them, in this room. Nobody goes in or out, and nobody but you gets to the phone. There's a fire escape in front of the window. The window's locked now. I'd keep it that way. If the deal turns out O.K. we'll let them go, but if they cut up on you while I'm gone there's no reason why you can't knock them around as much as you want."

MacMan nodded his hard round head and pulled a chair out between them and the door. I picked up my hat.

Joe Wales called, "Hey, you're not going to uncover me to Babe, are you? That's got to be part of the deal."

"Not unless I have to."

"I'd just as leave stand the rap," he said. "I'd be safer in jail."

"I'll give you the best break I can," I promised, "but you'll have to take what's dealt you."

Walking over to the St. Martin—only half a dozen blocks from Wales's place—I decided to go up against McCloor and the girl as a Continental op who suspected Babe of being in on a branch bank stick-up in Alameda the previous week. He hadn't been in on it—if the bank people had described half-correctly the men who had robbed them—so it wasn't likely my supposed suspicions would frighten him much. Clearing himself, he might give me some information I could use. The chief thing I wanted, of course, was a look at the girl, so I could report to her father that I had seen her. There was no reason for supposing that she and Babe knew her father was trying to keep an eye on her. Babe had a record. It was natural enough for sleuths to drop in now and then and try to hang something on him.

The St. Martin was a small three-story apartment house of red brick between two taller hotels. The vestibule register showed R. K. McCloor, 313, as Wales and Peggy had told me.

I pushed the bell button. Nothing happened. Nothing happened any of the four times I pushed it. I pushed the button labeled *Manager.*

The door clicked open. I went indoors. A beefy woman in a pink-striped cotton dress that needed pressing stood in an apartment doorway just inside the street door.

"Some people named McCloor live here?" I asked.

"Three-thirteen," she said.

"Been living here long?"

She pursed her fat mouth, looked intently at me, hesitated, but finally said, "Since last June."

"What do you know about them?"

She balked at that, raising her chin and her eyebrows.

I gave her my card. That was safe enough; it fit in with the pretext I intended using upstairs.

Her face, when she raised it from reading the card, was oily with curiosity.

"Come in here," she said in a husky whisper, backing through the doorway.

I followed her into her apartment. We sat on a chesterfield and she whispered, "What is it?"

"Maybe nothing." I kept my voice low, playing up to her theatricals. "He's done time for safe burglary. I'm trying to get a line on him now, on the off chance that he might have been tied up in a recent job. I don't know that he was. He may be going straight for all I know." I took his photograph—front and profile, taken at Leavenworth—out of my pocket. "This him?"

She seized it eagerly, nodded, said, "Yes, that's him, all right," turned it over to read the description on the back, and repeated, "Yes, that's him, all right."

"His wife is here with him?" I asked.

She nodded vigorously.

"I don't know her," I said. "What sort of looking girl is she?"

She described a girl who could have been Sue Hambleton. I couldn't show Sue's picture; that would have uncovered me if she and Babe heard about it.

I asked the woman what she knew about the Mc-Cloors. What she knew wasn't a great deal: paid their rent on time, kept irregular hours, had occasional drinking parties, quarreled a lot.

"Think they're in now?" I asked. "I got no answer on the bell."

"I don't know," she whispered. "I haven't seen either of them since night before last, when they had a fight."

"Much of a fight?"

"Not much worse than usual."

"Could you find out if they're in?" I asked.

She looked at me out of the ends of her eyes.

"I'm not going to make any trouble for you," I assured her. "But if they've blown I'd like to know it, and I reckon you would too."

"All right, I'll find out." She got up, patting a pocket in which keys jingled. "You wait here."

"I'll go as far as the third floor with you," I said, "and wait out of sight there."

"All right," she said reluctantly.

On the third floor, I remained by the elevator. She disappeared around a corner of the dim corridor, and presently a muffled electric bell rang. It rang three times. I heard her keys jingle and one of them grate in a lock. The lock clicked. I heard the doorknob rattle as she turned it.

Then a long moment of silence was ended by a scream that filled the corridor from wall to wall.

I jumped for the corner, swung around it, saw an open door ahead, went through it, and slammed the door shut behind me.

The scream stopped.

I was in a small dark vestibule with three doors beside the one I had come through. One door was shut. One opened into a bathroom. I went to the other.

The fat manager stood just inside it, her round back to me. I pushed past her and saw what she was looking at.

Sue Hambleton, in pale yellow pajamas trimmed with black lace, was lying across the bed. She lay on her back. Her arms were stretched out over her head. One leg was bent under her, one stretched out so that its bare foot rested on the floor. That bare foot was whiter than a live foot could be. Her face was white as her foot, except for a mottled swollen area from the right eyebrow to the right cheek-bone and dark bruises on her throat.

"Phone the police," I told the woman, and began poking into corners, closets and drawers.

It was late afternoon when I returned to the Agency. I asked the file clerk to see if we had anything on Joe Wales and Peggy Carroll, and then went into the Old Man's office.

He put down some reports he had been reading, gave me a nodded invitation to sit down, and asked, "You've seen her?"

"Yeah. She's dead."

The Old Man said, "Indeed," as if I had said it was raining, and smiled with polite attentiveness while I told him about it—from the time I had rung Wales's bell until I had joined the fat manager in the dead girl's apartment.

"She had been knocked around some, was bruised on the face and neck," I wound up. "But that didn't kill her."

"You think she was murdered?" he asked, still smiling gently.

"I don't know. Doc Jordan says he thinks it could have been arsenic. He's hunting for it in her now. We found a funny thing in the joint. Some thick sheets of dark gray paper were stuck in a book—*The Count of Monte Cristo*—wrapped in a month-old newspaper and wedged into a dark corner between the stove and the kitchen wall."

"Ah, arsenical fly paper," the Old Man murmured. "The Maybrick-Seddons trick. Mashed in water, four to six grains of arsenic can be soaked out of a sheet—enough to kill two people."

I nodded, saying, "I worked on one in Louisville in 1916. The mulatto janitor saw McCloor leaving at half-past nine yesterday morning. She was probably dead before that. Nobody's seen him since. Earlier in the morning the people in the next apartment had heard them talking, her groaning. But they had too many fights for the neighbors to pay much attention to that. The landlady told me they had a fight the night before that. The police are hunting for him."

"Did you tell the police who she was?"

"No. What do we do on that angle? We can't tell them about Wales without telling them all."

"I dare say the whole thing will have to come out," he said thoughtfully. "I'll wire New York."

I went out of his office. The file clerk gave me a couple of newspaper clippings. The first told me that fifteen months ago Joseph Wales, alias Holy Joe, had been arrested on the complaint of a farmer named Toomey that he had been taken for twenty-five hundred dollars on a phony "business opportunity" by Wales and three other men. The second clipping said the case had been dropped when Toomey failed to appear against Wales in court—bought off in the customary manner by the return of part or all of his money. That was all our files held on Wales, and they had nothing on Peggy Carroll.

* * *

MacMan opened the door for me when I returned to Wales's apartment.

"Anything doing?" I asked him.

"Nothing—except they've been belly-aching a lot." Wales came forward, asking eagerly, "Satisfied now?"

The girl stood by the window, looking at me with anxious eyes.

I didn't say anything.

"Did you find her?" Wales asked, frowning. "She was where I told you?"

"Yeah," I said.

"Well, then." Part of his frown went away. "That lets Peggy and me out, doesn't—" He broke off, ran his tongue over his lower lip, put a hand to his chin, asked sharply, "You didn't give them the tip-off on me, did you?"

I shook my head, no.

He took his hand from his chin and asked irritably, "What's the matter with you, then? What are you looking like that for?"

Behind him the girl spoke bitterly. "I knew damned well it would be like this," she said. "I knew damned well we weren't going to get out of it. Oh, what a smart guy you are!"

"Take Peggy into the kitchen, and shut both doors," I told MacMan. "Holy Joe and I are going to have a real heart-to-heart talk."

The girl went out willingly, but when MacMan was closing the door she put her head in again to tell Wales, "I hope he busts you in the nose if you try to hold out on him."

MacMan shut the door.

"Your playmate seems to think you know something," I said.

Wales scowled at the door and grumbled, "She's more help to me than a broken leg." He turned his face to me, trying to make it look frank and friendly. "What do you want? I came clean with you before. What's the matter now?"

"What do you guess?"

He pulled his lips in between his teeth. "What do you want to make me guess for?" he demanded. "I'm willing to play ball with you. But what can I do if you won't tell me what you want? I can't see inside your head."

"You'd get a kick out of it if you could."

He shook his head wearily and walked back to the sofa, sitting down bent forward, his hands together between his knees. "All right," he sighed. "Take your time about asking me. I'll wait for you."

I went over and stood in front of him. I took his chin between my left thumb and fingers, raising his head and bending my own down until our noses were almost touching. I said, "Where you stumbled, Joe, was in sending the telegram right after the murder."

"He's dead?" It popped out before his eyes had even had time to grow round and wide.

The question threw me off balance. I had to wrestle with my forehead to keep it from wrinkling, and I put too much calmness in my voice when I asked, "Is who dead?"

"Who? How do I know? Who do you mean?"

"Who did you think I meant?" I insisted.

"How do I know? Oh, all right! Old man Hambleton, Sue's father."

"That's right," I said, and took my hand away from his chin.

"And he was murdered, you say?" He hadn't moved his face an inch from the position into which I had lifted it. "How?"

"Arsenic fly paper."

"Arsenic fly paper." He looked thoughtful. "That's a funny one."

"Yeah, very funny. Where'd you go about buying some if you wanted it?"

"Buying it? I don't know. I haven't seen any since I was a kid. Nobody uses fly paper here in San Francisco anyway. There aren't enough flies."

"Somebody used some here," I said, "on Sue."

"Sue?" He jumped so that the sofa squeaked under him.

"Yeah. Murdered yesterday morning—arsenical fly paper."

"Both of them?" he asked incredulously.

"Both of who?"

"Her and her father."

"Yeah."

He put his chin far down on his chest and rubbed the back of one hand with the palm of the other. "Then I am in a hole," he said slowly.

"That's what," I cheerfully agreed. "Want to try talking yourself out of it?"

"Let me think."

I let him think, listening to the tick of the clock while he thought. Thinking brought drops of sweat out on his gray-white face. Presently he sat up straight, wiping his face with a fancily colored handkerchief. "I'll talk," he said. "I've got to talk now. Sue was getting ready to ditch Babe. She and I were going away. She— Here, I'll show you."

He put his hand in his pocket and held out a folded sheet of thick note paper to me. I took it and read:

Dear Joe:—

I can't stand this much longer—we've simply got to go soon. Babe beat me again tonight. Please, if you really love me, let's make it soon.

Sue

The handwriting was a nervous woman's, tall, angular, and piled up.

"That's why I made the play for Hambleton's grand," he said. "I've been shatting on my uppers for a couple of months, and when that letter came yesterday I just had to raise dough somehow to get her away. She wouldn't have stood for tapping her father though, so I tried to swing it without her knowing."

"When did you see her last?"

"Day before yesterday, the day she mailed that letter. Only I saw her in the afternoon—she was here—and she wrote it that night."

"Babe suspect what you were up to?"

"We didn't think he did. I don't know. He was jealous as hell all the time, whether he had any reason to be or not."

"How much reason did he have?"

Wales looked me straight in the eye and said, "Sue was a good kid."

I said, "Well, she's been murdered."

He didn't say anything.

Day was darkening into evening. I went to the door and pressed the light button. I didn't lose sight of Holy Joe Wales while I was doing it.

As I took my finger away from the button, something clicked at the window. The click was loud and sharp.

I looked at the window.

A man crouched there on the fire escape, looking in through the glass and lace curtain. He was a thick-featured dark man whose size identified him as Babe McCloor. The muzzle of a big black automatic was touching the glass in front of him. He had tapped the glass with it to catch our attention.

He had our attention.

There wasn't anything for me to do just then. I stood there and looked at him. I couldn't tell whether he was looking at me or at Wales. I could see him clearly enough, but the lace curtain spoiled my view of details like that. I imagined he wasn't neglecting either of us, and I didn't imagine the lace curtain hid much from him. He was closer to the curtain than we, and I had turned on the room's lights.

Wales, sitting dead-still on the sofa, was looking at McCloor. Wales's face wore a peculiar, stiffly sullen expression. His eyes were sullen. He wasn't breathing.

McCloor flicked the nose of his pistol against the pane, and a triangular piece of glass fell out, tinkling apart on the floor. It didn't, I was afraid, make enough noise to alarm MacMan in the kitchen. There were two closed doors between here and there.

Wales looked at the broken pane and closed his eyes. He closed them slowly, little by little, exactly as if he were falling asleep. He kept his stiffly sullen blank face turned straight to the window.

McCloor shot him three times.

The bullets knocked Wales down on the sofa, back against the wall. Wales's eyes popped open, bulging. His lips crawled back over his teeth, leaving them naked to the gums. His tongue came out. Then his head fell down and he didn't move any more.

When McCloor jumped away from the window I jumped to it. While I was pushing the curtain aside, unlocking the window and raising it, I heard his feet land on the cement paving below.

MacMan flung the door open and came in, the girl at his heels.

"Take care of this," I ordered as I scrambled over the sill. "McCloor shot him."

Wales's apartment was on the second floor. The fire escape ended there with a counter-weighted iron ladder that a man's weight would swing down into a cement-paved court.

I went down as Babe McCloor had gone, swinging down on the ladder till within dropping distance of the court, and then letting go.

There was only one street exit to the court. I took it.

A startled looking, smallish man was standing in the middle of the sidewalk close to the court, gaping at me as I dashed out.

I caught his arm, shook it. "A big guy running." Maybe I yelled. "Where?"

He tried to say something, couldn't, and waved his arm at billboards standing across the front of a vacant lot on the other side of the street.

I forgot to say, "Thank you," in my hurry to get over there.

I got behind the billboards by crawling under them instead of going to either end, where there were openings. The lot was large enough and weedy enough to give cover to anybody who wanted to lie down and bushwhack a pursuer—even anybody as large as Babe McCloor.

While I considered that, I heard a dog barking at one corner of the lot. He could have been barking at a man who had run by. I ran to that corner of the lot. The dog was in a board-fenced backyard, at the corner of a narrow alley that ran from the lot to a street.

I chinned myself on the board fence, saw a wire-haired terrier alone in the yard, and ran down the alley while he was charging my part of the fence.

I put my gun back into my pocket before I left the alley for the street.

A small touring car was parked at the curb in front of a cigar store some fifteen feet from the alley. A policeman was talking to a slim dark-faced man in the cigar store doorway.

"The big fellow that come out of the alley a minute ago," I said. "Which way did he go?"

The policeman looked dumb. The slim man nodded his head down the street, said, "Down that way," and went on with his conversation.

I said, "Thanks," and went on down to the corner. There was a taxi phone there and two idle taxis. A block and a half below, a streetcar was going away. "Did the big fellow who came down here a minute ago take a taxi or the streetcar?" I asked the two taxi chauffeurs who were leaning against one of the taxis.

The rattier-looking one said, "He didn't take a taxi."

I said, "I'll take one. Catch that streetcar for me."

The streetcar was three blocks away before we got going. The street wasn't clear enough for me to see who got on and off it. We caught it when it stopped at Market Street.

"Follow along," I told the driver as I jumped out.

On the rear platform of the streetcar I looked through the glass. There were only eight or ten people aboard.

"There was a great big fellow got on at Hyde Street," I said to the conductor. "Where'd he get off?"

The conductor looked at the silver dollar I was turning over in my fingers and remembered that the big man got off at Taylor Street. That won the silver dollar.

I dropped off as the streetcar turned into Market Street. The taxi, close behind, slowed down, and its door swung open. "Sixth and Mission," I said as I hopped in.

McCloor could have gone in any direction from Taylor Street. I had to guess. The best guess seemed to be that he would make for the other side of Market Street.

It was fairly dark by now. We had to go down to Fifth Street to get off Market, then over to Mission, and back up to Sixth. We got to Sixth Street without seeing McCloor. I couldn't see him on Sixth Street—either way from the crossing.

"On up to Ninth," I ordered, and while we rode told the driver what kind of man I was looking for.

We arrived at Ninth Street. No McCloor. I cursed and pushed my brains around.

The big man was a yegg. San Francisco was on fire for him. The yegg instinct would be to use a rattler to get away from trouble. The freight yards were in this end of town. Maybe he would be shifty enough to lie low instead of trying to powder. In that case, he probably hadn't crossed Market Street at all. If he stuck, there would still be a chance of picking him up tomorrow. If he was high-tailing, it was catch him now or not at all.

"Down to Harrison," I told the driver.

We went down to Harrison Street, and down Harrison to Third, up Bryant to Eighth, down Brannan to Third again, and over to Townsend—and we didn't see Babe McCloor.

"That's tough, that is," the driver sympathized as we stopped across the street from the Southern Pacific passenger station.

"I'm going over and look around in the station," I said. "Keep your eyes open while I'm gone."

When I told the copper in the station my trouble he introduced me to a couple of plain-clothes men who had been planted there to watch for McCloor. That had been done after Sue Hambleton's body was found. The shooting of Holy Joe Wales was news to them.

I went outside again and found my taxi in front of the door, its horn working overtime, but too asthmatically to be heard indoors. The ratty driver was excited.

"A guy like you said come up out of King Street just now and swung on a Number 16 car as it pulled away," he said.

"Going which way?"

"Thataway," pointing southeast.

"Catch him," I said, jumping in.

The streetcar was out of sight around a bend in Third Street two blocks below. When we rounded the bend, the streetcar was slowing up, four blocks ahead. It hadn't slowed up very much when a man leaned far out and stepped off. He was a tall man, but didn't look tall on account of his shoulder spread. He didn't check his momentum, but used it to carry him across the sidewalk and out of sight.

We stopped where the man had left the car.

I gave the driver too much money and told him, "Go back to Townsend Street and tell the copper in the station that I've chased Babe McCloor into the S. P. yards."

I thought I was moving silently down between two strings of box cars, but I had gone less than twenty feet when a light flashed in my face and a sharp voice ordered, "Stand still, you."

I stood still. Men came from between cars. One of them spoke my name, adding, "What are you doing here? Lost?" It was Harry Pebble, a police detective.

I stopped holding my breath and said, "Hello, Harry. Looking for Babe?"

"Yes. We've been going over the rattlers."

"He's here. I just tailed him in from the street."

Pebble swore and snapped the light off.

"Watch, Harry," I advised. "Don't play with him. He's packing plenty of gun and he's cut down one boy tonight."

"I'll play with him," Pebble promised, and told one of the men with him to go over and warn those on the other side of the yard that McCloor was in, and then to ring for reinforcements.

"We'll just sit on the edge and hold him in till they come," he said.

That seemed a sensible way to play it. We spread out and waited. Once Pebble and I turned back a lanky bum who tried to slip into the yard between us, and one of the men below us picked up a shivering kid who was trying to slip out. Otherwise nothing happened until Lieutenant Duff arrived with a couple of carloads of coppers.

Most of our force went into a cordon around the yard. The rest of us went through the yard in small groups, working it over car by car. We picked up a few hoboes that Pebble and his men had missed earlier, but we didn't find McCloor.

We didn't find any trace of him until somebody stumbled over a railroad bum huddled in the shadow of a gondola. It took a couple of minutes to bring him to, and he couldn't talk then. His jaw was broken. But when we asked if McCloor had slugged him, he nodded, and when we asked in which direction McCloor had been headed, he moved a feeble hand to the east.

We went over and searched the Santa Fe yards.

We didn't find McCloor.

I rode up to the Hall of Justice with Duff. MacMan was in the captain of detectives' office with three or four police sleuths.

"Wales die?" I asked.

"Yep."

"Say anything before he went?"

"He was gone before you were through the window."

"You held on to the girl?"

"She's here."

"She say anything?"

"We were waiting for you before we tapped her," detective-sergeant O'Gar said, "not knowing the angle on her."

"Let's have her in. I haven't had any dinner yet. How about the autopsy on Sue Hambleton?"

"Chronic arsenic poisoning."

"Chronic? That means it was fed to her little by little, and not in a lump?"

"Uh-huh. From what he found in her kidneys, intestines, liver, stomach and blood, Jordan figures there was less than a grain of it in her. That wouldn't be enough to knock her off. But he says he found arsenic in the tips of her hair, and she'd have to be given some at least a month ago for it to have worked out that far."

"Any chance that it wasn't arsenic that killed her?"

"Not unless Jordan's a bum doctor."

A policewoman came in with Peggy Carroll.

The blonde girl was tired. Her eyelids, mouth corners and body drooped, and when I pushed a chair out toward her she sagged down in it.

O'Gar ducked his grizzled bullet head at me.

"Now, Peggy," I said, "tell us where you fit into this mess."

"I don't fit into it." She didn't look up. Her voice was tired. "Joe dragged me into it. He told you."

"You his girl?"

"If you want to call it that," she admitted.

"You jealous?"

"What," she asked, looking up at me, her face puzzled, "has that got to do with it?"

"Sue Hambleton was getting ready to go away with him when she was murdered."

The girl sat up straight in the chair and said deliberately, "I swear to God I didn't know she was murdered."

"But you did know she was dead," I said positively.

"I didn't," she replied just as positively.

I nudged O'Gar with my elbow. He pushed his under-shot jaw at her and barked, "What are you trying to give us? You knew she was dead. How could you kill her without knowing it?"

While she looked at him I waved the others in. They crowded close around her and took up the chorus of the sergeant's song. She was barked, roared, and snarled at plenty in the next few minutes.

The instant she stopped trying to talk back to them I cut in again. "Wait," I said, very earnestly. "Maybe she didn't kill her."

"The hell she didn't," O'Gar stormed, holding the center of the stage so the others could move away from the girl without their retreat seeming too artificial. "Do you mean to tell me this baby—"

"I didn't say she didn't," I remonstrated. "I said maybe she didn't."

"Then who did?"

I passed the question to the girl. "Who did?"

"Babe," she said immediately.

O'Gar snorted to make her think he didn't believe her.

I asked, as if I were honestly perplexed, "How do you know that if you didn't know she was dead?"

"It stands to reason he did," she said. "Anybody can see that. He found out she was going away with Joe, so he killed her and then came to Joe's and killed him. That's just exactly what Babe would do when he found it out."

"Yeah? How long have *you* known they were going away together?"

"Since they decided to. Joe told me a month or two ago."

"And you didn't mind?"

"You've got this all wrong," she said. "Of course I didn't mind. I was being cut in on it. You know her father had the bees. That's what Joe was after. She didn't mean anything to him but an in to the old man's pockets. And I was to get my dib. And you needn't think I was crazy

enough about Joe or anybody else to step off in the air for
them. Babe got next and fixed the pair of them. That's a
cinch."

"Yeah? How do you figure Babe would kill her?"

"That guy? You don't think he'd—"

"I mean how would he go about killing her?"

"Oh!" She shrugged. "With his hands, likely as not."

"Once he'd made up his mind to do it, he'd do it quick
and violent?" I suggested.

"That would be Babe," she agreed.

"But you can't see him slow-poisoning her—spreading
it out over a month?"

Worry came into the girl's blue eyes. She put her lower
lip between her teeth, then said slowly, "No, I can't see
him doing it that way. Not Babe."

"Who can you see doing it that way?"

She opened her eyes wide, asking, "You mean Joe?"

I didn't say anything.

"Joe might have," she said persuasively. "God only
knows what he'd want to do it for, why he'd want to get
rid of the kind of meal ticket she was going to be. But you
couldn't always guess what he was getting at. He pulled
plenty of dumb ones. He was too slick without being
smart. If he was going to kill her, though, that would be
about the way he'd go about it."

"Were he and Babe friendly?"

"No."

"Did he go to Babe's much?"

"Not at all that I know about. He was too leery of
Babe to take a chance on being caught there. That's why I
moved upstairs, so Sue could come over to our place to see
him."

"Then how could Joe have hidden the fly paper he
poisoned her with in her apartment?"

"Fly paper!" Her bewilderment seemed honest enough.

"Show it to her," I told O'Gar.

He got a sheet from the desk and held it close to the
girl's face.

She stared at it for a moment and then jumped up and grabbed my arm with both hands.

"I didn't know what it was," she said excitedly. "Joe had some a couple of months ago. He was looking at it when I came in. I asked him what it was for, and he smiled that wisenheimer smile of his and said, 'You make angels out of it,' and wrapped it up again and put it in his pocket. I didn't pay much attention to him; he was always fooling with some kind of tricks that were supposed to make him wealthy, but never did."

"Ever see it again?"

"No."

"Did you know Sue very well?"

"I didn't know her at all. I never even saw her. I used to keep out of the way so I wouldn't gum Joe's play with her."

"But you know Babe?"

"Yes, I've been on a couple of parties where he was. That's all I know him."

"Who killed Sue?"

"Joe," she said. "Didn't he have that paper you say she was killed with?"

"Why did he kill her?"

"I don't know. He pulled some awful dumb tricks sometimes."

"You didn't kill her?"

"No, no, no!"

I jerked the corner of my mouth at O'Gar.

"You're a liar," he bawled, shaking the fly paper in her face. "You killed her." The rest of the team closed in, throwing accusations at her. They kept it up until she was groggy and the policewoman beginning to look worried.

Then I said angrily, "All right. Throw her in a cell and let her think it over." To her, "You know what you told Joe this afternoon: this is no time to dummy up. Do a lot of thinking tonight."

"Honest to God I didn't kill her," she said.

I turned my back to her. The policewoman took her away.

"Ho-hum," O'Gar yawned. "We gave her a pretty good ride at that, for a short one."

"Not bad," I agreed. "If anybody else looked likely, I'd say she didn't kill Sue. But if she's telling the truth, then Holy Joe did it. And why should he poison the goose that was going to lay nice yellow eggs for him? And how and why did he cache the poison in their apartment? Babe had the motive, but damned if he looks like a slow-poisoner to me. You can't tell, though; he and Holy Joe could even have been working together on it."

"Could," Duff said. "But it takes a lot of imagination to get that one down. Anyway you twist it, Peggy's our best bet so far. Go up against her again, hard, in the morning?"

"Yeah," I said. "And we've got to find Babe."

The others had had dinner. MacMan and I went out and got ours. When we returned to the detective bureau an hour later it was practically deserted of the regular operatives.

"All gone to Pier 42 on a tip that McCloor's there," Steve Ward told us.

"How long ago?"

"Ten minutes."

MacMan and I got a taxi and set out for Pier 42. We didn't get to Pier 42.

On First Street, half a block from the Embarcadero, the taxi suddenly shrieked and slid to a halt.

"What—?" I began, and saw a man standing in front of the machine. He was a big man with a big gun. "Babe," I grunted, and put my hand on MacMan's arm to keep him from getting his gun out.

"Take me to—" McCloor was saying to the frightened driver when he saw us. He came around to my side and pulled the door open, holding the gun on us.

He had no hat. His hair was wet, plastered to his head. Little streams of water trickled down from it. His clothes were dripping wet.

He looked surprised at us and ordered, "Get out."

As we got out he growled at the driver, "What the hell you got your flag up for if you had fares?"

The driver wasn't there. He had hopped out the other side and was scooting away down the street. McCloor cursed him and poked his gun at me, growling, "Go on, beat it."

Apparently he hadn't recognized me. The light here wasn't good, and I had a hat on now. He had seen me for only a few seconds in Wales's room.

I stepped aside. MacMan moved to the other side.

McCloor took a backward step to keep us from getting him between us and started an angry word.

MacMan threw himself on McCloor's gun arm.

I socked McCloor's jaw with my fist. I might just as well have hit somebody else for all it seemed to bother him.

He swept me out of his way and pasted MacMan in the mouth. MacMan fell back till the taxi stopped him, spit out a tooth, and came back for more.

I was trying to climb up McCloor's left side.

MacMan came in on his right, failed to dodge a chop of the gun, caught it square on the top of the noodle, and went down hard. He stayed down.

I kicked McCloor's ankle, but couldn't get his foot from under him. I rammed my right fist into the small of his back and got a left-handful of his wet hair, swinging on it. He shook his head, dragging me off my feet.

He punched me in the side and I could feel my ribs and guts flattening together like leaves in a book.

I swung my fist against the back of his neck. That bothered him. He made a rumbling noise down in his chest, crunched my shoulder in his left hand, and chopped at me with the gun in his right.

I kicked him somewhere and punched his neck again.

Down the street, at the Embarcadero, a police whistle was blowing. Men were running up First Street toward us.

McCloor snorted like a locomotive and threw me away from him. I didn't want to go. I tried to hang on. He threw me away from him and ran up the street.

I scrambled up and ran after him, dragging my gun out.

At the first corner he stopped to squirt metal at me—three shots. I squirted one at him. None of the four connected.

He disappeared around the corner. I swung wide around it, to make him miss if he were flattened to the wall waiting for me. He wasn't. He was a hundred feet ahead, going into a space between two warehouses. I went in after him, and out after him at the other end, making better time with my hundred and ninety pounds than he was making with his two-fifty.

He crossed a street, turning up, away from the waterfront. There was a light on the corner. When I came into its glare he wheeled and leveled his gun at me. I didn't hear it click, but I knew it had when he threw it at me. The gun went past with a couple of feet to spare and raised hell against a door behind me.

McCloor turned and ran up the street. I ran up the street after him.

I put a bullet past him to let the others know where we were. At the next corner he started to turn to the left, changed his mind, and went straight on.

I sprinted, cutting the distance between us to forty or fifty feet, and yelped, "Stop or I'll drop you."

He jumped sidewise into a narrow alley.

I passed it on the jump, saw he wasn't waiting for me, and went in. Enough light came in from the street to let us see each other and our surroundings. The alley was blind —walled on each side and at the other end by tall concrete buildings with steel-shuttered windows and doors.

McCloor faced me, less than twenty feet away. His jaw stuck out. His arms curved down free of his sides. His shoulders were bunched.

"Put them up," I ordered, holding my gun level.

"Get out of my way, little man," he grumbled, taking a stiff-legged step toward me. "I'll eat you up."

"Keep coming," I said, "and I'll put you down."

"Try it." He took another step, crouching a little. "I can still get to you *with* slugs in me."

"Not where I'll put them." I was wordy, trying to talk him into waiting till the others came up. I didn't want to have to kill him. We could have done that from the taxi. "I'm no Annie Oakley, but if I can't pop your kneecaps with two shots at this distance, you're welcome to me. And if you think smashed kneecaps are a lot of fun, give it a whirl."

"Hell with that," he said and charged.

I shot his right knee.

He lurched toward me.

I shot his left knee.

He tumbled down.

"You would have it," I complained.

He twisted around, and with his arms pushed himself into a sitting position facing me.

"I didn't think you had sense enough to do it," he said through his teeth.

I talked to McCloor in the hospital. He lay on his back in bed with a couple of pillows slanting his head up. The skin was pale and tight around his mouth and eyes, but there was nothing else to show he was in pain.

"You sure devastated me, bo," he said when I came in.

"Sorry," I said, "but—"

"I ain't beefing. I asked for it."

"Why'd you kill Holy Joe?" I asked, off-hand, as I pulled a chair up beside the bed.

"Uh-uh—you're tooting the wrong ringer."

I laughed and told him I was the man in the room with Joe when it happened.

McCloor grinned and said, "I thought I'd seen you somewheres before. So that's where it was. I didn't pay no attention to your mug, just so your hands didn't move."

"Why'd you kill him?"

He pursed his lips, screwed up his eyes at me, thought something over, and said, "He killed a broad I knew."

"He killed Sue Hambleton?" I asked.

He studied my face a while before he replied, "Yep."

"How do you figure that out?"

"Hell," he said, "I don't have to. Sue told me. Give me a butt."

I gave him a cigarette, held a lighter under it, and objected. "That doesn't exactly fit in with other things I know. Just what happened and what did she say? You might start back with the night you gave her the goog."

He looked thoughtful, letting smoke sneak slowly out of his nose, then said, "I hadn't ought to hit her in the eye, that's a fact. But, see, she had been out all afternoon and wouldn't tell me where she'd been, and we had a row about it. What's this—Thursday morning? That was Monday, then. After the row I went out and spent the night in a dump over on Army Street. I got home about seven the next morning. Sue was sick as hell, but she wouldn't let me get a croaker for her. That was kind of funny, because she was scared stiff."

McCloor scratched his head meditatively and suddenly drew in a great lungful of smoke, practically eating up the rest of the cigarette. He let the smoke leak out of mouth and nose together, looking dully through the cloud at me. Then he said brusquely, "Well, she went under. But before she went she told me she'd been poisoned by Holy Joe."

"She say how he'd given it to her?"

McCloor shook his head.

"I'd been asking her what was the matter, and not getting anything out of her. Then she starts whining that she's poisoned. 'I'm poisoned, Babe,' she whines. 'Arsenic. That damned Holy Joe,' she says. Then she won't say anything else, and it's not a hell of a while after that that she kicks off."

"Yeah? Then what'd you do?"

"I went gunning for Holy Joe. I knew him but didn't know where he jungled up, and didn't find out till yesterday. You was there when I came. You know about that. I had picked up a boiler and parked it over on Turk Street, for the getaway. When I got back to it, there was a copper standing close to it. I figured he might have spotted it as a hot one and was waiting to see who came for it, so I let it alone, and caught a streetcar instead, and cut for the yards. Down there I ran into a whole flock of hammer and saws and had to go overboard in China Basin, swimming up to a pier, being ranked again by a watchman there, swimming off to another, and finally getting through the line only to run into another bad break. I wouldn't of flagged that taxi if the *For Hire* flag hadn't been up."

"You knew Sue was planning to take a run-out on you with Joe?"

"I don't know it yet," he said. "I knew damned well she was cheating on me, but I didn't know who with."

"What would you have done if you had known that?" I asked.

"Me?" He grinned wolfishly. "Just what I did."

"Killed the pair of them," I said.

He rubbed his lower lip with a thumb and asked calmly, "You think I killed Sue?"

"You did."

"Serves me right," he said. "I must be getting simple in my old age. What the hell am I doing barbering with a lousy dick? That never got nobody nothing but grief. Well, you might just as well take it on the heel and toe now, my lad. I'm through spitting."

And he was. I couldn't get another word out of him.

The Old Man sat listening to me, tapping his desk lightly with the point of a long yellow pencil, staring past me with mild blue rimless-spectacled eyes. When I had brought my story up to date, he asked pleasantly, "How is MacMan?"

"He lost two teeth, but his skull wasn't cracked. He'll be out in a couple of days."

The Old Man nodded and asked, "What remains to be done?"

"Nothing. We can put Peggy Carroll on the mat again,

but it's not likely we'll squeeze much more out of her. Outside of that, the returns are pretty well all in."

"And what do you make of it?"

I squirmed in my chair and said, "Suicide."

The Old Man smiled at me, politely but skeptically.

"I don't like it either," I grumbled. "And I'm not ready to write in a report yet. But that's the only total that what we've got will add up to. That fly paper was hidden behind the kitchen stove. Nobody would be crazy enough to try to hide something from a woman in her own kitchen like that. But the woman might hide it there.

"According to Peggy, Holy Joe had the fly paper. If Sue hid it, she got it from him. For what? They were planning to go away together, and were only waiting till Joe, who was on the nut, raised enough dough. Maybe they were afraid of Babe, and had the poison there to slip him if he tumbled to their plan before they went. Maybe they meant to slip it to him before they went anyway.

"When I started talking to Holy Joe about murder, he thought Babe was the one who had been bumped off. He was surprised, maybe, but as if he was surprised that it had happened so soon. He was more surprised when he heard that Sue had died too, but even then he wasn't so surprised as when he saw McCloor alive at the window.

"She died cursing Holy Joe, and she knew she was poisoned, and she wouldn't let McCloor get a doctor. Can't that mean that she had turned against Joe, and had taken the poison herself instead of feeding it to Babe? The poison was hidden from Babe. But even if he found it, I can't figure him as a poisoner. He's too rough. Unless he caught her trying to poison him and made her swallow the stuff. But that doesn't account for the month-old arsenic in her hair."

"Does your suicide hypothesis take care of that?" the Old Man asked.

"It could," I said. "Don't be kicking holes in my theory. It's got enough as it stands. But, if she committed suicide this time, there's no reason why she couldn't have tried it

once before—say after a quarrel with Joe a month ago—
and failed to bring it off. That would have put the arsenic
in her. There's no real proof that she took any between a
month ago and day before yesterday."

"No real proof," the Old Man protested mildly, "except
the autopsy's finding—chronic poisoning."

I was never one to let experts' guesses stand in my way.
I said, "They base that on the small amount of arsenic they
found in her remains—less than a fatal dose. And the
amount they find in your stomach after you're dead depends on how much you vomit before you die."

The Old Man smiled benevolently at me and asked,
"But you're not, you say, ready to write this theory into a
report? Meanwhile, what do you propose doing?"

"If there's nothing else on tap, I'm going home, fumi-
gate my brains with Fatimas, and try to get this thing
straightened out in my head. I think I'll get a copy of *The
Count of Monte Cristo* and run through it. I haven't read it
since I was a kid. It looks like the book was wrapped up
with the fly paper to make a bundle large enough to
wedge tightly between the wall and stove, so it wouldn't
fall down. But there might be something in the book. I'll
see anyway."

"I did that last night," the Old Man murmured.

I asked, "And?"

He took a book from his desk drawer, opened it where
a slip of paper marked a place, and held it out to me, one
pink finger marking a paragraph.

"Suppose you were to take a milligramme of this
poison the first day, two milligrammes the second day,
and so on. Well, at the end of ten days you would have
taken a centigramme: at the end of twenty days increasing
another milligramme, you would have taken three hundred centigrammes; that is to say, a dose you would
support without inconvenience, and which would be very
dangerous for any other person who had not taken the
same precautions as yourself. Well, then, at the end of the
month, when drinking water from the same carafe, you

would kill the person who had drunk this water, without your perceiving otherwise than from slight inconvenience that there was any poisonous substance mingled with the water."

"That does it," I said. "That does it. They were afraid to go away without killing Babe, too certain he'd come after them. She tried to make herself immune from arsenic poisoning by getting her body accustomed to it, taking steadily increasing doses, so when she slipped the big shot in Babe's food she could eat it with him without danger. She'd be taken sick, but wouldn't die, and the police couldn't hang his death on her because she too had eaten the poisoned food.

"That clicks. After the row Monday night, when she wrote Joe the note urging him to make the getaway soon, she tried to hurry up her immunity, and increased her preparatory doses too quickly, took too large a shot. That's why she cursed Joe at the end; it was his plan."

"Possibly she overdosed herself in an attempt to speed it along," the Old Man agreed, "but not necessarily. There are people who can cultivate an ability to take large doses of arsenic without trouble, but it seems to be a sort of natural gift with them, a matter of some constitutional peculiarity. Ordinarily, anyone who tried it would do what Sue Hambleton did—slowly poison themselves until the cumulative effect was strong enough to cause death."

Babe McCloor was hanged, for killing Holy Joe Wales, six months later.

THE SCORCHED FACE

"We expected them home yesterday," Alfred Banbrock ended his story. "When they had not come by this morning, my wife telephoned Mrs. Walden. Mrs. Walden said they had not been down there—had not been expected, in fact."

"On the face of it, then," I suggested, "it seems that your daughters went away of their own accord, and are staying away on their own accord?"

Banbrock nodded gravely. Tired muscles sagged in his fleshy face.

"It would seem so," he agreed. "That is why I came to your agency for help instead of going to the police."

"Have they ever disappeared before?"

"No. If you read the papers and magazines, you've no doubt seen hints that the younger generation is given to irregularity. My daughters came and went pretty much as they pleased. But, though I can't say I ever knew what they were up to, we always knew where they were in a general way."

"Can you think of any reason for their going away like this?"

He shook his weary head.

"Any recent quarrels?" I probed.

"N—" He changed it to: "Yes—although I didn't attach any importance to it, and wouldn't have recalled it if you hadn't jogged my memory. It was Thursday evening—the evening before they went away."

"And it was about—?"

"Money, of course. We never disagreed over anything else. I gave each of my daughters an adequate allowance—perhaps a very liberal one. Nor did I keep them strictly within it. There were few months in which they didn't exceed it. Thursday evening they asked for an amount of money even more than usual in excess of what two girls should need. I wouldn't give it to them, though I finally did give them a somewhat smaller amount. We didn't exactly quarrel—not in the strict sense of the word—but there was a certain lack of friendliness between us."

"And it was after this disagreement that they said they were going down to Mrs. Walden's, in Monterey, for the weekend?"

"Possibly. I'm not sure of that point. I don't think I heard of it until the next morning, but they may have told my wife before that."

"And you know of no other possible reason for their running away?"

"None. I can't think that our dispute over money—by no means an unusual one—had anything to do with it."

"What does their mother think?"

"Their mother is dead," Banbrock corrected me. "My wife is their stepmother. She is only two years older than Myra, my older daughter. She is as much at sea as I."

"Did your daughters and their stepmother get along all right together?"

"Yes! Yes! Excellently! If there was a division in the family, I usually found them standing together against me."

"Your daughters left Friday afternoon?"

"At noon, or a few minutes after. They were going to drive down."

"The car, of course, is still missing?"

"Naturally."

"What was it?"

"A Locomobile, with a special cabriolet body. Black."

"You can give me the license and engine numbers?"

"I think so."

He turned in his chair to the big roll-top desk that hid a quarter of one office wall, fumbled with papers in a compartment, and read the numbers over his shoulder to me. I put them on the back of an envelope.

"I'm going to have this car put on the police department list of stolen machines," I told him. "It can be done without mentioning your daughters. The police bulletin might find the car for us. That would help us find your daughters."

"Very well," he agreed, "if it can be done without disagreeable publicity. As I told you at first, I don't want any more advertising than is absolutely necessary—unless it becomes likely that harm has come to the girls."

I nodded understanding, and got up.

"I want to go out and talk to your wife," I said. "Is she home now?"

"Yes, I think so. I'll phone her and tell her you are coming."

In a big limestone fortress on top of a hill in Sea Cliff, looking down on ocean and bay, I had my talk with Mrs. Banbrock. She was a tall dark girl of not more than twenty-two years, inclined to plumpness.

She couldn't tell me anything her husband hadn't at least mentioned, but she could give me finer details.

I got descriptions of the two girls:

Myra—20 years old; 5 feet 8 inches; 150 pounds; athletic; brisk, almost masculine manner and carriage; bobbed brown hair; brown eyes; medium complexion; square face, with large chin and short nose; scar over left ear, concealed by hair; fond of horses and all outdoor sports. When she left the house she wore a blue and green wool dress, small blue hat, short black seal coat, and black slippers.

Ruth—18 years; 5 feet 4 inches; 105 pounds; brown eyes; brown bobbed hair; medium complexion; small oval face; quiet, timid, inclined to lean on her more forceful sister. When last seen she had worn a tobacco-brown coat trimmed with brown fur over a gray silk dress, and a wide brown hat.

I got two photographs of each girl, and an additional snapshot of Myra standing in front of the cabriolet. I got a list of the things they had taken with them—such things as would naturally be taken on a weekend visit. What I valued most of what I got was a list of their friends, relatives, and other acquaintances, so far as Mrs. Banbrock knew them.

"Did they mention Mrs. Walden's invitation before their quarrel with Mr. Banbrock?" I asked, when I had my lists stowed away.

"I don't think so," Mrs. Banbrock said thoughtfully. "I didn't connect the two things at all. They didn't really quarrel with their father, you know. It wasn't harsh enough to be called a quarrel."

"Did you see them when they left?"

"Assuredly! They left about half-past twelve Friday afternoon. They kissed me as usual when they went, and there was certainly nothing in their manner to suggest anything out of the ordinary."

"You've no idea at all where they might have gone?"

"None."

"Can't even make a guess?"

"I can't. Among the names and addresses I have given you are some of friends and relatives of the girls in other cities. They may have gone to one of those. Do you think we should—?"

"I'll take care of that," I promised. "Could you pick out one or two of them as the most likely places for the girls to have gone?"

She wouldn't try it. "No," she said positively, "I could not."

From this interview I went back to the Agency, and put the Agency machinery in motion: arranging to have operatives from some of the Continental's other branches call on the out-of-town names on my list, having the missing Locomobile put on the police department list, turning one photograph of each girl over to a photographer to be copied.

That done, I set out to talk to the persons on the list Mrs. Banbrock had given me. My first call was on a Constance Delee, in an apartment building on Post Street. I saw a maid. The maid said Miss Delee was out of town. She wouldn't tell me where her mistress was, or when she would be back.

From there I went up on Van Ness Avenue and found a Wayne Ferris in an automobile salesroom: a sleek-haired young man whose very nice manners and clothes completely hid anything else—brains for instance—he might have had. He was very willing to help me, and he knew nothing. It took him a long time to tell me so. A nice boy.

Another blank: "Mrs. Scott is in Honolulu."

In a real estate office on Montgomery Street I found my next one—another sleek, stylish, smooth-haired young man with nice manners and nice clothes. His name was Raymond Elwood. I would have thought him a no more distant relative of Ferris than cousin if I hadn't known that the world—especially the dancing, teaing world—was full of their sort. I learned nothing from him.

Then I drew some more blanks: "Out of town," "Shopping," "I don't know where you can find him."

I found one more of the Banbrock girls' friends before I called it a day. Her name was Mrs. Stewart Correll. She lived in Presidio Terrace, not far from the Banbrocks. She was a small woman, or girl, of about Mrs. Banbrock's age. A little fluffy blonde person with wide eyes of that particular blue which always looks honest and candid no matter what is going on behind it.

"I haven't seen either Ruth or Myra for two weeks or more," she said in answer to my question.

"At that time—the last time you saw them—did either say anything about going away?"

"No."

Her eyes were wide and frank. A little muscle twitched in her upper lip.

"And you've no idea where they might have gone?"

"No."

Her fingers were rolling her lace handkerchief into a little ball.

"Have you heard from them since you last saw them?"

"No."

She moistened her mouth before she said it.

"Will you give me the names and addresses of all the people you know who were also known by the Banbrock girls?"

"Why—? Is there—?"

"There's a chance that some of them may have seen them more recently than you," I explained. "Or may even have seen them since Friday."

Without enthusiasm, she gave me a dozen names. All were already on my list. Twice she hesitated as if about to speak a name she did not want to speak. Her eyes stayed on mine, wide and honest. Her fingers, no longer balling the handkerchief, picked at the cloth of her skirt.

I didn't pretend to believe her. But my feet weren't solidly enough on the ground for me to put her on the grill. I gave her a promise before I left, one that she could get a threat out of if she liked.

"Thanks, very much," I said. "I know it's hard to remember things exactly. If I run across anything that will help your memory, I'll be back to let you know about it."

"Wha—? Yes, do!" she said.

Walking away from the house, I turned my head to look back just before I passed out of sight. A curtain swung into place at a second-floor window. The street lights weren't bright enough for me to be sure the curtain had swung in front of a blonde head.

My watch told me it was nine-thirty: too late to line up any more of the girls' friends. I went home, wrote my report for the day, and turned in, thinking more about Mrs. Correll than about the girls.

She seemed worth an investigation.

Some telegraphic reports were in when I got to the

office the next morning. None was of any value. Investigation of the names and addresses in other cities had revealed nothing. An investigation in Monterey had established reasonably—which is about as well as anything is ever established in the detecting business—that the girls had not been there recently, that the Locomobile had not been there.

The early editions of the afternoon papers were on the street when I went out to get some breakfast before taking up the grind where I had dropped it the previous night.

I bought a paper to prop behind my grapefruit.

It spoiled my breakfast for me:

BANKER'S WIFE SUICIDE

Mrs. Stewart Correll, wife of the vice-president of the Golden Gate Trust Company, was found dead early this morning by her maid in her bedroom, in her home in Presidio Terrace. A bottle believed to have contained poison was on the floor beside the bed.

The dead woman's husband could give no reason for his wife's suicide. He said she had not seemed depressed or . . .

At the Correll residence I had to do a lot of talking before I could get to Correll. He was a tall, slim man of less than thirty-five, with a sallow, nervous face and blue eyes that fidgeted.

"I'm sorry to disturb you at a time like this," I apologized when I had finally insisted my way into his presence. "I won't take up more of your time than necessary. I am an operative of the Continental Detective Agency. I have been trying to find Ruth and Myra Banbrock, who disappeared several days ago. You know them, I think."

"Yes," he said without interest. "I know them."

"You knew they had disappeared?"

"No." His eyes switched from a chair to a rug. "Why should I?"

"Have you seen either of them recently?" I asked, ignoring his question.

"Last week—Wednesday, I think. They were just leaving—standing at the door talking to my wife—when I came home from the bank."

"Didn't your wife say anything to you about their vanishing?"

"No. Really, I can't tell you anything about the Misses Banbrock. If you'll excuse me—"

"Just a moment longer," I said. "I wouldn't have bothered you if it hadn't been necessary. I was here last night to question Mrs. Correll. She seemed nervous. My impression was that some of her answers to my questions were—uh—evasive. I want—"

He was up out of his chair. His face was red in front of mine.

"You!" he cried. "I can thank you for—"

"Now, Mr. Correll," I tried to quiet him, "there's no use—"

But he had himself all worked up.

"You drove my wife to her death," he accused me. "You killed her with your damned prying—with your bulldozing threats, with your—"

That was silly. I felt sorry for this young man whose wife had killed herself. Apart from that, I had work to do. I tightened the screws.

"We won't argue, Correll," I told him. "The point is that I came here to see if your wife could tell me anything about the Banbrocks. She told me less than the truth. Later, she committed suicide. I want to know why. Come through for me, and I'll do what I can to keep the papers and the public from linking her death with the girls' disappearance."

"Linking her death with their disappearance?" he exclaimed. "That's absurd!"

"Maybe—but the connection is there!" I hammered

away at him. I felt sorry for him, but I had work to do. "It's there. If you'll give it to me, maybe it won't have to be advertised. I'm going to get it, though. You give it to me—or I'll go after it out in the open."

For a moment I thought he was going to take a poke at me. I wouldn't have blamed him. His body stiffened—then sagged, and he dropped back into his chair. His eyes fidgeted away from mine. "There's nothing I can tell," he mumbled. "When her maid went to her room to call her this morning, she was dead. There was no message, no reason, nothing."

"Did you see her last night?"

"No. I was not home for dinner. I came in late and went straight to my own room, not wanting to disturb her. I hadn't seen her since I left the house that morning."

"Did she seem disturbed or worried then?"

"No."

"Why do you think she did it?"

"My God, man, I don't know! I've thought and thought, but I don't know!"

"Health?"

"She seemed well. She was never ill, never complained."

"Any recent quarrels?"

"We never quarreled—never in the year and a half we have been married!"

"Financial trouble?"

He shook his head without speaking or looking up from the floor.

"Any other worry?"

He shook his head again.

"Did the maid notice anything peculiar in her behavior last night?"

"Nothing."

"Have you looked through her things—for papers, letters?"

"Yes—and found nothing." He raised his head to look at me. "The only thing"—he spoke very slowly—"there was a little pile of ashes in the grate in her room, as if she had burned papers, or letters."

Correll held nothing more for me—nothing I could get out of him, anyway.

The girl at the front gate in Alfred Banbrock's Shoreman's Building suite told me he was *in conference*. I sent my name in. He came out of conference to take me into his private office. His tired face was full of questions.

I didn't keep him waiting for the answers. He was a grown man. I didn't edge around the bad news.

"Things have taken a bad break," I said as soon as we were locked in together. "I think we'll have to go to the police and newspapers for help. A Mrs. Correll, a friend of your daughters, lied to me when I questioned her yesterday. Last night she committed suicide."

"Irma Correll? Suicide?"

"You knew her?"

"Yes! Intimately! She was—that is, she was a close friend of my wife and daughters. She killed herself?"

"Yes. Poison. Last night. Where does she fit in with your daughters' disappearance?"

"Where?" he repeated. "I don't know. Must she fit in?"

"I think she must. She told me she hadn't seen your daughters for a couple of weeks. Her husband told me just now that they were talking to her when he came home from the bank last Wednesday afternoon. She seemed nervous when I questioned her. She killed herself shortly afterward. There's hardly a doubt that she fits in somewhere."

"And that means—?"

"That means," I finished for him, "that your daughters may be perfectly safe, but that we can't afford to gamble on that possibility."

"You think harm has come to them?"

"I don't think anything," I evaded, "except that with a death tied up closely with their going, we can't afford to play around."

Banbrock got his attorney on the phone—a pink-faced, white-haired old boy named Norwall, who had the reputation of knowing more about corporations than all the Morgans, but who hadn't the least idea as to what police procedure was all about—and told him to meet us at the Hall of Justice.

We spent an hour and a half there, getting the police turned loose on the affair, and giving the newspapers what we wanted them to have. That was plenty of dope on the girls, plenty of photographs and so forth, but nothing about the connection between them and Mrs. Correll. Of course we let the police in on that angle.

After Banbrock and his attorney had gone away together, I went back to the detectives' assembly room to chew over the job with Pat Reddy, the police sleuth assigned to it.

Pat was the youngest member of the detective bureau —a big blond Irishman who went in for the spectacular in his lazy way.

A couple of years ago he was a new copper, pounding his feet in harness on a hillside beat. One night he tagged an automobile that was parked in front of a fireplug. The owner came out just then and gave him an argument. She was Althea Wallach, only and spoiled daughter of the owner of the Wallach Coffee Company—a slim, reckless youngster with hot eyes. She must have told Pat plenty. He took her over to the station and dumped her in a cell.

Old Wallach, so the story goes, showed up the next morning with a full head of steam and half the lawyers in San Francisco. But Pat made his charge stick, and the girl was fined. Old Wallach did everything but take a punch at Pat in the corridor afterward. Pat grinned his sleepy grin at the coffee importer, and drawled, "You better lay off me—or I'll stop drinking your coffee."

That crack got into most of the newspapers in the country, and even into a Broadway show.

But Pat didn't stop with the snappy comeback. Three days later he and Althea Wallach went over to Alameda and got themselves married. I was in on that part. I happened to be on the ferry they took, and they dragged me along to see the deed done.

Old Wallach immediately disowned his daughter, but that didn't seem to worry anybody else. Pat went on pounding his beat, but, now that he was conspicuous, it wasn't long before his qualities were noticed. He was boosted into the detective bureau.

Old Wallach relented before he died, and left Althea his millions.

Pat took the afternoon off to go to the funeral, and went back to work that night, catching a wagonload of gunmen. He kept on working. I don't know what his wife did with her money, but Pat didn't even improve the quality of his cigars—though he should have. He lived now in the Wallach mansion, true enough, and now and then on rainy mornings he would be driven down to the Hall in a Hispano-Suiza brougham; but there was no difference in him beyond that.

That was the big blond Irishman who sat across a desk from me in the assembly room and fumigated me with something shaped like a cigar.

He took the cigar-like thing out of his mouth presently, and spoke through the fumes. "This Correll woman you think's tied up with the Banbrocks—she was stuck-up a couple of months back and nicked for eight hundred dollars. Know that?"

I hadn't known it. "Lose anything besides cash?" I asked.

"No."

"You believe it?"

He grinned. "That's the point," he said. "We didn't catch the bird who did it. With women who lose things that way—especially money—it's always a question whether it's a hold-up or a hold-out."

He teased some more poison-gas out of the cigar-thing, and added, "The hold-up might have been on the level, though. What are you figuring on doing now?"

"Let's go up to the Agency and see if anything new has

turned up. Then I'd like to talk to Mrs. Banbrock again. Maybe she can tell us something about the Correll woman."

At the office I found that reports had come in on the rest of the out-of-town names and addresses. Apparently none of these people knew anything about the girls' whereabouts. Reddy and I went on up to Sea Cliff to the Banbrock home.

Banbrock had telephoned the news of Mrs. Correll's death to his wife, and she had read the papers. She told us she could think of no reason for the suicide. She could imagine no possible connection between the suicide and her stepdaughters' vanishing.

"Mrs. Correll seemed as nearly contented and happy as usual the last time I saw her, two or three weeks ago," Mrs. Banbrock said. "Of course she was by nature inclined to be dissatisfied with things, but not to the extent of doing a thing like this."

"Do you know of any trouble between her and her husband?"

"No. So far as I know, they were happy, though—"

She broke off. Hesitancy, embarrassment showed in her dark eyes.

"Though?" I repeated.

"If I don't tell you now, you'll think I am hiding something," she said, flushing, and laughing a little laugh that held more nervousness than amusement. "It hasn't any bearing, but I was always just a little jealous of Irma. She and my husband were—well, everyone thought they would marry. That was a little before he and I married. I never let it show, and I dare say it was a foolish idea, but I always had a suspicion that Irma married Stewart more in pique than for any other reason, and that she was still fond of Alfred—Mr. Banbrock."

"Was there anything definite to make you think that?"

"No, nothing—really! I never thoroughly believed it. It was just a sort of vague feeling. Cattiness, no doubt, more than anything else."

It was getting along toward evening when Pat and I

left the Banbrock house. Before we knocked off for the day, I called up the Old Man—the Continental's San Francisco branch manager, and therefore my boss—and asked him to sic an operative on Irma Correll's past.

I took a look at the morning papers—thanks to their custom of appearing almost as soon as the sun is out of sight—before I went to bed. They had given our job a good spread. All the facts except those having to do with the Correll angle were there, plus photographs, and the usual assortment of guesses and similar garbage.

The following morning I went after the friends of the missing girls to whom I had not yet talked. I found some of them and got nothing of value from them. Late in the morning I telephoned the office to see if anything new had turned up. It had.

"We've just had a call from the sheriff's office at Martinez," the Old Man told me. "An Italian grapegrower near Knob Valley picked up a charred photograph a couple of days ago, and recognized it as Ruth Banbrock when he saw her picture in this morning's paper. Will you get up there? A deputy sheriff and the Italian are waiting for you in the Knob Valley marshal's office."

"I'm on my way," I said.

At the ferry building I used the four minutes before my boat left trying to get Pat Reddy on the phone, with no success.

Knob Valley is a town of less than a thousand people, a dreary, dirty town in Contra Costa County. A San Francisco—Sacramento local set me down there while the afternoon was still young.

I knew the marshal slightly—Tom Orth. I found two men in the office with him. Orth introduced us. Abner Paget, a gawky man of forty-something, with a slack chin, scrawny face, and pale intelligent eyes, was the deputy sheriff. Gio Cereghino, the Italian grapegrower, was a small, nut-brown man with strong yellow teeth that showed in an everlasting smile under his black mustache, and soft brown eyes.

Paget showed me the photograph. A scorched piece of

paper the size of a half-dollar, apparently all that had not been burned of the original picture. It was Ruth Banbrock's face. There was little room for doubting that. She had a peculiarly excited—almost drunken—look, and her eyes were larger than in the other pictures of her I had seen. But it was her face.

"He says he found it day 'fore yesterday," Paget explained dryly, nodding at the Italian. "The wind blew it against his foot when he was walkin' up a piece of road near his place. He picked it up an' stuck it in his pocket, he says, for no special reason, I guess." He paused to regard the Italian meditatively. The Italian nodded his head in vigorous affirmation.

"Anyways," the deputy sheriff went on, "he was in town this mornin', an' seen the pictures in the papers from Frisco. So he come in here an' told Tom about it. Tom an' me decided the best thing was to phone your agency—since the papers said you was workin' on it."

I looked at the Italian. Paget, reading my mind, explained, "Cereghino lives over in the hills. Got a grape ranch there. Been around here five or six years, an' ain't killed nobody that I know of."

"Remember the place where you found the picture?" I asked the Italian.

His grin broadened under his mustache, and his head went up and down. "For sure, I remember that place."

"Let's go there," I suggested to Paget.

"Right. Comin' along, Tom?"

The marshal said he couldn't. He had something to do in town. Cereghino, Paget and I went out and got into a dusty Ford that the deputy sheriff drove.

We rode for nearly an hour, along a county road that bent up the slope of Mount Diablo. After a while, at a word from the Italian, we left the county road for a dustier and ruttier one. A mile of this one.

"This place," Cereghino said.

Paget stopped the Ford. We got out in a clearing. The trees and bushes that had crowded the road retreated here for twenty feet or so on either side, leaving a little dusty circle in the woods.

"About this place," the Italian was saying. "I think by this stump. But between that bend ahead and that one behind, I know for sure."

Paget was a countryman. I am not. I waited for him to move.

He looked around the clearing, slowly, standing still between the Italian and me. His pale eyes lighted presently. He went around the Ford to the far side of the clearing. Cereghino and I followed.

Near the fringe of brush at the edge of the clearing, the scrawny deputy stopped to grunt at the ground. The wheel-marks of an automobile were there. A car had turned around here.

Paget went on into the woods. The Italian kept close to his heels. I brought up the rear. Paget was following some sort of track. I couldn't see it, either because he and the Italian blotted it out ahead of me, or because I'm a shine Indian. We went back quite a way.

Paget stopped. The Italian stopped.

Paget said, "Uh-huh," as if he had found an expected thing.

The Italian said something with the name of God in it. I trampled a bush, coming beside them to see what they saw. I saw it.

At the base of a tree, on her side, her knees drawn up close to her body, a girl was dead. She wasn't nice to see. Birds had been at her.

A tobacco-brown coat was half on, half off her shoulders. I knew she was Ruth Banbrock before I turned her over to look at the side of her face the ground had saved from the birds.

Cereghino stood watching me while I examined the girl. His face was mournful in a calm way. The deputy sheriff paid little attention to the body. He was off in the brush, moving around, looking at the ground. He came back as I finished my examination.

"Shot," I told him, "once in the right temple. Before that, I think, there was a fight. There are marks on the arm that was under her body. There's nothing on her—no jewelry, money—nothing."

"That goes," Paget said. "Two women got out of the car back in the clearin', an' came here. Could've been three women—if the others carried this one. Can't make out how many went back. One of 'em was larger than this one. There was a scuffle here. Find the gun?"

"No," I said.

"Neither did I. It went away in the car, then. There's what's left of a fire over there." He ducked his head to the left. "Paper an' rags burnt. Not enough left to do us any good. I reckon the photo Cereghino found blew away from the fire. Late Friday, I'd put it, or maybe Saturday mornin' . . . No nearer than that."

I took the deputy sheriff's word for it. He seemed to know his stuff.

"Come here. I'll show you somethin'," he said, and led me over to a little black pile of ashes.

He hadn't anything to show me. He wanted to talk to me away from the Italian's ears.

"I think the Italian's all right," he said, "but I reckon I'd best hold him a while to make sure. This is some way from his place, an' he stuttered a little bit too much tellin' me how he happened to be passin' here. Course, that don't mean nothin' much. All these Italians peddle *vino*, an' I guess that's what brought him out this way. I'll hold him a day or two, anyways."

"Good," I agreed. "This is your country, and you know the people. Can you visit around and see what you can pick up? Whether anybody saw anything? Saw a Locomobile cabriolet? Or anything else? You can get more than I could."

"I'll do that," he promised.

"All right. Then I'll go back to San Francisco now. I suppose you'll want to camp here with the body?"

"Yeah. You drive the Ford back to Knob Valley, an' tell

Tom what's what. He'll come or send out. I'll keep the Italian here with me."

Waiting for the next west-bound train out of Knob Valley, I got the office on the telephone. The Old Man was out. I told my story to one of the office men and asked him to get the news to the Old Man as soon as he could.

Everybody was in the office when I got back to San Francisco. Alfred Banbrock, his face a pink-gray that was deader than solid gray could have been. His pink and white old lawyer. Pat Reddy, sprawled on his spine with his feet on another chair. The Old Man, with his gentle eyes behind gold spectacles and his mild smile, hiding the fact that fifty years of sleuthing had left him without any feelings at all on any subject.

Nobody said anything when I came in. I said my say as briefly as possible.

"Then the other woman—the woman who killed Ruth was—?"

Banbrock didn't finish his question. Nobody answered it.

"We don't know what happened," I said after a while. "Your daughter and someone we don't know may have gone there. Your daughter may have been dead before she was taken there. She may have—"

"But Myra!" Banbrock was pulling at his collar with a finger inside. "Where is Myra?"

I couldn't answer that, nor could any of the others.

"You are going up to Knob Valley now?" I asked him.

"Yes, at once. You will come with me?"

I wasn't sorry I could not. "No. There are things to be done here. I'll give you a note to the marshal. I want you to look carefully at the piece of your daughter's photograph the Italian found—to see if you remember it."

Banbrock and the lawyer left.

Reddy lit one of his awful cigars.

"We found the car," the Old Man said.

"Where was it?"

"In Sacramento. It was left in a garage there either late

Friday night or early Saturday. Foley has gone up to investigate it. And Reddy has uncovered a new angle."

Pat nodded through his smoke.

"A hockshop dealer came in this morning," Pat said, "and told us that Myra Banbrock and another girl came to his joint last week and hocked a lot of stuff. They gave him phoney names, but he swears one of them was Myra. He recognized her picture as soon as he saw it in the paper. Her companion wasn't Ruth. It was a little blonde."

"Mrs. Correll?"

"Uh-huh. The shark can't swear to that, but I think that's the answer. Some of the jewelry was Myra's, some Ruth's, and some we don't know. I mean we can't prove it belonged to Mrs. Correll—though we will."

"When did all this happen?"

"They soaked the stuff Monday before they went away."

"Have you seen Correll?"

"Uh-huh. I did a lot of talking to him, but the answers weren't worth much. He says he don't know whether any of her jewelry is gone or not, and doesn't care. It was hers, he says, and she could do anything she wanted with it. He was kind of disagreeable. I got along a little better with one of the maids. She says some of Mrs. Correll's pretties disappeared last week. Mrs. Correll said she had lent them to a friend. I'm going to show the stuff the hockshop has to the maid tomorrow to see if she can identify it. She didn't know anything else—except that Mrs. Correll was out of the picture for a while on Friday—the day the Banbrock girls went away."

"What do you mean, out of the picture?" I asked.

"She went out late in the morning and didn't show up until somewhere around three the next morning. She and Correll had a row over it, but she wouldn't tell him where she had been."

I liked that. It could mean something.

"And," Pat went on, "Correll has just remembered that his wife had an uncle who went crazy in Pittsburgh in 1902, and that she had a morbid fear of going crazy herself, and that she had often said she would kill herself if she thought she was going crazy. Wasn't it nice of him to remember those things at last? To account for her death?"

"It was," I agreed, "but it doesn't get us anywhere. It doesn't even prove that he knows anything. Now my guess is—"

"To hell with your guess," Pat said, getting up and pushing his hat in place. "Your guesses all sound like a lot of static to me. I'm going home, eat my dinner, read my Bible, and go to bed."

I suppose he did. Anyway, he left us.

We all might as well have spent the next three days in bed for all the profit that came out of our running around. No place we visited, nobody we questioned, added to our knowledge. We were in a blind alley.

We learned that the Locomobile was left in Sacramento by Myra Banbrock, and not by anyone else, but we didn't learn where she went afterward. We learned that some of the jewelry in the pawnshop was Mrs. Correll's. The Locomobile was brought back from Sacramento. Mrs. Correll was buried. Ruth Banbrock was buried. The newspapers found other mysteries. Reddy and I dug and dug, and all we brought up was dirt.

The following Monday brought me close to the end of my rope. There seemed nothing more to do but sit back and hope that the circulars with which we had plastered North America would bring results. Reddy had already been called off and put to running out fresher trails. I hung on because Banbrock wanted me to keep at it so long as there was the shadow of anything to keep at. But by Monday I had worked myself out.

Before going to Banbrock's office to tell him I was licked, I dropped in at the Hall of Justice to hold a wake over the job with Pat Reddy. He was crouched over his desk, writing a report on some other job.

"Hello!" he greeted me, pushing his report away and smearing it with ashes from his cigar. "How go the Banbrock doings?"

"They don't," I admitted. "It doesn't seem possible,

with the stack-up what it is, that we should have come to a dead stop! It's there for us, if we can find it. The need of money before both the Banbrock and the Correll calamities, Mrs. Correll's suicide after I had questioned her about the girls, her burning things before she died and the burning of things immediately before or after Ruth Banbrock's death."

"Maybe the trouble is," Pat suggested, "that you're not such a good sleuth."

"Maybe."

We smoked in silence for a minute or two after that insult.

"You understand," Pat said presently, "there doesn't have to be any connection between the Banbrock death and disappearance and the Correll death."

"Maybe not. But there has to be a connection between the Banbrock death and the Banbrock disappearance. There was a connection—in a pawnshop—between the Banbrock and Correll actions before these things. If there is that connection, then—" I broke off, all full of ideas.

"What's the matter?" Pat asked. "Swallow your gum?"

"Listen!" I let myself get almost enthusiastic. "We've got what happened to three women hooked up together. If we could tie up some more in the same string—I want the names and addresses of all the women and girls in San Francisco who have committed suicide, been murdered, or have disappeared within the past year."

"You think this is a wholesale deal?"

"I think the more we can tie up together, the more lines we'll have to run out. And they can't all lead nowhere. Let's get our list, Pat!"

We spent all the afternoon and most of the night getting it. Its size would have embarrassed the Chamber of Commerce. It looked like a hunk of the telephone book. Things happened in a city in a year. The section devoted to strayed wives and daughters was the largest; suicides next; and even the smallest division—murders—wasn't any too short.

We could check off most of the names against what the police department had already learned of them and their motives, weeding out those positively accounted for in a manner nowise connected with our present interest. The remainder we split into two classes; those of unlikely connection, and those of more possible connection. Even then, the second list was longer than I had expected, or hoped.

There were six suicides in it, three murders, and twenty-one disappearances.

Reddy had other work to do. I put the list in my pocket and went calling.

For four days I ground at the list. I hunted, found, questioned, and investigated friends and relatives of the women and girls on my list. My questions all hit in the same direction. Had she been acquainted with Myra Banbrock? Ruth? Mrs. Correll? Had she been in need of money before her death or disappearance? Had she destroyed anything before her death or disappearance? Had she known any of the other women on my list?

Three times I drew yesses.

Sylvia Varney, a girl of twenty, who had killed herself on November 5th, had drawn six hundred dollars from the bank the week before her death. No one in her family could say what she had done with the money. A friend of Sylvia Varney's—Ada Youngman, a married woman of twenty-five or -six—had disappeared on December 2nd, and was still gone. The Varney girl had been at Mrs. Youngman's home an hour before she—the Varney girl—killed herself.

Mrs. Dorothy Sawdon, a young widow, had shot herself on the night of January 13th. No trace was found of either the money her husband had left her or the funds of a club whose treasurer she was. A bulky letter her maid remembered having given her that afternoon was never found.

These three women's connection with the Banbrock-Correll affair was sketchy enough. None of them had done anything that isn't done by nine out of ten women who kill themselves or run away. But the troubles of all three had come to a head within the past few months—and all three were women of about the same financial and social position as Mrs. Correll and the Banbrocks.

Finishing my list with no fresh leads, I came back to these three.

I had the names and addresses of sixty-two friends of the Banbrock girls. I set about getting the same sort of catalogue on the three women I was trying to bring into the game. I didn't have to do all the digging myself. Fortunately, there were two or three operatives in the office with nothing else to do just then.

We got something.

Mrs. Sawdon had known Raymond Elwood. Sylvia Varney had known Raymond Elwood. There was nothing to show Mrs. Youngman had known him, but it was likely she had. She and the Varney girl had been thick.

I had already interviewed this Raymond Elwood in connection with the Banbrock girls, but had paid no especial attention to him. I had considered him just one of the sleek-headed, high-polished young men of whom there were quite a few listed.

I went back at him, all interest now. The results were promising.

He had, as I have said, a real estate office on Montgomery Street. We were unable to find a single client he had ever served, or any signs of one's existence. He had an apartment out in the Sunset District, where he lived alone. His local record seemed to go back no farther than ten months, though we couldn't find its definite starting point. Apparently he had no relatives in San Francisco. He belonged to a couple of fashionable clubs. He was vaguely supposed to be "well connected in the East." He spent money.

I couldn't shadow Elwood, having too recently interviewed him. Dick Foley did. Elwood was seldom in his office during the first three days Dick tailed him. He was seldom in the financial district. He visited his clubs, he danced and teaed and so forth, and each of those three days he visited a house on Telegraph Hill.

The first afternoon Dick had him, Elwood went to the Telegraph Hill house with a tall fair girl from Burlingame. The second day—in the evening—with a plump young woman who came out of a house out on Broadway. The third evening with a very young girl who seemed to live in the same building as he.

Usually Elwood and his companion spent from three to four hours in the house on Telegraph Hill. Other people—all apparently well-to-do—went in and out of the house while it was under Dick's eye.

I climbed Telegraph Hill to give the house the up-and-down. It was a large house—a big frame house painted egg-yellow. It hung dizzily on a shoulder of the hill, a shoulder that was sharp where rock had been quarried away. The house seemed about to go skiing down on the roofs far below.

It had no immediate neighbors. The approach was screened by bushes and trees.

I gave that section of the hill a good strong play, calling at all the houses within shooting distance of the yellow one. Nobody knew anything about it, or about its occupants. The folks on the Hill aren't a curious lot—perhaps because most of them have something to hide on their own account.

My climbing uphill and downhill got me nothing until I succeeded in learning who owned the yellow house. The owner was an estate whose affairs were in the hands of the West Coast Trust Company.

I took my investigations to the trust company, with some satisfaction. The house had been leased eight months ago by Raymond Elwood, acting for a client named T. F. Maxwell.

We couldn't find Maxwell. We couldn't find anybody who knew Maxwell. We couldn't find any evidence that Maxwell was anything but a name.

One of the operatives went up to the yellow house on the hill, and rang the bell for half an hour with no result.

We didn't try that again, not wanting to stir things up at this stage.

I made another trip up the hill, house-hunting. I couldn't find a place as near the yellow house as I would have liked, but I succeeded in renting a three-room flat from which the approach to it could be watched.

Dick and I camped in the flat—with Pat Reddy, when he wasn't off on other duties—and watched machines turn into the screened path that led to the egg-tinted house. Afternoon and night there were machines. Most of them carried women. We saw no one we could place as a resident of the house. Elwood came daily, once alone, the other time with women whose faces we couldn't see from our window.

We shadowed some of the visitors away. They were without exception reasonably well off financially, and some were socially prominent. We didn't go up against any of them with talk. Even a carefully planned pretext is as likely as not to tip your mitt when you're up against a blind game.

Three days of this—and our break came.

It was early evening, just dark. Pat Reddy had phoned that he had been up on a job for two days and a night, and was going to sleep the clock around. Dick and I were sitting at the window of our flat, watching automobiles turn toward the yellow house, writing down their license numbers as they passed through the blue-white patch of light an arc-lamp put in the road just beyond our window.

A woman came climbing the hill, afoot. She was a tall woman, strongly built. A dark veil not thick enough to advertise the fact that she wore it to hide her features, nevertheless did hide them. Her way was up the hill, past our flat, on the other side of the roadway.

A night wind from the Pacific was creaking a grocer's sign down below, swaying the arc-light above. The wind caught the woman as she passed out of our building's sheltered area. Coat and skirts tangled. She put her back to the wind, a hand to her hat. Her veil whipped out straight from her face.

Her face was a face from a photograph—Myra Banbrock's face.

Dick made her with me. "Our baby!" he cried, bouncing to his feet.

"Wait," I said. "She's going into the joint on the edge of the hill. Let her go. We'll go after her when she's inside. That's our excuse for frisking the joint."

I went into the next room, where our telephone was, and called Pat Reddy's number.

"She didn't go in," Dick called from the window. "She went past the path."

"After her!" I ordered. "There's no sense to that! What's the matter with her?" I felt sort of indignant about it. "She's got to go in! Tail her. I'll find you after I get Pat."

Dick went.

Pat's wife answered the telephone. I told her who I was.

"Will you shake Pat out of the covers and send him up here? He knows where I am. Tell him I want him in a hurry."

"I will," she promised. "I'll have him there in ten minutes—wherever it is."

Outdoors, I went up the road, hunting for Dick and Myra Banbrock. Neither was in sight. Passing the bushes that masked the yellow house, I went on, circling down a stony path to the left. No sign of either.

I turned back in time to see Dick going into our flat. I followed.

"She's in," he said when I joined him. "She went up the road, cut across through some bushes, came back to the edge of the cliff, and slid feet-first through a cellar window."

That was nice. The crazier the people you are sleuthing act, as a rule, the nearer you are to an ending of your troubles.

Reddy arrived within a minute or two of the time his wife had promised. He came in buttoning his clothes.

"What the hell did you tell Althea?" he growled at me.

"She gave me an overcoat to put over my pajamas, dumped the rest of my clothes in the car, and I had to get in them on the way over."

"I'll cry with you after a while," I dismissed his troubles. "Myra Banbrock just went into the joint through a cellar window. Elwood has been there an hour. Let's knock it off."

Pat is deliberate.

"We ought to have papers, even at that," he stalled.

"Sure," I agreed, "but you can get them fixed up afterward. That's what you're here for. Contra Costa County wants her—maybe to try her for murder. That's all the excuse we need to get into the joint. We go there for her. If we happen to run into anything else—well and good."

Pat finished buttoning his vest.

"Oh, all right!" he said sourly. "Have it your way. But if you get me smashed for searching a house without authority, you'll have to give me a job with your law-breaking agency."

"I will." I turned to Foley. "You'll have to stay outside, Dick. Keep your eye on the getaway. Don't bother anybody else, but if the Banbrock girl gets out, stay behind her."

"I expected it," Dick howled. "Any time there's any fun I can count on being stuck off somewhere on a street corner!"

Pat Reddy and I went straight up the bush-hidden path to the yellow house's front door, and rang the bell.

A big black man in a red fez, red silk jacket over red-striped silk shirt, red zouave pants and red slippers opened the door. He filled the opening, framed in the black of the hall behind him.

"Is Mr. Maxwell home?" I asked.

The black man shook his head and said words in a language I don't know.

"Mr. Elwood, then?"

Another shaking of the head. More strange language.

"Let's see whoever is home then," I insisted.

Out of the jumble of words that meant nothing to me, I picked three in garbled English, which I thought were "master," "not," and "home."

The door began to close. I put a foot against it.

Pat flashed his buzzer.

Though the black man had poor English, he had knowledge of police badges.

One of his feet stamped on the floor behind him. A gong boomed deafeningly in the rear of the house.

The black man bent his weight to the door.

My weight on the foot that blocked the door, I leaned sidewise, swaying to the Negro.

Slamming from the hip, I put my fist in the middle of him.

Reddy hit the door and we went into the hall.

" 'Fore God, Fat Shorty," the black man gasped in good Virginian, "you done hurt me!"

Reddy and I went by him, down the hall whose bounds were lost in darkness.

The bottom of a flight of steps stopped my feet.

A gun went off upstairs. It seemed to point at us. We didn't get the bullets.

A babble of voices—women screaming, men shouting—came and went upstairs; came and went as if a door was being opened and shut.

"Up, my boy!" Reddy yelped in my ear.

We went up the stairs. We didn't find the man who had shot at us.

At the head of the stairs, a door was locked. Reddy's bulk forced it.

We came into a bluish light. A large room, all purple and gold. Confusion of overturned furniture and rumpled rugs. A gray slipper lay near a far door. A green silk gown was in the center of the floor. No person was there.

I raced Pat to the curtained door beyond the slipper. The door was not locked. Reddy yanked it wide.

A room with three girls and a man crouching in a

corner, fear in their faces. Neither of them was Myra Banbrock, or Raymond Elwood, or anyone we knew.

Our glances went away from them after the first quick
look.

The open door across the room grabbed our attention.

The door gave to a small room.

The room was chaos.

A small room, packed and tangled with bodies. Live
bodies, seething, writhing. The room was a funnel into
which men and women had been poured. They boiled
noisily toward the one small window that was the funnel's
outlet. Men and women, youths and girls, screaming,
struggling, squirming, fighting. Some had no clothes.

"We'll get through and block the window!" Pat yelled
in my ear.

"Like hell—" I began, but he was gone ahead into the
confusion.

I went after him.

I didn't mean to block the window. I meant to save Pat
from his foolishness. No five men could have fought
through that boiling turmoil of maniacs. No ten men could
have turned them from the window.

Pat—big as he is—was down when I got to him. A
half-dressed girl—a child—was driving at his face with
sharp high-heels. Hands, feet, were tearing him apart.

I cleared him with a play of gun-barrel on chins and
wrists—dragged him back.

"Myra's not there!" I yelled into his ear as I helped him
up. "Elwood's not there!"

I wasn't sure, but I hadn't seen them, and I doubted
that they would be in this mess. These savages, boiling
again to the window, with no attention for us, whoever
they were, weren't insiders. They were the mob, and the
principals shouldn't be among them.

"We'll try the other rooms," I yelled again. "We don't
want these."

Pat rubbed the back of his hand across his torn face
and laughed.

"It's a cinch I don't want 'em any more," he said.

We went back to the head of the stairs the way we had come. We saw no one. The man and girls who had been in the next room were gone.

At the head of the stairs we paused. There was no noise behind us except the now fainter babble of the lunatics fighting for their exit.

A door shut sharply downstairs.

A body came out of nowhere, hit my back, flattened me to the landing.

The feel of silk was on my cheek. A brawny hand was fumbling at my throat.

I bent my wrist until my gun, upside down, lay against my cheek. Praying for my ear, I squeezed.

My cheek took fire. My head was a roaring thing, about to burst.

The silk slid away.

Pat hauled me upright.

We started down the stairs.

Swish!

A thing came past my face, stirring my bared hair.

A thousand pieces of glass, china, plaster, exploded upward at my left.

I tilted head and gun together.

A Negro's red-silk arms were still spread over the balustrade above.

I sent him two bullets. Pat sent him two.

The Negro teetered over the rail.

He came down on us, arms outflung—a deadman's swan-dive.

We scurried down the stairs from under him.

He shook the house when he landed, but we weren't watching him then.

The smooth sleek head of Raymond Elwood took our attention.

In the light from above, it showed for a furtive split second around the newel-post at the foot of the stairs. Showed and vanished.

Pat Reddy, closer to the rail than I, went over it in a one-hand vault down into the blackness below.

I made the foot of the stairs in two jumps, jerked myself around with a hand on the newel, and plunged into the suddenly noisy dark of the hall.

A wall I couldn't see hit me. Caroming off the opposite wall, I spun into a room whose curtained grayness was the light of day after the hall.

Pat Reddy stood with one hand on a chair-back, holding his belly with the other. His face was mouse-colored under its blood. His eyes were glass agonies. He had the look of a man who had been kicked.

The grin he tried failed. He nodded toward the rear of the house. I went back.

In a little passageway I found Raymond Elwood.

He was sobbing and pulling frantically at a locked door. His face was the hard white of utter terror.

I measured the distance between us.

He turned as I jumped.

I put everything I had in the downswing of my gun-barrel—

A ton of meat and bone crashed into my back.

I went over against the wall, breathless, giddy, sick.

Red-silk arms that ended in brown hands locked around me.

I wondered if there was a whole regiment of these gaudy Negroes—or if I was colliding with the same one over and over.

This one didn't let me do much thinking.

He was big. He was stong. He didn't mean any good.

My gun-arm was flat at my side, straight down. I tried a shot at one of the Negro's feet. Missed. Tried again. He moved his feet. I wriggled around, half facing him.

Elwood piled on my other side.

The Negro bent me backward, folding my spine on itself like an accordion.

I fought to hold my knees stiff. Too much weight was hanging on me. My knees sagged. My body curved back.

Pat Reddy, swaying in the doorway, shone over the Negro's shoulder like the Angel Gabriel.

Gray pain was in Pat's face, but his eyes were clear. His right hand held a gun. His left was getting a blackjack out of his hip pocket.

He swung the sap down on the Negro's shaven skull.

The black man wheeled away from me, shaking his head.

Pat hit him once more before the Negro closed with him—hit him full in the face, but couldn't beat him off.

Twisting my freed gun hand up, I drilled Elwood neatly through the chest, and let him slide down me to the floor.

The Negro had Pat against the wall, bothering him a lot. His broad red back was a target.

But I had used five of the six bullets in my gun. I had more in my pocket, but reloading takes time.

I stepped out of Elwood's feeble hands, and went to work with the flat of my gun on the Negro. There was a roll of fat where his skull and neck fit together. The third time I hit it, he flopped, taking Pat with him.

I rolled him off. The blond police detective—not very blond now—got up.

At the other end of the passageway an open door showed an empty kitchen.

Pat and I went to the door that Elwood had been playing with. It was a solid piece of carpentering, and neatly fastened.

Yoking ourselves together, we began to beat the door with our combined three hundred and seventy or eighty pounds.

It shook, but held. We hit again. Wood we couldn't see tore.

Again.

The door popped away from us. We went through—down a flight of steps—rolling, snowballing down—until a cement floor stopped us.

Pat came back to life first.

"You're a hell of an acrobat," he said. "Get off my neck!"

I stood up. He stood up. We seemed to be dividing the evening between falling on the floor and getting up from the floor.

A light switch was at my shoulder. I turned it on.

If I looked anything like Pat, we were a fine pair of nightmares. He was all raw meat and dirt, with not enough clothes left to hide much of either.

I didn't like his looks, so I looked around the basement in which we stood. To the rear was a furnace, coalbins and a woodpile. To the front was a hallway and rooms, after the manner of the upstairs.

The first door we tried was locked, but not strongly. We smashed through it into a photographer's dark-room.

The second door was unlocked, and put us in a chemical laboratory; retorts, tubes, burners and a small still. There was a little round iron stove in the middle of the room. No one was there.

We went out into the hallway and to the third door, not so cheerfully. This cellar looked like a bloomer. We were wasting time here, when we should have stayed upstairs. I tried the door.

It was firm beyond trembling.

We smacked it with our weight, together, experimentally. It didn't shake.

"Wait."

Pat went to the woodpile in the rear and came back with an axe.

He swung the axe against the door, flaking out a hunk of wood. Silvery points of light sparkled in the hole. The other side of the door was an iron or steel plate.

Pat put the axe down and leaned on the helve.

"You write the next prescription," he said.

I didn't have anything to suggest, except, "I'll camp here. You beat it upstairs, and see if any of your coppers have shown up. This is a God-forsaken hole, but somebody may have sent in an alarm. See if you can find another way into this room—a window, maybe—or manpower enough to get us in through this door."

Pat turned toward the steps.

A sound stopped him—the clicking of bolts on the other side of the iron-lined door.

A jump put Pat on one side of the frame. A step put me on the other.

Slowly the door moved in. Too slowly.

I kicked it open.

Pat and I went into the room on top of my kick.

His shoulder hit the woman. I managed to catch her before she fell.

Pat took her gun. I steadied her back on her feet.

Her face was a pale blank square.

She was Myra Banbrock, but she had none of the masculinity that had been in her photographs and description.

Steadying her with one arm—which also served to block her arms—I looked around the room.

A small cube of a room whose walls were brown-painted metal. On the floor lay a queer little dead man.

A little man in tight fitting black velvet and silk. Black velvet blouse and breeches, black silk stockings and skull cap, black patent leather pumps. His face was small and old and bony, but smooth as stone, without line or wrinkle.

A hole was in his blouse, where it fit high under his chin. The hole bled very slowly. The floor around him showed it had been bleeding faster a little while ago.

Beyond him, a safe was open. Papers were on the floor in front of it, as if the safe had been tilted to spill them out.

The girl moved against my arm.

"You killed him?" I asked.

"Yes," too faint to have been heard a yard away.

"Why?"

She shook her short brown hair out of her eyes with a tired jerk of her head.

"Does it make any difference?" she asked. "I did kill him."

"It might make a difference," I told her, taking my arm away, and going over to shut the door. People talk more freely in a room with a closed door. "I happen to be in your father's employ. Mr. Reddy is a police detective. Of course, neither of us can smash any laws, but if you'll tell us what's what, maybe we can help you."

"My father's employ?" she questioned.

"Yes. When you and your sister disappeared, he engaged me to find you. We found your sister, and—"

Life came into her face and eyes and voice.

"I didn't kill Ruth!" she cried. "The papers lied! I didn't kill her! I didn't know she had the revolver. I didn't know it! We were going away to hide from—from everything. We stopped in the woods to burn the—those things. That's the first time I knew she had the revolver. We had talked about suicide at first, but I had persuaded her— thought I had persuaded her—not to. I tried to take the revolver away from her, but I couldn't. She shot herself while I was trying to get it away. I tried to stop her. I didn't kill her!"

This was getting somewhere.

"And then?" I encouraged her.

"And then I went to Sacramento and left the car there, and came back to San Francisco. Ruth told me she had written Raymond Elwood a letter. She told me that before I persuaded her not to kill herself—the first time. I tried to get the letter from Raymond. She had written him she was going to kill herself. I tried to get the letter, but Raymond said he had given it to Hador.

"So I came here this evening to get it. I had just found it when there was a lot of noise upstairs. Then Hador came in and found me. He bolted the door. And—and I shot him with the revolver that was in the safe. I—I shot him when he turned around, before he could say anything. It had to be that way, or I couldn't."

"You mean you shot him without being threatened or attacked by him?" Pat asked.

"Yes. I was afraid of him, afraid to let him speak. I hated him! I couldn't help it. It had to be that way. If he had talked I couldn't have shot him. He—he wouldn't have let me!"

"Who was this Hador?" I asked.

She looked away from Pat and me, at the walls, at the ceiling, at the queer little dead man on the floor.

"He was a—" She cleared her throat, and started again, staring down at her feet. "Raymond Elwood brought us here the first time. We thought it was funny. But Hador was a devil. He told you things and you believed them. You couldn't help it. He told you *everything* and you believed it. Perhaps we were drugged. There was always a warm bluish wine. It must have been drugged. We couldn't have done those things if it hadn't. Nobody would— He called himself a priest—a priest of Alzoa. He taught a freeing of the spirit from the flesh by—"

Her voice broke huskily. She shuddered.

"It was horrible!" she went on presently in the silence Pat and I had left for her. "But you believed him. That is the whole thing. You can't understand it unless you understand that. The things he taught could not be so. But he said they were, and you *believed* they were. Or maybe—I don't know—maybe you pretended you believed them, because you were crazy and drugs were in your blood. We came back again and again, for weeks, months, before the disgust that had to come drove us away.

"We stopped coming, Ruth and I—and Irma. And then we found out what he was. He demanded money, more money than we had been paying while we believed—or pretended belief—in his cult. We couldn't give him the money he demanded. I told him we wouldn't. He sent us photographs—of us—taken during the—the times here. They were—*pictures—you—couldn't—explain*. And they were true! We knew them true! What could we do? He said he would send copies to our father, every friend, everyone we knew—unless we paid.

"What could we do—except pay? We got the money somehow. We gave him money—more—more—more. And then we had no more—could get no more. We didn't know what to do! There was nothing to do, except—Ruth and Irma wanted to kill themselves. I thought of that, too. But I persuaded Ruth not to. I said we'd go away. I'd take her away—keep her safe. And then—then—this!"

She stopped talking, went on staring at her feet.

I looked again at the little dead man on the floor, weird in his black cap and clothes. No more blood came from his throat.

It wasn't hard to put the pieces together. This dead Hador, self-ordained priest of something or other, staging orgies under the alias of religious ceremonies. Elwood, his confederate, bringing women of family and wealth to him. A room lighted for photography, with a concealed camera. Contributions from his converts so long as they were faithful to the cult. Blackmail—with the help of the photographs—afterward.

I looked from Hador to Pat Reddy. He was scowling at the dead man. No sound came from outside the room.

"You have the letter your sister wrote Elwood?" I asked the girl.

Her hand flashed to her bosom, and crinkled paper there.

"Yes."

"It says plainly she meant to kill herself?"

"Yes."

"That ought to square her with Contra Costa County," I said to Pat.

He nodded his battered head.

"It ought to," he agreed. "It's not likely that they could prove murder on her even without that letter. With it, they'll not take her into court. That's a safe bet. Another is that she won't have any trouble over this shooting. She'll come out of court free, and thanked in the bargain."

Myra Banbrock flinched away from Pat as if he had hit her in the face.

I was her father's hired man just now. I saw her side of the affair.

I lit a cigarette and studied what I could see of Pat's face through blood and grime. Pat is a right guy.

"Listen, Pat," I wheedled him, though with a voice that was as if I were not trying to wheedle him at all. "Miss Banbrock can go into court and come out free and thanked, as you say. But to do it, she's got to use everything she knows. She's got to have all the evidence there is. She's got to use all those photographs Hador took—or all we can find of them.

"Some of those pictures have sent women to suicide, Pat—at least two that we know. If Miss Banbrock goes into court, we've got to make the photographs of God knows how many other women public property. We've got to advertise things that will put Miss Banbrock—and you can't say how many other woman and girls—in a position that at least two women have killed themselves to escape."

Pat scowled at me and rubbed his dirty chin with a dirtier thumb.

I took a deep breath and made my play. "Pat, you and I came here to question Raymond Elwood, having traced him here. Maybe we suspected him of being tied up with the mob that knocked over the St. Louis bank last month. Maybe we suspected him of handling the stuff that was taken from the mail cars in that stick-up near Denver week before last. Anyway, we were after him, knowing that he had a lot of money that came from nowhere, and a real estate office that did no real estate business.

"We came here to question him in connection with one of these jobs I've mentioned. We were jumped by a couple of the Negroes upstairs when they found we were sleuths. The rest of it grew out of that. This religious cult business was just something we ran into, and didn't interest us especially. So far as we knew, all these folks jumped us just through friendship for the man we were trying to question. Hador was one of them, and, tussling with you, you shot him with his own gun, which, of course, is the one Miss Banbrock found in the safe."

Reddy didn't seem to like my suggestion at all. The eyes with which he regarded me were decidedly sour.

"You're goofy," he accused me. "What'll that get anybody? That won't keep Miss Banbrock out of it. She's here, isn't she, and the rest of it will come out like thread off a spool."

"But Miss Banbrock *wasn't* here," I explained. "Maybe the upstairs is full of coppers by now. Maybe not. Anyway, you're going to take Miss Banbrock out of here and turn her over to Dick Foley, who will take her home. She's got nothing to do with this party. Tomorrow she, and her father's lawyer, and I, will all go up to Martinez and make a deal with the prosecuting attorney of Contra Costa County. We'll show him how Ruth killed herself. If somebody happens to connect the Elwood who I hope is dead upstairs with the Elwood who knew the girls and Mrs. Correll, what of it? If we keep out of court—as we'll do by convincing the Contra Costa people they can't possibly convict her of her sister's murder—we'll keep out of the newspapers—and out of trouble."

Pat hung fire, thumb still to chin.

"Remember," I urged him, "it's not only Miss Banbrock we're doing this for. It's a couple of dead ones, and a flock of live ones, who certainly got mixed up with Hador of their own accords, but who don't stop being human beings on that account."

Pat shook his head stubbornly.

"I'm sorry," I told the girl with faked hopelessness. "I've done all I can, but it's a lot to ask of Reddy. I don't know that I blame him for being afraid to take a chance on—"

Pat is Irish. "Don't be so damned quick to fly off," he snapped at me, cutting short my hypocrisy. "But why do I have to be the one that shot this Hador? Why not you?"

I had him!

"Because," I explained, "you're a bull and I'm not. There'll be less chance of a slip-up if he was shot by a bona fide, star-wearing, flat-footed officer of the peace. I killed most of those birds upstairs. You ought to do something to show you were here."

That was only part of the truth. My idea was that if Pat took the credit, he couldn't very well ease himself out afterward, no matter what happened. Pat's a right guy, and I'd trust him anywhere—but you can trust a man just as easily if you have him sewed up.

Pat grumbled and shook his head, but, "I'm ruining myself, I don't doubt," he growled, "but I'll do it, this once."

"Attaboy!" I went over to pick up the girl's hat from the corner in which it lay. "I'll wait here until you come back from turning her over to Dick." I gave the girl her hat and orders together. "You go to your home with the man Reddy turns you over to. Stay there until I come, which will be as soon as I can make it. Don't tell anybody anything, except that I told you to keep quiet. That includes your father. Tell him I told you not to tell him even where you saw me. Got it?"

"Yes, and I—"

Gratitude is nice to think about afterward, but it takes time when there's work to be done.

"Get going, Pat!"

They went.

As soon as I was alone with the dead man I stepped over him and knelt in front of the safe, pushing letters and papers away, hunting for photographs. None was in sight. One compartment of the safe was locked.

I frisked the corpse. No key. The locked compartment wasn't very strong, but neither am I the best safe-burglar in the West. It took me a while to get into it.

What I wanted was there. A thick sheaf of negatives. A stack of prints—half a hundred of them.

I started to run through them, hunting for the Banbrock girls' pictures. I wanted to have them pocketed before Pat came back. I didn't know how much farther he would let me go.

Luck was against me—and the time I had wasted

getting into the compartment. He was back before I had got past the sixth print in the stack. Those six had been— pretty bad.

"Well, that's done," Pat growled at me as he came into the room. "Dick's got her. Elwood is dead, and so is the only one of the Negroes I saw upstairs. Everybody else seems to have beat it. No bulls have shown—so I put in a call for a wagonful."

I stood up, holding the sheaf of negatives in one hand, the prints in the other.

"What's all that?" he asked.

I went after him again. "Photographs. You've just done me a big favor, Pat, and I'm not hoggish enough to ask another. But I'm going to put something in front of you, Pat. I'll give you the lay, and you can name it.

"These"—I waved the pictures at him—"are Hador's meal-tickets—the photos he was either collecting on or planning to collect on. They're photographs of people, Pat, mostly women and girls, and some of them are pretty rotten.

"If tomorrow's papers say that a flock of photos were found in this house after the fireworks, there's going to be a fat suicide-list in the next day's papers, and a fatter list of disappearances. If the papers say nothing about the photos, the lists may be a little smaller, but not much. Some of the people whose pictures are here know they are here. They will expect the police to come hunting for them. We know this much about the photographs—two women have killed themselves to get away from them. This is an armful of stuff that can dynamite a lot of people, Pat, and a lot of families—no matter which of those two ways the paper read.

"But, suppose, Pat, the papers say that just before you shot Hador he succeeded in burning a lot of pictures and papers, burning them beyond recognition. Isn't it likely, then, that there won't be any suicides? That some of the disappearances of recent months may clear themselves up? There she is, Pat—you name it."

Looking back, it seems to me I had come a lot nearer being eloquent than ever before in my life.

But Pat didn't applaud. He cursed me. He cursed me thoroughly, bitterly, and with an amount of feeling that told me I had won another point in my little game. He called me more things than I ever listened to before from a man who was built of meat and bone, and who therefore could be smacked.

When he was through, we carried the papers and photographs and a small book of addresses we found in the safe into the next room, and fed them to the little round iron stove there. The last of them was ash before we heard the police overhead.

"That's absolutely all!" Pat declared when we got up from our work. "Don't ever ask me to do anything else for you if you live to be a thousand."

"That's absolutely all," I echoed.

I like Pat. He is a right guy. The sixth photograph in the stack had been of his wife—the coffee importer's reckless, hot-eyed daughter.

THIS KING BUSINESS

The train from Belgrade set me down in Stefania, capital of Muravia, in early afternoon—a rotten afternoon. Cold wind blew cold rain in my face and down my neck as I left the square granite barn of a railroad station to climb into a taxicab.

English meant nothing to the chauffeur, nor French. Good German might have failed. Mine wasn't good. It was a hodgepodge of grunts and gargles. This chauffeur was the first person who had ever pretended to understand it. I suspected him of guessing, and I expected to be taken to some distant suburban point. Maybe he was a good guesser. Anyhow, he took me to the Hotel of the Republic.

The hotel was a new six-story affair, very proud of its elevators, American plumbing, private baths, and other modern tricks. After I had washed and changed clothes I went down to the café for luncheon. Then, supplied with minute instructions in English, French, and sign-language by a highly uniformed head porter, I turned up my raincoat collar and crossed the muddy plaza to call on Roy Scanlan, United States *chargé d'affaires* in this youngest and smallest of the Balkan States.

He was a pudgy man of thirty, with smooth hair already far along the gray route, a nervous flabby face, plump white hands that twitched, and very nice clothes. He shook hands with me, patted me into a chair, barely glanced at my letter of introduction, and stared at my necktie while saying, "So you're a private detective from San Francisco?"

"Yes."

"And?"

"Lionel Grantham."

"Surely not!"

"Yes."

"But he's—" The diplomat realized he was looking into my eyes, hurriedly switched his gaze to my hair and forgot what he had started to say.

"But he's what?" I prodded him.

"Oh!"—with a vague upward motion of head and eyebrows—"not that sort."

"How long has he been here?" I asked.

"Two months. Possibly three or three and a half."

"You know him well?"

"Oh, no! By sight, of course, and to talk to. He and I are the only Americans here, so we're fairly well acquainted."

"Know what he's doing here?"

"No, I don't. He just happened to stop here in his travels, I imagine, unless, of course, he's here for some special reason. No doubt there's a girl in it—she is General Radnjak's daughter—though I don't think so."

"How does he spend his time?"

"I really haven't any idea. He lives at the Hotel of the Republic, is quite a favorite among our foreign colony, rides a bit, lives the usual life of a young man of family and wealth."

"Mixed up with anybody who isn't all he ought to be?"

"Not that I know of, except that I've seen him with Mahmoud and Einarson. They are certainly scoundrels, though they may not be."

"Who are they?"

"Nubar Mahmoud is private secretary to Doctor Semich, the President. Colonel Einarson is an Icelander, just now virtually the head of the army. I know nothing about either of them."

"Except that they are scoundrels?"

The *chargé d'affaires* wrinkled his round white forehead in pain and gave me a reproachful glance. "Not at all," he said. "Now, may I ask, of what is Grantham suspected?"

"Nothing."

"Then?"

"Seven months ago, on his twenty-first birthday, this Lionel Grantham got hold of the money his father had left him—a nice wad. Till then the boy had had a tough time of it. His mother had, and has, highly developed middle-class notions of refinement. His father had been a genuine aristocrat in the old manner—a hard-souled, soft-spoken individual who got what he wanted by simply taking it, with a liking for old wine and young women, and plenty of both, and for cards and dice and running horses—and fights, whether he was in them or watching them.

"While he lived the boy had a he-raising. Mrs. Grantham thought her husband's tastes low, but he was a man who had things his own way. Besides, the Grantham blood was the best in America. She was a woman to be impressed by that. Eleven years ago—when Lionel was a kid of ten—the old man died. Mrs. Grantham swapped the family roulette wheel for a box of dominoes and began to convert the kid into a patent-leather Galahad. •

"I've never seen him, but I'm told the job wasn't a success. However, she kept him bundled up for eleven years, not even letting him escape to college. So it went until the day when he was legally of age and in possession of his share of his father's estate. That morning he kisses Mamma and tells her casually that he's off for a little run around the world—alone. Mamma does and says all that might be expected of her, but it's no good. The Grantham blood is up. Lionel promises to drop her a postcard now and then, and departs.

"He seems to have behaved fairly well during his wandering. I suppose just being free gave him all the excitement he needed. But a few weeks ago the trust company that handles his affairs got instructions from him to turn some railroad bonds into cash and ship the money to him in care of a Belgrade bank. The amount was large—over the three million mark—so the trust company told Mrs. Grantham about it. She chucked a fit. She had been getting letters from him—from Paris, without a word said about Belgrade.

"Mamma was all for dashing over to Europe at once. Her brother, Senator Walbourn, talked her out of it. He did some cabling, and learned that Lionel was neither in Paris nor in Belgrade, unless he was hiding. Mrs. Grantham packed her trunks and made reservations. The Senator headed her off again, convincing her that the lad would resent her interference, telling her the best thing was to investigate on the quiet. He brought the job to the Agency. I went to Paris, learned that a friend of Lionel's there was relaying his mail, and that Lionel was here in Stefania. On the way down I stopped off in Belgrade and learned that the money was being sent here to him—most of it already has been. So here I am."

Scanlan smiled happily.

"There's nothing I can do," he said. "Grantham is of age, and it's his money."

"Right," I agreed, "and I'm in the same fix. All I can do is poke around, find out what he's up to, try to save his dough if he's being gypped. Can't you give me even a guess at the answer? Three million dollars—what could he put it into?"

"I don't know." The *chargé d'affaires* fidgeted uncomfortably. "There's no business here that amounts to anything. It's purely an agricultural country, split up among small landowners—ten, fifteen, twenty acre farms. There's his association with Einarson and Mahmoud, though. They'd certainly rob him if they got the chance. I'm positive they're robbing him. But I don't think they would. Perhaps he isn't acquainted with them. It's probably a woman."

"Well, whom should I see? I'm handicapped by not knowing the country, not knowing the language. To whom can I take my story and get help?"

"I don't know," he said gloomily. Then his face brightened. "Go to Vasilije Djudakovich. He is Minister of Police. He is the man for you! He can help you, and you may trust him. He has a digestion instead of a brain. He'll not understand a thing you tell him. Yes, Djudakovich is your man!"

"Thanks," I said, and staggered out into the muddy street.

I found the Minister of Police's offices in the Administration Building, a gloomy concrete pile next to the Executive Residence at the head of the plaza. In French that was even worse than my German, a thin, white-whiskered clerk, who looked like a consumptive Santa Claus, told me His Excellency was not in. Looking solemn, lowering my voice to a whisper, I repeated that I had come from the

United States *chargé d'affaires.* This hocus-pocus seemed to impress Saint Nicholas. He nodded understandingly and shuffled out of the room. Presently he was back, bowing at the door, asking me to follow him.

I tailed him along a dim corridor to a wide door marked "15." He opened it, bowed me through it, wheezed, *"Asseyez-vous, s'il vous plaît,"* closed the door and left me. I was in an office, a large, square one. Everything in it was large. The four windows were double-size. The chairs were young benches, except the leather one at the desk, which could have been the rear half of a touring car. A couple of men could have slept on the desk. Twenty could have eaten at the table.

A door opposite the one through which I had come opened, and a girl came in, closing the door behind her, shutting out a throbbing purr, as of some heavy machine, that had sounded through.

"I'm Romaine Frankl," she said in English, "His Excellency's secretary. Will you tell me what you wish?"

She might have been any age from twenty to thirty, something less than five feet in height, slim without boniness, with curly hair as near black as brown can get, black-lashed eyes whose gray irises had black rims, a small, delicate-featured face, and a voice that seemed too soft and faint to carry as well as it did. She wore a red woolen dress that had no shape except that which her body gave it, and when she moved—to walk or raise a hand—it was as if it cost her no energy—as if someone else were moving her.

"I'd like to see him," I said while I was accumulating this data.

"Later, certainly," she promised, "but it's impossible now." She turned, with her peculiar effortless grace, back to the door, opening it so that the throbbing purr sounded in the room again. "Hear?" she said. "He's taking his nap."

She shut the door against His Excellency's snoring and floated across the room to climb up in the immense leather chair at the desk.

"Do sit down," she said, wriggling a tiny forefinger at a

chair beside the desk. "It will save time if you will tell me your business, because, unless you speak our tongue, I'll have to interpret your message to His Excellency."

I told her about Lionel Grantham and my interest in him, in practically the same words I had used on Scanlan, winding up, "You see, there's nothing I can do except try to learn what the boy's up to and give him a hand if he needs it. I can't go to him—he's too much Grantham, I'm afraid, to take kindly to what he'd think was nursemaid stuff. Mr. Scanlan advised me to come to the Minister of Police for help."

"You were fortunate." She looked as if she wanted to make a joke about my country's representative but wasn't sure how I'd take it. "Your *chargé d'affaires* is not always easy to understand."

"Once you get the hang of it, it's not hard," I said. "You just throw out all his statements that have *no's* or *not's* or *nothing's* or *don't's* in them."

"That's it! That's it, exactly!" She leaned toward me, laughing. "I've always known there was some key to it, but nobody's been able to find it before. You've solved our national problem."

"For reward, then, I should be given all the information you have about Grantham."

"You should, but I'll have to speak to His Excellency first."

"You can tell me unofficially what you think of Grantham. You know him?"

"Yes. He's charming. A nice boy, delightfully naïve, inexperienced, but really charming."

"Who are his friends here?"

She shook her head and said, "No more of that until His Excellency wakes. You're from San Francisco? I remember the funny little streetcars, and the fog, and the salad right after the soup, and Coffee Dan's."

"You've been there?"

"Twice. I was in the United States for a year and a half, in vaudeville, bringing rabbits out of hats."

We were still talking about that half an hour later

when the door opened and the Minister of Police came in.

The oversize furniture immediately shrank to normal, the girl became a midget, and I felt like somebody's little boy.

This Vasilije Djudakovich stood nearly seven feet tall, and that was nothing to his girth. Maybe he wouldn't weigh more than five hundred pounds, but, looking at him, it was hard to think except in terms of tons. He was a blond-haired, blond-bearded mountain of meat in a black frock coat. He wore a necktie, so I suppose he had a collar, but it was hidden all the way around by the red rolls of his neck. His white vest was the size and shape of a hoop skirt, and in spite of that it strained at the buttons. His eyes were almost invisible between the cushions of flesh around them, and were shaded into a colorless darkness, like water in a deep well. His mouth was a fat red oval among the yellow hairs of his whiskers and mustache. He came into the room slowly, ponderously, and I was surprised that the floor didn't creak.

Romaine Frankl was watching me attentively as she slid out of the big leather chair and introduced me to the Minister. He gave me a fat, sleepy smile and a hand that had the general appearance of a naked baby, and let himself down slowly into the chair the girl had quit. Planted there, he lowered his head until it rested on the pillows of his several chins, and then he seemed to go to sleep.

I drew up another chair for the girl. She took another sharp look at me—she seemed to be hunting for something in my face—and began to talk to him in what I supposed was the native lingo. She talked rapidly for about twenty minutes, while he gave no sign that he was listening or that he was even awake.

When she was through, he said, *"Da."* He spoke dreamily, but there was a volume to the syllable that could have come from no place smaller than his gigantic belly. The girl turned to me, smiling.

"His Excellency will be glad to give you every possible

assistance. Officially, of course, he does not care to interfere in the affairs of a visitor from another country, but he
realizes the importance of keeping Mr. Grantham from
being victimized while here. If you will return tomorrow
afternoon, at, say, three o'clock . . ."

I promised to do that, thanked her, shook hands with
the mountain again and went out into the rain.

Back at the hotel, I had no trouble learning that Lionel
Grantham occupied a suite on the sixth floor and was in it
at that time. I had his photograph in my pocket and his
description in my head. I spent what was left of the afternoon and the early evening waiting for a look at him. At a
little after seven I got it.

He stepped out of the elevator, a tall, flat-backed boy
with a supple body that tapered from broad shoulders to
narrow hips, carried erectly on long, muscular legs—the
sort of frame that tailors like. His pink, regular-featured,
really handsome face wore an expression of aloof superior-
ity that was too marked to be anything else than a cover
for youthful self-consciousness.

Lighting a cigarette, he passed into the street. The rain
had stopped, though clouds overhead promised more
shortly. He turned down the street afoot. So did I.

We went to a much-gilded restaurant two blocks from
the hotel, where a gypsy orchestra played on a little balcony stuck insecurely high on one wall. All the waiters and
half the diners seemed to know the boy. He bowed and
smiled to this side and that as he walked down to a table
near the far end, where two men were waiting for him.

One of them was tall and thick-bodied, with bushy
dark hair and a flowing dark mustache. His florid, short-
nosed face wore the expression of a man who doesn't mind
a fight now and then. This one was dressed in a green and
gold military uniform, with high boots of the shiniest black
leather. His companion was in evening clothes, a plump,
swarthy man of medium height, with oily black hair and a
suave, oval face.

While young Grantham joined this pair I found a table some distance from them for myself. I ordered dinner and looked around at my neighbors. There was a sprinkling of uniforms in the room, some dress coats and evening gowns, but most of the diners were in ordinary daytime clothes. I saw a couple of faces that were probably British, a Greek or two, a few Turks. The food was good and so was my appetite. I was smoking a cigarette over a tiny cup of syrupy coffee when Grantham and the big florid officer got up and went away.

I couldn't have got my bill and paid it in time to follow them without raising a disturbance, so I let them go. Then I settled to my meal and waited until the dark, plump man they had left behind called for his check. I was in the street a minute ahead of him, standing, looking up toward the dimly electric-lighted plaza with what was meant for the expression of a tourist who didn't quite know where to go next.

He passed me, going up the muddy street with the soft, careful-where-you-put-your-foot tread of a cat.

A soldier—a bony man in sheepskin coat and cap, with a gray mustache bristling over gray, sneering lips—stepped out of a dark doorway and stopped the swarthy man with whining words.

The swarthy man lifted hands and shoulders in a gesture that held both anger and surprise.

The soldier whined again, but the sneer on his gray mouth became more pronounced. The plump man's voice was low, sharp, angry, but he moved a hand from pocket to soldier, and the brown of Muravian paper money showed in the hand. The soldier pocketed the money, raised a hand in a salute and went across the street.

When the swarthy man had stopped staring after the soldier, I moved toward the corner around which sheepskin coat and cap had vanished. My soldier was a block and a half down the street, striding along with bowed head. He was in a hurry. I got plenty of exercise keeping up with him. Presently the city began to thin out. The thinner it got, the less I liked this expedition. Shadowing is at its best in daytime, downtown in a familiar large city. This was shadowing at its worst.

He led me out of the city along a cement road bordered by few houses. I stayed as far back as I could, so he was a faint, blurred shadow ahead. He turned a sharp bend in the road. I hustled toward the bend, intending to drop back again as soon as I had rounded it. Speeding, I nearly gummed the works.

The soldier suddenly appeared around the curve, coming toward me.

A little behind me a small pile of lumber on the roadside was the only cover within a hundred feet. I stretched my short legs thither.

Irregularly piled boards made a shallow cavity in one end of the pile, almost large enough to hold me. On my knees in the mud I hunched into that cavity.

The soldier came into sight through a chink between boards. Bright metal gleamed in one of his hands. A knife, I thought. But when he halted in front of my shelter I saw it was a revolver of the old-style nickel-plated sort.

He stood still, looking at my shelter, looking up the road and down the road. He grunted, came toward me. Slivers stung my cheek as I rubbed myself flatter against the timber-ends. My gun was with my blackjack—in my Gladstone bag in my room in my hotel. A fine place to have them now! The soldier's gun was bright in his hand.

Rain began to patter on boards and ground. The soldier turned up the collar of his coat as he came. Nobody ever did anything I liked more. A man stalking another wouldn't have done that. He didn't know I was there. He was hunting a hiding place for himself. The game was even. If he found me, he had the gun, but I had seen him first.

His sheepskin coat rasped against the wood as he went by me, bending low as he passed my corner for the back of the pile, so close to me that the same raindrops seemed to be hitting both of us. I undid my fists after that. I couldn't see him, but I could hear him breathing, scratching himself, even humming.

A couple of weeks went by.

The mud I was kneeling in soaked through my pantslegs, wetting my knees and shins. The rough wood filed skin off my face every time I breathed. My mouth was as dry as my knees were wet, because I was breathing through it for silence.

An automobile came around the bend, headed for the city. I heard the soldier grunt softly, heard the click of his gun as he cocked it. The car came abreast, went on. The soldier blew out his breath and started scratching himself and humming again.

Another couple of weeks passed.

Men's voices came through the rain, barely audible, louder, quite clear. Four soldiers in sheepskin coats and hats walked down the road the way we had come, their voices presently shrinking into silence as they disappeared around the curve.

In the distance an automobile horn barked two ugly notes. The soldier grunted—a grunt that said clearly, "Here it is." His feet slopped in the mud, and the lumber pile creaked under his weight. I couldn't see what he was up to.

White light danced around the bend in the road, and an automobile came into view—a high-powered car going cityward with a speed that paid no attention to the wet slipperiness of the road. Rain and night and speed blurred its two occupants, who were in the front seat.

Over my head a heavy revolver roared. The soldier was working. The speeding car swayed crazily along the wet cement, its brakes screaming.

When the sixth shot told me the nickel-plated gun was probably empty, I jumped out of my hollow.

The soldier was leaning over the lumber pile, his gun still pointing at the skidding car while he peered through the rain.

He turned as I saw him, swung the gun around to me,

snarled an order I couldn't understand. I was betting the gun was empty. I raised both hands high over my head, made an astonished face and kicked him in the belly.

He folded over on me, wrapping himself around my leg. We both went down. I was underneath, but his head was against my thigh. His cap fell off. I caught his hair with both hands and yanked myself into a sitting position. His teeth went into my leg. I called him disagreeable things and put my thumbs in the hollows under his ears. It didn't take much pressure to teach him that he oughtn't to bite people. When he lifted his face to howl, I put my right fist in it, pulling him into the punch with my left hand in his hair. It was a nice solid sock.

I pushed him off my leg, got up, took a handful of his coat collar, and dragged him out into the road.

White light poured over us. Squinting into it, I saw the automobile standing down the road, its spotlight turned on me and my sparring partner. A big man in green and gold came into the light—the florid officer who had been one of Grantham's companions in the restaurant. An automatic was in one of his hands.

He strode over to us, stiff-legged in his high boots, ignored the soldier on the ground, and examined me carefully with sharp little dark eyes. "British?" he asked.

"American."

He bit a corner of his mustache and said meaninglessly, "Yes, that is better."

His English was guttural, with a German accent.

Lionel Grantham came from the car to us. His face wasn't as pink as it had been.

"What is it?" he asked the officer, but he looked at me.

"I don't know," I said. "I took a stroll after dinner and got mixed up on my directions. Finding myself out here, I decided I was headed the wrong way. When I turned around to go back I saw this fellow duck behind the lumber pile. He had a gun in his hand. I took him for a stick-up, so I played Indian on him. Just as I got to him he jumped up and began spraying you people. I reached him in time to spoil his aim. Friend of yours?"

"You're an American," the boy said. I'm Lionel Grantham. This is Colonel Einarson. We're very grateful to you." He screwed up his forehead and looked at Einarson. "What do you think of it?"

The officer shrugged his shoulders, growled, "One of my children—we'll see," and kicked the ribs of the man on the ground.

The kick brought the soldier to life. He sat up, rolled over on hands and knees, and began a broken, long-winded entreaty, plucking at the Colonel's tunic with dirty hands.

"Ach!" Einarson knocked the hands down with a tap of pistol barrel across knuckles, looked with disgust at the muddy marks on his tunic and growled an order.

The soldier jumped to his feet, stood at attention, got another order, did an about-face, and marched to the automobile. Colonel Einarson strode stiff-legged behind him, holding his automatic to the man's back. Grantham put a hand on my arm.

"Come along," he said. "We'll thank you properly and get better acquainted after we've taken care of this fellow."

Colonel Einarson got into the driver's seat, with the soldier beside him. Grantham waited while I found the soldier's revolver. Then we got into the rear seat. The officer looked doubtfully at me out of his eye-corners, but said nothing. He drove the car back the way it had come. He liked speed, and we hadn't far to go. By the time we were settled in our seats the car was whisking us through a gateway in a high stone wall, with a sentry on each side presenting arms. We did a sliding half-circle into a branching driveway and jerked to a standstill in front of a square whitewashed building.

Einarson prodded the soldier out ahead of him. Grantham and I got out. To the left a row of long, low buildings showed pale gray in the rain—barracks. The door of the square, white building was opened by a bearded orderly in green. We went in. Einarson pushed his prisoner across the small reception hall and through the open door of a bedroom. Grantham and I followed them in. The orderly stopped in the doorway, traded some words with Einarson, and went away, closing the door.

The room we were in looked like a cell, except that there were no bars over the one small window. It was a narrow room, with bare, whitewashed walls and ceiling. The wooden floor, scrubbed with lye until it was almost as white as the walls, was bare. For furniture there was a black iron cot, three folding chairs of wood and canvas and an unpainted chest of drawers, with comb, brush, and a few papers on top. That was all.

"Be seated, gentlemen," Einarson said, indicating the camp chairs. "We'll get at this thing now."

The boy and I sat down. The officer laid his pistol on the top of the chest of drawers, rested one elbow beside the pistol, took a corner of his mustache in one big red hand, and addressed the soldier. His voice was kindly, paternal. The soldier, standing rigidly upright in the middle of the floor, replied, whining, his eyes focused on the officer's with a blank, in-turned look.

They talked for five minutes or more. Impatience grew in the Colonel's voice and manner. The soldier kept his blank abjectness. Einarson ground his teeth together and looked angrily at the boy and me.

"This pig!" he exclaimed, and began to bellow at the soldier.

Sweat sprang out on the soldier's gray face, and he cringed out of his military stiffness. Einarson stopped bellowing at him and yelled two words at the door. It opened and the bearded orderly came in with a short, thick, leather whip. At a nod from Einarson he put the whip beside the automatic on the top of the chest of drawers and went out.

The soldier whimpered. Einarson spoke curtly to him. The soldier shuddered, began to unfasten his coat with shaking fingers, pleading all the while with whining, stuttering words. He took off his coat, his green blouse, his gray undershirt, letting them fall on the floor, and stood there, his hairy, not exactly clean body naked from the waist up. He worked his fingers together and cried.

Einarson grunted a word. The soldier stiffened at attention, hands at sides, facing us, his left side to Einarson.

Slowly Colonel Einarson removed his own belt, unbuttoned his tunic, took it off, folded it carefully, and laid it on the cot. Beneath it he wore a white cotton shirt. He rolled the sleeves up above his elbows and picked up the whip. "This pig!" he said again.

Lionel Grantham stirred uneasily on his chair. His face was white, his eyes dark.

Leaning his left elbow on the chest of drawers again, playing with his mustache-end with his left hand, standing indolently cross-legged, Einarson began to flog the soldier. His right arm raised the whip, brought the lash whistling down to the soldier's back, raised it again, brought it down again. It was especially nasty because he was not hurrying himself, not exerting himself. He meant to flog the man until he got what he wanted, and he was saving his strength so that he could keep it up as long as necessary.

With the first blow the terror went out of the soldier's eyes. They dulled sullenly and his lips stopped twitching. He stood woodenly under the beating, staring over Grantham's head. The officer's face had also become expressionless. Anger was gone. He showed no pleasure in his work, not even that of relieving his feelings. His air was the air of a stoker shoveling coal, of a carpenter sawing a board, of a stenographer typing a letter. Here was a job to be done in a workmanlike manner, without haste or excitement or wasted effort, without either enthusiasm or repulsion. It was nasty, but it taught me respect for this Colonel Einarson.

Lionel Grantham sat on the edge of his folding chair, staring at the soldier with white-ringed eyes. I offered the

boy a cigarette, making an unnecessary complicated operation out of lighting it and my own—to break up his score-
keeping. He had been counting the strokes, and that
wasn't good for him.

The whip curved up, swished down, cracked on the
naked back—up, down, up, down. Einarson's florid face
took on the damp glow of moderate exercise. The soldier's
gray face was a lump of putty. He was facing Grantham
and me. We couldn't see the marks of the whip.

Grantham said something to himself in a whisper.
Then he gasped, "I can't stand this!"

Einarson didn't look around from his work.

"Don't stop it now," I muttered. "We've gone this far."

The boy got up unsteadily and went to the window,
opened it and stood looking out into the rainy night.
Einarson paid no attention to him. He was putting more
weight into the whipping now, standing with his feet far
apart, leaning forward a little, his left hand on his hip, his
right carrying the whip up and down with increasing
swiftness.

The soldier swayed and a sob shook his hairy chest.
The whip cut out out. I looked at my watch. Einarson
had been at it for forty minutes, and looked good for the
rest of the night.

The soldier moaned and turned toward the officer.
Einarson did not break the rhythm of his stroke. The last
cut the man's shoulder. I caught a glimpse of his back—
raw meat. Einarson spoke sharply. The soldier jerked
himself to attention again, his left side to the officer. The
whip went on with its work—up, down, up, down, up,
down.

The soldier flung himself on hands and knees at Einarson's feet and began to pour out sob-broken words. Einarson looked down at him, listening carefully, holding the
lash of the whip in his left hand, the butt still in his right.
When the man had finished, Einarson asked questions, got
answers, nodded, and the soldier stood up. Einarson put a
friendly hand on the man's shoulder, turned him around,

looked at his mangled red back, and said something in a sympathetic tone. Then he called the orderly in and gave him some orders. The soldier, moaning as he bent, picked up his discarded clothes and followed the orderly out of the bedroom.

Einarson tossed the whip up on top of the chest of drawers and crossed to the bed to pick up his tunic. A leather pocketbook slid from an inside pocket to the floor. When he recovered it, a soiled newspaper clipping slipped out and floated across to my feet. I picked it up and gave it back to him—a photograph of a man, the Shah of Persia, according to the French caption under it.

"That pig!" he said—meaning the soldier, not the Shah—as he put on his tunic and buttoned it. "He has a son, also until last week of my troops. This son drinks too much of wine. I reprimand him. He is insolent. What kind of army is it without discipline? Pigs! I knock this pig down, and he produces a knife. Ach! What kind of army is it where a soldier may attack his officers with knives? After I—personally, you comprehend—have finished with this swine, I have him courtmartialed and sentenced to twenty years in the prison. This elder pig, his father, does not like that. So he will shoot me tonight. Ach! What kind of army is that?"

Lionel Grantham came away from his window. His young face was haggard. His young eyes were ashamed of the haggardness of his face.

Colonel Einarson made me a stiff bow and a formal speech of thanks for spoiling the soldier's aim—which I hadn't—and saving his life. Then the conversation turned to my presence in Muravia. I told them briefly that I held a captain's commission in the military intelligence department during the war. That much was the truth, and that was all the truth I gave them. After the war—so my fairy tale went—I had decided to stay in Europe, had taken my discharge there and had drifted around, doing odd jobs at one place and another. I was vague, trying to give them the impression that those odd jobs had not always, or usually, been ladylike. I gave them more definite—though still highly imaginary—details of my recent employment with a French syndicate, admitting that I had come to this corner of the world because I thought it better not to be seen in Western Europe for a year or so.

"Nothing I could be jailed for," I said, "but things could be made uncomfortable for me. So I roamed over into *Mitteleuropa,* learned that I might find a connection in Belgrade, got there to find it a false alarm, and came on down here. I may pick up something here. I've got a date with the Minister of Police tomorrow. I think I can show him where he can use me."

"The gross Djudakovich!" Einarson said with frank contempt. "You find him to your liking?"

"No work, no eat," I said.

"Einarson," Grantham began quickly, hesitated, then said, "Couldn't we—don't you think—" and didn't finish.

The Colonel frowned at him, saw I had noticed the frown, cleared his throat, and addressed me in a gruffly hearty tone, "Perhaps it would be well if you did not too speedily engage yourself to this fat minister. It may be—there is a possibility that we know of another field where your talents might find employment more to your taste—and profit."

I let the matter stand, saying neither yes nor no.

We returned to the city in the officer's car. He and Grantham sat in the rear. I sat beside the soldier who drove. The boy and I got out at our hotel. Einarson said good night and was driven away as if he were in a hurry.

"It's early," Grantham said as we went indoors. "Come up to my room."

I stopped at my own room to wash off the mud I'd gathered around the lumber stack and to change my clothes, and then went up with him. He had three rooms on the top floor, overlooking the plaza.

He set out a bottle of whisky, a syphon, lemons, cigars, and cigarettes, and we drank, smoked, and talked. Fifteen or twenty minutes of the talk came from no deeper than the mouth on either side—comments on the night's excitement, our opinions of Stefania, and so on. Each of us had something to say to the other. Each was weighing the other before he said it. I decided to put mine over first.

"Colonel Einarson was spoofing us tonight," I said.

"Spoofing?" The boy sat up straight, blinking.

"His soldier shot for money, not revenge."

"You mean—?" His mouth stayed open.

"I mean the little dark man you ate with gave the soldier money."

"Mahmoud! Why, that's— You are sure?"

"I saw it."

He looked at his feet, yanking his gaze away from mine as if he didn't want me to see that he thought I was lying.

"The soldier may have lied to Einarson," he said presently, still trying to keep me from knowing he thought me the liar. "I can understand some of the language, as spoken by the educated Muravians, but not the country dialect the soldier talked, so I don't know what he said, but he may have lied, you know."

"Not a chance," I said. "I'd bet my pants he told the truth."

He continued to stare at his outstretched feet, fighting to hold his face cool and calm. Part of what he was thinking slipped out in words. "Of course, I owe you a tremendous debt for saving us from—"

"You don't. You owe that to the soldier's bad aim. I didn't jump him till his gun was empty."

"But—" His young eyes were wide before mine, and if I had pulled a machine gun out of my cuff he wouldn't have been surprised. He suspected me of everything on the blotter. I cursed myself for overplaying my hand. There was nothing to do now but spread the cards.

"Listen, Grantham. Most of what I told you and Einarson about myself is the bunk. Your uncle, Senator Walbourn, sent me down here. You were supposed to be in Paris. A lot of your dough was being shipped to Belgrade.

The Senator was leery of the racket, didn't know whether you were playing a game or somebody was putting over a fast one. I went to Belgrade, traced you here, and came here, to run into what I ran into. I've traced the money to you, have talked to you. That's all I was hired to do. My job's done—unless there's anything I can do for you now."

"Not a thing," he said very calmly. "Thanks, just the same." He stood up, yawning. "Perhaps I'll see you again before you leave."

"Yeah." It was easy for me to make my voice match his indifference: I hadn't a cargo of rage to hide. "Good night."

I went down to my room, got into bed, and went to sleep.

I slept till late the next morning and then had breakfast in my room. I was in the middle of it when knuckles tapped my door. A stocky man in a wrinkled gray uniform, set off with a short, thick sword, came in, saluted, gave me a square white envelope, looked hungrily at the American cigarettes on my table, smiled and took one when I offered them, saluted again, and went out.

The square envelope had my name written on it in a small, very plain and round, but not childish, handwriting. Inside was a note from the same pen:

> The Minister of Police regrets that departmental affairs prevent his receiving you this afternoon.

It was signed "Romaine Frankl," and had a postscript:

> If it's convenient for you to call on me after nine this evening, perhaps I can save you some time.
>
> R. F.

Below this an address was written.

I put the note in my pocket and called, "Come in," to another set of knocking knuckles.

Lionel Grantham entered. His face was pale and set.

"Good morning," I said, making it cheerfully casual, as if I attached no importance to last night's rumpus. "Had breakfast yet? Sit down, and—"

"Oh, yes, thanks. I've eaten." His handsome red face was reddening. "About last night—I was—"

"Forget it! Nobody likes to have his business pried into."

"That's good of you," he said, twisting his hat in his hands. He cleared his throat. "You said you'd—ah—help me if I wished."

"Yeah. I will. Sit down."

He sat down, coughed, ran his tongue over his lips. "You haven't said anything to anyone about last night's affair with the soldier?"

"No," I said.

"Will you not say anything about it?"

"Why?"

He looked at the remains of my breakfast and didn't answer. I lit a cigarette to go with my coffee and waited. He stirred uneasily in his chair and without looking up, asked, "You know Mahmoud was killed last night?"

"The man in the restaurant with you and Einarson?"

"Yes. He was shot down in front of his house a little after midnight."

"Einarson?"

The boy jumped.

"No!" he cried. "Why do you say that?"

"Einarson knew Mahmoud had paid the soldier to wipe him out, so he plugged Mahmoud, or had him plugged. Did you tell him what I told you last night?"

"No." He blushed. "It's embarrassing to have one's family sending a guardian after one."

I made a guess. "He told you to offer me the job he spoke of last night, and to caution me against talking about the soldier. Didn't he?"

"Y-e-s."

"Well, go ahead and offer."

"But he doesn't know you're—"

"What are you going to do, then?" I asked. "If you don't make me the offer, you'll have to tell him why."

"Oh, Lord, what a mess!" he said wearily, putting elbows on knees, face between palms, looking at me with the harried eyes of a boy finding life too complicated.

He was ripe for talk. I grinned at him, finished my coffee, and waited.

"You know I'm not going to be led home by an ear," he said with a sudden burst of rather childish defiance.

"You know I'm not going to try to take you," I soothed him.

We had some more silence after that. I smoked while he held his head and worried. After a while he squirmed in his chair, sat stiffly upright, and his face turned perfectly crimson from hair to collar.

"I'm going to ask for your help," he said, pretending he didn't know he was blushing. "I'm going to tell you the whole foolish thing. If you laugh, I'll— You won't laugh, will you?"

"If it's funny I probably will, but that needn't keep me from helping you."

"Yes, do laugh! It's silly! You ought to laugh!" He took a deep breath. "Did you ever—did you ever think you'd like to be a—" He stopped, looked at me with a desperate sort of shyness, pulled himself together, and almost shouted the last word—"king?"

"Maybe. I've thought of a lot of things I'd like to be, and that might be one of 'em."

"I met Mahmoud at an embassy ball in Constantinople," he dashed into the story, dropping his words quickly as if glad to get rid of them. "He was President Semich's secretary. We got quite friendly, though I wasn't especially fond of him. He persuaded me to come here with him, and introduced me to Colonel Einarson. Then they—there's really no doubt that the country is wretchedly governed. I wouldn't have gone into it if that hadn't been so.

"A revolution was being prepared. The man who was to lead it had just died. It was handicapped, too, by a lack of money. Believe this—it wasn't all vanity that made me go into it. I believed—I still believe—that it would have been—will be—for the good of the country. The offer they made me was that if I would finance the revolution I could be—could be king.

"Now wait! The Lord knows it's bad enough, but don't think it sillier than it is. The money I have would go a long way in this small, impoverished country. Then, with an American ruler, it would be easier—it ought to be—for the country to borrow in America or England. Then there's the political angle. Muravia is surrounded by four countries, any one of which is strong enough to annex it if it wants. Muravia has stayed independent so far only because of the jealousy among its stronger neighbors and because it hasn't a seaport.

"But with an American ruler—and if loans in America and England were arranged, so we had their capital invested here—there would be a change in the situation. Muravia would be in a stronger position, would have at least some slight claim on the friendship of stronger powers. That would be enough to make the neighbors cautious.

"Albania, shortly after the First World War, thought of the same thing, and offered its crown to one of the wealthy American Bonapartes. He didn't want it. He was an older man and had already made his career. I did want my chance when it came. There were"—some of the embarrassment that had left him during his talking returned—"there were kings back in the Grantham lines. We trace our descent from James the Fourth of Scotland. I wanted —it was nice to think of carrying the line back to a crown.

"We weren't planning a violent revolution. Einarson holds the army. We simply had to use the army to force the Deputies—those who were not already with us—to change the form of government and elect me king. My descent would make it easier than if the candidate were one who hadn't royal blood in him. It would give me a certain standing in spite—in spite of my being young, and—and the people really want a king, especially the peasants. They don't think they're really entitled to call themselves a nation without one. A president means nothing to them—he's simply an ordinary man like themselves. So, you see, I— It was— Go ahead, laugh! You've heard enough to know how silly it is!" His voice was high-pitched, screechy. "Laugh! Why don't you laugh?"

"What for?" I asked. "It's crazy, God knows, but not silly. Your judgment was gummy, but your nerve's all right. You've been talking as if this were all dead and buried. Has it flopped?"

"No, it hasn't," he said slowly, frowning, "but I keep thinking it has. Mahmoud's death shouldn't change the situation, yet I've a feeling it's all over."

"Much of your money sunk?"

"I don't mind that. But—well—suppose the American newspapers get hold of the story, and they probably will. You know how ridiculous they could make it. And then the others who'll know about it—my mother and uncle and the trust company. I won't pretend I'm not ashamed to face them. And then—" His face got red and shiny. "And then Valeska—Miss Radnjak—her father was to have led the revolution. He did lead it—until he was murdered. She is I never could be good enough for her." He said this in a peculiarly idiotic tone of awe. "But I've hoped that perhaps by carrying on her father's work, and if I had something besides mere money to offer her—if I had done something—made a place for myself—perhaps she'd—you know."

I said, "Uh-huh."

"What shall I do?" he asked earnestly. "I can't run away. I've got to see it through for her, and to keep my own self-respect. But I've got the feeling that it's all over. You offered to help me. Help me. Tell me what I ought to do!"

"You'll do what I tell you—if I promise to bring you

through with a clean face?" I asked, just as if steering millionaire descendants of Scotch kings through Balkan plots were an old story to me, merely part of the day's work.

"Yes!"

"What's the next thing on the revolutionary program?"

"There's a meeting tonight. I'm to bring you."

"What time?"

"Midnight."

"I'll meet you here at eleven-thirty. How much am I supposed to know?"

"I was to tell you about the plot, and to offer you whatever inducements were necessary to bring you in. There was no definite arrangement as to how much or how little I was to tell you."

At nine-thirty that night a cab set me down in front of the address the Minister of Police's secretary had given in her note. It was a small two-story house in a badly paved street on the city's eastern edge. A middle-aged woman in very clean, stiffly starched, ill-fitting clothes opened the door for me. Before I could speak, Romaine Frankl, in a sleeveless pink satin gown, floated into sight behind the woman, smiling, holding out a small hand to me.

"I didn't know you'd come," she said.

"Why?" I asked, with a great show of surprise at the notion that any man would ignore an invitation from her, while the servant closed the door and took my coat and hat.

We were standing in a dull-rose-papered room, finished and carpeted with oriental richness. There was one discordant note in the room—an immense leather chair.

"We'll go upstairs," the girl said, and addressed the servant with words that meant nothing to me, except the name Marya. "Or would you"—she turned to me and English again—"prefer beer to wine?"

I said I wouldn't, and we went upstairs, the girl climbing ahead of me with her effortless appearance of being carried. She took me into a black, white, and gray room that was very daintily furnished with as few pieces as possible, its otherwise perfect feminine atmosphere spoiled by the presence of another of the big padded chairs.

The girl sat on a gray divan, pushing away a stack of French and Austrian magazines to make a place for me beside her. Through an open door I could see the painted foot of a Spanish bed, a short stretch of purple counterpane, and half of a purple-curtained window.

"His Excellency was very sorry," the girl began, and stopped.

I was looking—not staring—at the big leather chair. I knew she had stopped because I was looking at it, so I wouldn't take my eyes away.

"Vasilije," she said, more distinctly than was really necessary, "was very sorry he had to postpone this afternoon's appointment. The assassination of the President's secretary—you heard of it?—made us put everything else aside for the moment."

"Oh, yes, that fellow Mahmoud—" slowly shifting my eyes from the leather chair to her. "Found out who killed him?"

Her black-ringed, black-centered eyes seemed to study me from a distance while she shook her head, jiggling the nearly black curls.

"Probably Einarson," I said.

"You haven't been idle." Her lower lids lifted when she smiled, giving her eyes a twinkling effect.

The servant Marya came in with wine and fruit, put them on a small table beside the divan, and went away. The girl poured wine and offered me cigarettes in a silver box. I passed them up for one of my own. She smoked a king-size Egyptian cigarette—big as a cigar. It accentuated the smallness of her face and hand—which is probably why she favored that size.

"What sort of revolution is this they've sold my boy?" I asked.

"It was a very nice one until it died."

"How come it died?"

"It—do you know anything about our history?"

"No."

"Well, Muravia came into existence as a result of the fear and jealousy of four countries. The nine or ten thousand square miles that make this country aren't very valuable land. There's little here that any of those four countries especially wanted, but no three of them would agree to let the fourth have it. The only way to settle the thing was to make a separate country out of it. That was done in 1923.

"Doctor Semich was elected the first president, for a ten-year term. He is not a statesman, not a politician, and never will be. But since he was the only Muravian who had ever been heard of outside his own town, it was thought that his election would give the new country some prestige. Besides, it was a fitting honor for Muravia's only great man. He was not meant to be anything but a figurehead. The real governing was to be done by General Danilo Radnjak, who was elected vice-president, which, here, is more than equivalent to prime minister. General Radnjak was a capable man. The army worshiped him, the peasants trusted him, and our *bourgeoisie* knew him to be honest, conservative, intelligent, and as good a business administrator as a military one.

"Doctor Semich is a very mild, elderly scholar with no knowledge whatever of worldly affairs. You can understand him from this—he is easily the greatest of living bacteriologists, but he'll tell you, if you are on intimate terms with him, that he doesn't believe in the value of bacteriology at all. 'Mankind must learn to live with bacteria as with friends,' he'll say. 'Our bodies must adapt themselves to diseases, so there will be little difference between having tuberculosis, for example, or not having it. That way lies victory. This making war on bacteria is a futile business. Futile but interesting. So we do it. Our poking around in laboratories is perfectly useless—but it amuses us.'

"Now when this delightful old dreamer was honored

by his countrymen with the presidency, he took it in the worst possible way. He determined to show his appreciation by locking up his laboratory and applying himself heart and soul to running the government. Nobody expected or wanted that. Radnjak was to have been the government. For a while he did control the situation, and everything went well.

"But Mahmoud had designs of his own. He was Doctor Semich's secretary, and he was trusted. He began calling the President's attentions to various trespasses of Radnjak's on the presidential powers. Radnjak, in an attempt to keep Mahmoud from control, made a terrible mistake. He went to Doctor Semich and told him frankly and honestly that no one expected him, the President, to give all his time to executive business, and that it had been the intention of his countrymen to give him the honor of being the first president rather than the duties.

"Radnjak had played into Mahmoud's hands—the secretary became the actual government. Doctor Semich was now thoroughly convinced that Radnjak was trying to steal his authority, and from that day on Radnjak's hands were tied. Doctor Semich insisted on handling every governmental detail himself, which meant that Mahmoud handled it, because the President knows as little about statesmanship today as he did when he took office. Complaints—no matter who made them—did no good. Doctor Semich considered every dissatisfied citizen a fellow-conspirator of Radnjak's. The more Mahmoud was criticized in the Chamber of Deputies, the more faith Doctor Semich had in him. Last year the situation became intolerable, and the revolution began to form.

"Radnjak headed it, of course, and at least ninety percent of the influential men in Muravia were in it. The attitude of people as a whole it is difficult to judge. They are mostly peasants, small landowners, who ask only to be let alone. But there's no doubt they'd rather have a king than a president, so the form was to be changed to please them. The army, which worshiped Radnjak, was in it. The revolution matured slowly. General Radnjak was a cautious, careful man, and, as this is not a wealthy country, there was not much money available.

"Two months before the date set for the outbreak, Radnjak was assassinated. And the revolution went to pieces, split up into half a dozen factions. There was no other man strong enough to hold them together. Some of these groups still meet and conspire, but they are without general influence, without real purpose. And this is the revolution that has been sold Lionel Grantham. We'll have more information in a day or two, but what we've learned so far is that Mahmoud, who spent a month's vacation in Constantinople, brought Grantham back here with him and joined forces with Einarson to swindle the boy.

"Mahmoud was very much out of the revolution, of course, since it was aimed at him. But Einarson had been in it with his superior, Radnjak. Since Radnjak's death Einarson has succeeded in transferring to himself much of the allegiance that the soldiers gave the dead general. They do not love the Icelander as they did Radnjak, but Einarson is spectacular, theatrical—has all the qualities that simple men like to see in their leaders. So Einarson had the army and could get enough of the late revolution's machinery in his hands to impress Grantham. For money he'd do it. So he and Mahmoud put on a show for your boy. They used Valeska Radnjak, the general's daughter, too. She, I think, was also a dupe. I've heard that the boy and she are planning to be king and queen. How much did he invest in this farce?"

"Maybe as much as three million American dollars."

Romaine Frankl whistled softly and poured more wine.

"How did the Minister of Police stand, when the revolution was alive?" I asked.

"Vasilije," she told me, sipping wine between phrases, "is a peculiar man, an original. He is interested in nothing except his comfort. Comfort to him means enormous amounts of food and drink and at least sixteen hours of sleep each day, and not having to move around much during his eight waking hours. Outside of that he cares for nothing. To guard his comfort he has made the police department a model one. They've got to do their work smoothly and neatly. If they don't crimes will go unpunished, people will complain, and those complaints might disturb His Excellency. He might even have to shorten his afternoon nap to attend a conference or meeting. That wouldn't do. So he insists on an organization that will keep crime down to a minimum, and catch the perpetrators of that minimum. And he gets it."

"Catch Radnjak's assassin?"

"Killed resisting arrest ten minutes after the murder."

"One of Mahmoud's men?"

The girl emptied her glass, frowning at me, her lifted lower lids putting a twinkle in the frown.

"You're not so bad," she said slowly, "but now it's my turn to ask. Why did you say Einarson killed Mahmoud?"

"Einarson knew Mahmoud had tried to have him and Grantham shot earlier in the evening."

"Really?"

"I saw a soldier take money from Mahmoud, ambush Einarson and Grantham and miss 'em with six shots."

She clicked a fingernail against her teeth.

"That's not like Mahmoud," she objected, "to be seen paying for his murders."

"Probably not," I agreed. "But suppose his hired man decided he wanted more pay, or maybe he'd only been paid part of his wages. What better way to collect than to pop out and ask for it in the street a few minutes before he was scheduled to turn the trick?"

She nodded, and spoke as if thinking aloud, "Then they've got all they expect to get from Grantham, and each was trying to hog it by removing the other."

"Where you go wrong," I told her, "is in thinking that the revolution is dead."

"But Mahmoud wouldn't, even for three million dollars, conspire to remove himself from power."

"Right! Mahmoud thought he was putting on a show

for the boy. When he learned it wasn't a show—learned Einarson was in earnest—he tried to have him knocked off."

"Perhaps." She shrugged her smooth bare shoulders. "But now you're guessing."

"Yes? Einarson carries a picture of the Shah of Persia. It's worn, as if he handled it a lot. The Shah of Persia is a Russian soldier who went in there after the war, worked himself up until he had the army in his hands, became dictator, then Shah. Correct me if I'm wrong. Einarson is an Icelandic soldier who came in here after the war and has worked himself up until he's got the army in his hands. If he carries the Shah's picture and looks at it often enough to have it shabby from handling, does it mean he hopes to follow his example? Or doesn't it?"

Romaine Frankl got up and roamed around the room, moving a chair two inches here, adjusting an ornament there, shaking out the folds of a window curtain, pretending a picture wasn't quite straight on the wall, moving from place to place with the appearance of being carried—a graceful small girl in pink satin.

She stopped in front of a mirror, moved a little to one side so she could see my reflection in it, and fluffed her curls while saying almost absently, "Very well, Einarson wants a revolution. What will your boy do?"

"What I tell him."

"What will you tell him?"

"Whatever pays best. I want to take him home with all his money."

She left the mirror and came over to me, rumpled my hair, kissed my mouth, and sat on my knees, holding my face between small warm hands.

"Give me a revolution, nice man!" Her eyes were black with excitement, her voice throaty, her mouth laughing, her body trembling. "I detest Einarson. Use him and break him for me. But give me a revolution!"

I laughed, kissed her, and turned her around on my lap so her head would fit against my shoulder.

"We'll see," I promised. "I'm to meet the folks at midnight. Maybe I'll know then."

"You'll come back after the meeting?"

"Try to keep me away!"

I got back to the hotel at eleven-thirty, loaded my hips with gun and blackjack, and went upstairs to Grantham's suite. He was alone, but said he expected Einarson. He seemed glad to see me.

"Tell me, did Mahmoud go to any of the meetings?" I asked.

"No. His part in the revolution was hidden even from most of those in it. There were reasons why he couldn't appear."

"There were. The chief one was that everybody knew he didn't want any revolts, didn't want anything but money."

Grantham chewed his lower lip and said, "Oh, Lord, what a mess!"

Colonel Einarson arrived, in a dinner coat, but very much the soldier, the man of action. His hand-clasp was stronger than it needed to be. His little dark eyes were hard and bright.

"You are ready, gentlemen?" he addressed the boy and me as if we were a multitude. "Excellent! We shall go now. There will be difficulties tonight. Mahmoud is dead. There will be those of our friends who will ask, 'Why now revolt?' Ach!" He yanked a corner of his flowing dark mustache. "I will answer that. Good souls, our confrères, but given to timidity. There is no timidity under capable leadership. You shall see!" And he yanked his mustache again. This military gent seemed to be feeling Napoleonic this evening. But I didn't write him off as a musical-comedy revolutionist—I remembered what he had done to the soldier.

We left the hotel, got into a machine, rode seven blocks, and went into a small hotel on a side street. The porter bowed to the belt when he opened the door for Einarson. Grantham and I followed the officer up a flight of stairs, down a dim hall. A fat, greasy man in his fifties came bowing and clucking to meet us. Einarson introduced him to me—the proprietor of the hotel. He took us into a low-ceilinged room where thirty or forty men got up from chairs and looked at us through tobacco smoke.

Einarson made a short, very formal speech which I couldn't understand, introducing me to the gang. I ducked my head at them and found a seat beside Grantham. Einsaron sat on his other side. Everybody else sat down again, in no especial order.

Colonel Einarson smoothed his mustache and began to talk to this one and that, shouting over the clamor of other voices when necessary. In an undertone Lionel Grantham pointed out the more important conspirators to me—a dozen or more members of the Chamber of Deputies, a banker, a brother of the Minister of Finance (supposed to represent that official), half a dozen officers (all in civilian clothes tonight), three professors from the university, the president of a labor union, a newspaper publisher and his editor, the secretary of a students' club, a politician from out in the country, and a handful of small-business men.

The banker, a white-bearded fat man of sixty, stood up and began a speech, staring intently at Einarson. He spoke deliberately, softly, but with a faintly defiant air. The Colonel didn't let him get far.

"Ach!" Einarson barked and reared up on his feet. None of the words he said meant anything to me, but they took the pinkness out of the banker's cheeks and brought uneasiness into the eyes around us.

"They want to call it off," Grantham whispered in my ear. "They won't go through with it now. I know they won't."

The meeting became rough. A lot of people were yelping at once, but nobody talked down Einarson's bellow. Everybody was standing up, either very red or very white in the face. Fists, fingers and heads were shaking. The Minister of Finance's brother—a slender, elegantly dressed man with a long, intelligent face—took off his noseglasses so savagely that they broke in half, screamed words at Einarson, spun on his heel, and walked to the door.

He pulled it open and stopped.

The hall was full of green uniforms. Soldiers leaned against the wall, sat on their heels, stood in little groups. They hadn't guns—only bayonets in scabbards at their sides. The Minister of Finance's brother stood very still at the door, looking at the soldiers.

A brown-whiskered, dark-skinned, big man, in coarse clothes and heavy boots, glared with red-rimmed eyes from the soldiers to Einarson, and took two heavy steps toward the Colonel. This was the country politician. Einarson blew out his lips and stepped forward to meet him. Those who were between them got out of the way.

Einarson roared and the countryman roared. Einarson made the most noise, but the countryman wouldn't stop on that account.

Colonel Einarson said, "Ach!" and spat in the countryman's face.

The countryman staggered back a step and one of his paws went under his brown coat. I stepped around Einarson and shoved the muzzle of my gun in the countryman's ribs.

Einarson laughed, called two soldiers into the room. They took the countryman by the arms and led him out. Somebody closed the door. Everybody sat down. Einarson made another speech. Nobody interrupted him. The white-whiskered banker made another speech. The Minister of Finance's brother rose to say half a dozen polite words, staring near-sightedly at Einarson, holding half of his broken glasses in each slender hand. Grantham, at a word from Einarson, got up and talked. Everybody listened very respectfully.

Einarson spoke again. Everybody got excited. Everybody talked at once. It went on for a long time. Grantham explained to me that the revolution would start early Thursday morning—it was now early Wednesday morning—and that the details were now being arranged for the last time. I doubted that anybody was going to know anything about the details, with all this hubbub going on. They kept it up until half-past three. The last couple of hours I spent dozing in a chair, tilted back against the wall in a corner.

Grantham and I walked back to our hotel after the meeting. He told me we were to gather in the plaza at four o'clock the next morning. It would be daylight by six, and by then the government buildings, the President, most of the officials and Deputies who were not on our side, would be in our hands. A meeting of the Chamber of Deputies would be held under the eyes of Einarson's troops, and everything would be done as swiftly and regularly as possible.

I was to accompany Grantham as a sort of bodyguard, which meant, I imagined, that both of us were to be kept out of the way as much as possible. That was all right with me.

I left Grantham at the fifth floor, went to my room, ran cold water over my face and hands, and then left the hotel again. There was no chance of getting a cab at this hour, so I set out afoot for Romaine Frankl's house. I had a little excitement on the way.

A wind was blowing in my face as I walked. I stopped and put my back to it to light a cigarette. A shadow down the street slid over into a building's shadow. I was being tailed, and not very skillfully. I finished lighting my cigarette and went on my way until I came to a sufficiently dark side street. Turning into it, I stopped in a street-level dark doorway.

A man came puffing around the corner. My first crack at him went wrong—the blackjack took him too far forward, on the cheek. The second one got him fairly behind the ear. I left him sleeping there and went on to Romaine Frankl's house.

The servant Marya, in a woolly gray bathrobe, opened the door and sent me up to the black, white, and gray room, where the Minister's secretary, still in the pink gown, was propped up among cushions on the divan. A tray full of cigarette butts showed how she'd been spending her time.

"Well?" she asked as I moved her over to make a seat for myself beside her.

"Thursday morning at four we revolute."

"I knew you'd do it," she said, patting my hand.

"It did itself, though there were a few minutes when I could have stopped it by simply knocking our Colonel behind the ear and letting the rest of them tear him apart. That reminds me—somebody's hired man tried to follow me here tonight."

"What sort of a man?"

"Short, beefy, forty—just about my size and age."

"But he didn't succeed?"

"I slapped him flat and left him sleeping there."

She laughed and pulled my ear. "That was Gopchek, our very best detective. He'll be furious."

"Well, don't sic any more of 'em on me. You can tell him I'm sorry I had to hit him twice, but it was his own fault. He shouldn't have jerked his head back the first time."

She laughed, then frowned, finally settling on an expression that held half of each. "Tell me about the meeting," she commanded.

I told her what I knew. When I had finished she pulled my head down to kiss me, and held it down to whisper, "You do trust me, don't you, dear?"

"Yeah. Just as much as you trust me."

"That's far from being enough," she said, pushing my face away.

Marya came in with a tray of food. We pulled the table around in front of the divan and ate.

"I don't quite understand you," Romaine said over a stalk of asparagus. "If you don't trust me why do you tell me things? As far as I know, you haven't done much lying to me. Why should you tell me the truth if you've no faith in me?"

"My susceptible nature," I explained. "I'm so overwhelmed by your beauty and charm that I can't refuse you anything."

"Don't!" she exclaimed, suddenly serious. "I've capitalized on that beauty and charm in half the countries in the world. Don't say things like that to me ever again. It hurts, because—because—" She pushed her plate back, started to reach for a cigarette, stopped her hand in midair, and looked at me with disagreeable eyes. "I love you," she said.

I took the hand that was hanging in the air, kissed the palm of it, and asked, "You love me more than anyone else in the world?"

She pulled the hand away from me.

"Are you a bookkeeper?" she demanded. "Must you have amounts, weights, and measurements for everything?"

I grinned at her and tried to go on with my meal. I had been hungry. Now, though I had eaten only a couple of mouthfuls, my appetite was gone. I tried to pretend I still had the hunger I had lost, but it was no go. The food didn't want to be swallowed. I gave up the attempt and lighted a cigarette.

She used her left hand to fan away the smoke between us. "You don't trust me," she insisted. "Then why do you put yourself in my hands?"

"Why not? You can make a flop of the revolution. That's nothing to me. It's not my party, and its failure needn't mean that I can't get the boy out of the country with his money."

"You don't mind a prison, an execution, perhaps?"

"I'll take my chances," I said. But what I was thinking was, if after twenty years of scheming and slickering in bigtime cities I let myself get trapped in this hill village, I'd deserve all I got.

"And you've no feeling at all for me?"

"Don't be foolish." I waved my cigarette at my uneaten meal. "I haven't had anything to eat since eight o'clock last night."

She laughed, put a hand over my mouth, and said, "I

understand. You love me, but not enough to let me interfere with your plans. I don't like that. It's effeminate."

"You going to turn out for the revolution?" I asked.

"I'm not going to run through the streets throwing
bombs, if that's what you mean."

"And Djudakovich?"

"He sleeps till eleven in the morning. If you start at
four, you'll have seven hours before he's up." She said all
this perfectly seriously. "Get it done in that time. Or he
might decide to stop it."

"Yeah? I had a notion he wanted it."

"Vasilije wants nothing but peace and comfort."

"But listen, sweetheart," I protested. "If your Vasilije is
any good at all, he can't help finding out about it ahead of
time. Einarson and his army are the revolution. These
bankers and deputies and the like that he's carrying with
him to give the party a responsible look are a lot of movie
conspirators. Look at 'em! They hold their meetings at
midnight, and all that kind of foolishness. Now that
they're actually signed up to something, they won't be able
to keep from spreading the news. All day they'll be going
around trembling and whispering together in odd corners."

"They've been doing that for months," she said. "Nobody pays any attention to them. And I promise you
Vasilije shan't hear anything new. I certainly won't tell
him, and he never listens to anything anyone else says."

"All right." I wasn't sure it was all right, but it might
be. "Now this row is going through—if the army follows
Einarson?"

"Yes, and the army will follow him."

"Then, after it's over, our real job begins?"

She rubbed a flake of cigarette ash into the table cloth
with a small pointed finger, and said nothing.

"Einarson's got to be dumped," I continued.

"We'll have to kill him," she said thoughtfully. "You'd
better do it yourself."

I saw Einarson and Grantham that evening, and spent
several hours with them. The boy was fidgety, nervous,

without confidence in the revolution's success, though he
tried to pretend he was taking things as a matter of course.
Einarson was full of words. He gave us every detail of the
next day's plans. I was more interested in him than in
what he was saying. He could put the revolution over, I
thought, and I was willing to leave it to him. So while he
talked I studied him, combing him over for weak spots.

I took him physically first—a tall, thick-bodied man in
his prime, not as quick as he might have been, but strong
and tough. He had an amply jawed, short-nosed, florid
face that a fist wouldn't bother much. He wasn't fat, but
he ate and drank too much to be hardboiled, and your
florid man can seldom stand much poking around the belt.
So much for the gent's body.

Mentally he wasn't a heavyweight. His revolution was
crude stuff. It would get over chiefly because there wasn't
much opposition. He had plenty of will-power, I imagined,
but I didn't put a big number on that. People who haven't
much brains have to develop will-power to get anywhere. I
didn't know whether he had guts or not, but before an
audience I guessed he'd make a grand showing, and most
of this act would be before an audience. Off in a dark
corner I had an idea he would go watery. He believed in
himself—absolutely. That's ninety percent of leadership,
so there was no flaw in him there. He didn't trust me. He
had taken me in because as things turned out it was easier
to do so than to shut the door against me.

He kept on talking about his plans. There was nothing
to talk about. He was going to bring his soldiers in town in
the early morning and take over the government. That was
all the plan that was needed. The rest of it was the lettuce
around the dish, but this lettuce part was the only part we
could discuss. It was dull.

At eleven o'clock Einarson stopped talking and left us,
making this sort of speech, "Until four o'clock, gentlemen,
when Muravia's history begins." He put a hand on my
shoulder and commanded me, "Guard His Majesty!"

I said, "Uh-huh," and immediately sent His Majesty to

bed. He wasn't going to sleep, but he was too young to confess it, so he went off willingly enough. I got a taxi and went out to Romaine's.

She was like a child the night before a picnic. She kissed me and she kissed the servant Marya. She sat on my knees, beside me, on the floor, on all the chairs, changing her location every half-minute. She laughed and talked incessantly, about the revolution, about me, about herself, about anything at all. She nearly strangled herself trying to talk while swallowing wine. She lit her big cigarettes and forgot to smoke them, or forgot to stop smoking them until they scorched her lips. She sang lines from songs in half a dozen languages.

I left at three o'clock. She went down to the door with me, pulled my head down to kiss my eyes and mouth.

"If anything goes wrong," she said, "come to the prison. We'll hold that until—"

"If it goes wrong enough I'll be brought there," I promised.

She wouldn't joke now. "I'm going there now," she said. "I'm afraid Einarson's got my house on his list."

"Good idea," I said. "If you hit a bad spot get word to me."

I walked back to the hotel through the dark streets— the lights were turned off at midnight—without seeing a single other person, not even one of the gray-uniformed policemen. By the time I reached home rain was falling steadily.

In my room I changed into heavier clothes and shoes, dug an extra gun—an automatic—out of my bag and hung it in a shoulder holster. Then I filled my pockets with enough ammunition to make me bow-legged, picked up hat and raincoat, and went upstairs to Lionel Grantham's suite.

"It's ten to four," I told him. "We might as well go down to the plaza. Better put a gun in your pocket."

He hadn't slept. His handsome young face was as cool and pink and composed as it had been the first time I saw him, though his eyes were brighter now. He got into an overcoat, and we went downstairs.

Rain drove into our faces as we went toward the center of the dark plaza. Other figures moved around us, though none came near. We halted at the foot of an iron statue of somebody on a horse.

A pale young man of extraordinary thinness came up and began to talk rapidly, gesturing with both hands, sniffing every now and then, as if he had a cold in his head. I couldn't understand a word he said.

The rumble of other voices began to compete with the patter of rain. The fat, white-whiskered face of the banker who had been at the meeting appeared suddenly out of the darkness and went back into it just as suddenly, as if he didn't want to be recognized. Men I hadn't seen before gathered around us, saluting Grantham with a sheepish sort of respect. A little man in a too big cape ran up and began to tell us something in a cracked, jerky voice. A thin, stooped man with glasses freckled by raindrops translated the little man's story into English, "He says the artillery has betrayed us, and guns are being mounted in the government buildings to sweep the plaza at daybreak." There was an odd sort of hopefulness in his voice, and he added, "In that event we can, naturally, do nothing."

"We can die," Lionel Grantham said gently.

There wasn't the least bit of sense to that crack. Nobody was here to die. They were all here because it was so unlikely that anybody would have to die, except perhaps a few of Einarson's soldiers. That's the sensible view of the boy's speech. But it's God's own truth that even I—a middle-aged detective who had forgotten what it was like to believe in fairies—felt suddenly warm inside my wet clothes. And if anybody had said to me, "This boy is a real king," I wouldn't have argued the point.

An abrupt hush came in the murmuring around us, leaving only the rustle of rain, and the tramp, tramp, tramp of orderly marching up the street—Einarson's men. Everybody commenced to talk at once, happily, expectantly, cheered by the approach of those whose part it was to do the heavy work.

An officer in a glistening slicker pushed through the crowd—a small, dapper boy with too large a sword. He saluted Grantham elaborately, and said in English, of which he seemed proud, "Colonel Einarson's respects, Mister, and this progress goes betune."

I wondered what the last word meant.

Grantham smiled and said, "Convey my thanks to Colonel Einarson."

The banker appeared again, bold enough now to join us. Others who had been at the meeting appeared. We made an inner group around the statue, with the mob around us—more easily seen now in the gray of early morning. I didn't see the countryman into whose face Einarson had spat.

The rain soaked us. We shifted our feet, shivered, and talked. Daylight came slowly, showing more and more who stood around us wet and curious-eyed. On the edge of the crowd men burst into cheers. The rest of them took it up. They forgot their wet misery, laughed and danced, hugged and kissed one another. A bearded man in a leather coat came to us, bowed to Grantham, and explained that Einarson's own regiment could be seen occupying the Administration Building.

Day came fully. The mob around us opened to make way for an automobile that was surrounded by a squad of cavalrymen. It stopped in front of us. Colonel Einarson, holding a bare sword in his hand, stepped out of the car, saluted, and held the door open for Grantham and me. He followed us in, smelling of victory like a chorus girl of Coty. The cavalrymen closed around the car again, and we were driven to the Administration Building, through a crowd that yelled and ran red-faced and happy after us. It was all quite theatrical.

"The city is ours," said Einarson, leaning forward in his seat, his sword's point on the car floor, his hands on its hilt. "The President, the Deputies, nearly every official of importance, is taken. Not a single shot fired, not a window broken!"

He was proud of his revolution, and I didn't blame him. I wasn't sure that he might not have brains, after all. He had had sense enough to park his civilian adherents in the plaza until his soldiers had done their work.

We got out at the Administration Building, walking up the steps between rows of infantrymen at present-arms, rain sparkling on their fixed bayonets. More green-uniformed soldiers presented arms along the corridors. We went into an elaborately furnished dining room, where fifteen or twenty officers stood up to receive us. There were lots of speeches made. Everybody was triumphant. All through breakfast there was much talking. I didn't understand any of it.

After the meal we went to the Deputies' Chamber, a large, oval room with curved rows of benches and desks facing a raised platform. Besides three desks on the platform, some twenty chairs had been put there, facing the curved seats. Our breakfast party occupied these chairs. I noticed that Grantham and I were the only civilians on the platform. None of our fellow conspirators were there, except those who were in Einarson's army. I wasn't so fond of that.

Grantham sat in the first row of chairs, between Einarson and me. We looked down on the Deputies. There were perhaps a hundred of them distributed among the curved benches, split sharply in two groups. Half of them, on the right side of the room, were revolutionists. They stood up and hurrahed at us. The other half, on the left, were prisoners. Most of them seemed to have dressed hurriedly.

Around the room, shoulder to shoulder against the wall except on the platform and where the doors were, stood Einarson's soldiers.

An old man came in between two soldiers—a mild-eyed old gentleman, bald, stooped, with a wrinkled, clean-shaven, scholarly face.

"Doctor Semich," Grantham whispered.

The President's guards took him to the center one of the three desks on the platform. He paid no attention to us who were sitting on the platform, and he did not sit down.

A red-haired Deputy—one of the revolutionary party —got up and talked. His fellows cheered when he had finished. The President spoke—three words in a very dry, very calm voice, and left the platform to walk back the way he had come, the two soldiers accompanying him.

"Refused to resign," Grantham informed me.

The red-haired Deputy came up on the platform and took the center desk. The legislative machinery began to grind. Men talked briefly, apparently to the point—revolutionists. None of the prisoner Deputies rose. A vote was taken. A few of the in-wrongs didn't vote. Most of them seemed to vote with the ins.

"They've revoked the constitution," Grantham whispered.

The Deputies were hurrahing again—those who were there voluntarily. Einarson leaned over and mumbled to Grantham and me, "That is as far as we may safely go today. It leaves all in our hands."

"Time to listen to a suggestion?" I asked.

"Yes."

"Will you excuse us a moment?" I said to Grantham, and got up and walked to one of the rear corners of the platform.

Einarson followed me, frowning suspiciously.

"Why not give Grantham his crown now?" I asked when we were standing in the corner, my right shoulder touching his left, half facing each other, half facing the corner, our backs to the officers who sat on the platform, the nearest less than ten feet away. "Push it through. You can do it. There'll be a howl, of course. Tomorrow, as a concession to that howl, you'll make him abdicate. You'll get credit for that. You'll be fifty percent stronger with the people. Then you will be in a position to make it look as if the revolution was his party, and that you were the patriot who kept this newcomer from grabbing the throne. Meanwhile you'll be dictator, and whatever else you want to be when the time comes. See what I mean? Let him bear the brunt. You catch yours on the rebound."

He liked the idea, but he didn't like it to come from me. His little dark eyes pried into mine. "Why should you suggest this?" he asked.

"What do you care? I promise you he'll abdicate within twenty-four hours."

He smiled under his mustache and raised his head. I knew a major in the A. E. F. who always raised his head like that when he was going to issue an unpleasant order. I spoke quickly. "My raincoat—do you see it's folded over my left arm?"

He said nothing, but his eyelids crept together.

"You can't see my left hand," I went on.

His eyes were slits, but he said nothing.

"There's an automatic in it," I wound up.

"Well?" he asked contemptuously.

"Nothing, only—get funny, and I'll let your guts out."

"Ach!"—he didn't take me seriously—"and after that?"

"I don't know. Think it over carefully, Einarson. I've deliberately put myself in a position where I've got to go ahead if you don't give in. I can kill you before you do anything. I'm going to do it if you don't give Grantham his crown now. Understand? I've got to. Maybe—most likely —your boys would get me afterward, but you'd be dead. If I back down now, you'll certainly have me shot. So I can't back down. If neither of us backs down, we'll both take the leap. *I've* gone too far to weaken now. *You'll* have to give in. Think it over."

He thought it over. Some of the color washed out of his face, and a little rippling movement appeared in the flesh of his chin. I crowded him along by moving the raincoat enough to show him the muzzle of the gun that actually was there in my left hand. I had the big heater—he hadn't nerve enough to take a chance on dying in his hour of victory.

He strode across the platform to the desk at which the

redhead sat, drove the redhead away with a snarl and a gesture, leaned over the desk, and bellowed down into the chamber. I stood a little to one side of him, a little behind, so no one could get between us.

No Deputy made a sound for a long minute after the Colonel's bellow had stopped. Then one of the anti-revolutionists jumped to his feet and yelped bitterly. Einarson pointed a long brown finger at him. Two soldiers left their places by the wall, took the Deputy roughly by neck and arms, and dragged him out. Another Deputy stood up, talked, and was removed. After the fifth drag-out everything was peaceful. Einarson put a question and got a unanimous answer.

He turned to me, his gaze darting from my face to my raincoat and back, and said, "That is done."

"We'll have the coronation now," I commanded.

I missed most of the ceremony. I was busy keeping my hold on the florid officer, but finally Lionel Grantham was officially installed as Lionel the First, King of Muravia. Einarson and I congratulated him, or whatever it was, together. Then I took the officer aside.

"We're going to take a walk," I said. "No foolishness. Take me out of a side door."

I had him now, almost without needing the gun. He would have to deal quietly with Grantham and me—kill us without any publicity—if he were to avoid being laughed at—this man who had let himself be stuck up and robbed of a throne in the middle of his army.

We went roundabout from the Administration Building to the Hotel of the Republic without meeting anyone who knew us. The population was all in the plaza. We found the hotel deserted. I made him run the elevator to my floor, and herded him to my room.

I tried the door, found it unlocked, let go the knob, and told him to go in. He pushed the door open and stopped.

Romaine Frankl was sitting crosslegged in the middle of my bed, sewing a button on one of my union suits.

I prodded Einarson into the room and closed the door. Romaine looked at him and at the automatic that was now uncovered in my hand. With burlesque disappointment she said, "Oh, you haven't killed him yet!"

Colonel Einarson stiffened. He had an audience now— one that saw his humiliation. He was likely to do something. I'd have to handle him with gloves, or—maybe the other way was better. I kicked him on the ankle and snarled, "Get over in the corner and sit down!"

He spun around to me. I jabbed the muzzle of the pistol in his face, grinding his lip between it and his teeth. When his head jerked back I slammed him in the belly with my other fist. He grabbed for air with a wide mouth. I pushed him over to a chair in one corner.

Romaine laughed and shook a finger at me, saying, "You're a rowdy!"

"What else can I do?" I protested, chiefly for my prisoner's benefit. "When somebody's watching him he gets notions that he's a hero. I stuck him up and made him crown the boy king. But this bird has still got the army, which is the government. I can't let go of him, or both Lionel the Once and I will gather lead. It hurts me more than it does him to have to knock him around, but I can't help myself. I've got to keep him sensible."

"You're doing wrong by him," she replied. "You've got no right to mistreat him. The only polite thing for you to do is to cut his throat in a gentlemanly manner."

"Ach!" Einarson's lungs were working again.

"Shut up," I yelled at him, "or I'll knock you double-jointed."

He glared at me, and I asked the girl, "What'll we do with him? I'd be glad to cut his throat, but the trouble is, his army might avenge him, and I'm not a fellow who likes to have anybody's army avenging on him."

"We'll give him to Vasilije," she said, swinging her feet over the side of the bed and standing up. "He'll know what to do."

"Where is he?"

"Upstairs in Grantham's suite, finishing his morning nap."

Then she said lightly, casually, as if she hadn't been thinking seriously about it, "So you had the boy crowned?"

"I did. You want it for your Vasilije? Good! We want five million American dollars for our abdication. Grantham put in three to finance the doings, and he deserves a profit. He's been regularly elected by the Deputies. He's got no real backing here, but he can get support from the neighbors. Don't overlook that. There are a couple of countries not a million miles away that would gladly send in an army to support a legitimate king in exchange for whatever concessions they liked. But Lionel the First isn't unreasonable. He thinks it would be better for you to have a native ruler. All he asks is a decent provision from the government. Five million is low enough, and he'll abdicate tomorrow. Tell that to your Vasilije."

She went around me to avoid passing between my gun and its target, stood on tiptoe to kiss my ear, and said, "You and your king are brigands. I'll be back in a few minutes."

She went out.

"Ten millions," Colonel Einarson said.

"I can't trust you now," I said. "You'd pay us off in front of a firing squad."

"You can trust this pig Djudakovich?"

"He's got no reason to hate us."

"He will when he's told of you and his Romaine."

I laughed.

"Besides, how can he be king? Ach! What is his promise to pay if he cannot become in a position to pay? Suppose even I am dead. What will he do with my army? Ach! You have seen the pig! What kind of king is he?"

"I don't know," I said truthfully. "I'm told he was a good Minister of Police because inefficiency would spoil his comfort. Maybe he'd be a good king for the same reason. I've seen him once. He's a bloated mountain, but there's nothing ridiculous about him. He weighs a ton, and moves without shaking the floor. I'd be afraid to try on him what I did to you."

This insult brought the soldier up on his feet, very tall and straight. His eyes burned at me while his mouth hardened in a thin line. He was going to make trouble for me before I was rid of him.

The door opened and Vasilije Djudakovich came in, followed by the girl. I grinned at the fat Minister. He nodded without smiling. His little dark eyes moved coldly from me to Einarson.

The girl said, "The government will give Lionel the First a draft for four million dollars, American, on either a Vienna or Athens bank, in exchange for his abdication." She dropped her official tone and added, "That's every nickel I could get out of him."

"You and your Vasilije are a couple of rotten bargain hunters," I complained. "But we'll take it. We've got to have a special train to Saloniki—one that will put us across the border before the abdication goes into effect."

"That will be arranged," she promised.

"Good! Now to do all this your Vasilije has got to take the army away from Einarson. Can he do it?"

"Ach!" Colonel Einarson reared up his head, swelled his thick chest. "That is precisely what he has got to do!"

The fat man grumbled sleepily through his yellow beard. Romaine came over and put a hand on my arm.

"Vasilije wants a private talk with Einarson. Leave it to him."

I agreed and offered Djudakovich my automatic. He paid no attention to the gun or to me. He was looking with a clammy sort of patience at the officer. I went out with the girl and closed the door. At the foot of the stairs I took her by the shoulders.

"Can I trust your Vasilije?" I asked.

"Oh my dear, he could handle half a dozen Einarsons."

"I don't mean that. He won't try to gyp me?"

"Why should you start worrying about that now?"

"He doesn't seem to be exactly all broken out with friendliness."

She laughed, and twisted her face around to bite at one of my hands.

"He's got ideals," she explained. "He despises you and your king for a pair of adventurers who are making a profit out of his country's troubles. That's why he's so sniffy. But he'll keep his word."

Maybe he would, I thought, but he hadn't given me his word—the girl had.

"I'm going over to see His Majesty," I said. "I won't be long—then I'll join you up in his suite. What was the idea of the sewing act? I had no buttons off."

"You did," she contradicted me, rummaging in my pocket for cigarettes. "I pulled one off when one of our men told me you and Einarson were headed this way. I thought it would look domestic."

I found my king in a wine and gold drawing-room in the Executive Residence, surrounded by Muravia's socially and politically ambitious. Uniforms were still in the majority, but a sprinkling of civilians had finally got to him, along with their wives and daughters. He was too occupied to see me for a few minutes, so I stood around, looking the folks over. Particularly one—a tall girl in black, who stood apart from the others, at a window.

I noticed her first because she was beautiful in face and body, and then I studied her more closely because of the expression in the brown eyes with which she watched the new king. If ever anybody looked proud of anybody else, this girl did of Grantham. The way she stood there, alone by the window, and looked at him—he would have had to be at least a combination of Apollo, Socrates, and Alexander to deserve half of it. Valeska Radnjak, I supposed.

I looked at the boy. His face was proud and flushed, and every two seconds turned toward the girl at the window while he listened to the jabbering of the worshipful group around him. I knew he wasn't any Apollo-Socrates-Alexander, but he managed to look the part. He had found a spot in the world that he liked. I was half sorry he couldn't hang on to it, but my regrets didn't keep me from deciding that I had wasted enough time.

I pushed through the crowd toward him. He recognized me with the eyes of a park sleeper being awakened from sweet dreams by a nightstick on his shoe-soles. He excused himself from the others and took me down a corridor to a room with stained glass windows and richly carved office furniture.

"This was Doctor Semich's office," he told me. "I shall—"

"You'll be in Greece by tomorrow," I said bluntly.

He frowned at his feet, a stubborn frown.

"You ought to know you can't hold on," I argued. "You may think everything is going smoothly. If you do, you're deaf, dumb, and blind. I put you in with the muzzle of a gun against Einarson's liver. I've kept you in this long by kidnaping him. I've made a deal with Djudakovich—the only strong man I've seen here. It's up to him to handle Einarson. I can't hold him any longer. Djudakovich will make a good king, if he wants to. He promises you four million dollars and a special train and safe-conduct to Saloniki. You go out with your head up. You've been a king. You've taken a country out of bad hands and put it into good—this fat guy is real. And you've made yourself a million profit."

"No. You go. I shall see it through. These people have trusted me, and I shall—"

"My God, that's old Doc Semich's line! These people haven't trusted you—not a bit of it. I'm the people who trusted you. I made you king, understand? I made you king so you could go home with your chin up—not so you could stay here and make an ass of yourself! I bought help with promises. One of them was that you'd get out within twenty-four hours. You've got to keep the promises I made in your name. The people trusted you, huh? You were crammed down their throats, my son! And I did the cramming! Now I'm going to uncram you. If it happens to be tough on your romance—if your Valeska won't take any price less than this dinky country's throne—"

"That's enough." His voice came from some point at least fifty feet above me. "You shall have your abdication. I don't want the money. You will send word to me when the train is ready."

"Write the get-out now," I ordered.

He went over to the desk, found a sheet of paper, and with a steady hand wrote that in leaving Muravia he renounced his throne and all rights to it. He signed the paper *Lionel Rex* and gave it to me. I pocketed it and began sympathetically, "I can understand your feelings, and I'm sorry that—"

He put his back to me and walked out. I returned to the hotel.

At the fifth floor I left the elevator and walked softly to the door of my room. No sound came through. I tried the door, found it unlocked, and went in. Emptiness. Even my clothes and bags were gone. I went up to Grantham's suite.

Djudakovich, Romaine, Einarson, and half the police force were there.

Colonel Einarson sat very erect in an armchair in the middle of the room. Dark hair and mustache bristled. His chin was out, muscles bulged everywhere in his florid face, his eyes were hot—he was in one of his finest scrapping moods. That came of giving him an audience.

I scowled at Djudakovich, who stood on wide-spread giant's legs with his back to a window. Why hadn't the fat fool known enough to keep Einarson off in a lonely corner, where he could be handled?

Romaine floated around and past the policemen who stood or sat everywhere in the room, and came to where I stood, inside the door.

"Are your arrangements all made?" she asked.

"Got the abdication in my pocket."

"Give it to me."

"Not yet," I said. "First I've got to know that your Vasilije is as big as he looks. Einarson doesn't look squelched to me. Your fat boy ought to have known he'd blossom out in front of an audience."

"There's no telling what Vasilije is up to," she said lightly, "except that it will be adequate."

I wasn't as sure of that as she was. Djudakovich rumbled a question at her, and she gave him a quick answer. He rumbled some more—at the policemen. They began to go away from us, singly, in pairs, in groups. When the last one had gone the fat man pushed words out between his yellow whiskers at Einarson. Einarson stood up, chest out, shoulders back, grinning confidently under his dark mustache.

"What now?" I asked the girl.

"Come along and you'll see," she said.

The four of us went downstairs and out the hotel's front door. The rain had stopped. In the plaza was gathered most of Stefania's population, thickest in front of the Administration Building and Executive Residence. Over their heads we could see the sheepskin caps of Einarson's regiment, still around those buildings as he had left them.

We—or at least Einarson—were recognized and cheered as we crossed the plaza. Einarson and Djudakovich went side by side in front, the soldier marching, the fat giant waddling. Romaine and I went close behind them. We headed straight for the Administration Building.

"What is he up to?" I asked irritably.

She patted my arm, smiled excitedly, and said, "Wait and see."

There didn't seem to be anything else to do—except worry.

We arrived at the foot of the Administration Building's stone steps. Bayonets had an uncomfortably cold gleam in the early evening light as Einarson's troops presented arms. We climbed the steps. On the broad top step Einarson and Djudakovich turned to face soldiers and citizens below. The girl and I moved around behind the pair. Her teeth were chattering, her fingers were digging into my arm, but her lips and eyes were smiling recklessly.

The soldiers who were around the Executive Residence came to join those already before us, pushing back the citizens to make room. Another detachment came up. Einarson raised his hand, bawled a dozen words, growled at Djudakovich, and stepped back.

Djudakovich spoke, a drowsy, effortless roar that could have been heard as far as the hotel. As he spoke he took a paper out of his pocket and held it before him. There was nothing theatrical in his voice or manner. He might have been talking about anything not too important. But—looking at his audience, you'd have known it was important.

The soldiers had broken ranks to crowd nearer, faces were reddening, a bayoneted gun was shaken aloft here and there. Behind them the citizens were looking at one another with frightened faces, jostling each other, some trying to get nearer, some trying to get away.

Djudakovich talked on. The turmoil grew. A soldier pushed through his fellows and started up the steps, others at his heels.

Einarson cut in on the fat man's speech, stepping to the edge of the top step, bawling down at the upturned faces, with the voice of a man accustomed to being obeyed.

The soldiers on the steps tumbled down. Einarson bawled again. The broken ranks were slowly straightened, flourished guns were grounded. Einarson stood silent a moment, glowering at his troops, and then began an address. I couldn't understand his words any more than I had the fat man's, but there was no question about his impressiveness. And there was no doubt that the anger was going out of the faces below.

I looked at Romaine. She shivered and was no longer smiling. I looked at Djudakovich. He was as still and as emotionless as the mountain he resembled.

I wished I knew what it was all about, so I'd know

whether it was wisest to shoot Einarson and duck through the apparently empty building behind us or not. I could guess that the paper in Djudakovich's hand had been evidence of some sort against the Colonel, evidence that would have stirred the soldiers to the point of attacking him if they hadn't been too accustomed to obeying him.

While I was wishing and guessing, Einarson finished his address, stepped to one side, pointed a finger at Djudakovich, barked an order.

Down below, soldiers' faces were indecisive, shifty-eyed, but four of them stepped briskly out at their colonel's order and came up the steps. "So," I thought, "my fat candidate has lost! Well, he can have the firing squad. The back door for mine." My hand had been holding the gun in my coat pocket for a long time. I kept it there while I took a slow step back, drawing the girl with me.

"Move when I tell you," I muttered.

"Wait!" she gasped. "Look!"

The fat giant, sleepy-eyed as ever, put out an enormous paw and caught the wrist of Einarson's pointing hand. Pulled Einarson down. Let go the wrist and caught the Colonel's shoulder. Lifted him off his feet with that one hand that held his shoulder. Shook him at the soldiers below. Shook Einarson at them with one hand. Shook his piece of paper—whatever it was—at them with the other. And I'm damned if one seemed any more strain on his arms than the other!

While he shook them—man and paper—he roared sleepily, and when he had finished roaring he flung his two handfuls down to the wild-eyed ranks. Flung them with a gesture that said, *"Here is the man and here is the evidence against him. Do what you like."*

And the soldiers who had cringed back into ranks at Einarson's command when he stood tall and domineering above them, did what could have been expected when he was tossed down to them.

They tore him apart—actually—piece by piece. They dropped their guns and fought to get at him. Those farther away climbed over those nearer, smothering them, trampling them. They surged back and forth in front of the steps, an insane pack of men turned wolves, savagely struggling to destroy a man who must have died before he had been down half a minute.

I put the girl's hand off my arm and went to face Djudakovich.

"Muravia's yours," I said. "I don't want anything but our draft and train. Here's the abdication."

Romaine swiftly translated my words and then Djudakovich's, "The train is ready now. The draft will be delivered there. Do you wish to go over for Grantham?"

"No. Send him down. How do I find the train?"

"I'll take you," she said. "We'll go through the building and out a side door."

One of Djudakovich's detectives sat at the wheel of a car in front of the hotel. Romaine and I got in it. Across the plaza tumult was still boiling. Neither of us said anything while the car whisked us through darkening streets.

Presently she asked very softly, "And now you despise me?"

"No." I reached for her. "But I hate mobs, lynchings—they sicken me. No matter how wrong the man is, if a mob's against him, I'm for him. The only thing I ever pray to God for is a chance some day to squat down behind a machine gun with a lynching party in front of me. I had no use for Einarson, but I wouldn't have given him that! Well, what's done is done. What was the document?"

"A letter from Mahmoud. He had left it with a friend to be given to Vasilije if anything ever happened to him. He knew Einarson, it seems, and prepared his revenge. The letter confessed his—Mahmoud's—part in the assassination of General Radnjak, and said that Einarson was also implicated. The army worshiped Radnjak, and Einarson wanted the army."

"Your Vasilije could have used that to chase Einarson out—without feeding him to the wolves," I complained.

"Vasilije was right. Bad as it was, that was the way to

do it. It's over and settled forever, with Vasilije in power. An Einarson alive, an army not knowing he had killed their idol—too risky. Up to the end Einarson thought he had power enough to hold his troops, no matter what they knew. He—"

"All right—it's done. And I'm glad to be through with this king business. Kiss me."

She did, and whispered, "When Vasilije dies—and he can't live long, the way he eats—I'm coming to San Francisco."

"You're a cold-blooded hussy," I said.

Lionel Grantham, ex-king of Muravia, was only five minutes behind us in reaching our train. He wasn't alone. Valeska Radnjak, looking as much like the queen of something as if she had been, was with him. She didn't seem to be all broken up over the loss of her throne.

The boy was pleasant and polite enough to me during our rattling trip to Saloniki, but obviously not very comfortable in my company. His bride-to-be didn't know anybody but the boy existed, unless she happened to find someone else directly in front of her. So I didn't wait for their wedding, but left Saloniki on a boat that pulled out a couple of hours after we arrived.

I left the draft with them, of course. They decided to take out Lionel's three millions and return the fourth to Muravia. And I went back to San Francisco to quarrel with my boss over what he thought were unnecessary five-and ten-dollar items in my expense account.

THE GATEWOOD CAPER

Harvey Gatewood had issued orders that I was to be admitted as soon as I arrived, so it took me only a little less than fifteen minutes to thread my way past the door-keepers, office boys, and secretaries who filled up most of the space between the Gatewood Lumber Corporation's front door and the president's private office. His office was large, all mahogany and bronze and green plush, with a mahogany desk as big as a bed in the center of the floor.

Gatewood, leaning across the desk, began to bark at me as soon as the obsequious clerk who had bowed me in bowed himself out.

"My daughter was kidnaped last night! I want the gang that did it if it takes every cent I got!"

"Tell me about it," I suggested.

But he wanted results, it seemed, and not questions, and so I wasted nearly an hour getting information that he could have given me in fifteen minutes.

He was a big bruiser of a man, something over 200 pounds of hard red flesh, and a czar from the top of his bullet head to the toes of his shoes that would have been at least number twelves if they hadn't been made to measure.

He had made his several millions by sandbagging everybody that stood in his way, and the rage he was burning up with now didn't make him any easier to deal with.

His wicked jaw was sticking out like a knob of granite

and his eyes were filmed with blood—he was in a lovely frame of mind. For a while it looked as if the Continental Detective Agency was going to lose a client, because I'd made up my mind that he was going to tell me all I wanted to know, or I'd chuck the job.

But finally I got the story out of him.

His daughter Audrey had left their house on Clay Street at about 7 o'clock the preceding evening, telling her maid that she was going for a walk. She had not returned that night—though Gatewood had not known that until after he had read the letter that came this morning.

The letter had been from someone who said that she had been kidnaped. It demanded $50,000 for her release, and instructed Gatewood to get the money ready in hundred-dollar bills—so that there would be no delay when he was told the manner in which the money was to be paid over to his daughter's captors. As proof that the demand was not a hoax, a lock of the girl's hair, a ring she always wore, and a brief note from her, asking her father to comply with the demands, had been enclosed.

Gatewood had received the letter at his office and had telephoned to his house immediately. He had been told that the girl's bed had not been slept in the previous night and that none of the servants had seen her since she started out for her walk. He had then notified the police, turning the letter over to them, and a few minutes later he had decided to employ private detectives also.

"Now," he burst out, after I had wormed these things out of him, and he had told me that he knew nothing of his daughter's associates or habits, "go ahead and do something! I'm not paying you to sit around and talk about it!"

"What are you going to do?" I asked.

"Me? I'm going to put those——behind bars if it takes every cent I've got in the world!"

"Sure! But first you get that $50,000 ready, so you can give it to them when they ask for it."

He clicked his jaw shut and thrust his face into mine.

"I've never been clubbed into doing anything in my

life! And I'm too old to start now!" he said. "I'm going to call these people's bluff!"

"That's going to make it lovely for your daughter. But, aside from what it'll do to her, it's the wrong play. Fifty thousand isn't a whole lot to you, and paying it over will give us two chances that we haven't got now. One when the payment is made—a chance either to nab whoever comes for it or get a line on them. And the other when your daughter is returned. No matter how careful they are, it's a cinch she'll be able to tell us something that will help us grab them."

He shook his head angrily, and I was tired of arguing with him. So I left, hoping he'd see the wisdom of the course I had advised before it was too late.

At the Gatewood residence I found butlers, second men, chauffeurs, cooks, maids, upstairs girls, downstairs girls, and a raft of miscellaneous flunkies—he had enough servants to run a hotel.

What they told me amounted to this: the girl had not received a phone call, note by messenger or telegram—the time-honored devices for luring a victim out to a murder or abduction—before she left the house. She had told her maid that she would be back within an hour or two; but the maid had not been alarmed when her mistress failed to return all that night.

Audrey was the only child, and since her mother's death she had come and gone to suit herself. She and her father didn't hit it off very well together—their natures were too much alike, I gathered—and he never knew where she was. There was nothing unusual about her remaining away all night. She seldom bothered to leave word when she was going to stay overnight with friends.

She was nineteen years old, but looked several years older, about five feet five inches tall, and slender. She had blue eyes, brown hair—very thick and long—was pale and very nervous. Her photographs, of which I took a handful, showed that her eyes were large, her nose small and regular and her chin pointed.

She was not beautiful, but in the one photograph where a smile had wiped off the sullenness of her mouth, she was at least pretty.

When she left the house she was wearing a light tweed skirt and jacket with a London tailor's label in them, a buff silk shirtwaist with stripes a shade darker, brown wool stockings, low-heeled brown oxfords, and an untrimmed gray felt hat.

I went up to her rooms—she had three on the third floor—and looked through all her stuff. I found nearly a bushel of photographs of men, boys, and girls; and a great stack of letters of varying degrees of intimacy, signed with a wide assortment of names and nicknames. I made notes of all the addresses I found.

Nothing in her rooms seemed to have any bearing on her abduction, but there was a chance that one of the names and addresses might be of someone who had served as a decoy. Also, some of her friends might be able to tell us something of value.

I dropped in at the Agency and distributed the names and addresses among the three operatives who were idle, sending them out to see what they could dig up.

Then I reached the police detectives who were working on the case—O'Gar and Thode—by telephone, and went down to the Hall of Justice to meet them. Lusk, a post office inspector, was also there. We turned the job around and around, looking at it from every angle, but not getting very far. We were all agreed, however, that we couldn't take a chance on any publicity, or work in the open, until the girl was safe.

They had had a worse time with Gatewood than I—he had wanted to put the whole thing in the newspapers, with the offer of a reward, photographs and all. Of course, Gatewood was right in claiming that this was the most effective way of catching the kidnapers—but it would have been tough on his daughter if her captors happened to be persons of sufficiently hardened character. And kidnapers as a rule aren't lambs.

I looked at the letter they had sent. It was printed with

pencil on ruled paper of the kind that is sold in pads by every stationery dealer in the world. The envelope was just as common, also addressed in pencil, and postmarked *San Francisco, September 20,* 9 P.M. That was the night she had been seized.

The letter read:

Sir:

    We have your charming daughter and place a value of $50,000 upon her. You will get the money ready in $100 bills at once so there will be no delay when we tell you how it is to be paid over to us.

    We beg to assure you that things will go badly with your daughter should you not do as you are told, or should you bring the police into this matter, or should you do anything foolish.

    $50,000 is only a small fraction of what you stole while we were living in mud and blood in France for you, and we mean to get that much or else!

                            Three.

A peculiar note in several ways. They are usually written with a great pretense of partial illiterateness. Almost always there's an attempt to lead suspicion astray. Perhaps the ex-service stuff was there for that purpose—or perhaps not.

Then there was a postscript:

    We know someone who will buy her even after we are through with her—in case you won't listen to reason.

The letter from the girl was written jerkily on the same kind of paper, apparently with the same pencil.

Daddy—
    Please do as they ask! I am so afraid—
                            Audrey

A door at the other end of the room opened, and a head came through.

"O'Gar! Thode! Gatewood just called up. Get up to his office right away!"

The four of us tumbled out of the Hall of Justice and into a police car.

Gatewood was pacing his office like a maniac when we pushed aside enough hirelings to get to him. His face was hot with blood and his eyes had an insane glare in them.

"She just phoned me!" he cried thickly, when he saw us.

It took a minute or two to get him calm enough to tell us about it.

"She called me on the phone. Said, 'Oh, Daddy! Do something! I can't stand this—they're killing me!' I asked her if she knew where she was, and she said, 'No, but I can see Twin Peaks from here. There's three men and a woman, and—' And then I heard a man curse, and a sound as if he had struck her, and the phone went dead. I tried to get central to give me the number, but she couldn't! It's a damned outrage the way the telephone system is run. We pay enough for service, God knows, and we . . ."

O'Gar scratched his head and turned away from Gatewood. "In sight of Twin Peaks! There are hundreds of houses that are!"

Gatewood meanwhile had finished denouncing the telephone company and was pounding on his desk with a paperweight to attract our attention.

"Have you people done anything at all?" he demanded.

I answered him with another question: "Have you got the money ready?"

"No," he said, "I won't be held up by anybody!"

But he said it mechanically, without his usual conviction—the talk with his daughter had shaken him out of some of his stubbornness. He was thinking of her safety a little now instead of only his own fighting spirit.

We went at him hammer and tongs for a few minutes, and after a while he sent a clerk out for the money.

We split up the field then. Thode was to take some men from headquarters and see what he could find in the Twin Peaks end of town; but we weren't very optimistic over the prospects there—the territory was too large.

Lusk and O'Gar were to carefully mark the bills that the clerk brought from the bank, and then stick as close to Gatewood as they could without attracting attention. I was to go out to Gatewood's house and stay there.

The abductors had plainly instructed Gatewood to get the money ready immediately so that they could arrange to get it on short notice—not giving him time to communicate with anyone or make plans.

Gatewood was to get hold of the newspapers, give them the whole story, with the $10,000 reward he was offering for the abductors' capture, to be published as soon as the girl was safe—so we would get the help of publicity at the earliest possible moment without jeopardizing the girl.

The police in all the neighboring towns had already been notified—that had been done before the girl's phone message had assured us that she was held in San Francisco.

Nothing happened at the Gatewood residence all that evening. Harvey Gatewood came home early; and after dinner he paced his library floor and drank whiskey until bedtime, demanding every few minutes that we, the detectives in the case, do something besides sit around like a lot of damned mummies. O'Gar, Lusk, and Thode were out in the street, keeping an eye on the house and neighborhood.

At midnight Harvey Gatewood went to bed. I declined a bed in favor of the library couch, which I dragged over beside the telephone, an extension of which was in Gatewood's bedroom.

At 2:30 the telephone bell rang. I listened in while Gatewood talked from his bed.

A man's voice, crisp and curt: "Gatewood?"

"Yes."

"Got the dough?"

"Yes."

Gatewood's voice was thick and blurred—I could imagine the boiling that was going on inside him.

"Good!" came the brisk voice. "Put a piece of paper around it and leave the house with it, right away! Walk down Clay Street, keeping on the same side as your house. Don't walk too fast and keep walking. If everything's all right, and there's no elbows tagging along, somebody'll come up to you between your house and the waterfront. They'll have a handkerchief up to their face for a second, and then they'll let it fall to the ground.

"When you see that, you'll lay the money on the pavement, turn around, and walk back to your house. If the money isn't marked, and you don't try any fancy tricks, you'll get your daughter back in an hour or two. If you try to pull anything—remember what we wrote you! Got it straight?"

Gatewood sputtered something that was meant for an affirmative, and the telephone clicked silent.

I didn't waste any of my precious time tracing the call—it would be from a public telephone, I knew—but yelled up the stairs to Gatewood, "You do as you were told, and don't try any foolishness!"

Then I ran out into the early morning air to find the police detectives and the post office inspector.

They had been joined by two plainclothesmen, and had two automobiles waiting. I told them what the situation was, and we laid hurried plans.

O'Gar was to drive in one of the cars down Sacramento Street, and Thode, in the other, down Washington Street. These streets parallel Clay, one on each side. They were to drive slowly, keeping pace with Gatewood, and stopping at each cross street to see that he passed.

When he failed to cross within a reasonable time they were to turn up to Clay Street—and their actions from then on would have to be guided by chance and their own wits.

Lusk was to wander along a block or two ahead of Gatewood, on the opposite side of the street, pretending to be mildly intoxicated.

I was to shadow Gatewood down the street, with one of the plainclothesmen behind me. The other plainclothesman was to turn in a call at headquarters for every available man to be sent to City Street. They would arrive too late, of course, and as likely as not it would take them some time to find us; but we had no way of knowing what was going to turn up before the night was over.

Our plan was sketchy enough, but it was the best we could do—we were afraid to grab whoever got the money from Gatewood. The girl's talk with her father that afternoon had sounded too much as if her captors were desperate for us to take any chances on going after them roughshod until she was out of their hands.

We had hardly finished our plans when Gatewood, wearing a heavy overcoat, left his house and turned down the street.

Farther down, Lusk, weaving along, talking to himself, was almost invisible in the shadows. There was no one else in sight. That meant that I had to give Gatewood at least two blocks' lead, so that the man who came for the money wouldn't tumble to me. One of the plainclothesmen was half a block behind me, on the other side of the street.

We walked two blocks down, and then a chunky man in a derby hat came into sight. He passed Gatewood, passed me, went on.

Three blocks more.

A touring car, large, black, powerfully engined and with lowered curtains, came from the rear, passed us, went on. Possibly a scout. I scrawled its license number down on my pad without taking my hand out of my overcoat pocket.

Another three blocks.

A policeman passed, strolling in ignorance of the game

being played under his nose; and then a taxicab with a single male passenger. I wrote down its license number.

Four blocks with no one in sight of me but Gatewood—I couldn't see Lusk any more.

Just ahead of Gatewood a man stepped out of a black doorway, turned around, called up to a window for someone to come down and open the door for him.

We went on.

Coming from nowhere, a woman stood on the sidewalk fifty feet ahead of Gatewood, a handkerchief to her face. It fluttered to the pavement.

Gatewood stopped, standing stiff-legged. I could see his right hand come up, lifting the side of the overcoat in which it was pocketed—and I knew his hand was gripped around a pistol.

For perhaps half a minute he stood like a statue. Then his left hand came out of his pocket, and the bundle of money fell to the sidewalk in front of him, where it made a bright blur in the darkness. Gatewood turned abruptly, and began to retrace his steps homeward.

The woman had recovered her handkerchief. Now she ran to the bundle, picked it up, and scuttled to the black mouth of an alley a few feet distant—a rather tall woman, bent, and in dark clothes from head to feet.

In the black mouth of the alley she vanished.

I had been compelled to slow up while Gatewood and the woman stood facing each other, and I was more than a block away now. As soon as the woman disappeared, I took a chance and started pounding my rubber soles against the pavement.

The alley was empty when I reached it.

It ran all the way through to the next street, but I knew that the woman couldn't have reached the other end before I got to this one. I carry a lot of weight these days, but I can still step a block or two in good time. Along both sides of the alley were the rears of apartment buildings, each with its back door looking blankly, secretively, at me.

The plainclothesman who had been trailing behind me came up, then O'Gar and Thode in their cars, and soon, Lusk. O'Gar and Thode rode off immediately to wind through the neighboring streets, hunting for the woman. Lusk and the plainclothesman each planted himself on a corner from which two of the streets enclosing the block could be watched.

I went through the alley, hunting vainly for an un-locked door, an open window, a fire escape that would show recent use—any of the signs that a hurried departure from the alley might leave.

Nothing!

O'Gar came back shortly with some reinforcements from headquarters that he had picked up, and Gatewood.

Gatewood was burning.

"Bungled the damn thing again! I won't pay your agency a nickel, and I'll see that some of these so-called detectives get put back in a uniform and set to walking beats!"

"What'd the woman look like?" I asked him.

"I don't know! I thought you were hanging around to take care of her! She was old and bent, kind of, I guess, but I couldn't see her face for her veil. I don't know! What the hell were you men doing? It's a damned outrage the way . . ."

I finally got him quieted down and took him home, leaving the city men to keep the neighborhood under surveillance. There were fourteen or fifteen of them on the job now, and every shadow held at least one.

The girl would head for home as soon as she was released and I wanted to be there to pump her. There was an excellent chance of catching her abductors before they got very far, if she could tell us anything at all about them.

Home, Gatewood went up against the whiskey bottle again, while I kept one ear cocked at the telephone and the other at the front door. O'Gar or Thode phoned every half-hour or so to ask if we'd heard from the girl.

They had still found nothing.

At 9 o'clock they, with Lusk, arrived at the house. The woman in black had turned out to be a man and got away.

In the rear of one of the apartment buildings that touched the alley—just a foot or so within the back door—they found a woman's skirt, long coat, hat and veil—all black. Investigating the occupants of the house, they had learned that an apartment had been rented to a young man named Leighton three days before.

Leighton was not home, when they went up to his apartment. His rooms held a lot of cold cigarette butts, an empty bottle, and nothing else that had not been there when he rented it.

The inference was clear; he had rented the apartment so that he might have access to the building. Wearing women's clothes over his own, he had gone out of the back door—leaving it unlatched behind him—to meet Gatewood. Then he had run back into the building, discarded his disguise and hurried through the building, out the front door, and away before we had our feeble net around the block—perhaps dodging into dark doorways here and there to avoid O'Gar and Thode in their cars.

Leighton, it seemed, was a man of about thirty, slender, about five feet eight or nine inches tall, with dark hair and eyes; rather good-looking, and well-dressed on the two occasions when people living in the building had seen him, in a brown suit and a light brown felt hat.

There was no possibility, according to both of the detectives and the post office inspector, that the girl might have been held, even temporarily, in Leighton's apartment.

Ten o'clock came, and no word from the girl.

Gatewood had lost his domineering bullheadedness by now and was breaking up. The suspense was getting him, and the liquor he had put away wasn't helping him. I didn't like him either personally or by reputation, but this morning I felt sorry for him.

I talked to the Agency over the phone and got the

reports of the operatives who had been looking up Audrey's friends. The last person to see her had been an Agnes Dangerfield, who had seen her walking down Market Street near Sixth, alone, on the night of her abduction—some time between 8:15 and 8:45. Audrey had been too far away from the Dangerfield girl to speak to her.

For the rest, the boys had learned nothing except that Audrey was a wild, spoiled youngster who hadn't shown any great care in selecting her friends—just the sort of girl who could easily fall into the hands of a mob of highbinders.

Noon struck. No sign of the girl. We told the newspapers to turn loose the story, with the added developments of the past few hours.

Gatewood was broken; he sat with his head in his hands, looking at nothing. Just before I left to follow a hunch I had, he looked up at me, and I'd never have recognized him if I hadn't seen the change take place.

"What do you think is keeping her away?" he asked.

I didn't have the heart to tell him what I had every reason to suspect, now that the money had been paid and she had failed to show up. So I stalled with some vague assurances and left.

I caught a cab and dropped off in the shopping district. I visited the five largest department stores, going to all the women's wear departments from shoes to hats, and trying to learn if a man—perhaps one answering Leighton's description—had been buying clothes in the past couple days that would fit Audrey Gatewood.

Failing to get any results, I turned the rest of the local stores over to one of the boys from the Agency, and went across the bay to canvass the Oakland stores.

At the first one I got action. A man who might easily have been Leighton had been in the day before, buying clothes of Audrey's size. He had bought lots of them, everything from lingerie to a coat, and—my luck was hitting on all cylinders—had had his purchases delivered to T. Offord, at an address on Fourteenth Street.

At the Fourteenth Street address, an apartment house, I found Mr. and Mrs. Theodore Offord's names in the vestibule for Apartment 202.

I had just found the apartment number when the front door opened and a stout, middle-aged woman in a gingham housedress came out. She looked at me a bit curiously, so I asked, "Do you know where I can find the superintendent?"

"I'm the superintendent," she said.

I handed her a card and stepped indoors with her. "I'm from the bonding department of the North American Casualty Company"—a repetition of the lie that was printed on the card I had given her—"and a bond for Mr. Offord has been applied for. Is he all right so far as you know?" With the slightly apologetic air of one going through with a necessary but not too important formality.

"A bond? That's funny! He is going away tomorrow."

"Well, I can't say what the bond is for," I said lightly. "We investigators just get the names and addresses. It may be for his present employer, or perhaps the man he is going to work for has applied for it. Or some firms have us look up prospective employees before they hire them, just to be safe."

"Mr. Offord, so far as I know, is a very nice young man," she said, "but he has been here only a week."

"Not staying long, then?"

"No. They came here from Denver, intending to stay, but the low altitude doesn't agree with Mrs. Offord, so they are going back."

"Are you sure they came from Denver?"

"Well," she said, "they told me they did."

"How many of them are there?"

"Only the two of them; they're young people."

"Well, how do they impress you?" I asked, trying to get over the impression that I thought her a woman of shrewd judgment.

"They seem to be a very nice young couple. You'd hardly know they were in their apartment most of the time, they're so quiet. I'm sorry they can't stay."

"Do they go out much?"

"I really don't know. They have their keys, and unless I should happen to pass them going in or out I'd never see them."

"Then, as a matter of fact you couldn't say whether they stayed away all night some nights or not. Could you?"

She eyed me doubtfully—I was stepping way over my pretext now, but I didn't think it mattered—and shook her head. "No, I couldn't say."

"They have many visitors?"

"I don't know. Mr. Offord is not—"

She broke off as a man came in quietly from the street, brushed past me, and started to mount the steps to the second floor.

"Oh, dear!" she whispered. "I hope he didn't hear me talking about him. That's Mr. Offord."

A slender man in brown, with a light brown hat—Leighton, perhaps.

I hadn't seen anything of him except his back, nor he anything except mine. I watched him as he climbed the stairs. If he had heard the women mention his name he would use the turn at the head of the stairs to sneak a look at me.

He did.

I kept my face stolid, but I knew him.

He was "Penny" Quayle, a con man who had been active in the east four or five years before.

His face was as expressionless as mine. But he knew me.

A door on the second floor shut. I left the woman and started for the stairs.

"I think I'll go up and talk to him," I told her.

Coming silently to the door of Apartment 202, I listened. Not a sound. This was no time for hesitation. I pressed the bell-button.

As close together as the tapping of three keys under the fingers of an expert typist, but a thousand times more vicious, came three pistol shots. And waist-high in the door of Apartment 202 were three bullet holes.

The three bullets would have been in my fat carcass if I hadn't learned years ago to stand to one side of strange doors when making uninvited calls.

Inside the apartment sounded a man's voice, sharp, commanding. "Cut it, kid! For God's sake, not that!"

A woman's voice, shrill, spiteful, screaming blasphemies.

Two more bullets came through the door.

"Stop! No! No!" The man's voice had a note of fear in it now.

The woman's voice, cursing hotly. A scuffle. A shot that didn't hit the door.

I hurled my foot against the door, near the knob, and the lock broke away.

On the floor of the room, a man—Quayle—and a woman were tussling. He was bending over her, holding her wrists, trying to keep her down. A smoking pistol was in one of her hands. I got to it in a jump and tore it loose.

"That's enough!" I called to them when I was planted. "Get up and receive company."

Quayle released his antagonist's wrists, whereupon she struck at his eyes with curved, sharp-nailed fingers, tearing his cheek open. He scrambled away from her on hands and knees, and both of them got to their feet.

He sat down on a chair immediately, panting and wiping his bleeding cheek with a handkerchief.

She stood, hands on hips, in the center of the room, glaring at me. "I suppose," she spat, "you think you've raised hell!"

I laughed—I could afford to.

"If your father is in his right mind," I told her, "he'll do it with a razor strap when he gets you home again. A fine joke you picked out to play on him!"

"If *you'd* been tied to him as long as I have and had been bullied and held down as much, I guess *you'd* do most anything to get enough money so that you could go away and live your own life."

I didn't say anything to that. Remembering some of

the business methods Harvey Gatewood had used—particularly some of his war contracts that the Department of Justice was still investigating—I suppose the worst that could be said about Audrey was that she was her father's own daughter.

"How'd you rap to it?" Quayle asked me, politely.

"Several ways," I said. "First, one of Audrey's friends saw her on Market Street between 8:15 and 8:45 the night she disappeared, and your letter to Gatewood was postmarked 9 P.M. Pretty fast work. You should have waited a while before mailing it. I suppose she dropped it in the post office on her way over here?"

Quayle nodded.

"Then second," I went on, "there was that phone call of hers. She knew it took anywhere from ten to fifteen minutes to get her father on the wire at the office. If she had gotten to a phone while imprisoned, time would have been so valuable that she'd have told her story to the first person she got hold of—the switchboard operator, most likely. So that made it look as if, besides wanting to throw out that Twin Peaks line, she wanted to stir the old man out of his bullheadedness.

"When she failed to show up after the money was paid, I figured it was a sure bet that she had kidnaped herself. I knew that if she came back home after faking this thing, we'd find out before we'd talked to her very long—and I figured she knew that too and would stay away.

"The rest was easy—I got some good breaks. We knew a man was working with her after we found the woman's clothes you left behind, and I took a chance on there being no one else in it. Then I figured she'd need clothes—she couldn't have taken any from home without tipping her mitt—and there was an even chance that she hadn't laid in a stock beforehand. She's got too many girl friends of the sort that do a lot of shopping to make it safe for her to have risked showing herself in stores. Maybe, then, the man would buy what she needed. And it turned out that he did, and that he was too lazy to carry away his purchases, or perhaps there were too many of them, and so he had them sent out. That's the story."

Quayle nodded again.

"I was damned careless," he said, and then, jerking a contemptuous thumb toward the girl, "But what can you expect? She's had a skinful of hop ever since we started. Took all my time and attention keeping her from running wild and gumming the works. Just now was a sample—I told her you were coming up and she goes crazy and tries to add your corpse to the wreckage!"

The Gatewood reunion took place in the office of the captain of inspectors on the second floor of the Oakland City Hall, and it was a merry little party.

For over an hour it was a tossup whether Harvey Gatewood would die of apoplexy, strangle his daughter or send her off to the state reformatory until she was of age. But Audrey licked him. Besides being a chip off the old block, she was young enough to be careless of consequences, while her father, for all his bullheadedness, had had some caution hammered into him.

The card she beat him with was a threat of spilling everything she knew about him to the newspapers, and at least one of the San Francisco papers had been trying to get his scalp for years.

I don't know what she had on him, and I don't think he was any too sure himself; but with his war contracts still being investigated by the Department of Justice, he couldn't afford to take a chance. There was no doubt at all that she would have done as she threatened.

And so, together, they left for home, sweating hate for each other from every pore.

We took Quayle upstairs and put him in a cell, but he was too experienced to let that worry him. He knew that if the girl was to be spared, he himself couldn't very easily be convicted of anything.

I was glad it was over. It had been a tough caper.

DEAD YELLOW WOMEN

She was sitting straight and stiff in one of the Old Man's chairs when he called me into his office—a tall girl of perhaps twenty-four, broad-shouldered, deep-bosomed, in mannish gray clothes. That she was Oriental showed only in the black shine of her bobbed hair, in the pale yellow of her unpowdered skin, and in the fold of her upper lids at the outer eye-corners, half hidden by the dark rims of her spectacles. But there was no slant to her eyes, her nose was almost aquiline, and she had more chin than Mongolians usually have. She was modern Chinese-American from the flat heels of her tan shoes to the crown of her untrimmed felt hat.

I knew her before the Old Man introduced me. The San Francisco papers had been full of her affairs for a couple of days. They had printed photographs and diagrams, interviews, editorials, and more or less expert opinions from various sources. They had gone back to 1912 to remember the stubborn fight of the local Chinese—mostly from Fokien and Kwangtung, where democratic ideas and hatred of Manchus go together—to have her father kept out of the United States, to which he had scooted when the Manchu rule flopped. The papers had recalled the excitement in Chinatown when Shan Fang was allowed to land—insulting placards had been hung in the streets, an unpleasant reception had been planned.

But Shan Fang had fooled the Cantonese. Chinatown

had never seen him. He had taken his daughter and his gold—presumably the accumulated profits of a lifetime of provincial misrule—down to San Mateo County, where he had built what the papers described as a palace on the edge of the Pacific. There he had lived and died in a manner suitable to a Ta Jen and a millionaire.

So much for the father. For the daughter—this young woman who was coolly studying me as I sat down across the table from her—she had been ten-year-old Ai Ho, a very Chinese little girl, when her father had brought her to California. All that was Oriental of her now were the features I have mentioned and the money her father had left her. Her name, translated into English, had become Water Lily, and then, by another step, Lillian. It was as Lillian Shan that she had attended an eastern university, acquired several degrees, won a tennis championship of some sort in 1919, and published a book on the nature and significance of fetishes, whatever all that is or are.

Since her father's death, in 1921, she had lived with her four Chinese servants in the house on the shore, where she had written her first book and was now at work on another. A couple of weeks ago, she had found herself stumped, so she said—had run into a blind alley. There was, she said, a certain old cabalistic manuscript in the Arsenal Library in Paris that she believed would solve her troubles for her. So she had packed some clothes and, accompanied by her maid, a Chinese woman named Wang Ma, had taken a train for New York, leaving the three other servants to take care of the house during her absence. The decision to go to France for a look at the manuscript had been formed one morning—she was on the train before dark.

On the train between Chicago and New York, the key to the problem that had puzzled her suddenly popped into her head. Without pausing even for a night's rest in New York, she had turned around and headed back for San Francisco. At the ferry here she had tried to telephone her chauffeur to bring a car for her. No answer. A taxicab had carried her and her maid to her house. She rang the doorbell to no effect.

When her key was in the lock the door had been suddenly opened by a young Chinese man—a stranger to her. He had refused her admittance until she told him who she was. He mumbled an unintelligible explanation as she and the maid went into the hall. Both of them were neatly bundled up in some curtains.

Two hours later Lillian Shan got herself loose—in a linen closet on the second floor. Switching on the light, she started to untie the maid. She stopped. Wang Ma was dead. The rope around her neck had been drawn too tight.

Lillian Shan went out into the empty house and telephoned the sheriff's office in Redwood City.

Two deputy sheriffs had come to the house, had listened to her story, had poked around, and had found another Chinese body—another strangled woman—buried in the cellar. Apparently she had been dead a week or a week and a half; the dampness of the ground made more positive dating impossible. Lillian Shan identified her as another of her servants—Wan Lan, the cook.

The other servants—Hoo Lun and Yin Hung—had vanished. Of the several hundred thousand dollars' worth of furnishings old Shan Fang had put into the house during his life, not a nickel's worth had been removed. There were no signs of a struggle. Everything was in order. The closest neighboring house was nearly half a mile away. The neighbors had seen nothing, knew nothing.

That's the story the newspapers had hung headlines over, and that's the story this girl, sitting very erect in her chair, speaking with businesslike briskness, shaping each word as exactly as if it were printed in black type, told the Old Man and me.

"I am not at all satisfied with the effort the San Mateo County authorities have made to apprehend the murderer or murderers," she wound up. "I wish to engage your agency."

The Old Man tapped the table with the point of his inevitable long yellow pencil and nodded to me.

"Have you any idea of your own on the murders, Miss Shan?" I asked.

"I have not."

"What do you know about the servants—the missing ones as well as the dead?"

"I really know little or nothing about them." She didn't seem very interested. "Wang Ma was the most recent of them to come to the house, and she has been with me for nearly seven years. My father employed them, and I suppose he knew something about them."

"Don't you know where they came from? Whether they have relatives? Whether they have friends? What they did when they weren't working?"

"No," she said. "I did not pry into their lives."

"The two who disappeared—what do they look like?"

"Hoo Lun is an old man, quite white-haired and thin and stooped. He did the housework. Yin Hung, who was my chauffeur and gardener, is younger, about thirty years old, I think. He is quite short, even for a Cantonese, but sturdy. His nose has been broken at some time and not set properly. It is very flat, with a pronounced bend in the bridge."

"Do you think this pair, or either of them, could have killed the women?"

"I do not think they did."

"The younger Chinese—the stranger who let you in the house—what did he look like?"

"He was quite slender, and not more than twenty or twenty-one years old, with large gold fillings in his front teeth. I think he was quite dark."

"Will you tell me exactly why you are dissatisfied with what the sheriff is doing, Miss Shan?"

"In the first place, I am not sure they are competent. The ones I saw certainly did not impress me with their brilliance."

"And in the second place?"

"Really," she asked coldly, "is it necessary to go into all my mental processes?"

"It is."

She looked at the Old Man, who smiled at her with his polite, meaningless smile—a mask through which you can read nothing.

For a moment she hung fire. Then, "I don't think they are looking in very likely places. They seem to spend the greater part of their time in the vicinity of the house. It is absurd to think the murderers are going to return."

I turned that over in my mind.

"Miss Shan," I asked, "don't you think they suspect you?"

Her dark eyes burned through her glasses at me and, if possible, she made herself more rigidly straight in her chair.

"Preposterous!"

"That isn't the point," I insisted. "Do they?"

"I am not able to penetrate the police mind," she came back. "Do *you?*"

"I don't know anything about this job but what I've read and what you've just told me. I need more foundation than that to suspect anybody. But I can understand why the sheriff's office would be a little doubtful. You left in a hurry. They've got your word for why you went and why you came back, and your word is all. The woman found in the cellar could have been killed just before you left as well as just after. Wang Ma, who could have told things, is dead. The other servants are missing. Nothing was stolen. That's plenty to make the sheriff think about you!"

"Do you suspect me?" she asked again.

"No," I said truthfully. "But that proves nothing."

She spoke to the Old Man, with a chin-tilting motion, as if she were talking over my head.

"Do you wish to undertake this work for me?"

"We shall be very glad to do what we can," he said, and then to me, after they had talked terms and while she was writing a check, "You handle it. Use what men you need."

"I want to go out to the house first and look the place over," I said.

Lillian Shan was putting away her checkbook.

"Very well. I am returning home now. I will drive you down."

It was a restful ride. Neither the girl nor I wasted energy on conversation. My client and I didn't seem to like each other very much. She drove well.

The Shan house was a big brownstone affair, set among sodded lawns. The place was hedged shoulder-high on three sides. The fourth boundary was the ocean, where it came in to make a notch in the shoreline between two rocky points.

The house was full of hangings, rugs, pictures, and so on—a mixture of things American, European and Asiatic. I didn't spend much time inside. After a look at the linen closet, at the still-open cellar grave, and at the pale, thick-featured Danish woman who was taking care of the house until Lillian Shan could get a new corps of servants, I went outdoors again. I poked around the lawns for a few minutes, stuck my head in the garage, where two cars, besides the one in which we had come from town, stood, and then went off to waste the rest of the afternoon talking to the girl's neighbors. None of them knew anything. Since we were on opposite sides of the game, I didn't hunt up the sheriff's men.

By twilight I was back in the city, going into the apartment building in which I lived during my first year in San Francisco. I found the lad I wanted in his cubbyhole room, getting his small body into a cerise silk shirt that was something to look at. Cipriano was the bright-faced Filipino boy who looked after the building's front door in the daytime. At night, like all the Filipinos in San Francisco, he could be found down on Kearny Street, just below Chinatown, except when he was in a Chinese gambling-house passing his money over to the yellow brothers.

I had once, half joking, promised to give the lad a fling at gumshoeing if the opportunity ever came. I thought I could use him now.

"Come in, sir!"

He was dragging a chair out of a corner for me, bowing and smiling. Whatever else the Spaniards do for the people they rule, they make them polite.

"What's doing in Chinatown these days?" I asked as he went on with his dressing.

He gave me a white-toothed smile. "I take eleven bucks out of bean game last night."

"And you're getting ready to take it back tonight?"

"Not all of 'em, sir! Five bucks I spend for this shirt."

"That's the stuff." I applauded his wisdom in investing part of his fan tan profits. "What else is doing down there?"

"Nothing unusual, sir. You want to find something?"

"Yeah. Hear any talk about the killings down the country last week? The two Chinese women?"

"No, sir. Chinaboy don't talk much about things like that. Not like us Americans. I read about those things in newspapers, but I have not heard."

"Many strangers in Chinatown nowadays?"

"All the time there's strangers, sir. But I guess maybe some new Chinaboys are there. Maybe not, though."

"How would you like to do a little work for me?"

"Yes, sir! Yes, sir! Yes, sir!" He said it oftener than that, but that will give you the idea. While he was saying it he was down on his knees, dragging a valise from under the bed. Out of the valise he took a pair of brass knuckles and a shiny revolver.

"Here! I want some information. I don't want you to knock anybody off for me."

"I don't knock 'em," he assured me, stuffing his weapons in his hip pockets. "Just carry these—maybe I need 'em."

"Here's what I want. Two of the servants ducked out of the house down there." I described Yin Hung and Hoo Lun. "I want to find them. I want to find what anybody in Chinatown knows about the killings. I want to find who the dead women's friends and relatives are, where they came from, and the same thing for the two men. I want to know about those strange Chinese—where they hang out, where they sleep, what they're up to.

"Now, don't try to get all this in a night. You'll be doing fine if you get any of it in a week. Here's twenty dollars. Five of it is your night's pay. You can use the other to carry you around. Don't be foolish and poke your nose into a lot of grief. Take it easy and see what you can turn up for me. I'll drop in tomorrow."

From the Filipino's room I went to the office. Everybody except Fiske, the night man, was gone, but Fiske thought the Old Man would drop in for a few minutes later in the night.

I smoked, pretended to listen to Fiske's report on all the jokes that were at the Orpheum that week, and grouched over my job. I was too well known to get anything on the quiet in Chinatown. I wasn't sure Cipriano was going to be much help. I needed somebody who was in right down there.

This line of thinking brought me around to Dummy Uhl. Uhl was a dummerer who had lost his store. Five years before, he had been sitting on the world. Any day on which his sad face, his package of pins, and his *I am deaf and dumb* sign didn't take twenty dollars out of the office buildings along his route was a rotten day. His big card was his ability to play the statue when skeptical people yelled or made sudden noises behind him. When the Dummy was right, a gun going off beside his ear wouldn't make him twitch an eyelid. But too much heroin broke his nerves until a whisper was enough to make him jump. He put away his pins and his sign—another man whose social life had ruined him.

Since then Dummy had become an errand boy for

whoever would stake him to the price of his necessary nose-candy. He slept somewhere in Chinatown, and he didn't care especially how he played the game. I had used him to get me some information on a window-smashing six months before. I decided to try him again.

I called Loop Pigatti's place—a dive down on Pacific Street, where Chinatown fringes into the Latin Quarter. Loop is a tough citizen, who runs a tough hole, and who minds his own business, which is making his dive show a profit. Everybody looks alike to Loop. Whether you're a yegg, stool-pigeon, detective, or settlement worker, you get an even break out of Loop and nothing else. But you can be sure that, unless it's something that might hurt his business, anything you tell Loop will get no further. And anything he tells you is more than likely to be right.

He answered the phone himself.

"Can you get hold of Dummy Uhl for me?" I asked after I had told him who I was.

"Maybe."

"Thanks. I'd like to see him tonight."

"You got nothin' on him?"

"No, Loop, and I don't expect to. I want him to get something for me."

"All right. Where d'you want him?"

"Send him up to my joint. I'll wait there for him."

"If ho'll come," Loop promised and hung up.

I left word with Fiske to have the Old Man call me up when he came in, and then I went up to my rooms to wait for my informant.

He came in a little after ten—a short, stocky, pasty-faced man of forty or so, with mouse-colored hair streaked with yellow-white.

"Loop says y'got sumpin' f'r me."

"Yes," I said, waving him to a chair, and closing the door. "I'm buying news."

He fumbled with his hat, started to spit on the floor, changed his mind, licked his lips, and looked up at me.

"What kind o' news? I don't know nothin'."

I was puzzled. The Dummy's yellowish eyes should have showed the pinpoint pupils of the heroin addict. They didn't. The pupils were normal. That didn't mean he was off the stuff—he had put belladonna into them to distend them to normal. The puzzle was—why? He wasn't usually particular enough about his appearance to go to that trouble.

"Did you hear about the Chinese killings down the shore last week?" I asked him.

"No."

"Well," I said, paying no attention to the denial, "I'm hunting for the pair of yellow men who ducked out—Hoo Lun and Yin Hung. Know anything about them?"

"No."

"It's worth a couple of hundred dollars to you to find either of them for me. It's worth another couple hundred to find out about the killings for me. It's worth another to find the slim Chinese youngster with gold teeth who opened the door for the Shan girl and her maid."

"I don't know nothin' about them things," he said.

But he said it automatically while his mind was busy counting up the hundreds I had dangled before him. I suppose his dope-addled brains made the total somewhere in the thousands. He jumped up.

"I'll see what I c'n do. S'pose you slip me a hundred now, on account."

I didn't see that. "You get it when you deliver."

We had to argue that point, but finally he went grumbling and growling to get me my news.

I went back to the office. The Old Man hadn't come in yet. It was nearly midnight when he arrived.

"I'm using Dummy Uhl again," I told him, "and I've put a Filipino boy down there too. I've got another scheme, but I don't know anybody to handle it. I think if we offered the missing chauffeur and houseman jobs in some out-of-the-way place up the country, perhaps they'd fall for it. Do you know anybody who could pull it for us?"

"Exactly what have you in mind?"

"It must be somebody who has a house out in the country, the farther the better, the more secluded the better. They would phone one of the Chinese employment offices that they needed three servants—cook, houseman, and chauffeur. We throw in the cook for good measure, to cover the game. It's got to be air-tight on the other end, and, if we're going to catch our fish, we have to give 'em time to investigate. So whoever does it must have some servants, and must put up a bluff—I mean in his own neighborhood—that they are leaving, and the servants must be in on it. And we've got to wait a couple of days so our friends here will have time to investigate. I think we'd better use Fong Yick's employment agency, on Washington Street.

"Whoever does it could phone Fong Yick tomorrow morning, and say he'd be in Thursday morning to look the applicants over. This is Monday—that'll be long enough. Our helper gets to the employment office at ten Thursday morning. Miss Shan and I arrive in a taxicab ten minutes later, when he'll be in the middle of questioning the applicants. I'll slide out of the taxi into Fong Yick's, grab anybody that looks like one of our missing servants. Miss Shan will come in a minute or two behind me and check me up—so there won't be any false-arrest mixups."

The Old Man nodded approval.

"Very well," he said. "I think I can arrange it. I will let you know tomorrow."

I went home to bed. Thus ended the first day.

At nine the next morning, Tuesday, I was talking to Cipriano in the lobby of the apartment building that employs him. His eyes were black drops of ink in white saucers. He thought he had got something.

"Yes, sir! Strange Chinaboys are in town, some of them. They sleep in a house on Waverly Place—on the western side, four houses from the house of Jair Quon, where I sometimes play dice. And there is more—I talk to

a white man who knows they are hatchetmen from Portland and Eureka and Sacramento. They are Hip Sing
men—a tong war starts—pretty soon, maybe."

"Do these birds look like gunmen to you?"

Cipriano scratched his head.

"No, sir, maybe not. But a fellow can shoot sometimes
if he don't look like it. This man tells me they are Hip Sing
men."

"Who was this white man?"

"I don't know the name, but he lives there. A short
man—snowbird."

"Gray hair, yellowish eyes?"

"Yes, sir."

That, as likely as not, would be Dummy Uhl. One of
my men was stringing the other. The tong stuff hadn't
sounded right to me anyhow. Once in a while they mix
things, but usually they are blamed for somebody else's
crimes. Most wholesale killings in Chinatown are the result
of family or clan feuds—such as the ones the "Four
Brothers" used to stage.

"This house where you think the strangers are living—
know anything about it?"

"No, sir. But maybe you could go through there to the
house of Chang Li Ching on the other street—Spofford
Alley."

"So? And who is this Chang Li Ching?"

"I don't know, sir. But he is there. Nobody sees him,
but all Chinaboys say he is great man."

"So? And his house is in Spofford Alley?"

"Yes, sir, a house with red door and red steps. You find
it easy, but better not fool with Chang Li Ching."

I didn't know whether that was advice or just a general
remark.

"A big gun, huh?" I probed.

But my Filipino didn't really know anything about this
Chang Li Ching. He was basing his opinion of the
Chinese's greatness on the attitude of his fellow country-
men when they mentioned him.

"Learn anything about the two Chinese men?" I asked after I had fixed this point.

"No, sir, but I will—you bet!"

I praised him for what he had done, told him to try it again that night, and went back to my rooms to wait for Dummy Uhl, who had promised to come there at ten-thirty. It was not quite ten when I got there, so I used some of my spare time to call up the office. The Old Man said Dick Foley—our shadow ace—was idle, so I borrowed him. Then I fixed my gun and sat down to wait for my stool-pigeon.

He rang the bell at eleven o'clock. He came in frowning tremendously.

"I don't know what t' hell to make of it, kid," he spoke importantly over the cigarette he was rolling: "There's sumpin' makin' down there, an' that's a fact. Things ain't been anyways quiet since the Japs began buyin' stores in the Chink streets, an' maybe that's got sumpin' to do with it. But there ain't no strange Chinks in town—not a damn one! I got a hunch your men have gone down to L. A., but I expec' t' know f'r certain tonight. I got a Chink ribbed up t' get the dope; 'f I was you, I'd put a watch on the boats at San Pedro. Maybe those fellas'll swap papers wit' a couple Chink sailors that'd like t' stay here."

"And there are no strangers in town?"

"Not any."

"Dummy," I said bitterly, "you're a liar, and you're a boob, and I've been playing you for a sucker. You were in on that killing, and so were your friends, and I'm going to throw you in the can, and your friends on top of you!"

I put my gun in sight, close to his scared gray face.

"Keep yourself still while I do my phoning!"

Reaching for the telephone with my free hand, I kept one eye on the Dummy.

It wasn't enough. My gun was too close to him.

He yanked it out of my hand. I jumped for him.

The gun turned in his fingers. I grabbed it—too late. It

went off, its muzzle less than a foot from where I'm thickest. Fire stung my body.

Clutching the gun with both hands, I folded down to the floor. Dummy went away from there, leaving the door open behind him.

One hand on my burning belly, I crossed to the window and waved an arm at Dick Foley, stalling on a corner down the street. Then I went to the bathroom and looked to my wound. A blank cartridge does hurt if you catch it close up!

My vest and shirt and union suit were ruined, and I had a nasty scorch on my body. I greased it, taped a cushion over it, changed my clothes, loaded the gun again, and went down to the office to wait for word from Dick. The first trick in the game looked like mine. Heroin or no heroin, Dummy Uhl would not have jumped me if my guess—based on the trouble he was taking to make his eyes look right and the lie he had sprung on me about there being no strangers in Chinatown—hadn't hit close to the mark.

Dick wasn't long in joining me.

"Good pickings!" he said when he came in. The little Canadian talks like a thrifty man's telegram. "Beat it for phone. Called Hotel Irvington. Booth—couldn't get anything but number. Ought to be enough. Then Chinatown. Dived in cellar west side Waverly Place. Couldn't stick close enough to spot place. Afraid to take chance hanging around. How do you like it?"

"I like it all right. Let's look up The Whistler's record."

A file clerk got it for us—a bulky envelope the size of a briefcase, crammed with memoranda, clippings and letters. The gentleman's biography, as we had it, ran like this:

Neil Conyers, alias The Whistler, was born in Philadelphia—out on Whiskey Hill—in 1883. In '94, at the age of eleven, he was picked up by the Washington police. He had gone there to join Coxey's Army. They sent him home. In '98 he was arrested in his home town for stabbing another lad in a row over an election-night bonfire. This time he was released in his parents' custody. In 1901 the Philadelphia police grabbed him again, charging him with being the head of the first organized automobile-stealing ring. He was released without trial for lack of evidence. But the district attorney lost his job in the resultant scandal. In 1908 Conyers appeared on the Pacific Coast—at Seattle, Portland, San Francisco, and Los Angeles—in company with a con man known as "Duster" Hughes. Hughes was shot and killed the following year by a man whom he'd swindled in a fake airplane-manufacturing deal. Conyers was arrested on the same deal. Two juries disagreed and he was turned loose. In 1910 the Post Office Department's famous raid on get-rich-quick promoters caught him. Again there wasn't enough evidence against him to put him away. In 1915 the law scored on him for the first time. He went to San Quentin for buncoing some visitors to the Panama-Pacific International Exposition. He stayed there for three years. In 1919 he and a Jap named Hasegawa nicked the Japanese colony of Seattle for $20,000, Conyers posing as an American who had held a commission in the Japanese army during the late war. He had a counterfeit medal of the Order of the Rising Sun which the emperor was supposed to have pinned on him. When the game fell through, Hasegawa's family made good the $20,000—Conyers got out of it with a good profit and not even any disagreeable publicity. The thing had been hushed. He returned to San Francisco after that, bought the Hotel Irvington, and had been living there now for five years without anybody being able to add another word to his criminal record. He was up to something, but nobody could learn what. There wasn't a chance in the world of getting a detective into his hotel as a guest. Apparently the joint was always without vacant rooms. It was as exclusive as the Pacific-Union Club.

This, then, was the proprietor of the hotel Dummy Uhl had got on the phone before diving into his hole in Chinatown.

I had never seen Conyers. Neither had Dick. There were a couple of photographs in his envelope. One was the profile and full-face photograph of the local police, taken when he had been picked up on the charge that led him to San Quentin. The other was a group picture: all rung up in evening clothes, with the phony Japanese medal on his chest, he stood among half a dozen of the Seattle Japs he had trimmed—a flashlight picture taken while he was leading them to the slaughter.

These pictures showed him to be a big bird, fleshy, pompous-looking, with a heavy, square chin and shrewd eyes.

"Think you could pick him up?" I asked Dick.

"Sure."

"Suppose you go up there and see if you can get a room or apartment somewhere in the neighborhood—one you can watch the hotel from. Maybe you'll get a chance to tail him around now and then."

I put the pictures in my pocket, in case they'd come in handy, dumped the rest of the stuff back in its envelope, and went into the Old Man's office.

"I arranged that employment office stratagem," he said. "A Frank Paul, who has a ranch out beyond Martinez, will be in Fong Yick's establishment at ten Thursday morning, carrying out his part."

"That's fine! I'm going calling in Chinatown now. If you don't hear from me for a couple of days, will you ask the streetcleaners to watch what they're sweeping up?"

He said he would.

San Francisco's Chinatown jumps out of the shopping district at California Street and runs north to the Latin Quarter—a strip two blocks wide by six long. Before the fire nearly twenty-five thousand Chinese lived in those dozen blocks. I don't suppose the population is a third of that now.

Grant Avenue, the main street and spine of this strip, is for most of its length a street of gaudy shops and flashy chop-suey houses catering to the tourist trade, where the racket of American jazz orchestras drowns the occasional squeak of a Chinese flute. Farther out, there isn't so much paint and gilt, and you can catch the proper Chinese smell of spices and vinegar and dried things. If you leave the main thoroughfares and showplaces and start poking around in alleys and dark corners, and nothing happens to you, the chances are you'll find some interesting things—though you won't like some of them.

However, I wasn't poking around as I turned off Grant Avenue at Clay Street, and went up to Spofford Alley, hunting for the house with red steps and red door, which Cipriano had said was Chang Li Ching's. I did pause for a few seconds to look up Waverly Place when I passed it. The Filipino had told me the strange Chinese were living there, and that he thought their house might lead through to Chang Li Ching's; and Dick Foley had shadowed Dummy Uhl there.

But I couldn't guess which was the important house. Four doors from Jair Quon's gambling house, Cipriano had said, but I didn't know where Jair Quon's was. Waverly Place was a picture of peace and quiet just now. A fat Chinese was stacking crates of green vegetables in front of a grocery. Half a dozen small yellow boys were playing at marbles in the middle of the street. On the other side, a blond young man in tweeds was climbing the six steps from a cellar to the street, a painted Chinese woman's face showing for an instant before she closed the door behind him. Up the street a truck was unloading rolls of paper in front of one of the Chinese newspaper plants. A shabby guide was bringing four sightseers out of the Temple of the Queen of Heaven—a joss house over the Sue Hing headquarters.

I went on up to Spofford Alley and found my house with no difficulty at all. It was a shabby building with steps and door the color of dried blood, its windows solidly shuttered with thick, tight-nailed planking. What made it stand out from its neighbors was that its ground floor wasn't a shop or place of business. Purely residential buildings are rare in Chinatown: almost always the street floor is given to business, with the living quarters in cellar or upper stories.

I went up the three steps and tapped the red door with my knuckles.

Nothing happened.

I hit it again, harder. Still nothing. I tried it again, and this time was rewarded by the sounds of scraping and clicking inside.

At least two minutes of this scraping and clicking, and the door swung open—a bare four inches.

One slanting eye and a slice of wrinkled brown face looked out of the crack at me, above the heavy chain that held the door.

"Whata wan'?"

"I want to see Chang Li Ching."

"No savvy. Maybe closs stleet."

"Bunk! You fix your little door and run back and tell Chang Li Ching I want to see him."

"No can do! No savvy Chang."

"You tell him I'm here," I said, turning my back on the door. I sat down on the top step, and added, without looking around, "I'll wait."

While I got my cigarettes out there was silence behind me. Then the door closed softly and the scraping and clicking broke out behind it. I smoked a cigarette and another and let time go by, trying to look like I had all the patience there was. I hoped this yellow man wasn't going to make a chump of me by letting me sit there until I got tired of it.

Chinese passed up and down the alley, scuffling along in American shoes that can never be made to fit them. Some of them looked curiously at me, some gave me no attention at all. An hour went to waste, and a few minutes, and then the familiar scraping and clicking disturbed the door.

The chain rattled as the door swung open. I wouldn't turn my head.

"Go 'way! No catch 'em Chang!"

I said nothing. If he wasn't going to let me in he would have let me sit there without further attention.

A pause.

"Whata wan'?"

"I want to see Chang Li Ching," I said without looking around.

Another pause, ended by the banging of the chain against the doorframe.

"All light."

I chucked my cigarette into the street, got up and stepped into the house. In the dimness I could make out a few pieces of cheap and battered furniture. I had to wait while the Chinese put four arm-thick bars across the door and padlocked them there. Then he nodded at me and scuffled across the floor, a small, bent man with hairless yellow head and a neck like a piece of rope.

Out of this room, he led me into another, darker still, into a hallway, and down a flight of rickety steps. The odors of musty clothing and damp earth were strong. We walked through the dark across a dirt floor for a while, turned to the left, and cement was under my feet. We turned twice more in the dark, and then climbed a flight of unplaned wooden steps into a hall that was fairly light with the glow from shaded electric lights.

In this hall my guide unlocked a door, and we crossed a room where cones of incense burned, and where, in the light of an oil lamp, little red tables with cups of tea stood in front of wooden panels, marked with Chinese characters in gold paint, which hung on the walls. A door on the opposite side of this room let us into pitch blackness, where I had to hold the tail of my guide's loose made-to-order blue coat.

So far he hadn't once looked back at me since our tour began, and neither of us had said anything. This running upstairs and downstairs, turning to the right and turning to the left, seemed harmless enough. If he got any fun out of confusing me, he was welcome. I was confused enough now, so far as the directions were concerned. I hadn't the least idea where I might be. But that didn't disturb me so much. If I was going to be cut down, a knowledge of my geographical position wouldn't make it any more pleasant. If I was going to come out all right, one place was still as good as another.

We did a lot more of the winding around, we did some stair climbing and some stair descending, and the rest of the foolishness. I figured I'd been indoors nearly half an hour by now, and I had seen nobody but my guide.

Then I saw something else.

We were going down a long, narrow hall that had brown-painted doors close together on either side. All these doors were closed—secretive-looking in the dim light. Abreast of one of them, a glint of dull metal caught my eye—a dark ring in the door's center.

I went to the floor.

Going down as if I'd been knocked, I missed the flash. But I heard the roar, smelled the powder.

My guide spun around, twisting out of one slipper. In each of his hands was an automatic as big as a coal scuttle. Even while trying to get my own gun out I wondered how so puny a man could have concealed so much machinery on him.

The big guns in the little man's hands flamed at me. Chinese-fashion, he was emptying them—crash! crash! crash!

I thought he was missing me until I had my finger tight on my trigger. Then I woke up in time to hold my fire.

He wasn't shooting at me. He was pouring metal into the door behind me—the door from which I had been shot at.

I rolled away from it, across the hall.

The scrawny little man stepped closer and finished his bombardment. His slugs shredded the wood as if it had been paper. His guns clicked empty.

The door swung open, pushed by the wreck of a man who was trying to hold himself up by clinging to the sliding panel in the door's center.

Dummy Uhl—all the middle of him gone—slid down to the floor and made more of a puddle than a pile there.

The hall filled with yellow men, black guns sticking out like briars in a blackberry patch.

I got up. My guide dropped his guns to his side and sang out a guttural solo. Chinese began to disappear through various doors, except four who began gathering up what twenty bullets had left of Dummy Uhl.

The stringy old boy tucked his empty guns away and came down the hall to me, one hand held out toward my gun.

"You give 'em," he said politely.

I gave 'em. He could have had my pants.

My gun stowed away in his shirtbosom, he looked casually at what the four Chinese were carrying away, and then at me.

"No like 'em fella, huh?" he asked.

"Not so much," I admitted.

"All light. I take you."

Our two-man parade got under way again. The ring-around-the-rosy game went on for another flight of stairs and some right and left turns, and then my guide stopped before a door and scratched it with his fingernails.

The door was opened by another Chinese. But this one was none of your Cantonese runts. He was a big meateating wrestler—bull-throated, mountain-shouldered, gorilla-armed, leather-skinned. The god that made him had plenty of material, and gave it time to harden.

Holding back the curtain that covered the door, he stepped to one side. I went in, and found his twin standing on the other side of the door.

The room was large and cubical, its doors and windows—if any—hidden behind velvet hangings of green and blue and silver. In a big black chair, elaborately carved, behind an inlaid black table, sat an old Chinese man. His face was round and plump and shrewd, with a straggle of thin white whiskers on his chin. A dark, close-fitting cap was on his head; a purple robe, tight around his neck, showed its sable lining at the bottom, where it had fallen back in a fold over his blue satin trousers.

He did not get up from his chair, but smiled mildly over his whiskers and bent his head almost to the tea things on the table.

"It was only the inability to believe that one of your excellency's heaven-born splendor would waste his costly time on so mean a clod that kept the least of your slaves from running down to prostrate himself at your noble feet as soon as he heard the Father of Detectives was at his unworthy door."

That came out smoothly in English that was a lot clearer than my own. I kept my face straight, waiting.

"If the Terror of Evildoers will honor one of my deplorable chairs by resting his divine body on it, I can assure him the chair shall be burned afterward, so no lesser being may use it. Or will the Prince of Thief-catchers permit me to send a servant to his palace for a chair worthy of him?"

I went slowly to a chair, trying to arrange words in my mind. This old joker was spoofing me with an exaggeration—a burlesque—of the well-known Chinese politeness. I'm not hard to get along with; I'll play anybody's game up to a certain point.

"It's only because I'm weak-kneed with awe of the mighty Chang Li Ching that I dare to sit down," I explained, letting myself down on the chair, and turning my head to notice that the giants who had stood beside the door were gone.

I had a hunch they had gone no farther than the other side of the velvet hangings that hid the door.

"If it were not that the King of Finders-out"—he was at it again—"knows everything, I should marvel that he had heard my lowly name."

"Heard it? Who hasn't?" I kidded back. "Isn't the word *change*, in English, derived from Chang? Change, meaning alter, is what happens to the wisest man's opinions after he has heard the wisdom of Chang Li Ching!" I tried to get away from this vaudeville stuff, which was a strain on my head. "Thanks for having your man save my life back there in the passage."

He spread his hands out over the table.

"It was only because I feared the Emperor of Hawkshaws would find the odor of such low blood distasteful to his elegant nostrils that the foul one who disturbed your excellency was struck down quickly. If I have erred, and you would have chosen that he be cut to pieces inch by inch, I can only offer to torture one of my sons in his place."

"Let the boy live," I said carelessly, and turned to business. "I wouldn't have bothered you except that I am so ignorant that only the help of your great wisdom could ever bring me up to normal."

"Does one ask the way of a blind man?" the old duffer asked, cocking his head to one side. "Can a star, however willing, help the moon? If it pleases the Grandfather of Bloodhounds to flatter Chang Li Ching into thinking he can add to the great one's knowledge, who is Chang to thwart his master by refusing to make himself ridiculous?"

I took that to mean he was willing to listen to my questions.

"What I'd like to know is who killed Lillian Shan's servants, Wang Ma and Wan Lan?"

He played with a thin strand of his white beard, twisting it with a pale, small finger.

"Does the stag-hunter look at the hare?" he wanted to know. "And when so mighty a hunter pretends to concern himself with the death of servants, can Chang think anything except that it pleases the great one to conceal his real object? Yet it may be, because the dead were servants and not girdle-wearers, that the Lord of Snares thought the lowly Chang Li Ching, insignificant one of the Hundred Names, might have knowledge of them. Do not rats know the way of rats?"

He kept this stuff up for some minutes, while I sat and listened and studied his round, shrewd yellow mask of a face, and hoped that something clear would come of it all. Nothing did.

"My ignorance is even greater than I had arrogantly supposed," he brought his speech to an end. "This simple question you put is beyond the power of my muddled mind. I do not know who killed Wang Ma and Wan Lan."

I grinned at him, and put another question, "Where can I find Hoo Lun and Yin Hung?"

"Again I must grovel in my ignorance," he murmured, "only consoling myself with the thought that the Master of Mysteries knows the answers to his questions, and is pleased to conceal his infallibly accomplished purpose from Chang."

And that was as far as I got.

There were more crazy compliments, more bowing and scraping, more assurances of eternal reverence and love, and then I was following my rope-necked guide through winding, dark halls, across dim rooms, and up and down rickety stairs again.

At the street door—after he had taken down the bars—he slid my gun out of his shirt and handed it to me. I squelched the impulse to look at it then and there to see if anything had been done to it. Instead I stuck it in my pocket and stepped through the door.

"Thanks for the killing upstairs," I said.

The Chinese grunted, bowed, and closed the door.

I went up to Stockton Street, and turned toward the office, walking along slowly, punishing my brains.

First, there was Dummy Uhl's death to think over. Had it been arranged beforehand: to punish him for bungling that morning and, at the same time, to impress me? And how? And why? Or was it supposed to put me under obligations to the Chinese? And, if so, why? Or was it just one of those complicated tricks the Chinese like? I put the subject away and pointed my thoughts at the little plump yellow man in the purple robe.

I liked him. He had humor, brains, nerve, everything. To jam him in a cell would be a trick you'd want to write home about. He was my idea of a man worth working against.

But I didn't kid myself into thinking I had anything on him. Dummy Uhl had given me a connection between The Whistler's Hotel Irvington and Chang Li Ching. Dummy Uhl had gone into action when I accused him of being mixed up in the Shan killings. That much I had—and that was all, except that Chang had said nothing to show he wasn't interested in the Shan troubles.

In this light, the chances were that Dummy's death had not been a planned performance. It was more likely that he had seen me coming, had tried to wipe me out, and had been knocked off by my guide because he was interfering with the audience Chang had granted me. Dummy couldn't have had a very valuable life in the Chinese's eye—or in anybody else's.

I wasn't at all dissatisfied with the day's work so far. I hadn't done anything brilliant, but I had got a look at my destination, or thought I had. If I was butting my head against a stone wall, I at least knew where the wall was and had seen the man who owned it.

In the office, a message from Dick Foley was waiting for me. He had rented a front apartment up the street from the Irvington and had put in a couple of hours trailing The Whistler.

The Whistler had spent half an hour in Big Fat Thomson's place on Market Street, talking to the proprietor and some of the sure-thing gamblers who congregate there. Then he had taxicabbed out to an apartment house on O'Farrell Street—the Glenway—where he had rung one of the bells. Getting no answer, he had let himself into the building with a key. An hour later he had come out and returned to his hotel. Dick hadn't been able to determine which bell he had rung, or which apartment he had visited.

I got Lillian Shan on the telephone.

"Will you be in this evening?" I asked. "I've something I want to go into with you, and I can't give it to you over the wire."

"I will be at home until seven-thirty."

"All right, I'll be down."

It was seven-fifteen when the car I had hired put me down at her front door. She opened the door for me. The Danish woman who was filling in until new servants were employed stayed there only in the daytime, returning to her own home—a mile back from the shore—at night.

The evening gown Lillian Shan wore was severe enough, but it suggested that if she would throw away her glasses and do something for herself, she might not be so unfeminine-looking after all. She took me upstairs to the library, where a clean-cut lad of twenty-something in evening clothes got up from a chair as we came in—a well-set-up boy with fair hair and skin.

His name, I learned when we were introduced, was Garthorne. The girl seemed willing enough to hold our conference in his presence. I wasn't. After I had done everything but insist pointblank on seeing her alone, she excused herself—calling him Jack—and took me out into another room.

By then I was a bit impatient.

"Who's that?" I demanded.

She put her eyebrows up for me.

"Mr. John Garthorne," she said.

"How well do you know him?"

"May I ask why you are so interested?"

"You may. Mr. John Garthorne is all wrong, I think."

"Wrong?"

I had another idea.

"Where does he live?"

She gave me an O'Farrell Street number.

"The Glenway Apartments?"

"I think so." She was looking at me without any affectation at all. "Will you please explain?"

"One more question and I will. Do you know a Chinese named Chang Li Ching?"

"No."

"All right. I'll tell you about Garthorne. So far I've run into two angles on this trouble of yours. One of them has to do with this Chang Li Ching in Chinatown, and one with an ex-convict named Conyers. This John Garthorne was in Chinatown today. I saw him coming out of a cellar that probably connects with Chang Li Ching's house. The ex-convict Conyers visited the building where Garthorne lives, early this afternoon."

Her mouth popped open and then shut.

"That is absurd!" she snapped. "I have known Mr. Garthorne for some time, and—"

"Exactly how long?"

"A long—several months."

"Where'd you meet him?"

"Through a girl I knew at college."

"What does he do for a living?"

She stood stiff and silent.

"Listen, Miss Shan," I said. "Garthorne may be all right, but I've got to look him up. If he's in the clear there'll be no harm done. I want to know what you know about him."

I got it, little by little. He was, or she thought he was, the youngest son of a prominent Richmond, Virginia, family, in disgrace just now because of some sort of boyish prank. He had come to San Francisco four months ago, to wait until his father's anger cooled. Meanwhile his mother kept him in money, leaving him without the necessity of toiling during his exile. He had brought a letter of introduction from one of Lillian Shan's schoolmates. Lillian Shan had, I gathered, a lot of liking for him.

"You're going out with him tonight?" I asked when I had got this.

"Yes."

"In his car or yours?"

She frowned, but she answered my question.

"In his. We are going to drive down to Half Moon for dinner."

"I'll need a key, then, because I am coming back here after you have gone."

"You're what?"

"I'm coming back here. I'll ask you not to say anything about my more or less unworthy suspicions to him, but my honest opinion is that he's drawing you away for the evening. So if the engine breaks down on the way back, just pretend you see nothing unusual in it."

That worried her, but she wouldn't admit I might be right. I got the key, though, and then I told her of my employment agency scheme that needed her assistance, and she promised to be at the office at half past nine Thursday morning.

I didn't see Garthorne again before I left the house.

In my hired car again, I had the driver take me to the nearest village, where I bought a plug of chewing tobacco, a flashlight, and a box of cartridges at the general store. My gun is a .38 Special, but I had to take the shorter, weaker cartridges, because the storekeeper didn't keep the specials in stock.

My purchases in my pocket, we started back toward the Shan house again. Two bends in the road this side of it, I stopped the car, paid the chauffeur, and sent him on his way, finishing the trip afoot.

The house was dark all around.

Letting myself in as quietly as possible, and going easy with the flashlight, I gave the interior a combing from cellar to roof. I was the only occupant. In the kitchen, I looted the icebox for a bite or two, which I washed down with milk. I could have used some coffee, but coffee is too fragrant.

The supper done, I made myself comfortable on a chair in the passageway between the kitchen and the rest of the house. On one side of the passageway, steps led down to the basement. On the other, steps led upstairs. With every door in the house except the outer ones open, the passageway was the center of things so far as hearing noises was concerned.

An hour went by—quietly except for the passing of cars on the road a hundred yards away and the washing of the Pacific down in the little cove. I chewed on my plug of tobacco—a substitute for cigarettes—and tried to count up the hours of my life I'd spent like this, sitting or standing around waiting for something to happen.

The telephone rang.

I let it ring. It might be Lillian Shan needing help, but I couldn't take a chance. It was too likely to be some egg trying to find out if anybody was in the house.

Another half-hour went by with a breeze springing up from the ocean, rustling trees outside.

A noise came that was neither wind nor surf nor passing car.

Something clicked somewhere.

It was at a window, but I didn't know which. I got rid of my chew, got gun and flashlight out.

It sounded again, harshly.

Somebody was giving a window a strong play—too strong. The catch rattled, and something clicked against the pane. It was a stall. Whoever he was, he could have smashed the glass with less noise than he was making.

I stood up, but I didn't leave the passageway. The window noise was a fake to draw the attention of anyone who might be in the house. I turned my back on it, trying to see into the kitchen.

The kitchen was too black to see anything.

I saw nothing there. I heard nothing there.

Damp air blew on me from the kitchen.

That was something to worry about. I had company, and he was slicker than I. He could open doors or windows under my nose. That wasn't so good.

Weight on rubber heels, I backed away from my chair until the frame of the cellar door touched my shoulder. I wasn't sure I was going to like this party. I like an even break or better, and this didn't look like one.

So when a thin line of light danced out of the kitchen to hit the chair in the passageway, I was three steps cellarward, my back flat against the stair-wall.

The light fixed itself on the chair for a couple of

seconds, and then began to dart around the passageway, through it into the room beyond. I could see nothing but the light.

Fresh sounds came to me—the purr of automobile engines close to the house on the road side, the soft padding of feet on the back porch, on the kitchen linoleum, quite a few feet. An odor came to me—an unmistakable odor—the smell of unwashed Chinese.

Then I lost track of these things. I had plenty to occupy me close up.

The proprietor of the flashlight was at the head of the cellar steps. I had ruined my eyes watching the light; I couldn't see him.

The first thin ray he sent downstairs missed me by an inch—which gave me time to make a map there in the dark. If he was of medium size, holding the light in his left hand, a gun in his right, and exposing as little of himself as possible—his noodle should have been a foot and a half above the beginning of the light-beam, the same distance behind it, six inches to the left—my left.

The light swung sideways and hit one of my legs.

I swung the barrel of my gun at the point I had marked X in the night.

His gun-fire cooked my cheek. One of his arms tried to take me with him. I twisted away and let him dive alone into the cellar, showing me a flash of gold teeth as he went past.

The house was full of "Ah yahs" and pattering feet.

I had to move—or I'd be pushed.

Downstairs might be a trap. I went up to the passageway again.

The passageway was solid and alive with stinking bodies. Hands and teeth began to take my clothes away from me. I knew damned well I had declared myself in on something!

I was one of a struggling, tearing, grunting and groaning mob of invisibles. An eddy of them swept me toward the kitchen. Hitting, kicking, butting, I went along.

A high-pitched voice was screaming Chinese orders.

My shoulder scraped the door-frame as I was carried into the kitchen, fighting as best I could against enemies I couldn't see, afraid to use the gun I still gripped.

I was only one part of the mad scramble. The flash of my gun might have made me the center of it. These lunatics were fighting panic now; I didn't want to show them something tangible to tear apart.

I went along with them, cracking everything that got in my way, and being cracked back. A bucket got between my feet.

I crashed down, upsetting my neighbors, rolled over a body, felt a foot on my face, squirmed from under it, and came to rest in a corner, still tangled up with the galvanized bucket.

Thank God for that bucket!

I wanted these people to go away. I didn't care who or what they were. If they'd depart in peace I'd forgive their sins.

I put my gun inside the bucket and squeezed the trigger. I got the worst of the racket, but there was enough to go around. It sounded like a crump going off.

I cut loose in the bucket again, and had another idea. Two fingers of my left hand in my mouth, I whistled as shrill as I could while I emptied the gun.

It was a sweet racket!

When my gun had run out of bullets and my lungs out of air, I was alone. I was glad to be alone. I knew why men go off and live in caves by themselves. And I didn't blame them!

Sitting there alone in the dark, I reloaded my gun.

On hands and knees I found my way to the open kitchen door, and peeped out into the blackness that told me nothing. The surf made guzzling sounds in the cove. From the other side of the house came the noise of cars. I hoped it was my friends going away.

I shut the door, locked it, and turned on the kitchen light.

The place wasn't as badly upset as I had expected. Some pans and dishes were down and a chair had been broken, and the place smelled of unwashed bodies. But that was all—except a blue cotton sleeve in the middle of the floor, a straw sandal near the passageway door, and a handful of short black hairs, a bit blood-smeared, beside the sandal.

In the cellar I did not find the man I had sent down there. An open door showed how he had left me. His flashlight was there, and my own, and some of his blood.

Upstairs again, I went through the front of the house. The front door was open. Rugs had been rumpled. A blue vase was broken on the floor. A table was pushed out of place, and a couple of chairs had been upset. I found an old and greasy brown felt hat that had neither sweatband nor hatband. I found a grimy photograph of President Coolidge—apparently cut from a Chinese newspaper—and six wheat-straw cigarette papers.

I found nothing upstairs to show that any of my guests had gone up there.

It was half past two in the morning when I heard a car drive up to the front door. I peeped out of Lillian Shan's bedroom window on the second floor. She was saying goodnight to Jack Garthorne.

I went back to the library to wait for her.

"Nothing happened?" were her first words, and they sounded more like a prayer than anything else.

"It did," I told her, "and I suppose you had your breakdown."

For a moment I thought she was going to lie to me, but she nodded, and dropped into a chair, not as erect as usual.

"I had a lot of company," I said, "but I can't say I found out much about them. The fact is, I bit off more than I could chew, and had to be satisfied with chasing them out."

"You didn't call the sheriff's office?" There was something strange about the tone in which she put the question.

"No—I don't want Garthorne arrested yet."

That shook the dejection out of her. She was up, tall and straight in front of me, and cold. "I'd rather not go into that again," she said.

That was all right with me, but, "You didn't say anything to him, I hope."

"Say anything to him?" She seemed amazed. "Do you think I would insult him by repeating your guesses—your absurd guesses?"

"That's fine." I applauded her silence if not her opinion of my theories. "Now, I'm going to stay here tonight. There isn't a chance in a hundred of anything happening, but I'll play it safe."

She didn't seem very enthusiastic about that, but she finally went off to bed.

Nothing happened between then and sunup, of course. I left the house as soon as daylight came and gave the grounds the once over. Footprints were all over the place, from water's edge to driveway. Along the driveway some of the sod was cut where machines had been turned carelessly.

Borrowing one of the cars from the garage, I was back in San Francisco before the morning was far gone.

In the office, I asked the Old Man to put an operative behind Jack Garthorne; to have the old hat, flashlight, sandal and the rest of my souvenirs put under the microscope and searched for fingerprints, footprints, toothprints or what have you; and to have our Richmond branch look up the Garthornes. Then I went up to see my Filipino assistant.

He was gloomy.

"What's the matter?" I asked. "Somebody knock you over?"

"Oh, no, sir!" he protested. "But maybe I am not so good a detective. I try to follow one fella, and he turns a corner and he is gone."

"Who was he, and what was he up to?"

"I do not know, sir. There is four automobiles with men getting out of them into that cellar of which I tell you the strange Chinese live. After they are gone in, one man comes out. He wears his hat down over bandage on his upper face, and he walks away rapidly. I try to follow him, but he turns that corner, and where is he?"

"What time did all this happen?"

"Twelve o'clock, maybe."

"Could it have been later than that, or earlier?"

"Yes, sir."

My visitors, no doubt, and the man Cipriano had tried to shadow could have been the one I swatted. The Filipino hadn't thought to get the license numbers of the automobiles. He didn't know whether they had been driven by white men or Chinese, or even what make cars they were.

"You've done fine," I assured him. "Try it again tonight. Take it easy, and you'll get there."

From him I went to a telephone and called the Hall of Justice. Dummy Uhl's death had not been reported, I learned.

Twenty minutes later I was skinning my knuckles on Chang Li Ching's front door.

The little old Chinese with the rope neck didn't open for me this time. Instead, a young Chinese with a smallpox-pitted face and a wide grin.

"You wanna see Chang Li Ching," he said before I could speak, and stepped back for me to enter.

I went in and waited while he replaced all the bars and locks. We went to Chang by a shorter route than before, but it was still far from direct. For a while I amused myself trying to map the route in my head as he went along, but it was too complicated, so I gave it up.

The velvet-hung room was empty when my guide showed me in, bowed, grinned, and left me. I sat down in a chair near the table and waited.

Chang Li Ching didn't put on the theatricals for me by materializing silently, or anything of the sort. I heard his soft slippers on the floor before he parted the hangings and came in. He was alone, his white whiskers ruffled in a smile that was grandfatherly.

"The Scatterer of Hordes honors my poor residence again," he greeted me, and went on at great length with the same sort of nonsense that I'd had to listen to on my first visit.

The Scatterer of Hordes part was cool enough—if it was a reference to last night's doings.

"Not knowing who he was until too late, I beaned one of your servants last night," I said when he had run out of flowers for the time. "I know there's nothing I can do to square myself for such a terrible act, but I hope you'll let me cut my throat and bleed to death in one of your garbage cans as a sort of apology."

A little sighing noise that could have been a smothered chuckle disturbed the old man's lips, and the purple cap twitched on his round head.

"The Disperser of Marauders knows all things," he murmured blandly, "even to the value of noise in driving away demons. If he says the man he struck was Chang Li Ching's servant, who is Chang to deny it?"

I tried him with my other barrel.

"I don't know much—not even why the police haven't yet heard of the death of the man who was killed here yesterday."

One of his hands made little curls in his white beard.

"I had not heard of the death," he said.

I could guess what was coming, but I wanted to take a look at it.

"You might ask the man who brought me here yesterday," I suggested.

Chang Li Ching picked up a little padded stick from the table and struck a tasseled gong that hung at his shoulder. Across the room the hangings parted to admit the pock-marked Chinese who had brought me in.

"Did death honor our hovel yesterday?" Chang asked in English.

"No, Ta Jen," the pock-marked one said.

"It was the nobleman who guided me here yesterday," I explained, "not this son of an emperor."

Chang imitated surprise.

"Who welcomed the King of Spies yesterday?" he asked the man at the door.

"I bring 'em, Ta Jen."

I grinned at the pock-marked man, he grinned back, and Chang smiled benevolently.

"An excellent jest," he said.

It was.

The pock-marked man bowed and started to duck back through the hangings. Loose shoes rattled on the boards behind him. He spun around. One of the big wrestlers I had seen the previous day loomed above him. The wrestler's eyes were bright with excitement, and grunted Chinese syllables poured out of his mouth. The pock-marked one talked back. Chang Li Ching silenced them with a sharp command. All this was in Chinese—out of my reach.

"Will the Grand Duke of Manhunters permit his servant to depart for a moment to attend to his distressing domestic affairs?"

"Sure."

Chang bowed with his hands together, and spoke to the wrestler.

"You will remain here to see that the great one is not disturbed and that any wishes he expresses are gratified."

The wrestler bowed and stood aside for Chang to pass through the door with the pock-marked man. The hangings swung over the door behind them.

I didn't waste any language on the man at the door, but got a cigarette going and waited for Chang to come back. The cigarette was half gone when a shot sounded in the building, not far away.

The giant at the door scowled.

Another shot sounded, and running feet thumped in the hall. The pock-marked man's face came through the hangings. He poured grunts at the wrestler. The wrestler scowled at me and protested. The other insisted.

The wrestler scowled at me again, rumbled, "You wait," and was gone with the other.

I finished my cigarette to the tune of muffled struggle-sounds that seemed to come from the floor below. There were two more shots, far apart. Feet ran past the door of the room I was in. Perhaps ten minutes had gone since I had been left alone.

I found I wasn't alone.

Across the room from the door, the hangings that covered the wall were disturbed. The blue, green and silver velvet bulged out an inch and settled back in place.

The disturbance happened the second time perhaps ten feet farther along the wall. No movement for a while, and then a tremor in the far corner.

Somebody was creeping along between hangings and wall.

I let him creep, still slumping in my chair with idle hands. If the bulge meant trouble, action on my part would bring it that much quicker.

I traced the disturbance down the length of that wall and halfway across the other, to where I knew the door was. Then I lost it for some time. I had just decided that the creeper had gone through the door when the curtains opened and the creeper stepped out.

She wasn't four and a half feet high—a living ornament from somebody's shelf. Her face was a tiny oval of painted beauty, its perfection emphasized by the lacquer-black hair that was flat and glossy around her temples. Gold earrings swung beside her smooth cheeks, a jade butterfly was in her hair. A lavender jacket, glittering with white stones, covered her from under her chin to her knees. Lavender stockings showed under her short lavender trousers, and her bound-small feet were in slippers of the same color, shaped like kittens, with yellow stones for eyes and aigrettes for whiskers.

The point of all this our-young-ladies'-fashion stuff is that she was impossibly dainty. But there she was—neither a carving nor a painting, but a living small woman with fear in her black eyes and nervous, tiny fingers worrying the silk at her bosom.

Twice as she came toward me—hurrying with the

awkward, quick step of the foot-bound Chinese woman—
her head twisted around for a look at the hangings over
the door.

I was on my feet by now, going to meet her.

Her English wasn't much. Most of what she babbled at
me I missed, though I thought "yung hel-lup" might have
been meant for "You help?"

I nodded, catching her under the elbows as she stumbled against me.

She gave me some more language that didn't make the
situation any clearer—unless "sul-lay-vee gull" meant slave-
girl and "tak-ka wah" meant take away.

"You want me to get you out of here?" I asked.

Her head, close under my chin, went up and down,
and her red flower of a mouth shaped a smile that made all
the other smiles I could remember look like leers.

She did some more talking. I got nothing out of it.
Taking one of her elbows out of my hand, she pushed up
her sleeve, baring a forearm that an artist had spent a lifetime carving out of ivory. On it were five finger-shaped
bruises ending in cuts where the nails had punctured the
flesh.

She let the sleeve fall over it again, and gave me more
words. They didn't mean anything to me, but they tinkled
prettily.

"All right," I said, sliding my gun out. "If you want to
go, we'll go."

Both her hands went to the gun, pushing it down, and
she talked excitedly into my face, winding up with a
flicking of one hand across her collar—a pantomime of a
throat being cut.

I shook my head from side to side and urged her toward the door.

She balked, fright large in her eyes.

One of her hands went to my watch-pocket. I let her
take the watch out.

She put the tiny tip of one pointed finger over the
twelve and then circled the dial three times. I thought I

got that. Thirty-six hours from noon would be midnight of the following night—Thursday.

"Yes," I said.

She shot a look at the door and led me to the table where the tea things were. With a finger dipped in cold tea she began to draw on the table's inlaid top. Two parallel lines I took for a street. Another pair crossed them. The third pair crossed the second and paralleled the first.

"Waverly Place?" I guessed.

Her face bobbed up and down, delightedly.

On what I took for the east side of Waverly Place, she drew a square—perhaps a house. In the square she set what could have been a rose. I frowned at that. She erased the rose and in its place put a crooked circle, adding dots. I thought I had it. The rose had been a cabbage. This thing was a potato. The square represented the grocery store I had noticed on Waverly Place. I nodded.

Her finger crossed the street and put a square on the other side, and her face turned up to mine, begging me to understand her.

"The house across the street from the grocer's," I said slowly, and then, as she tapped my watch-pocket, I added, "at midnight tomorrow."

I don't know how much of it she caught, but she nodded her little head until her earrings were swinging like crazy pendulums.

With a quick diving motion, she caught my right hand, kissed it, and with a tottering, hoppy run vanished behind the velvet curtains.

I used my handkerchief to wipe the map off the table and was smoking in my chair when Chang Li Ching returned some twenty minutes later.

I left shortly after that, as soon as we had traded a few dizzy compliments. The pock-marked man ushered me out.

At the office there was nothing new for me. Foley hadn't been able to shadow The Whistler the night before.

I went home for the sleep I had not got last night.

* * *

At ten minutes after ten the next morning Lillian Shan and I arrived at the front door of Fong Yick's employment agency on Washington Street.

"Give me just two minutes," I told her as I climbed out. "Then come in."

"Better keep your steam up," I suggested to the driver. "We might have to slide away in a hurry."

In Fong Yick's, a lanky, gray-haired man who I thought was the Old Man's Frank Paul was talking around a chewed cigar to half a dozen Chinese. Across the battered counter a fat Chinese was watching them boredly through immense steel-rimmed spectacles.

I looked at the half-dozen. The third from me had a crooked nose—a short, squat man.

I pushed aside the others and reached for him.

I don't know what the stuff he tried on me was—jiu jitsu, maybe, or its Chinese equivalent. Anyhow, he crouched and moved his stiffly open hands trickily.

I took hold of him here and there, and presently had him by the nape of the neck, with one of his arms bent up behind him.

Another Chinese piled on my back. The lean, gray-haired man did something to his face, and the Chinese went over in a corner and stayed there.

That was the situation when Lillian Shan came in.

I shook the flat-nosed boy at her.

"Yin Hung!" she exclaimed.

"Hoo Lun isn't one of the others?" I asked, pointing to the spectators.

She shook her head emphatically and began jabbering Chinese at my prisoner. He jabbered back, meeting her gaze.

"What are you going to do with him?" she asked me in a voice that wasn't quite right.

"Turn him over to the police to hold for the San Mateo sheriff. Can you get anything out of him?"

"No."

I began to push him toward the door. The steel-spectacled Chinese blocked the way, one hand behind him.

"No can do," he said.

I slammed Yin Hung into him. He went back against the wall.

"Get out!" I yelled at the girl.

The gray-haired man stopped two Chinese who dashed for the door, sent them the other way—back hard against the wall.

We left the place.

There was no excitement in the street. We climbed into the taxicab and drove the block and a half to the Hall of Justice, where I yanked my prisoner out. The rancher Paul said he wouldn't go in, that he had enjoyed the party, but now had some of his own business to look after. He went on up Kearny Street afoot.

Half out of the taxicab, Lillian Shan changed her mind.

"Unless it's necessary," she said, "I'd rather not go in either. I'll wait here for you."

"Righto," and I pushed my captive across the sidewalk and up the steps.

Inside, an interesting situation developed.

The San Francisco police weren't especially interested in Yin Hung, though willing enough, of course, to hold him for the sheriff of San Mateo County.

Yin Hung pretended he didn't know any English, and I was curious to know what sort of story he had to tell, so I hunted around in the detectives' assembly room until I found Bill Thode of the Chinatown detail, who talks the language some.

He and Yin Hung jabbered at each other for some time.

Then Bill looked at me, laughed, bit off the end of a cigar, and leaned back in his chair.

"According to the way he tells it," Bill said, "that Wan Lan woman and Lillian Shan had a row. The next day Wan Lan's not anywheres around. The Shan girl and Wang Ma, her maid, say Wan Lan has left, but Hoo Lun tells this fellow he saw Wang Ma burning some of Wan Lan's clothes.

"So Hoo Lun and this fellow think something's wrong and the next day they're damned sure of it, because this fellow misses a spade from his garden tools. He finds it again that night, and it's still wet with damp dirt, and he says no dirt was dug up anywheres around the place—not outside of the house anyways. So him and Hoo Lun put their heads together, didn't like the result, and decided they'd better dust out before they went wherever Wan Lan had gone. That's the message."

"Where is Hoo Lun now?"

"He says he don't know."

"So Lillian Shan and Wang Ma were still in the house when this pair left?" I asked. "They hadn't started for the East yet?"

"So he says."

"Has he got any idea why Wan Lan was killed?"

"Not that I've been able to get out of him."

"Thanks, Bill! You'll notify the sheriff that you're holding him?"

"Sure."

Of course Lillian Shan and the taxicab were gone when I came out of the Hall of Justice door.

I went back into the lobby and used one of the booths to phone the office. Still no report from Dick Foley—nothing of any value—and none from the operative who was trying to shadow Jack Garthorne. A wire had come from the Richmond branch. It was to the effect that the Garthornes were a wealthy and well-known local family, that young Jack was usually in trouble, that he had slugged a Prohibition agent during a café raid a few months ago, that his father had taken him out of his will and chased him from the house, but that his mother was believed to be sending him money.

That fit in with what the girl had told me.

A streetcar carried me to the garage where I had stuck the roadster I had borrowed from the girl's garage the previous morning. I drove around to Cipriano's apartment building. He had no news of any importance for me. He had spent the night hanging around Chinatown, but had picked up nothing.

I was a little inclined toward grouchiness as I turned the roadster west, driving out through Golden Gate Park to the Ocean Boulevard. The job wasn't getting along as snappily as I wanted it to.

I let the roadster slide down the boulevard at a good clip, and the salt air blew some of my kinks away.

A bony-faced man with pinkish mustache opened the door when I rang Lillian Shan's bell. I knew him—Tucker, a deputy sheriff.

"Hullo," he said. "What d'you want?"

"I'm hunting for her too."

"Keep on hunting," he grinned. "Don't let me stop you."

"Not here, huh?"

"Nope. The Swede woman that works for her says she was in and out half an hour before I got here, and I've been here about ten minutes now."

"Got a warrant for her?" I asked.

"You bet you! Her chauffeur squawked."

"Yes, I heard him," I said. "I'm the bright boy who gathered him in."

I spent five or ten minutes more talking to Tucker and then climbed in the roadster again.

"Will you give the Agency a ring when you nab her?" I asked as I closed the door.

"You bet you."

I pointed the roadster at San Francisco again.

Just outside of Daly City a taxicab passed me, going south. Jack Garthorne's face looked through the window.

I snapped on the brakes and waved my arm. The taxicab turned and came back to me. Garthorne opened the door, but did not get out.

I got down into the road and went over to him.

"There's a deputy sheriff waiting in Miss Shan's house, if that's where you're headed."

His blue eyes jumped wide, and then narrowed as he looked suspiciously at me.

"Let's go over to the side of the road and have a little talk," I invited.

He got out of the taxicab and we crossed to a couple of comfortable-looking boulders on the other side.

"Where is Lil—Miss Shan?" he asked.

"Ask The Whistler," I suggested.

This blond kid wasn't so good. It took him a long time to get his gun out. I let him go through with it.

"What do you mean?" he demanded.

I hadn't meant anything. I had just wanted to see how the remark would hit him. I kept quiet.

"Has The Whistler got her?"

"I don't think so," I admitted, though I hated to do it. "But the point is that she has had to go in hiding to keep from being hanged for the murders The Whistler framed."

"Hanged?"

"Uh-huh. The deputy waiting in her house has a warrant for her—for murder."

He put away his gun and made gurgling noises in his throat.

"I'll go there! I'll tell everything I know!"

He started for the taxicab.

"Wait!" I called. "Maybe you'd better tell me what you know first. I'm working for her, you know."

He spun around and came back.

"Yes, that's right. You'll know what to do."

"Now what do you really know, if anything?" I asked when he was standing in front of me.

"I know the whole thing!" he cried. "About the deaths and the booze and—".

"Easy! Easy! There's no use wasting all that knowledge on the chauffeur."

He quieted down, and I began to pump him. I spent nearly an hour getting all of it.

The history of his young life, as he told it to me, began with his departure from home after falling into disgrace through slugging the Prohi. He had come to San Francisco to wait until his father cooled off. Meanwhile his mother kept him in funds, but she didn't send him all the money a young fellow in a wild city could use.

That was the situation when he ran into The Whistler, who suggested that a chap with Garthorne's front could pick up some easy money in the rum-running game if he did what he was told to do. Garthorne was willing enough. He didn't like Prohibition—it had caused most of his troubles. Rum-running sounded romantic to him—shots in the dark, signal lights off the starboard bow, and so on.

The Whistler, it seemed, had boats and booze and waiting customers, but his landing arrangements were out of whack. He had his eye on a little cove down the shore line that was an ideal spot to land hooch. It was neither too close nor too far from San Francisco. It was sheltered on either side by rocky points, and screened from the road by a large house and high hedges. Given the use of that house, his troubles would be over. He could land his hooch in the cove, run it into the house, repack it innocently there, put it through the front door into his automobiles, and shoot it to the thirsty city.

The house, he told Garthorne, belonged to a Chinese girl named Lillian Shan, who would neither sell nor rent it. Garthorne was to make her acquaintance—The Whistler was already supplied with a letter of introduction written by a former classmate of the girl's, a classmate who had fallen a lot since university days—and try to work himself in with her to a degree of intimacy that would permit him to make her an offer for the use of the house. That is, he was to find out if she was the sort of person who could be approached with a more or less frank offer of a share in the profits of The Whistler's game.

Garthorne had gone through with his part, or the first of it, and had become fairly intimate with the girl, when she suddenly left for the East, sending him a note saying she would be gone several months. That was fine for the rum-runners. Garthorne, calling at the house the next day, had learned that Wang Ma had gone with her mistress, and that the three other servants had been left in charge of the house.

That was all Garthorne knew first-hand. He had not taken part in the landing of the booze, though he would have liked to. But The Whistler had ordered him to stay away, so that he could continue his original part when the girl returned.

The Whistler told Garthorne he had bought the help of the three Chinese servants, but that the woman, Wan Lan, had been killed by the two men in a fight over their shares of the money. Booze had been run through the house once during Lillian Shan's absence. Her unexpected return gummed things. The house still held some of the booze. They had to grab her and Wung Ma and stick them in a closet until they got the stuff away. The strangling of Wang Ma had been accidental—a rope tied too tight.

The worst complication, however, was that another cargo was scheduled to land in the cove the following Tuesday night, and there was no way of getting word out to the boat that the place was closed. The Whistler sent for our hero and ordered him to get the girl out of the way and keep her out of the way until at least two o'clock Wednesday morning.

Garthorne had invited her to drive down to Half Moon with him for dinner that night. She had accepted. He had faked engine trouble, and had kept her away from the house until two-thirty, and The Whistler had told him later that everything had gone through without a hitch.

After this I had to guess at what Garthorne was driving at—he stuttered and stammered and let his ideas rattle looser than ever. I think it added up to this: he hadn't thought much about the ethics of his play with the girl. She had no attraction for him—too severe and serious to seem really feminine. And he had not pretended—hadn't carried on what could possibly be called a flirtation with her. Then he suddenly woke up to the fact that she wasn't as indifferent as he. That had been a shock to him—one he couldn't stand. He had seen things straight for the first time. He had thought of it before as simply a wit-matching game. Affection made it different—even though the affection was all on one side.

"I told The Whistler I was through this afternoon," he finished.

"How did he like it?"

"Not a lot. In fact, I had to hit him."

"So? And what were you planning to do next?"

"I was going to see Miss Shan, tell her the truth, and then—then I thought I'd better lay low."

"I think you'd better. The Whistler might not like being hit."

"I won't hide now! I'll go give myself up and tell the truth."

"Forget it!" I advised him. "That's no good. You don't know enough to help her."

That wasn't exactly the truth, because he did know that the chauffeur and Hoo Lun had still been in the house the day after her departure for the East. But I didn't want him to get out of the game yet.

"If I were you," I went on, "I'd pick out a quiet hiding place and stay there until I can get word to you. Know a good place?"

"Yes," slowly. "I have a—a friend who will hide me—down near—near the Latin Quarter."

"Near the Latin Quarter?" That could be Chinatown. I did some sharpshooting. "Waverly Place?"

He jumped.

"How did you know?"

"I'm a detective. I know everything. Ever hear of Chang Li Ching?"

"No."

I tried to keep from laughing into his puzzled face.

The first time I had seen this cut-up he was leaving a house in Waverly Place, with a Chinese woman's face showing dimly in the doorway behind him. The house had been across the street from a grocery. The Chinese girl with whom I had talked at Chang's had given me a slave-

girl yarn and an invitation to that same house. Big-hearted
Jack here had fallen for the same game, but he didn't
know that the girl had anything to do with Chang Li
Ching, didn't know that Chang existed, didn't know Chang
and The Whistler were playmates. Now Jack is in trouble,
and he's going to the girl to hide!

I didn't dislike this angle of the game. He was walking
into a trap, but that was nothing to me—or, rather, I
hoped it was going to help me.

"What's your friend's name?" I asked.

He hesitated.

"What is the name of the tiny woman whose door is
across the street from the grocery?" I made myself plain.

"Hsiu Hsiu."

"All right," I encouraged him in his foolishness. "You
go there. That's an excellent hiding place. Now if I want
to get a Chinese boy to you with a message, how will he
find you?"

"There's a flight of steps to the left as you go in. He'll
have to skip the second and third steps, because they are
fitted with some sort of alarm. So is the handrail. On the
second floor you turn to the left again. The hall is dark.
The second door to the right—on the right-hand side of
the hall—lets you into a room. On the other side of the
room is a closet, with a door hidden behind old clothes.
There are usually people in the room the door opens into,
so he'll have to wait for a chance to get through it. This
room has a little balcony outside, that you can get to from
either side of the windows. The balcony's sides are solid,
so if you crouch low you can't be seen from the street or
from other houses. At the other end of the balcony there
are two loose floorboards. You slide down under them into
a little room between walls. The trap door there will let
you down into another just like it where I'll probably be.
There's another way out of the bottom room down a flight
of steps, but I've never been that way."

A fine mess! It sounded like a child's game. But even
with all this frosting on the cake our young chump hadn't
tumbled. He took it seriously.

"So that's how it's done!" I said. "You'd better get there as soon as you can, and stay there until my messenger gets to you. You'll know him by the cast in one of his eyes, and maybe I'd better give him a password. Haphazard—that'll be the word. The street door—is it locked?"

"No. I've never found it locked. There are forty or fifty Chinamen—or perhaps a hundred—living in that building, so I don't suppose the door is ever locked."

"Good. Beat it now."

At 10:15 that night I was pushing open the door opposite the grocery in Waverly Place—an hour and three-quarters early for my date with Hsiu Hsiu. At 9:55 Dick Foley had phoned that The Whistler had gone into the red-painted door on Spofford Alley.

I found the interior dark, and closed the door softly, concentrating on the childish directions Garthorne had given me. That I knew they were silly didn't help me, since I didn't know any other route.

The stairs gave me some trouble, but I got over the second and third without touching the handrail, and went on up. I found the second door in the hall, the closet in the room behind it, and the door in the closet. Light came through the cracks around it. Listening, I heard nothing.

I pushed the door open—the room was empty. A smoking oil lamp stunk there. The nearest window made no sound as I raised it. That was inartistic—a squeak would have impressed Garthorne with his danger.

I crouched low on the balcony, in accordance with instructions, and found the loose floorboards that opened up a black hole. Feet first, I went down in, slanting at an angle that made descent easy. It seemed to be a sort of slot cut diagonally through the wall. It was stuffy, and I don't like narrow holes. I went down swiftly, coming into a small room, long and narrow, as if placed inside a thick wall.

No light was there. My flashlight showed a room perhaps eighteen feet long by four wide, furnished with table, couch and two chairs. I looked under the one rug on the floor. The trap door was there—a crude affair that didn't pretend it was part of the floor.

Flat on my belly, I put an ear to the trap door. No sound. I raised it a couple of inches. Darkness and a faint murmuring of voices. I pushed the trap door wide, let it down easily on the floor and stuck head and shoulders into the opening, discovering then that it was a double arrangement. Another door was below, fitting no doubt in the ceiling of the room below.

Cautiously I let myself down on it. It gave under my foot. I could have pulled myself up again, but since I had disturbed it I chose to keep going.

I put both feet on it. I swung down. I dropped into light. The door snapped up over my head. I grabbed Hsiu Hsiu and clapped a hand over her tiny mouth in time to keep her quiet.

"Hello," I said to the startled Garthorne, "this is my boy's evening off, so I came myself."

"Hello," he gasped.

This room, I saw, was a duplicate of the one from which I had dropped, another cupboard between walls, though this one had an unpainted wooden door at one end.

I handed Hsiu Hsiu to Garthorne.

"Keep her quiet," I ordered, "while—"

The clicking of the door's latch silenced me. I jumped to the wall on the hinged side of the door just as it swung open—the opener hidden from me by the door.

The door opened wide, but not much wider than Jack Garthorne's blue eyes, nor than his mouth. I let the door go back against the wall and stepped out behind my balanced gun.

The queen of something stood there!

She was a tall woman, straight-bodied and proud. A butterfly-shaped headdress decked with the loot of a dozen jewelry stores exaggerated her height. Her gown was amethyst filigreed with gold above, a living rainbow below. The clothes were nothing!

She was—maybe I can make it clear this way. Hsiu Hsiu was as perfect a bit of feminine beauty as could be imagined. She was perfect! Then comes this queen of something—and Hsiu Hsiu's beauty went away. She was a candle in the sun. She was still pretty—prettier than the woman in the doorway, if it came to that—but you didn't pay any attention to her. Hsiu Hsiu was a pretty girl: this royal woman in the doorway was—I don't know the words.

"My God!" Garthorne was whispering harshly. "I never knew it!"

"What are you doing here?" I challenged the woman.

She didn't hear me. She was looking at Hsiu Hsiu as a tigress might look at an alley cat. Hsiu Hsiu was looking at her as an alley cat might look at a tigress. Sweat was on Garthorne's face and his mouth was the mouth of a sick man.

"What are you doing here?" I repeated, stepping closer to Lillian Shan.

"I am here where I belong," she said slowly, not taking her eyes from the slave-girl. "I have come back to my people."

That was a lot of bunk. I turned to the goggling Garthorne.

"Take Hsiu Hsiu to the upper room, and keep her quiet, if you have to strangle her. I want to talk to Miss Shan."

Still dazed, he pushed the table under the trap door, climbed up on it, hoisted himself through the ceiling, and reached down. Hsiu Hsiu kicked and scratched, but I heaved her up to him. Then I closed the door through which Lillian Shan had come, and faced her.

"How did you get here?" I demanded.

"I went home after I left you, knowing what Yin Hung would say, because he had told me in the employment office, and when I got home— When I got home I decided to come here where I belong."

"Nonsense!" I corrected her. "When you got home you found a message there from Chang Li Ching, asking you—ordering you to come here."

She looked at me, saying nothing.

"What did Chang want?"

"He thought perhaps he could help me," she said, "and so I stayed here."

More nonsense.

"Chang told you Garthorne was in danger—had split with The Whistler."

"The Whistler?"

"You made a bargain with Chang," I accused her, paying no attention to her question. The chances were she didn't know The Whistler by that name.

She shook her head, jiggling the ornaments on her headdress.

"There was no bargain," she said, holding my gaze too steadily.

I didn't believe her. I said so.

"You gave Chang your house—or the use of it—in exchange for his promise that"—the boob were the first words I thought of, but I changed them—"Garthorne would be saved from The Whistler, and that you would be saved from the law."

She drew herself up.

"I did," she said calmly.

I caught myself weakening. This woman who looked like the queen of something wasn't easy to handle the way I wanted to handle her. I made myself remember that I knew her when she was homely as hell in mannish clothes.

"You ought to be spanked!" I growled at her. "Haven't you had enough trouble without mixing yourself now with a flock of highbinders? Did you see The Whistler?"

"There was a man up there," she said. "I don't know his name."

I hunted through my pocket and found the picture of him taken when he was sent to San Quentin.

"That is he," she told me when I showed it to her.

"A fine partner you picked," I raged. "What do you think his word or anything is worth?"

"I did not take his word for anything. I took Chang Li Ching's word."

"That's just as bad. They're mates. What was your bargain?"

She balked again, straight, stiff-necked and level-eyed. Because she was getting away from me with this Manchu princess stuff I got peevish.

"Don't be a chump all your life!" I pleaded. "You think you made a deal. They took you in! What do you think they're using your house for?"

She tried to look me down. I tried another angle of attack.

"Here, you don't mind who you make bargains with. Make one with me. I'm still one prison sentence ahead of The Whistler, so if his word is any good at all, mine ought to be highly valuable. You tell me what the deal was. If it's halfway decent, I'll promise you to crawl out of here and forget it. If you don't tell me, I'm going to empty a gun out of the first window I can find. And you'd be surprised how many cops a shot will draw in this part of town, and how fast it'll draw them."

The threat took some of the color out of her face.

"If I tell, you will promise to do nothing?"

"You missed part of it," I reminded her. "If I think the deal is halfway on the level I'll keep quiet."

She bit her lips and let her fingers twist together, and then it came.

"Chang Li Ching is one of the leaders of the anti-Japanese movement in China. Since the death of Sun Wen—or Sun Yat-Sen, as he is called in the south of China and here—the Japanese have increased their hold on the Chinese government until it is greater than it ever was. It is Sun Wen's work that Chang Li Ching and his friends are carrying on.

"With their own government against them, their immediate necessity is to arm enough patriots to resist Japanese aggression when the time comes. That is what my house is used for. Rifles and ammunition are loaded into boats there and sent out to ships lying far offshore. This man you call The Whistler is the owner of the ships that carry the arms to China."

"And the death of the servants?" I asked.

"Wan Lan was a spy for the Chinese government—for the Japanese. Wang Ma's death was an accident, I think, though she, too, was suspected of being a spy. To a patriot, the death of traitors is a necessary thing, you can understand that? Your people are like that too when your country is in danger."

"Garthorne told me a rum-running story," I said. "How about it?"

"He believed it," she said, smiling softly at the trap door through which he had gone. "They told him that, because they did not know him well enough to trust him. That is why they would not let him help in the loading."

One of her hands came out to rest on my arm.

"You will go away and keep silent?" she pleaded. "These things are against the law of your country, but would you not break another country's law to save your own country's life? Have not four hundred million people the right to fight an alien race that would exploit them? Since the day of Taou-kwang my country has been the plaything of more aggressive nations. Is any price too great for patriotic Chinese to pay to end that period of dishonor? You will not put yourself in the way of my people's liberty?"

"I hope they win," I said, "but you've been tricked. The only guns that have gone through your house have gone through in pocket! It would take a year to get a shipload through there. Maybe Chang is running guns to China. It's likely. But they don't go through your place.

"The night I was there coolies went through—coming in not going out. They came from the beach, and they left in machines. Maybe The Whistler is running the guns over for Chang and bringing coolies back. He can get anything from a thousand dollars up for each one he lands. That's about the how of it. He runs the guns over for Chang, and brings his own stuff—coolies and no doubt some opium—

back, getting his big profit on the return trip. There wouldn't be enough money in the guns to interest him.

"The guns would be loaded at a pier, all regular, masquerading as something else. Your house is used for the return. Chang may or may not be tied up with the coolie and opium game, but it's a cinch he'll let The Whistler do whatever he likes if only The Whistler will run his guns across. So, you see, you have been gypped!"

"But—"

"But nothing! You're helping Chang by taking part in the coolie traffic. And, my guess is, your servants were killed, not because they were spies, but because they wouldn't sell you out."

She was white-faced and unsteady on her feet. I didn't let her recover. "Do you think Chang trusts The Whistler? Did they seem friendly?"

I knew he couldn't trust him, but I wanted something specific.

"No-o-o," she said slowly. "There was some talk about a missing boat."

That was good.

"They still together?"

"Yes."

"How do I get there?"

"Down these steps, across the cellar—straight across—and up two flights of steps on the other side. They were in a room to the right of the second-floor landing."

Thank God I had a direct set of instructions for once!

I jumped up on the table and rapped on the ceiling.

"Come on down, Garthorne, and bring your chaperon."

"Don't either of you budge out of here until I'm back," I told the boob and Lillian Shan when we were all together again. "I'm going to take Hsiu Hsiu with me. Come on, sister, I want you to talk to any bad men I meet. We go to see Chang Li Ching, you understand?" I made faces. "One yell out of you, and—" I put my fingers around her collar and pressed them lightly.

She giggled, which spoiled the effect a little.

"To Chang," I ordered, and, holding her by one shoulder, urged her toward the door.

We went down into the dark cellar, across it, found the other stairs, and started to climb them. Our progress was slow. The girl's bound feet weren't made for fast walking.

A dim light burned on the first floor, where we had to turn to go up to the second floor. We had just made the turn when footsteps sounded behind us.

I lifted the girl up two steps, out of the light, and crouched beside her, holding her still. Four Chinese in wrinkled street clothes came down the first-floor hall, passed our stairs without a glance, and started on.

Hsiu Hsiu opened her red flower of a mouth and let out a squeal that could have been heard over in Oakland.

I cursed, turned her loose, and started up the steps. The four Chinese came after me. On the landing ahead one of Chang's big wrestlers appeared—a foot of thin steel in his paw. I looked back.

Hsiu Hsiu sat on the bottom step, her head over her shoulder, experimenting with different sorts of yells and screams, enjoyment all over her laughing doll's face. One of the climbing yellow men was loosening an automatic.

My legs pushed me on up toward the man-eater at the head of the steps.

When he crouched close above me I let him have it.

My bullet cut the gullet out of him.

I patted his face with my gun as he tumbled down past me.

A hand caught one of my ankles.

Clinging to the railing, I drove my other foot back. Something stopped my foot. Nothing stopped me.

A bullet flaked some of the ceiling down as I made the head of the stairs and jumped for the door to the right.

Pulling it open, I plunged in.

The other of the big man-eaters caught me—caught my plunging hundred and eighty-some pounds as a boy would catch a rubber ball.

Across the room, Chang Li Ching ran plump fingers

through his thin whiskers and smiled at me. Beside him, a man I knew for The Whistler started up from his chair, his beefy face twitching.

"The Prince of Hunters is welcome," Chang said, and added something in Chinese to the man-eater who held me.

The man-eater set me down on my feet, and turned to shut the door on my pursuers.

The Whistler sat down again, his red-veined eyes shifty on me, his bloated face empty of enjoyment.

I tucked my gun inside my clothes before I started across the room toward Chang. And crossing the room, I noticed something.

Behind The Whistler's chair the velvet hangings bulged just the least bit, not enough to have been noticed by anyone who hadn't seen them bulge before. So Chang didn't trust his confederate at all!

"I have something I want you to see," I told the old Chinese when I was standing in front of him, or, rather, in front of the table that was in front of him.

"That eye is privileged indeed which may gaze on anything brought by the Father of Avengers."

"I have heard," I said, as I put my hand in my pocket, "that all that starts for China doesn't get there."

The Whistler jumped up from his chair again, his mouth a snarl, his face a dirty pink. Chang Li Ching looked at him, and he sat down again.

I brought out the photograph of The Whistler standing in a group of Japs, the medal of the Order of the Rising Sun on his chest. Hoping Chang had not heard of the swindle and would not know the medal for a counterfeit, I dropped the photograph on the table.

The Whistler craned his neck, but could not see the picture.

Chang Li Ching looked at it for a long moment over his clasped hands, his old eyes shrewd and kindly, his face gentle. No muscle in his face moved. Nothing changed in his eyes.

The nails of his right hand slowly cut a red gash across the back of the clasped left hand.

"It is true," he said softly, "that one acquires wisdom in the company of the wise."

He unclasped his hands, picked up the photograph, and held it out to the beefy man. The Whistler seized it. His faced drained gray, his eyes bulged out.

"Why, that's—" he began, and stopped, let the photograph drop to his lap, and slumped down in an attitude of defeat.

That puzzled me. I had expected to argue with him, to convince Chang that the medal was not the fake it was.

"You may have what you wish in payment for this," Chang Li Ching was saying to me.

"I want Lillian Shan and Garthorne cleared, and I want your fat friend here, and I want anybody else who was in on the killings."

Chang's eyes closed for a moment—the first sign of weariness I had seen on his round face.

"You may have them," he said.

"The bargain you made with Miss Shan is all off, of course," I pointed out. "I may need a little evidence to make sure I can hang this baby," nodding at The Whistler.

Chang smiled dreamily.

"That, I am regretful, is not possible."

"Why—?" I began, and stopped.

There was no bulge in the velvet curtain behind The Whistler now, I saw. One of the chair legs glistened in the light. A red pool spread on the floor under him. I didn't have to see his back to know he was beyond hanging.

"That's different," I said, kicking a chair over to the table. "Now we'll talk business."

I sat down and we went into conference.

Two days later everything was cleared up to the satisfaction of police, press and public. The Whistler had been found in a dark street, hours dead from a cut in his back, killed in a bootlegging war, I heard. Hoo Lun was found.

The gold-toothed Chinese who had opened the door for Lillian Shan was found. Five others were found. These seven, with Yin Hung, the chauffeur, eventually drew a life sentence apiece. They were The Whistler's men, and Chang sacrificed them without batting an eye. They had as little proof of Chang's complicity as I had, so they couldn't hit back, even if they knew that Chang had given me most of my evidence against them.

Nobody but the girl, Chang and I knew anything about Garthorne's part, so he was out, with liberty to spend most of his time at the girl's house.

I had no proof that I could tie on Chang, couldn't get any. Regardless of his patriotism, I'd have given my right eye to put the old boy away. That would have been something to write home about. But there hadn't been a chance of nailing him, so I had had to be content with making a bargain whereby he turned everything over to me except himself and his friends.

I don't know what happened to Hsiu Hsiu, the squealing slave-girl. She deserved to come through all right. I might have gone back to Chang's to ask about her, but I stayed away. Chang had learned that the medal in the photo was a trick one. I had a note from him:

Greetings and Great Love to the Unveiler of Secrets:
    One whose patriotic fervor and inherent stupidity combined to blind him, so that he broke a valuable tool, trusts that the fortunes of worldly traffic will not again ever place his feeble wits in opposition to the irresistible will and dazzling intellect of the Emperor of Untanglers.

You can take that any way you like. But I know the man who wrote it, and I don't mind admitting that I've stopped eating in Chinese restaurants, and that if I never have to visit Chinatown again it'll be soon enough.

CORKSCREW

Boiling like a coffeepot before we were five miles out of Filmer, the automobile stage carried me south into the shimmering heat and bitter white dust of the Arizona desert.

I was the only passenger. The driver felt as little like talking as I. All morning we rode through cactus-spiked sage-studded oven country, without conversation except when the driver cursed the necessity of stopping to feed his clattering machine more water. The car crept through soft sifting sand, wound between steep-walled red mesas, dipped into dry arroyos where clumps of dusty mesquite were like white lace in the glare, and skirted sharp-edged barrancas.

The sun climbed up in the brazen sky. The higher it got, the larger and hotter it got. I wondered how much hotter it would have to get to explode the cartridges in the gun under my arm. Not that it mattered—if it got any hotter, we would all blow up anyway: car, desert, chauffeur and I would all bang out of existence in one explosive flash. I didn't care if we did!

That was my frame of mind as we pushed up a long slope, topped a sharp ridge and slid down into Corkscrew.

Corkscrew wouldn't have been impressive at any time. It especially wasn't this white-hot Sunday afternoon. One sandy street following the crooked edge of the Tirabuzon Cañon, from which, by translation, the town took its name.

A town, it was called, but village would have been flattery: fifteen or eighteen shabby buildings slumped along the irregular street, with tumble-down shacks leaning against them, squatting close to them and trying to sneak away from them.

In the street four dusty automobiles cooked. Between two buildings I could see a corral where half a dozen horses bunched their dejection under a shed. No person was in sight. Even the stage driver, carrying a limp and apparently empty mail sack, had vanished into a building labeled *Adderly's Emporium.*

Gathering up my two gray-powdered bags, I climbed out and crossed the road to where a weather-washed sign, on which the words *Cañon House* were barely visible, hung over the door of a two-story, iron-roofed, adobe house.

I crossed the wide, unpainted and unpeopled porch and pushed a door open with my foot, going into a dining room where a dozen men and a woman sat eating at oil-cloth-covered tables. In one corner of the room was a cashier's desk; and, on the wall behind it, a key rack. Between rack and desk, a pudgy man whose few remaining hairs were the exact shade of his sallow skin sat on a stool and pretended he didn't see me.

"A room and a lot of water," I said, dropping my bags.

"You can have your room," the sallow man growled, "but water won't do you no good. You won't no sooner drink and wash than you'll be thirsty and dirty all over again. Where in hell is that register?"

He couldn't find it, so he pushed an old envelope across the desk at me. "Register on the back of that. Be with us a spell?"

"Most likely."

A chair upset behind me.

I turned around as a lanky man with enormous red ears reared himself upright with the help of his hands on the table. "Ladiesh an' gentsh," he solemnly declaimed, "th' time hash came for yuh t' give up y'r evil ways an' git out y'r knittin'. Th' law hash came to Orilla County!"

The drunk bowed to me, upset his ham and eggs, and sat down again. The other diners applauded with thump of knives and forks on tables.

I looked them over while they looked me over. A miscellaneous assortment: weather-beaten horsemen, clumsily muscled laborers, men with the pasty complexions of night workers. The one woman in the room didn't belong to Arizona. She was a thin girl of maybe twenty-five, with too-bright dark eyes, dark short hair, and a sharp prettiness that was the mark of a larger settlement than this. You've seen her, or her sisters, in the larger cities, in the places that get going after the theaters let out.

The man with her was range country—a slim lad in the early twenties, not very tall, with pale blue eyes that were startling in so dark-tanned a face. His features were a bit too perfect in their clean-cut regularity.

"So you're the new deputy sheriff?" the sallow man questioned the back of my head.

Somebody had kept my secret right out in the open!

"Yes." I hid my annoyance under a grin that took in him and the diners. "But I'll trade my star right now for that room and water we were talking about."

He took me through the dining room and upstairs to a board-walled room in the rear on the second floor, said, "This is it," and left me.

I did what I could with the water in a pitcher on the washstand to free myself from the white grime I had accumulated. Then I dug a gray shirt and a suit of whipcords out of my bags and holstered my gun under my left shoulder, where it wouldn't be a secret.

In each side pocket of my coat I stowed a new .32 automatic—small, snub-nosed affairs that weren't much better than toys. Their smallness let me carry them where they'd be close to my hands without advertising the fact that the gun under my shoulder wasn't all my arsenal.

* * *

The dining room was empty when I went downstairs again. The sallow pessimist who ran the place stuck his head out of a door.

"Any chance of getting something to eat?" I asked.

"Hardly any"—jerking his head toward a sign that said: *Meals 6 to 8 A.M., 12 to 2 and 5 to 7 P.M.*

"You can grub up at the Toad's—if you ain't particular," he added sourly.

I went out, across the porch that was too hot for idlers, and into the street that was empty for the same reason. I found the Toad's huddled against the wall of a large one-story adobe building, which had *Border Palace* painted all across its front.

It was a small shack—three wooden walls stuck against the adobe wall of the Border Palace—jammed with a lunch counter, eight stools, a stove, a handful of cooking implements, half the flies in the world, an iron cot behind a half-drawn burlap curtain, and the proprietor. The interior had once been painted white. It was a smoky grease-color now, except where homemade signs said: *Meals At All Hours. No Credit*, and gave the prices of various foods. These signs were a fly-specked yellow-gray.

The proprietor was a small man, old, scrawny, dark-skinned, wrinkled, and cheerful.

"You the new sheriff?" he asked, and when he grinned I saw he had no teeth.

"Deputy," I admitted, "and hungry. I'll eat anything you've got that won't bite back, and that won't take long to get ready."

"Sure!" He turned to his stove and began banging pans around. "We need sheriffs," he said over his shoulder.

"Somebody been picking on you?"

"Nobody pick on me—I tell you that!" He flourished a stringy hand at a sugar barrel under the shelves behind his counter. "I fix them decidedly!"

A shotgun butt stuck out of the barrel. I pulled it out: a double-barreled shotgun with the barrels sawed off short; a mean weapon close up.

I slid it back into its resting-place as the old man begun thumping dishes down in front of me.

The food inside me and a cigarette burning, I went out into the crooked street again. From the Border Palace came the clicking of pool balls. I followed the sound through the door.

In a large room four men were leaning over a couple of pool tables, while five or six more watched them from chairs along the wall. On one side of the room was an oak bar. Through an open door in the rear came the sound of shuffling cards.

A big man whose paunch was dressed in a white vest, over a shirt in the bosom of which a diamond sparkled, came toward me, his triple-chinned red face expanding into a professionally jovial smile.

"I'm Bardell," he greeted me, stretching out a fat and shiny-nailed hand on which more diamonds glittered. "This is my joint. I'm glad to know you, sheriff! By God, we need you, and I hope you can spend a lot of your time here. These waddies"—and he chuckled, nodding at the pool players—"cut up rough on me sometimes."

I let him pump my hand up and down.

"Let me make you known to the boys," he went on, turning with one arm across my shoulders. "These are Circle H.A.R. riders"—waving some of his rings at the pool players—"except this Milk River hombre, who, being a peeler, kind of looks down on ordinary hands."

The Milk River hombre was the slender youth who had sat beside the girl in the Cañon House dining room. His companions were young—though not quite so young as he—sun-marked, wind-marked, pigeon-toed in high-heeled boots. Buck Small was sandy and popeyed; Smith was sandy and short; Dunne a rangy Irishman.

The men watching the game were mostly laborers from the Orilla Colony or hands from some of the smaller ranches in the neighborhood. There were two exceptions:

Chick Orr, short, thick-bodied, heavy-armed, with the shapeless nose, battered ears, gold front teeth, and gnarled hands of a pugilist; and Gyp Rainey, a slack-chinned, ratty individual whose whole front spelled cocaine.

Conducted by Bardell, I went into the back room to meet the poker players. There were only four of them. The other card tables, the keno outfit and the dice table were idle.

One of the players was the big-eared drunk who had made the welcoming speech at the hotel. Slim Vogel was the name. He was a Circle H.A.R. hand, as was Red Wheelan, who sat beside him. Both of them were full of hooch. The third player was a quiet, middle-aged man named Keefe. Number four was Mark Nisbet, a pale, slim man. Gambler was written all over him, from his heavy-lidded brown eyes to the slender sureness of his white fingers.

Nisbet and Vogel didn't seem to be getting along so good.

It was Nisbet's deal, and the pot had already been opened. Vogel, who had twice as many chips as anybody else, threw away two cards.

"I want both of 'em off'n th' top—this time!" and he didn't say it nicely. Nisbet dealt the cards, with nothing in his appearance to show he had heard the crack. Red Wheelan took three cards. Keefe was out. Nisbet drew one. Wheelan bet. Nisbet stayed. Vogel raised. Wheelan stayed. Nisbet raised. Vogel bumped it again. Wheelan dropped out. Nisbet raised once more.

"I'm bettin' you took *your* draw off'n th' top, too," Vogel snarled across the table at Nisbet, and tilted the pot again.

Nisbet called. He had aces over kings. The cow-puncher three nines.

Vogel laughed noisily as he raked in the chips. "'F I could keep a sheriff behind you t' watch you all th' time, I'd do somethin' for myself!"

Nisbet pretended to be busy straightening his chips. I

sympathized with him. He had played his hand rotten—
but how else can you play against a drunk?

"How d'you like our little town?" Red Wheelan asked
me.

"I haven't seen much of it yet," I stalled. "The hotel,
the lunch counter—they're all I've seen."

Wheelan laughed. "So you met the Toad? That's Slim's
friend!"

Everybody except Nisbet laughed, including Slim
Vogel.

"Slim tried to beat the Toad out of two bits' worth of
Java and sinkers once. He says he forgot to pay for 'em,
but it's more likely he sneaked out. Anyway, the next day,
here comes the Toad, stirring dust into the ranch, a
shotgun under his arm. He'd lugged that instrument of
destruction fifteen miles across the desert, on foot, to collect his two bits. He collected, too! He took his little two
bits away from Slim right there between the corral and the
bunkhouse—at the cannon's mouth, as you might say!"

Slim Vogel grinned ruefully and scratched one of his
big ears.

"The old son-of-a-gun done came after me just like I
was a damned thief! 'F he'd of been a man I'd of seen him
in hell 'fore I'd of gave it to him. But what can y' do with
an old buzzard that ain't even got no teeth to bite you
with?"

His bleary eyes went back to the table, and the laugh
on his loose lips changed to a sneer. "Let's play," he
growled, glaring at Nisbet. "It's a honest man's deal this
time!"

Bardell and I went back to the front of the building,
where the cowboys were still knocking the balls around. I
sat in one of the chairs against the wall and let them talk
around me. The conversation wasn't exactly fluent. Anybody could tell there was a stranger present.

My first job was to get over that. "Got any idea," I
asked nobody in particular, "where I could pick up a
horse? One that isn't too tricky for a bum rider to sit."

"You might get one at Echlin's stable," Milk River said

slowly, meeting my gaze with guileless blue eyes, "though it ain't likely he's got anything that'll live long if you hurry it. I tell you what—Peery, out to the ranch, has got a buckskin that'd just fit you. He won't want to let him go, but if you took some real money along and flapped it in his face, maybe you could deal."

"You're not steering me into a horse I can't handle, are you?" I asked.

The pale eyes went blank. "I ain't steering you into nothing whatsomever, mister," he said. "You asked for information. I give it to you. But I don't mind telling you that anybody that can stay in a rocking chair can sit that buckskin."

"That's fine. I'll go out tomorrow."

Milk River put his cue down, frowning. "Come to think of it, Peery's going down to the lower camp tomorrow. I tell you—if you got nothing else to do, we'll mosey out there right now."

"Good," I said, and stood up.

"You boys going home?" Milk River asked his companions.

"Yeah," Smith spoke casually. "We gotta roll out early in the mornin', so I s'pose we'd ought to be shakin' along out there. I'll see if Slim an' Red are ready."

They weren't. Vogel's disagreeable voice came through the open door. "I'm camped right here! I got this reptile on th' run, an' it's only a matter o' time 'fore he'll have t' take a chance of pullin' 'em off'n th' bottom t' save his hide. An' that's exac'ly what I'm awaitin' for! Th' first time he gets fancy, I'm goin' t' open up his Adam's apple for him!"

Smith returned to us.

"Slim an' Red are gonna play 'em a while. They'll git a lift out when they git enough."

Milk River, Smith, Dunne, Small and I went out of the Border Palace.

Three steps from the door a stooped, white-mustached man in a collarless stiff-bosomed shirt swooped down on me.

"My name's Adderly," he introduced himself, holding out one hand toward me while flicking the other at Adderly's Emporium. "Got a minute to spare? I'd like to make you acquainted with some of the folks."

The Circle H.A.R. men were walking slowly toward one of the machines in the street.

"Can you wait a couple of minutes?" I called after them.

Milk River looked back. "Yes. We got to gas and water the flivver. Take your time."

Adderly led me toward his store, talking as he walked. "Some of the better element is at my house—danged near all the better element. The folks who'll back you up if you'll put the fear of God in Corkscrew. We're tired and sick of this perpetual hell-raising."

We went through his store, across a yard and into his house. There were a dozen or more people there.

The Reverend Dierks—a gangling, emaciated man with a tight mouth in a long, thin face—made a speech at me. He called me brother; he told me what a wicked place Corkscrew was; and he told me he and his friends were prepared to swear out warrants for the arrest of various men who had committed sixty-some crimes during the past two years.

He had a list of them, with names, dates, and hours, which he read to me. Everybody I had met that day—except those here—was on that list at least once, along with a lot of names I didn't know. The crimes ranged from murder to intoxication and the use of profane language.

"If you'll let me have this list, I'll study it," I promised.

He gave it to me, but he wasn't to be put off with promises. "To refrain even for an hour from punishing wickedness is to be a partner to that wickedness, brother. You have been inside that house of sin operated by Bardell. You have heard the Sabbath desecrated with the sound of pool balls. You have smelled the foul odor of illegal rum on men's breaths! Strike now, brother! Let it not be said that you condoned evil from your first day in

Corkscrew! Go into those hells and do your duty as an officer of the law and a Christian!"

This was a minister; I didn't like to laugh.

I looked at the others. They were sitting—men and women—on the edges of their chairs. On their faces were the same expressions you see around a prize ring just before the gong rings.

Mrs. Echlin, the liveryman's wife, an angular-faced, angular-bodied woman, caught my gaze with her pebble-hard eyes. "And that brazen scarlet woman who calls herself Señora Gaia—and the three hussies who pretend they're her daughters! You ain't much of a deputy sheriff if you leave 'em in that house of theirs one night longer—to poison the manhood of Orilla County!"

The others nodded vigorously.

Miss Janey, schoolteacher, false-toothed, sour-faced, put in her part: "And even worse than those—those creatures—is that Clio Landes! Worse, because at least those —those hussies"—she looked down, managed a blush, looked out of the corners of her eyes at the minister—"those hussies are at least openly what they are. While she—who knows how bad she really is?"

"I don't know about her," Adderly began, but his wife shut him up.

"I do!" she snapped. She was a large, mustached woman whose corsets made knobs and points in her shiny black dress. "Miss Janey is perfectly right."

"Is this Clio Landes person on your list?" I asked, not remembering it.

"No, brother, she is not," the Reverend Dierks said regretfully. "But only because she is more subtle than the others. Corkscrew would indeed be better without her—a woman of obviously low moral standards with no visible means of support, associating with our worse element."

"I'm glad to have met you folks," I said as I folded the list and put it in my pocket. "And I'm glad to know you'll back me up."

I edged toward the door, hoping to get away without

much more talk. Not a chance. The Reverend Dierks followed me up. "You will strike now, brother? You will carry
God's war immediately into brothel and gambling hell?"

"I'm glad to have your support," I said, "but there
isn't going to be any wholesale raiding—not for a while
anyway. This list you've given me—I'll do what I think
ought to be done after I've examined it, but I'm not going
to worry a lot over a batch of petty misdemeanors that
happened a year ago. I'm starting from scratch. What
happens from now on is what interests me. See you later."
And I left.

The cowboys' car was standing in front of the store
when I came out.

"I've been meeting the better element," I explained as
I found a place between Milk River and Buck Small.

Milk River's brown face wrinkled around his eyes.
"Then you know what kind of riffraff we are," he said.

Dunne driving, the car carried us out of Corkscrew at
the street's southern end, and then west along the sandy
and rocky bottom of a shallow draw. The sand was deep
and the rocks were numerous; we didn't make very good
time. An hour and a half of jolting, sweltering and
smothering in this draw, and we climbed up out of it and
crossed to a larger and greener draw.

Around a bend in this draw the Circle H.A.R. buildings sat. We got out of the automobile under a low shed,
where another car already stood. A heavily muscled,
heavily boned man came around a whitewashed building
toward us. His face was square and dark. His close-clipped
mustache and deep-set small eyes were dark. This, I
learned, was Peery, who bossed the ranch for the owner,
who lived in the East.

"He wants a nice, mild horse," Milk River told Peery,
"and we thought maybe you might sell him that Rollo
horse of yours. That's the mildest horse I ever heard tell
of."

Peery tilted his high-crowned sombrero back on his
head and rocked on his heels. "What was you figuring on
paying for this here horse?"

"If it suits me," I said, "I'm willing to pay what it takes to buy him."

"That ain't so bad," he said. "S'pose one of you boys dab a rope on that buckskin and bring him around for the gent to look at."

Smith and Dunne set out together, pretending they weren't going eagerly.

Presently the two cowhands came back, riding, with the buckskin between them, already saddled and bridled. I noticed each of them had a rope on him. He was a loose-jointed pony of an unripe lemon color, with a sad, drooping, Roman-nosed head.

"There he is," Peery said. "Try him out and we'll talk dinero."

I chucked away my cigarette and went over to the buckskin. He cocked one mournful eye at me, twitched one ear, and went on looking sadly at the ground. Dunne and Smith took their lines off him, and I got into the saddle.

Rollo stood still under me until the other horses had left his side.

Then he showed me what he had.

He went straight up in the air—and hung there long enough to turn around before he came down. He stood on his front feet and then on his hind ones, and then he got off all of them again.

I didn't like this, but it wasn't a surprise. I had known I was a lamb being led to the slaughter. This was the third time it had happened to me. I might as well get it over with. A city man in range country is bound to find himself sitting on a disagreeable bone sooner or later. I'm a city man but I can even ride a horse if he'll co-operate. But when the horse doesn't want to stay under me—the horse wins.

Rollo was going to win. I wasn't foolish enough to waste strength fighting him.

So the next time he traded ends, I went away from him, holding myself limp so the tumble wouldn't ruin me.

Smith had caught the yellow pony, and was holding its

head when I took my knees off my forehead and stood up.

Peery, squatting in his heels, was frowning at me. Milk River was looking at Rollo with what was supposed to be a look of utter amazement.

"Now whatever did you do to Rollo to make him act thataway?" Peery asked me.

"Maybe he was only fooling," I suggested. "I'll try him again."

Once more Rollo stood still and sad until I was securely up on him. Then he went into convulsions under me—until I piled on my neck and one shoulder in a clump of brush.

I stood up, rubbing my left shoulder, which had hit a rock. Smith was holding the buckskin. The faces of all five men were serious and solemn—too serious and solemn.

"Maybe he don't like you," Buck Small gave his opinion.

"Might be," I admitted as I climbed into the saddle for the third time.

The lemon-tinted devil was getting warmed up by now, was beginning to take pride in his work. He let me stay aboard longer than before, so he could slam me off harder.

I was sick when I hit the ground in front of Peery and Milk River. It took me a little while to get up, and I had to stand still for a moment until I could feel the ground under my feet.

"Hold him a couple of seconds—" I began.

Peery's big frame stood in front of me. "That's enough," he said. "I ain't going to have you killed."

"Get out of my way," I growled. "I like this. I want more of it."

"You don't top my pony no more," he growled back at me. "He ain't used to playing so rough. You're liable to hurt him, falling off carelessly."

I tried to get past him. He barred my way with a thick arm. I drove my right fist at his dark face.

He went back, busy trying to keep his feet under him.

I went over and hoisted myself up on Rollo.

I had the buckskin's confidence by this time. We were old friends. He didn't mind showing me his secret stuff. He did things no horse could possibly do.

I landed in the same clump of brush that had got me once before and stayed where I landed.

I didn't know whether I could have got up again if I had wanted to. But I didn't want to. I closed my eyes and rested. If I hadn't done what I had set out to do, I was willing to fail.

Small, Dunne and Milk River carried me indoors and spread me on a bunk. "I don't think that horse would be much good to me," I told them. "Maybe I'd better look at another."

"You don't want to get discouraged like that," Small advised me.

"You better lay still and rest, fella," Milk River said. "You're liable to fall apart if you start moving around."

I took his advice.

When I woke up it was morning, and Milk River was prodding me.

"You're figuring on getting up for breakfast, or would you like it brung to you in bed?"

I moved cautiously until I found I was all in one piece. "I can crawl that far."

He sat down on a bunk across the room and rolled a cigarette while I put on my shoes—the only things except my hat I hadn't slept in.

Presently he said, "I always had the idea that nobody that couldn't sit a horse some couldn't amount to nothing much. I ain't so sure now. You can't ride any, and never will. You don't seem to have the least notion what to do after you get in the middle of the animal! But, still and all, a hombre that'll let a bronc dirty him up three times hand-running and then ties into a gent who tries to keep him from making it permanent ain't exactly haywire."

He lit his cigarette, and broke the match in half. "I got a sorrel horse you can have for a hundred dollars. He don't take no interest in handling cows, but he's all horse and he ain't mean."

I went into my money belt and slid five twenties over into his lap.

"Better look at him first," he objected.

"You've seen him," I yawned, standing up. "Where's breakfast?"

Six men were eating in the chuck shack when we came in. Three of them were hands I hadn't seen before. Neither Peery, Wheelan nor Vogel was there. Milk River introduced me to the strangers as the high-diving deputy sheriff, and, between bites of the food the one-eyed Chinese cook put on the table, the meal was devoted almost exclusively to wisecracks about my riding ability.

That suited me. I was sore and stiff, but my bruises weren't wasted. I had bought myself a place of some sort in this desert community, and maybe even a friend or two.

We were following the smoke of our cigarettes outdoors when running hoofs brought a swirl of dust up the draw.

Red Wheelan slid off his horse and staggered out of the sand cloud. "Slim's dead!" he said thickly.

Half a dozen voices shot questions at him. He stood swaying, trying to answer them. He was drunk as a lord!

"Nisbet shot him. I heard about it when I woke up this mornin'. He was shot early this mornin'—in front of Bardell's. I left 'em aroun' midnight last night, an' went down to Gaia's. I heard about it this mornin'. I went after Nisbet, but"—he looked down sheepishly at his empty belt—"Bardell took m' gun away."

He swayed again. I caught him, steadying him.

"Horses!" Peery bawled over my shoulder. "We're going to town!"

I let go of Wheelan and turned around.

"We're going to town," I repeated, "but no foolishness when we get there. This is my job."

Peery's eyes met mine.

"Slim belonged to us," he said.

"And whoever killed Slim belongs to me," I said.

That was all on the subject, but I didn't think I had made the point stick.

An hour later we were dismounting in front of the Border Palace.

A long, thin, blanket-wrapped body lay on two tables that had been pushed together. Half the citizens of Corkscrew were there. Behind the bar, Chick Orr's battered face showed, hard and watchful. Gyp Rainey was sitting in a corner, rolling a cigarette with shaky fingers that sprinkled the floor with tobacco crumbs. Beside him, paying no attention to anything, Mark Nisbet sat.

"By God, I'm glad to see you!" Bardell was telling me, his fat face not quite so red as it had been the day before. "This thing of having men killed at my front door has got to stop, and you're the man to stop it!"

I lifted a flap of the blanket and looked at the dead man. A small hole was in his forehead, over his right eye.

"Has a doctor seen him?" I asked.

"Yes," Bardell said. "Doc Haley saw him, but couldn't do anything. He must have been dead before he fell."

"Can you send for Haley?"

"I reckon I can." Bardell called to Gyp Rainey. "Run across the street and tell Doc Haley that the deputy sheriff wants to talk to him."

Gyp went gingerly through the cowboys grouped at the door and vanished.

"What do you know about the killing, Bardell?" I began.

"Nothing," he said emphatically, and went on to tell me what he knew. "Nisbet and I were in the back room, counting the day's receipts. Chick was straightening the bar up. Nobody else was in here. It was about half-past one this morning, maybe.

"We heard the shot—right out front, and all run out

there, of course. Chick was closest, so he got there first. Slim was laying in the street—dead."

"And what happened after that?"

"Nothing. We brought him in here. Adderly and Doc Haley—who lives right across the street—and the Toad next door had heard the shot, too, and they came out and—and that's all there was to it."

I turned to Gyp.

"Bardell's give it all to you," he said.

"Don't know who shot him?"

"Nope."

I saw Adderly's white mustache near the front of the room and put him on the stand next. He couldn't contribute anything. He had heard the shot, had jumped out of bed, put on pants and shoes, and had arrived in time to see Chick kneeling beside the dead man. He hadn't seen anything Bardell hadn't mentioned.

Dr. Haley had not arrived by the time I was through with Adderly, and I wasn't ready to open on Nisbet yet. Nobody else there seemed to know anything.

"Be back in a minute," I said, and went through the cowboys at the door to the street.

The Toad was giving his joint a much-needed cleaning.

"Good work," I praised him. "It needed it."

He climbed down from the counter on which he had been standing to reach the ceiling. The walls and floor were already comparatively clean.

"I not think it was so dirty," he grinned, showing his empty gums, "but when the sheriff come in to eat and make faces at my place, what am I going to do but clean him up?"

"Know anything about the killing?"

"Sure, I know. I am in my bed, and I hear that shot. I jump out of my bed, grab that shotgun and run to the door. There is that Slim Vogel in the street, and that Chick Orr on his knees alongside him. I stick my head out. There is Mr. Bardell and that Nisbet standing in their door.

"Mr. Bardell says, 'How is he?'

"That Chick Orr, he say, 'He's dead enough.'

"That Nisbet, he does not say anything, but he turn around and go back into the place. And then comes the doctor and Mr. Adderly, and I go out, and after the doctor looks at him and says he is dead, we carry him into Mr. Bardell's place."

That was all the Toad knew. I returned to the Border Palace. Dr. Haley—a fussy little man—was there.

The sound of the shot had awakened him, he said, but he had seen nothing beyond what the others had already told me. The bullet was a .38. Death had been instantaneous. So much for that.

I sat on a corner of a pool table, facing Nisbet. Feet shuffled on the floor behind me and I could feel tension. "What can you tell me, Nisbet?" I asked.

"Nothing that is likely to help," he said, picking his words slowly and carefully. "You were in in the afternoon and saw Slim, Wheelan, Keefe, and me playing. Well, the game went on like that. He won a lot of money—or he seemed to think it was a lot—as long as we played poker. But Keefe left before midnight, and Wheelan shortly after. Nobody else came in the game, so we were kind of short-handed for poker. We quit and played some highcard. I cleaned Vogel—got his last nickel. It was about one o'clock when he left, say half an hour before he was shot."

"You and Vogel get along pretty well?"

The gambler's eyes switched up to mine, turned to the floor again. "You know better than that. You heard him riding me ragged. Well, he kept that up—maybe was a little rawer toward the last."

"And you let him ride?"

"I did just that. I make my living out of cards, not out of fights."

"There was no trouble over the table, then?"

"I didn't say that. There was trouble. He made a break for his gun after I cleaned him."

"And you?"

"I shaded him on the draw—took his gun—unloaded it—gave it back to him—told him to beat it."

"And you didn't see him again until after he had been killed?"

"That's right."

I walked over to Nisbet, holding out one hand.

"Let me look at your gun."

He slid it swiftly out of his clothes—butt first—into my hand. A .38 S.&W., loaded in all six chambers.

"Don't lose it," I said as I handed it back to him, "I may want it later."

A roar from Peery turned me around. As I turned I let my hands go into my coat pockets to rest on the .32 toys.

Peery's right hand was near his neck, within striking distance of the gun I knew he had under his vest. Spread out behind him, his men were as ready for action as he.

"Maybe that's a deputy sheriff's idea of what had ought to be done," Peery was bellowing, "but it ain't mine! That skunk killed Slim. Slim went out of here toting too much money. That skunk shot him down without even giving him a chance to go for his iron, and took his dirty money back. If you think we're going to stand for—"

"Maybe somebody's got some evidence I haven't heard," I cut in. "The way it stands, I haven't got enough to convict Nisbet."

"Evidence be damned! Facts are facts, and you know this—"

"The first fact for you to study," I interrupted him again, "is that I'm running this show—running it my own way. Got anything against that?"

"Plenty!" A worn .45 appeared in his fist. Guns blossomed in the hands of all the men behind him.

I got between Peery's gun and Nisbet, feeling ashamed of the little popping noise my .32's were going to make compared with the roar of the guns facing me.

"What I'd like"—Milk River had stepped away from his fellows, and was leaning his elbows on the bar, facing them, a gun in each hand, a purring quality in his drawl-ing voice—"would be for whosoever wants to swap lead with our high-diving deputy to wait his turn. One at a time is my idea. I don't like this idea of crowding him."

Peery's face went purple.

"What I don't like," he bellowed at the boy, "is a yellow puppy that'll throw down the men he rides with!"

Milk River's face flushed, but his voice was still a purring drawl.

"Mister jigger, what you don't like and what you do like are so damned similar to me that I can't tell 'em apart. And you don't want to forget that I ain't one of your rannies. I got a contract to gentle some horses for you at ten dollars per gentle. Outside of that, you and yours are strangers to me."

The excitement was over. The action that had been brewing had been talked to death by now.

"Your contract expired just about a minute and a half ago," Peery was telling Milk River. "You can show up at the Circle H.A.R. just once more—that's when you come for whatever stuff you left behind you. You're through!"

He pushed his square-jawed face at me. "And you needn't think all the bets are in!"

He spun on his heel, and his hands trailed him out to their horses.

Milk River and I were sitting in my room at the Cañon House an hour later, talking. I had sent word to the county seat that the coroner had a job down here, and had found a place to stow Vogel's body until he came.

"Can you tell me who spread the grand news that I was a deputy sheriff?" I asked Milk River. "It was sup-posed to be a secret."

"Was it? Nobody would of thought of it. Our Mr. Turney didn't do nothing else for two days but run around telling folks what was going to happen when the new deputy come."

"Who is this Turney?"

"He's the gent that bosses the Orilla Colony Company outfit."

So my client's local manager was the boy who had tipped my mitt!

"Got anything special to do the next few days?" I asked.

"Nothing downright special."

"I've got a place on the payroll for a man who knows this country and can chaperon me around it."

"I'd have to know what the play was before I'd set in," he said slowly. "You ain't a regular deputy, and you don't belong in this country. It ain't none of my business, but I wouldn't want to tie in with a blind game."

That was sensible enough.

"I'll spread it out for you," I offered. "I'm a private detective—the San Francisco branch of the Continental Detective Agency. The stockholders of the Orilla Colony Company sent me down here. They've spent a lot of money irrigating and developing their land, and now they're ready to sell it.

"According to them, the combination of heat and water makes it ideal farm land—as good as the Imperial Valley. Nevertheless, there doesn't seem to be any great rush of customers. What's the matter, so the stockholders figure, is that you original inhabitants of this end of the state are such a hard lot that peaceful farmers don't want to come among you.

"It's no secret from anybody that both borders of this United States are sprinkled with sections that are as lawless now as they ever were in the old days. There's too much money in running immigrants over the line, and it's too easy, not to have attracted a lot of gentlemen who don't care how they get their money. With only 450 immigration inspectors divided between the two borders, the government hasn't been able to do much. The official guess is that some 135,000 foreigners were run into the country last year through back and side doors.

"Because this end of Orilla County isn't railroaded or

telephoned up, it has got to be one of the chief smuggling sections, and therefore, according to these men who hired me, full of assorted thugs. On another job a couple of months ago, I happened to run into a smuggling game and knocked it over. The Orilla Colony people thought I could do the same thing for them down here. So hither I come to make this part of Arizona ladylike.

"I stopped over at the county seat and got myself sworn in as deputy sheriff, in case the official standing came in handy. The sheriff said he didn't have a deputy down here and hadn't the money to hire one, so he was glad to sign me on. But we thought it was supposed to be a secret."

"I think you're going to have one hell of a lot of fun," Milk River grinned at me, "so I reckon I'll take that job you was offering. But I ain't going to be no deputy myself. I'll play around with you, but I don't want to tie myself up, so I'll have to enforce no laws I don't like."

"It's a bargain. Now what can you tell me that I ought to know?"

"Well, you needn't bother none about the Circle H.A.R. They're plenty tough, but they ain't running nothing over the line."

"That's all right as far as it goes," I agreed, "but my job is to clean out troublemakers, and from what I've seen of them they come under that heading."

"You're going to have one hell of a lot of fun," Milk River repeated. "Of course they're troublesome! But how could Peery raise cows down here if he didn't get hisself a crew that's a match for the gunmen your Orilla Colony people don't like? And you know how cowhands are. Set 'em down in a hard neighborhood and they're hellbent on proving to everybody that they're just as tough as the next one."

"I've nothing against them—if they behave. Now about these border-running folks?"

"I reckon Bardell's your big meat. Next to him—Big 'Nacio. You ain't seen him yet? A big, black-whiskered

Mex that's got a rancho down the cañon—four-five mile this side of the line. Anything that comes over the line comes through that rancho. But, proving that's another item for you to beat your head about."

"He and Bardell work together?"

"Uh-huh—I reckon he works for Bardell. Another thing you got to include in your tally is that these foreign gents who buy their way across the line don't always—nor even mostly—wind up where they want to. It ain't nothing unusual these days to find some bones out in the desert beside what was a grave until the coyotes opened it. And the buzzards are getting fat! If the immigrant's got anything worth taking on him, or if a couple of government men happen to be nosing around, or if anything happens to make the smuggling gents nervous, they usually drop their customer and dig him in where he falls."

The racket of the dinner-bell downstairs cut off our conference at this point.

There were only eight or ten diners in the dining room. None of Peery's men was there. Milk River and I sat at a table back in one corner of the room. Our meal was about half-eaten when the dark-eyed girl I had seen the previous day came in.

She came straight to our table. I stood up to learn her name was Clio Landes. She was the girl the better element wanted floated. She gave me a flashing smile, a strong, thin hand, and sat down.

"I hear you've lost your job again, you big bum," she laughed at Milk River.

I had known she didn't belong to Arizona. Her voice was New York.

"If that's all you heard, I'm still 'way ahead of you," Milk River grinned back at her. "I gone and got me another job—riding herd on law and order."

From the distance came the sound of a shot.

I went on eating.

Clio Landes said, "Don't you coppers get excited over things like that?"

"The first rule," I told her, "is never to let anything interfere with your meals, if you can help it."

An overalled man came in from the street.

"Nisbet's been killed down in Bardell's!" he yelled.

To Bardell's Border Palace Milk River and I went, half the diners running ahead of us, with half the town.

We found Nisbet in the back room, stretched out on the floor, dead. A hole that a .45 could have made was in his chest, which the men around him had bared.

Bardell's fingers gripped my arm. "Never give him a chance, the dogs!" he cried. "Cold murder!"

"Who shot him?"

"One of the Circle H.A.R., you can bet your neck on that!"

"Didn't anybody see it?"

"Nobody here admits they saw it."

"How did it happen?"

"Mark was out front. Me and Chick and five or six of these men were there. Mark came back here. Just as he stepped through the door—bang!"

Bardell shook his fist at the open window.

I crossed to the window and looked out. A five-foot strip of rocky ground lay between the building and the sharp edge of the Tirabuzon Cañon. A close-twisted rope was tight around a small knob of rock at the cañon's edge.

I pointed at the rope.

Bardell swore savagely. "If I'd of seen that we'd of got him! We didn't think anybody could get down there and didn't look very close. We ran up and down the ledge, looking between buildings."

We went outside, where I lay on my belly and looked down into the cañon. The rope—one end fastened to the knob—ran straight down the rock wall for twenty feet, and disappeared among the trees and bushes of a narrow shelf that ran along the wall there. Once on that shelf, a man could find ample cover to shield his retreat.

"What do you think?" I asked Milk River, who lay beside me.

"A clean getaway."

I stood up, pulling the rope and handing it to Milk River.

"It don't mean nothing to me. Might be anybody's," he said.

"The ground tell you anything?"

He shook his head again.

"You go down into the cañon and see what you can pick up," I told him. "I'll ride out to the Circle H.A.R. If you don't find anything, ride out that way."

I went back indoors for further questioning. Of the seven men who had been in Bardell's place at the time of the shooting, three seemed to be fairly trustworthy. The testimony of those three agreed with Bardell's in every detail.

"Didn't you say you were going out to see Peery?" Bardell asked.

"Yes."

"Chick, get horses! Me and you'll ride out there with the deputy, and as many of you other men as want to go. He'll need guns behind him!"

"Nothing doing!" I stopped Chick. "I'm going by myself. This posse stuff is out of my line."

Bardell scowled, but he nodded his head in agreement. "You're running it," he said. "I'd like to go out there with you, but if you want to play it different, I'm gambling you're right."

In the livery stable where we had put our horses I found Milk River saddling them, and we rode out of town together.

Half a mile out, we split. He turned to the left, down a trail that led into the cañon, calling over his shoulder to me, "If you get through out there sooner than you think, you can maybe pick me up by following the draw the ranch house is in down to the cañon."

I turned into the draw that led toward the Circle H.A.R., the long-legged, long-bodied horse Milk River had sold me carrying me along easily and swiftly. It was too soon after midday for riding to be pleasant. Heat waves boiled out of the draw bottom, the sun hurt my eyes, dust caked my throat.

Crossing from this draw into the larger one the Circle H.A.R. occupied, I found Peery waiting for me.

He didn't say anything, didn't move a hand. He just sat his horse and watched me approach. Two .45's were holstered on his legs.

I came alongside and held out the lariat I had taken from the rear of the Border Palace. As I held it out I noticed that no rope decorated his saddle.

"Know anything about this?" I asked.

He looked at the rope. "Looks like one of those things hombres use to drag steers around with."

"Can't fool you, can I?" I grunted. "Ever see this particular one before?"

He took a minute or more to think up an answer. "Yeah," finally. "Fact is, I lost that same rope somewheres between here and town this morning."

"Know where I found it?"

"Don't hardly make no difference." He reached for it. "The main thing is you found it."

"It might make a difference," I said, moving the rope out of his reach. "I found it strung down the cañon wall behind Bardell's, where you could slide down it after you potted Nisbet."

His hands went to his guns. I turned so he could see the shape of one of the pocketed automatics I was holding.

"Don't do anything you'll be sorry for," I advised him.

"Shall I gun this la-ad now?" Dunne's brogue rolled from behind me, "or will we wa-ait a bit?"

I looked around to see him standing behind a boulder, a .30-.30 rifle held on me. Above other rocks, other heads and other weapons showed.

I took my hand out of my pocket and put it on my saddle horn.

Peery spoke past me to the others. "He tells me Nisbet's been shot."

"Now ain't that provokin'?" Buck Small grieved. "I hope it didn't hurt him none."

"Dead," I supplied.

"Whoever could 'a' done th' like o' that?" Dunne wanted to know.

"It wasn't Santa Claus," I gave my opinion.

"Got anything else to tell me?" Peery demanded.

"Isn't that enough?"

"Yeah. Now if I was you, I'd ride right back to Corkscrew."

"You mean you don't want to go back with me?"

"Not any. If you want to try and take me, now—"

I didn't want to try, and I said so.

"Then there's nothing keeping you here," he pointed out.

I grinned at him and his friends, pulled the sorrel around and started back the way I had come.

A few miles down, I swung off to the south again, found the lower end of the Circle H.A.R. draw and followed it down into the Tirabuzon Cañon. Then I started to work up toward the point where the rope had been let down.

The cañon deserved its name—a rough and stony, tree-and bush-choked, winding gutter across the face of Arizona.

I hadn't gone far when I ran into Milk River, leading his horse toward me. He shook his head. "Not a damned thing! I can cut sign with the rest of 'em, but there's too many rocky ridges here."

I dismounted. We sat under a tree and smoked some tobacco.

"How'd you come out?" he wanted to know.

"So-so. The rope is Peery's, but he didn't want to come along with me. I figure we can find him when we want him, so I didn't insist. It would have been kind of uncomfortable."

He looked at me out of the end of his pale eyes. "A hombre might guess," he said slowly, "that you was playing the Circle H.A.R. against Bardell's crew, encouraging each side to eat up the other and save you the trouble of making any strong play of your own."

"You could be right. Do you think that'd be a dumb play?"

"I don't know. I reckon not—if you're making it, and if you're sure you're strong enough to take hold when you have to."

Night was coming on when Milk River and I turned into Corkscrew's crooked street. It was too late for the Cañon House's dining room, so we got down in front of the Toad's shack.

Chick Orr was standing in the Border Palace doorway. He turned his hammered mug to call something over his shoulder. Bardell appeared beside him, looked at me with a question in his eyes, and the pair of them stepped out into the street. "What result?" Bardell asked.

"No visible ones."

"You didn't make the pinch?" Chick Orr demanded, incredulously.

"That's right. I invited a man to ride back with me, but he said no."

The ex-pug looked me up and down and spit on the ground at my feet. "Ain't you a swell mornin'-glory?" he snarled. "I got a great mind to smack you down!"

"Go ahead," I invited him. "I don't mind skinning a knuckle on you."

His little eyes brightened. Stepping in, he let an open hand go at my face. I took my face out of the way, and turned my back, taking off coat and shoulder holster.

"Hold these, Milk River, while I take this pork-and-beaner for a romp."

Corkscrew came running as Chick and I faced each other. We were pretty much alike in size and age, but his fat was softer than mine, I thought. He had been a professional. I had battled around a little, but there was no doubt that he had me shaded on smartness. To offset that, his hands were lumpy and battered, while mine weren't. And he was—or had been—used to gloves, while bare knuckles were more in my line.

He crouched, waiting for me to come to him. I went, trying to play the boob, faking a right swing for a lead.

Not so good! He stepped outside instead of in. The left I chucked at him went wide. He rapped me on the cheekbone.

I stopped trying to outsmart him, smacked both hands into his body, and felt happy when the flesh folded softly around them. He got away quicker than I could follow, and shook me up with a sock on the jaw.

He left-handed me some more—in the eye, in the nose. His right scraped my forehead, and I was in again.

Left, right, left, I dug into his middle. He slashed me across the face with forearm and fist, and got clear.

He fed me some more lefts, splitting my lip, spreading my nose, stinging my face from forehead to chin. And when I finally got past that left hand I walked into a right uppercut that came up from his ankle to click on my jaw with a shock that threw me back half a dozen steps.

Keeping after me, he swarmed all over me. The evening air was full of fists. I pushed my feet into the ground and stopped the hurricane with a couple of pokes just above where his shirt ran into his pants.

He copped me with his right again—but not so hard. I laughed at him, remembering that something had clicked in his hand when he landed that uppercut, and plowed into him, hammering at him with both hands.

He got away again—cut me up with his left. I smothered his left arm with my right, hung on to it, and whaled him with my own left, keeping it low. His right banged into me. I let it bang. It was dead.

He nailed me once more before the fight ended—with a high straight left that smoked as it came. I managed to keep my feet under me, and the rest of it wasn't so bad. He chopped me a lot more, but his steam was gone.

He went down after a while, from an accumulation of

punches rather than from any especial one, and couldn't get up.

His face didn't have a mark on it that I was responsible for. Mine must have looked as if it had been run through a grinder.

"Maybe I ought to wash up before we eat," I said to Milk River as I took my coat and gun.

"Hell, yes!" he agreed, staring at my face.

A plump man in a Palm Beach suit got in front of me, taking my attention.

"I am Mr. Turney of the Orilla Colony Company," he introduced himself. "Am I to understand that you have not made an arrest since you have been here?"

This was the bird who had advertised me! I didn't like that, and I didn't like his round, aggressive face.

"Yes," I confessed.

"There have been two murders in two days," he ran on, "concerning which you have done nothing, though in each case the evidence seems clear enough. Do you think that is satisfactory?"

I didn't say anything.

"Let me tell you that it is not at all satisfactory." He supplied the answers to his own questions. "Neither is it satisfactory that you should have employed this man"—stabbing a plump finger in Milk River's direction—"who is notoriously one of the most lawless men in the county. I want you to understand clearly that unless there is a distinct improvement in your work—unless you show some disposition to do the things we were engaged to do—that engagement will be terminated!"

"Who'd you say you are?" I asked, when he had talked himself out.

"Mr. Turney, general superintendent of the Orilla Colony."

"So? Well, Mr. General Superintendent Turney, your owners forgot to tell me anything about you when they employed me. So I don't know you at all. Any time you've got anything to say to me, you turn it over to your owners, and if it's important enough, maybe they'll pass it on to me."

He puffed himself up. "I shall certainly inform them that you have been extremely remiss in your duty, however proficient you may be in street brawls!"

"Will you put a postscript on for me," I called after him as he walked away. "Tell 'em I'm kind of busy just now and can't use any advice—no matter who it comes from."

Milk River and I went on to the Cañon House.

Vickers, the sallow, pudgy proprietor, was at the door.

"If you think I got towels to mop up the blood from every hombre that gets himself beat up, you're mistaken," he growled at me. "And I don't want no sheets torn up for bandages, neither!"

"I never seen such a disagreeable cuss as you are," Milk River insisted as we climbed the stairs. "Seems like you can't get along with nobody. Don't you ever make no friends?"

"Only with saps!"

I did what I could with water and adhesive tape to reclaim my face, but the result was a long way from beauty. Milk River sat on the bed and grinned and watched me.

My patching finished, we went down to the Toad's for food. Three eaters were sitting at the counter. I had to exchange comments on the battle with them while I ate.

We were interrupted by the running of horses in the street. A dozen or more men went past the door, and we could hear them pulling up sharply, dismounting in front of Bardell's.

Milk River leaned sidewise until his mouth was close to my ear. "Big 'Nacio's crew from down the cañon. You better hold on tight, chief, or they'll shake the town from under you."

We finished our meal and went out to the street.

In the glow from the big lamp over Bardell's door a

Mexican lounged against the wall. A big black-bearded man, his clothes gay with silver buttons, two white-handled guns holstered low on his thighs.

"Will you take the horses over to the stable?" I asked Milk River. "I'm going up and lie across the bed and grow strength again."

He looked at me curiously, and went over to where we had left the ponies.

I stopped in front of the bearded Mexican, and pointed with my cigarette at his guns.

"You're supposed to take those things off when you come to town," I said pleasantly. "Matter of fact, you're not supposed to bring 'em in at all, but I'm not inquisitive enough to look under a man's coat for them."

Beard and mustache parted to show a smiling curve of yellow teeth.

"Mebbe if *el señor jerife* no lak t'ese t'ings, he lak try take t'em 'way?"

"No. *You* put 'em away."

"I lak t'em here. I wear t'em here."

"You do what I tell you," I said, still pleasantly, and left him, going back to the Toad's shack.

Leaning over the counter, I picked the sawed-off shotgun out of its nest.

"Can I borrow this? I want to make a believer out of a guy."

"Yes, sir, sure! You help yourself!"

I cocked both barrels before I stepped outdoors.

The big Mexican wasn't in sight. I found him inside, telling his friends about it. Some of his friends were Mexican, some American, some God knows what. All wore guns.

The big Mexican turned when his friends gaped past him at me. His hands dropped to his guns as he turned, but he didn't draw.

"I don't know what's in this cannon," I told the truth, centering the riot gun on the company, "maybe pieces of barbed wire and dynamite shavings. We'll find out if you birds don't start piling your guns on the bar right away—because I'll sure-God splash you with it!"

They piled their weapons on the bar. I didn't blame them. This thing in my hands would have mangled them plenty!

"After this, when you come to Corkscrew, put your guns out of sight."

Fat Bardell pushed through them, putting joviality back on his face.

"Will you tuck these guns away until your customers are ready to leave town?" I asked him.

"Yes! Yes! Be glad to!" he exclaimed when he had got over his surprise.

I returned the shotgun to its owner and went up to the Cañon House.

A door just a room or two from mine opened as I walked down the hall. Chick Orr came out, saying, "Don't do nothin' I wouldn't do," over his shoulder.

I saw Clio Landes standing inside the door.

Chick turned from the door, saw me, and stopped, scowling at me.

"You can't fight worth a damn!" he said. "All you know is how to hit!"

"That's right."

He rubbed a swollen hand over his belly. "I never could learn to take 'em down there. That's what beat me in the profesh. But don't pick no more fights with me—I might hurt you!" He poked me in the ribs with a thumb, and went on past me, down the stairs.

The girl's door was closed when I passed it. In my room, I dug out my fountain pen and paper, and had three words of my report written when a knock sounded on my door.

"Come in," I called, having left the door unlocked for Milk River.

Clio Landes pushed the door open. "Busy?"

"No. Come in and make yourself comfortable. Milk River will be along in a few minutes."

"You're not foxing Milk River, are you?" she asked point-blank.

"No. I got nothing to hang on him. He's right so far as I'm concerned. Why?"

"Nothing, only I thought there might be a caper or two you were trying to cop him for. You're not fooling me. These hicks think you're a bust, but I know different."

"Thanks for those few kind words. But don't be press-agenting my wisdom around. I've had enough advertising. What are you doing out here in the sticks?"

"Lunger!" She tapped her chest. "A croaker told me I'd last longer out here. Like a boob, I fell for it. Living out here isn't any different from dying in the big city."

"How long have you been away from the noise?" I asked her.

"Three years—a couple up in Colorado, and then this hole. Seems like three centuries."

"I was back there on a job in April," I led her on, "for two or three weeks."

"You were?"

It was just as if I'd said I had been to heaven. She began to shoot questions at me: Was this still so-and-so? Was that still thus?

We had quite a little gabfest, and I found I knew some of her friends. A couple of them were high-class swindlers, one was a bootleg magnate, and the rest were a mixture of bookies, con men, and the like.

I couldn't find out what her grift was. She talked a blend of thieves' slang and high-school English, and didn't say much about herself.

We were getting along fine when Milk River came in.

"My friends still in town?" I asked.

"Yes. I hear 'em bubbling around down in Bardell's. I hear you've been makin' yourself more unpopular."

"What now?"

"Your friends among the better element don't seem to think a whole lot of that trick of yours of giving Big

'Nacio's guns, and his hombres', to Bardell to keep. The general opinion seems to be you took the guns out of their right hands and put 'em back in the left."

"I only took 'em to show that I could," I explained. "I didn't want 'em. They would have got more anyway. I think I'll go down and show myself to 'em. I won't be long."

The Border Palace was noisy and busy. None of Big 'Nacio's friends paid any attention to me. Bardell came across the room to tell me, "I'm glad you backed the boys down. Saved me a lot of trouble."

I nodded and went out, around to the livery stable, where I found the night man hugging a little iron stove in the office.

"Got anybody who can ride to Filmer with a message tonight?"

"Maybe I can find somebody," he said without enthusiasm.

"Give him a good horse and send him up to the hotel as soon as you can," I requested.

I sat on the edge of the Cañon House porch until a long-legged lad of eighteen or so arrived on a pinto pony and asked for the deputy sheriff. I left the shadow I had been sitting in, and went down into the street, where I could talk to the boy without having an audience.

"Th' old man said yuh wanted to send somethin' to Filmer."

"Can you head out of here toward Filmer, and then cross over to the Circle H.A.R.?"

"Yes, suh, I c'n do that."

"Well, that's what I want. When you get there, tell Peery that Big 'Nacio and his men are in town, and might be riding that way before morning."

"I'll do jus' that, suh."

"This is yours. I'll pay the stable bill later." I slid a bill into his hand. "Get going, and don't let the information get out to anybody else."

Up in my room again, I found Milk River and the girl sitting around a bottle of liquor. We talked and smoked a while, and then the party broke up. Milk River told me he had the room next to mine.

Milk River's knuckles on the door brought me out of bed to shiver in the cold of five-something in the morning.

"This isn't a farm!" I grumbled at him as I let him in. "You're in the city now. You're supposed to sleep until the sun comes up."

"The eye of the law ain't never supposed to sleep," he grinned at me, his teeth clicking together, because he hadn't any more clothes on than I. "Fisher, who's got a ranch out that-a-way, sent a man in to tell you that there's a battle going on out at the Circle H.A.R. He hit my door instead of yours. Do we ride out that-a-way, chief?"

"We do. Hunt up some rifles, water, and the horses. I'll be down at the Toad's, ordering breakfast and getting some lunch wrapped up."

Forty minutes later Milk River and I were out of Corkscrew.

The morning warmed as we rode, the sun making long violet pictures on the desert, raising the dew in a softening mist. The mesquite was fragrant, and even the sand—which would be as nice as a dusty stove top later—had a fresh, pleasant odor.

Up over the ranch buildings, as we approached, three blue spots that were buzzards circled, and a moving animal showed against the sky for an instant on a distant ridge.

"A bronc that ought to have a rider and ain't," Milk River pronounced it.

Farther along we passed a bullet-riddled Mexican sombrero, and then the sun sparkled on a handful of empty brass cartridges.

One of the ranch buildings was a charred black pile. Near by another one of the men I had disarmed in Bardell's lay dead on his back.

A bandaged head poked around a building corner, and its owner stepped out, his right arm in a sling, a revolver in his left. Behind him trotted the one-eyed Chinese cook, swinging a cleaver.

Milk River recognized the bandaged man.

"Howdy, Red! Been quarreling?"

"Some. We took all th' advantage we could of th' warnin' you sent out, an' when Big 'Nacio an' his herd showed up just 'fore daylight, we Injuned them all over the country. I stopped a couple o' slugs, so I stayed to home whilst th' rest o' th' boys followed south. 'F you listen sharp, you can hear a pop now an' then."

"Do we follow 'em, or head 'em?" Milk River asked me.

"Can we head 'em?"

"Might. If Big 'Nacio's running, he'll circle back to his rancho along about dark. If we cut into the cañon and slide along down, maybe we can be there first. He won't make much speed having to fight off Peery and the boys as he goes."

"We'll try it."

Milk River leading, we went past the ranch buildings and on down the draw, going into the cañon at the point where I had entered it the previous day. After a while the footing got better, and we made better time.

At noon we stopped to rest the horses, eat a couple of sandwiches and smoke a bit. Then we went on.

Presently the sun passed, began to crawl down on our right, and shadows grew in the cañon. The welcome shade had reached the east wall when Milk River, in front, stopped. "Around this next bend it is."

We dismounted, took a drink apiece, blew the sand off our rifles, and went forward afoot toward a clump of bushes that covered the crooked cañon's next twist.

Beyond the bend the floor of the cañon ran downhill into a round saucer. The saucer's sides sloped gently up to the desert floor. In the middle of the saucer four adobe buildings sat. In spite of their exposure to the desert sun they looked, somehow, damp and dark. From one of them a thin plume of smoke rose. No man, no animal was in sight.

"I'm going to prospect down there," Milk River said, handing me his hat and rifle.

"Right," I agreed. "I'll cover you, but if anything breaks, you'd better get out of the way. I'm not the most dependable rifle-shot in the world!"

For the first part of his trip Milk River had plenty of cover. He went ahead rapidly. The screening plants grew fewer. His pace fell off. Flat on the ground, he squirmed from clump to boulder, from hummock to bush.

Thirty feet from the nearest building he ran out of places to hide, and he jumped up and sprinted to the shelter of the nearest building.

Nothing happened. He crouched against the wall for several long minutes, and then began to work his way toward the rear.

A Mexican came around the corner.

I couldn't make out his features, but I saw his body stiffen. His hand went to his waist.

Milk River's gun flashed.

The Mexican dropped. The bright steel of his knife glittered high over Milk River's head and rang when it landed on a stone.

Milk River went out of my sight around the building. When I saw him again he was charging at the black doorway of the second building.

Fire streaks came out of the door to meet him.

I did what I could with the two rifles—laying a barrage ahead of him—pumping lead at the open door as fast as I could get it out. I emptied the second rifle just as he got too close to the door for me to risk another shot.

Dropping the rifle, I ran back to my horse and rode to my crazy assistant's assistance.

He didn't need any. It was all over when I arrived.

He was driving another Mexican and Gyp Rainey out of the building with the nozzles of his guns. "This is the crop," he greeted me. "Leastways, I couldn't find no more."

"What are you doing here?" I asked Rainey.

But the hophead looked sullenly at the ground and made no reply.

"We'll tie 'em up," I decided, "and then look around."

Milk River did most of the tying, having had more experience with ropes. He trussed them back to back on the ground, and we went exploring.

Except for plenty of guns of all sizes and more than plenty of ammunition to fit, we didn't find anything very exciting until .we came to a heavy door—barred and padlocked—set half in the foundation of the principal building, half in the mound on which the building sat.

I found a broken piece of rusty pick and knocked the padlock off with it. Then we took the bar off and swung the door open.

Men came eagerly toward us out of an unventilated, unlighted cellar. Seven men who talked a medley of languages as they came.

We used our guns to stop them. Their jabbering went high, excited.

"Quiet!" I yelled to them.

They knew what I meant, even if they didn't understand the word. The babble stopped and we looked them over. All seven seemed to be foreigners—and a hard-looking gang of cutthroats.

Milk River and I tried them out with English first, and then with what Spanish we could scrape up between us. Both attempts brought a lot of jabbering from them, but nothing in either of those languages.

"Got anything else?" I asked Milk River.

"Chinook is all that's left."

That wouldn't help much. I tried to remember some of the words we used to think were French in the A.E.F.

"*Que désirez-vous?*" brought a bright smile to the fat face of a blue-eyed man.

I caught "*Nous allons aux Etats-Unis*" before the speed with which he threw the words at me confused me beyond recognizing anything else.

That was funny. Big 'Nacio hadn't let these birds know that they were already in the United States. I suppose he could manage them better if they thought they were still in Mexico.

"Montrez-moi votre passeport."

That brought a sputtering protest from Blue Eyes. They had been told no passports were necessary. It was because they had been refused passports that they were paying to be smuggled in.

"Quand êtes-vous venu ici?"

Hier meant yesterday, regardless of what the other things he put in his answer were. Big 'Nacio had come straight to Corkscrew after bringing these men across the border and sticking them in his cellar, then.

We locked the immigrants in their cellar again, putting Rainey and the Mexican in with them. Rainey howled like a wolf when I took his hypodermic needle and his coke away from him.

"Sneak up and take a look at the country," I told Milk River, "while I plant the man you killed."

By the time he came back I had the dead Mexican arranged to suit me: slumped down in a chair a little off from the front door of the principal building, his back against the wall, a sombrero tilted down over his face.

"There's dust kicking up some ways off," Milk River reported. "Wouldn't surprise me none if we got our company along toward dark."

Darkness had been solid for an hour when they came.

By then, fed and rested, we were ready for them. A light was burning in the house. Milk River was in there, tinkling a mandolin. Light came out of the open front door to show the dead Mexican dimly—a statue of a sleeper. Beyond him, around the corner except for my eyes and forehead, I lay close to the wall.

We could hear our company long before we could see them. Two horses—but they made enough noise for ten—coming lickety-split.

Big 'Nacio, in front, was out of the saddle and had one foot in the doorway before his horse's front feet—thrown high by the violence with which the big man had pulled him up—hit the ground again. The second rider was close behind him.

The bearded man saw the corpse. He jumped at it, swinging his quirt, roaring, *"Arriba, piojo!"*

The mandolin's tinkling stopped.

I scrambled up.

Big 'Nacio's whiskers went down in surprise.

His quirt caught a button of the dead man's clothes, tangled there, the loop on its other end holding one of Big 'Nacio's wrists. His other hand went to his thigh.

My gun had been in my hand for an hour. I was close. I had leisure to pick my target. When his hand touched his gun butt, I put a bullet through hand and thigh.

As he fell, I saw Milk River knock the second man down with a clout of gun barrel on the back of his head.

"Seems like we team up pretty good," the sunburned boy said as he stooped to take the enemy's weapons from them.

The bearded man's bellowing oaths made conversation difficult.

"I'll put this one you beaned in the cooler," I said. "Watch 'Nacio, and we'll patch him up when I come back."

I dragged the unconscious man halfway to the cellar door before he came to. I goaded him the rest of the way with my gun, shooed him indoors, shooed the other prisoners away from the door and closed and barred it.

The bearded man had stopped howling when I returned.

"Anybody riding after you?" I asked, as I knelt beside him and began cutting his pants away with my pocket-knife.

For answer to that I got a lot of information about myself, my habits, my ancestors. None of it happened to be the truth, but it was colorful.

"Maybe we'd better put a hobble on his tongue," Milk River suggested.

"No. Let him cry!" I spoke to the bearded man again. "If I were you, I'd answer that question. If it happens that the Circle H.A.R. riders trail you here and take us unawares, it's a gut that you're in for a lynching."

He hadn't thought of that.

"Sí, sí. T'at Peery an' hees hombres. T'ey seguir—mucha rapidez!"

"Any of you men left besides you and this other?"

"No! Ningún!"

"Suppose you build as much fire as you can out here in front while I'm stopping this egg's bleeding, Milk River."

The lad looked disappointed. "Ain't we going to bushwack them waddies none?"

"Not unless we have to."

By the time I had put a couple of tourniquets on the Mexican, Milk River had a roaring fire lighting the buildings and most of the saucer in which they sat. I had intended stowing 'Nacio and Milk River indoors, in case I couldn't make Peery talk sense. But there wasn't time. I had just started to explain my plan to Milk River when Perry's bass voice came from outside the ring of light. "Put 'em up, everybody!"

"Easy!" I cautioned Milk River, and stood up. But I didn't raise my hands.

"The excitement's over," I called. "Come on down."

Ten minutes passed. Peery rode into the light. His square-jawed face was grime-streaked and grim. His horse was muddy lather all over. His guns were in his hands.

Behind him rode Dunne—as dirty, as grim, as ready with his firearms.

Nobody followed Dunne. The others were spread around us in the darkness, then.

Peery leaned over his pony's head to look at Big 'Nacio, who was lying breathlessly still on the ground.

"Dead?"

"No—a slug through hand and leg. I've got some of his friends under lock and key indoors."

Mad red rims showed around Peery's eyes in the firelight.

"You can keep the others," he said harshly. "This hombre will do us."

I didn't misunderstand him. "I'm keeping all of them."

"I ain't got a damned bit of confidence in you," Peery growled down at me. "I'm making sure that this Big 'Nacio's riding stops right here. I'm taking care of him myself."

"Nothing stirring!"

"How you figuring on keeping me from taking him?" he laughed viciously at me. "You don't think me and Irish are alone, do you? If you don't believe you're corralled, make a play!"

I believed him, but—"That doesn't make any difference. If I were a grubline rider, or a desert rat, or any lone guy with no connections, you'd rub me out quick enough. But I'm not, and you know I'm not. I'm counting on that. You've got to kill me to take 'Nacio. That's flat! I don't think you want him bad enough to go that far."

He stared at me for a while. Then his knees urged his horse toward the Mexican. 'Nacio sat up and began pleading with me to save him.

Slowly I raised my right hand to my shoulder-holstered gun.

"Drop it!" Peery ordered, both his guns close to my head.

I grinned at him, took my gun out slowly, slowly turned it until it was level between his two.

We held that pose long enough to work up a good sweat apiece. It wasn't restful!

A queer light flickered in his red-rimmed eyes. I didn't guess what was coming until too late. His left-hand gun swung away from me—exploded.

A hole opened in the top of Big 'Nacio's head. He pitched over on his side.

The grinning Milk River shot Peery out of the saddle.

I was under Peery's right-hand gun when it went off. I was scrambling under his rearing horse's feet. Dunne's revolvers coughed.

"Inside!" I yelled to Milk River, and put two bullets into Dunne's pony.

Rifle bullets sang every which way across, around, under, over us.

Inside the lighted doorway Milk River hugged the floor, spouting fire and lead from both hands. Dunne's horse was down. Dunne got up—caught both hands to his face—went down beside his horse.

Milk River turned off the fireworks long enough for me to dash over him into the house.

While I smashed the lamp chimney, blew out the flame, he slammed the door. Bullets made music on door and wall.

"Did I do right, shooting that jigger?" Milk River asked.

"Good work!" I lied.

There was no use bellyaching over what was done, but I hadn't wanted Peery dead. Dunne's death was unnecessary, too. The proper place for guns is after talk has failed, and I hadn't run out of words by any means when this brown-skinned lad had gone into action.

The bullets stopped punching holes in our door.

"The boys have got their heads together," Milk River guessed. "They can't have a hell of a lot of caps left if they've been snapping them at 'Nacio since early morning."

I found a white handkerchief in my pocket and began stuffing one corner in a rifle muzzle.

"What's that for?" Milk River asked.

"Talk." I moved to the door. "And you're to hold your hand until I'm through."

"I never seen such a hombre for making talk," he complained.

I opened the door a cautious crack. Nothing happened. I eased the rifle through the crack and waved it in the light of the still burning fire. Nothing happened. I opened the door and stepped out.

"Send somebody down to talk!" I yelled at the outer darkness.

A voice I didn't recognize cursed bitterly and began a threat: "We'll give yuh—"

It broke off in silence.

Metal glinted off to one side.

Buck Small, his bulging eyes dark-circled, a smear of blood on one cheek, came into the light.

"What are you people figuring on doing?" I asked.

He looked sullenly at me. "We're figurin' on gettin' that Milk River party. We ain't got nothin' against you. You're doin' what you're paid to do. But Milk River hadn't ought to of killed Peery!"

"You boys want to take a tumble to yourselves, Buck. The wild and woolly days are over. You're in the clear so far. 'Nacio jumped you, and you did what was right when you massacred his riders all over the desert. But you've got no right to fool with my prisoners. Peery wouldn't understand that. And if we hadn't shot him, he'd have swung later!

"For Milk River's end of it: he doesn't owe you anything. He dropped Peery under your guns—dropped him with less than an even break! You people had the cards stacked against us. Milk River took a chance you or I wouldn't have taken. You've got nothing to howl about.

"I've got ten prisoners in there, and I've got a lot of guns, and stuff to put in 'em. If you make me do it, I'm going to deal out the guns to my prisoners and let 'em fight. I'd rather lose every damned one of them that way than let you take 'em.

"All that you boys can get out of fighting us is a lot of grief—whether you win or lose. This end of Orilla County has been left to itself longer than most of the Southwest. But those days are over. Outside money has come into it; outside people are coming. You can't buck it! Men tried that in the old days and failed. Will you talk it over with the others?"

"Yeah," and he went away in the darkness.

I went indoors.

"I think they'll be sensible," I told Milk River, "but you can't tell. So maybe you better hunt around and see if you can find a way through the floor to our basement hoosegow, because I meant what I said about giving guns to our captives."

Twenty minutes later Buck Small was back.

"You win," he said. "We want to take Peery and Dunne with us."

Nothing ever looked better to me than my bed in the Cañon House the next—Wednesday—night. My grandstand play with the yellow horse, my fight with Chick Orr, the unaccustomed riding I had been doing—these things had filled me fuller of aches than Orilla County was of sand.

Our ten prisoners were resting in an old outdoor storeroom of Adderly's, guarded by volunteers from among the better element under the supervision of Milk River. They would be safe there, I thought, until the immigration inspectors—to whom I had sent word—could come for them. Most of Big 'Nacio's men had been killed in the fight with the Circle H.A.R. hands, and I didn't think Bardell could collect men enough to try to open my prison.

The Circle H.A.R. riders would behave reasonably well from now on, I thought. There were two angles still open, but the end of my job in Corkscrew wasn't far away. So I wasn't dissatisfied with myself as I got stiffly out of my clothes and climbed into bed for the sleep I had earned.

Did I get it? No.

I was just comfortably bedded down when somebody began thumping on my door.

It was fussy little Dr. Haley.

"I was called into your temporary prison a few minutes ago to look at Rainey," the doctor said. "He tried to escape and broke his arm in a fight with one of the guards. That isn't serious, but the man's condition is. He should be given some cocaine. I don't think that it is safe to leave him without the drug any longer."

"Is he really in bad shape?"

"Yes."

"I'll go down and talk to him," I said, reluctantly starting to dress again. "I gave him a shot now and then on the way up from the rancho—enough to keep him from falling down on us. But I want to get some information out of him now, and he gets no more until he'll talk."

We could hear Rainey's howling before we reached the jail.

Milk River was talking to one of the guards.

"He's going to throw a joe on you, chief, if you don't give him a pill," Milk River told me. "I got him tied up now, so's he can't pull the splints off his arm. He's plumb crazy!"

The doctor and I went inside, the guard holding a lantern high at the door so we could see.

In one corner of the room, Gyp Rainey sat in the chair to which Milk River had tied him. Froth was in the corners of his mouth. He was writhing with cramps.

"For Christ's sake, give me a shot!" Rainey whined at me.

"Gimme a hand, Doctor, and we'll carry him out."

We lifted him, chair and all, and carried him outside.

"Now stop your bawling and listen to me," I ordered. "You shot Nisbet. I want the straight story of it. The straight story will bring you a shot."

"I didn't kill him!" he screamed.

"That's a lie. You stole Peery's rope while the rest of us were in Bardell's place Monday morning, talking over Slim's death. You tied the rope where it would look like the murderer had made a getaway down the cañon. Then you stood at the window until Nisbet came into the back room—and you shot him. Nobody went down that rope—or Milk River would have found some sign. Will you come through?"

He wouldn't. He screamed and cursed and pleaded and denied knowledge of the murder.

"Back you go!" I said.

Dr. Haley put a hand on my arm. "I don't want you to think I am interfering, but I really must warn you that what you're doing is dangerous. It is my belief, and my duty to advise you, that you are endangering this man's life by refusing him the drug."

"I know it, Doctor, but I'll have to risk it. He's not so

far gone, or he wouldn't be lying. When the sharp edge of the drug hunger hits him, he'll talk!"

Gyp Rainey stowed away again, I went back to my room. But not to bed.

Clio Landes was waiting for me, sitting there—I had left the door unlocked—with a bottle of whiskey. She was about three-quarters lit up—one of those melancholy lushes.

She was a poor, sick, lonely, homesick girl, far away from her world. She dosed herself with alcohol, remembered her dead parents, sad bits of her childhood and unfortunate slices of her past, and cried over them.

It was close to four o'clock Thursday morning when the whisky finally answered my prayers, and she went to sleep on my shoulder.

I picked her up and carried her down the hall to her own room. Just as I reached her door, fat Bardell came up the stairs.

"More work for the sheriff," he commented, jovially, and went on.

The sun was high and the room was hot when I woke to the familiar sound of someone knocking on the door. This time it was one of the volunteer guards—the long-legged boy who had carried the warning to Peery Monday night.

"Gyp wants t' see yuh." The boy's face was haggard. "He wants yuh more'n I ever seen a man want anything."

Rainey was a wreck when I got to him.

"I killed him! I killed him!" he shrieked at me. "Bardell knowed the Circle H.A.R. would hit back f'r Slim's killin'. He made me kill Nisbet an' stack th' deal agin Peery so's it'd be up t' you t' go up agin 'em. He'd tried it before an' got th' worst of it!

"Gimme a shot! That's th' God's truth! I stoled th' rope, planted it, an' shot Nisbet wit' Bardell's gun when Bardell sent him back there! Th' gun's under th' tin-can dump in back o' Adderly's. Gimme th' shot!"

"Where's Milk River?" I asked the long-legged boy.

"Sleepin', I reckon. He left along about daylight."

"All right, Gyp! Hold it until the doc gets here. I'll send him over!"

I found Dr. Haley in his house. A minute later he was carrying a charge over to the hypo.

The Border Palace didn't open until noon. Its doors were locked. I went up the street to the Cañon House. Milk River came out just as I stepped up on the porch.

"Hello, young fellow," I greeted him. "Got any idea which room your friend Bardell reposes in?"

He looked at me as if he had never seen me before.

"S'pose you find out for yourself. I'm through doing your chores. You can find yourself a new wet nurse, mister, or you can go to hell!"

The odor of whiskey came out with the words, but he wasn't drunk enough for that to be the whole explanation.

"What's the matter with you?" I asked.

"What's the matter is I think you're a lousy—"

I didn't let it get any farther.

His right hand whipped to his side as I stepped in.

I jammed him between the wall and my hip before he could draw, and got one of my hands on each of his arms.

"You may be a curly wolf with your rod," I growled, shaking him, a lot more peeved than if he had been a stranger, "but if you try any of your monkey business on me, I'll turn you over my knee!"

Clio Landes's thin fingers dug into my arm.

"Stop it!" she cried. "Stop it! Why don't you behave?" to Milk River, and to me, "He's sore over something this morning. He doesn't mean what he says!"

I was sore myself.

"I mean what I said," I insisted.

But I took my hands off him, and went indoors. Inside the door I ran into sallow Vickers.

"What room is Bardell's?"

"214. Why?"

I went on past him and upstairs.

My gun in one hand, I used the other to knock on Bardell's door.

"Who is it?" came through.

I told him.

"What do you want?"

I said I wanted to talk to him.

He kept me waiting for a couple of minutes before he opened. He was half-dressed. All his clothes below the waist were on. Above, he had a coat on over his undershirt, and one of his hands was in his coat pocket.

His eyes jumped big when they lit on the gun in my hand.

"You're arrested for Nisbet's murder!" I informed him. "Take your hand out of your pocket."

He tried to look as if he thought I was kidding him.

"For Nisbet's murder?"

"Uh-huh. Rainey came through. Take your hand out of your pocket."

His eyes moved from mine to look past my head, a flash of triumph burning in them.

I beat him to the first shot by a hairline, since he had wasted time waiting for me to fall for that ancient trick.

His bullet cut my neck.

Mine took him where his undershirt was tight over his fat chest.

He fell, tugging at his pocket, trying to get the gun out for another shot.

I could have jumped him, but he was going to die anyhow. That first bullet had got his lungs. I put another into him.

The hall filled with people.

"Get the doctor!" I called to them.

But Bardell didn't need him. He was dead before I had the words out.

Chick Orr came through the crowd, into the room.

I stood up, sticking my gun back in its holster.

"I've got nothing on you, Chick, yet," I said slowly. "You know better than I do whether there is anything to

get or not. If I were you, I'd drift out of Corkscrew
without wasting too much time packing up."

The ex-pug squinted his eyes at me, rubbed his chin,
and made a clucking sound in his mouth.

"'F anybody asks for me, you tell 'em I'm off on a
tour," and he pushed out through the crowd again.

When the doctor came, I took him up the hall to my
room, where he patched my neck. The wound wasn't
much, but it bled a lot.

After he had finished, I got fresh clothes from my bag
and undressed. But when I went to wash, I found the
doctor had used all my water. Getting into coat, pants and
shoes, I went down to the kitchen for more.

The hall was empty when I came upstairs again,
except for Clio Landes.

She went past me deliberately not looking at me.

I washed, dressed and strapped on my gun. One more
angle to be cleaned up, and I would be through. I didn't
think I'd need the .32 toys any more, so I put them away.
One more angle, and I was done. I was pleased with the
idea of getting away from Corkscrew. I didn't like the
place, had never liked it, liked it less than ever since Milk
River's break.

I was thinking about him when I stepped out of the
hotel—to see him standing across the street.

I didn't give him a tumble, but turned toward the
lower end of the street.

One step. A bullet kicked up dirt at my feet.

I stopped.

"Go for it, fat boy!" Milk River yelled. "It's me or
you!"

I turned slowly to face him, looking for an out. But
there wasn't any.

His eyes were insane-lighted slits. His face was a
ghastly savage mask. He was beyond reasoning with.

"It's me or you!" he repeated and put another bullet
into the ground in front of me. "Warm your iron!"

I stopped looking for an out and went for my gun.

He gave me an even break.

His gun swung down to me as mine straightened to him.

We pulled triggers together.

Flame jumped at me.

I smacked the ground—my right side all numb.

He was staring at me—bewildered. I stopped staring at him and looked at my gun—the gun that had only clicked when I pulled the trigger!

When I looked up again, he was coming toward me, slowly, his gun hanging at his side.

"Played it safe, huh?" I raised my gun so he could see the broken firing-pin. "Serves me right for leaving it on the bed when I went downstairs for water."

Milk River dropped his gun—grabbed mine.

Clio Landes came running from the hotel to him.

"You're not—?"

Milk River stuck my gun in her face. "You done that?"

"I was afraid he—" she began.

"You—— ——!" With the back of an open hand, Milk River struck the girl's mouth.

He dropped down beside me, his face a boy's face. A tear fell hot on my hand. "Chief, I didn't—"

"That's all right," I assured him, and I meant it.

I missed whatever else he said. The numbness was leaving my side, and the feeling that came in its place wasn't pleasant. Everything stirred inside me . . .

I was in bed when I came to. Dr. Haley was doing disagreeable things to my side. Behind him Milk River held a basin in unsteady hands.

"Milk River," I whispered, because that was the best I could do in the way of talk. He bent his ear to me.

"Get the Toad. He killed Vogel. Careful—gun on him. Talk self-defense—maybe confess. Lock him up with others."

Sweet sleep again.

Night, dim lamplight was in the room when I opened

my eyes again. Clio Landes sat beside my bed, staring at the floor, woebegone.

"Good evening," I managed.

I was sorry I had said anything.

She cried all over me and kept me busy assuring her she had been forgiven for the trickery with my gun. I don't know how many times I forgave her. It got to be a damned nuisance.

I had to shut my eyes and pretend I had passed out to shut her up.

I must have slept some, because when I looked around again it was day, and Milk River was in the chair.

He stood up, not looking at me, his head hanging.

"I'll be moving on, Chief, now that you're coming around all right. I want you to know, though, that if I'd knowed what that——done to your gun I wouldn't never have throwed down on you."

"What was the matter with you, anyhow?" I growled at him.

"Crazy, I reckon," he mumbled. "I had a couple of drinks, and then Bardell filled me full of stuff about you and her, and that you was playing me for a sucker. And—and I just went plumb loco, I reckon."

"Any of it left in your system?"

"Hell, no, Chief!"

"Then suppose you stop this foolishness and sit down and talk sense. Are you and the girl still on the outs?"

They were, most emphatically, most profanely.

"You're a big boob!" I told him. "She's a stranger out here, and homesick for her New York. I could talk her language and knew the people she knew. That's all there was—"

"But that ain't the big point, Chief! Any woman that would pull a—"

"Bunk! It was a shabby trick, right enough. But a woman who'll pull a trick like that for you when you are in a jam is worth a million an ounce. Now you run out and find this Clio person, and bring her back with you!"

He pretended he was going reluctantly. But I heard her voice when he knocked on her door. And they let me lay there in my bed of pain for one solid hour before they remembered me. They came in walking so close together that they were stumbling over each other's feet.

"Now let's talk business," I grumbled. "What day is this?"

"Monday."

"Did you get the Toad?"

"I done that thing," Milk River said, dividing the one chair with the girl. "He's over to the county seat now—went over with the others. He swallowed that self-defense bait and told me all about it. How'd you ever figure it out, Chief?"

"Figure what out?"

"That the Toad killed poor old Slim. He says Slim come in there that night, woke him up, ate a dollar and ten cents' worth of grub on him, and then dared him to try and collect. In the argument that follows, Slim goes for his gun, and the Toad gets scared and shoots him—after which Slim obligingly staggers out o' doors to die. But how'd you hit on it?"

"I oughtn't give away my professional secrets, but I will this once. The Toad was cleaning house when I went in to ask him for what he knew about the killing, and he had scrubbed his floor before he started on the ceiling. If that meant anything at all, it meant that he had had to scrub his floor and was making the cleaning general to cover it up. So maybe Slim had bled some on the floor.

"Starting from that point, the rest came easily enough. Slim left the Border Palace in a wicked frame of mind, broke after his earlier winning, humiliated by Nisbet's triumph in the gun-pulling, soured further by the stuff he had been drinking all day. Red Wheelan had reminded him that afternoon of the time the Toad had followed him to the ranch to collect two bits. What more likely than he'd carry his meanness into the Toad's shack? That Slim hadn't been shot with the shotgun didn't mean anything. I never had any faith in that shotgun from the first. If the Toad had been depending on that for his protection, he wouldn't have put it in plain sight, and under a shelf where it wasn't easy to get out. I figured the shotgun was there for moral effect, and he'd have another one stowed out of sight for use.

"Another point you folks missed was that Nisbet seemed to be telling a straight story—not at all the sort of tale he'd have told if he were guilty. Bardell's and Chick's weren't so good, but the chances are they really thought Nisbet had killed Slim and were trying to cover him up."

Milk River grinned at me, pulling the girl closer.

"You ain't so downright dumb," he said. "Clio done warned me the first time she seen you that I'd best not try to run no sandies on you."

A faraway look came into his pale eyes.

"Think of all them folks that were killed and maimed and jailed—all over a dollar and ten cents. It's a good thing Slim didn't eat five dollars' worth of grub. He'd of depopulated the state of Arizona complete!"

TULIP

I was sitting in a roothole the wind had toppled a blue spruce out of a couple of years back, watching a red fox in the shelter of a deadish blackberry clump make up its mind what to do about the odor of skunk carried across the clearing by a breeze that had also, till just a moment ago, carried the sound of field mice squeaking. Then the fox

turned its head to one side to look back the way it had
come and slid deftly out of sight, going the way foxes go,
with a neatness that makes the whole thing seem sudden
but unhurried. I thought the dogs were out; dogs make a
great deal of noise in the woods and at that time I believed
foxes treated dogs and men with the same sort of contemptuous wariness, but presently I heard a man's footsteps.

Tulip pushed aside some brambles a dozen feet from
where the fox had stood and came into the clearing. "Hi,
Pop," he said when he saw me, grinning all the way across
his broad face; then, as he came nearer, "You're skinnier
than ever, but they'll never kill you, will they?"

"How'd you find me?" I asked.

He jerked a big thumb back towards the house.
"Somebody told me I'd maybe find you up here, but if
you're hiding I don't mind jumping out and yelling peek-
aboo." He looked at the shotgun in my hand. "What's that
for? The shooting season's over."

"There are still crows."

He shrugged his thick shoulders. "A man's silly to
shoot things he doesn't want to eat. How was it in the
clink?"

"You're asking me?"

He grinned. "I've never been in federal prisons, just
state and local stuff. What are federal clinks like?"

"The cream of the crop, I guess, but any prison you're
in is a hole."

"Don't I know it! Did I ever tell you about the time
I—"

I said, "Oh, for God's sake," and reached down to fold
the stool I had been using.

"All right," he said good-naturedly. "Remind me to tell
you about it later. Where'd you get this dingus?" He
looked down at the stool, a folding metal frame with dark-
green duck seat and zippered compartments below.

"Gokey."

"What's that green and brown junk on the sides?"

"Mystik tape wrapped around the metal to keep it from shining too much in the woods."

He nodded. "You do all right by yourself, but I guess a man of your age can't be expected to squat on the ground."

"You're in your fifties yourself," I said.

"You're a lot older than that."

"Nonsense, I'll be fifty-eight this year."

"That's what I mean, Pop! You've got to take care of yourself." He stood at the edge of the roothole while I went back a dozen yards to get the Mason jar I had wedged in the fork of a young maple and asked, "And what's that?" as I returned screwing down the top.

"Rags soaked in skunk essence," I explained. "It brings deer pretty close, maybe just because it kills man-smell. I was trying it out on fox."

"You get awful childish sometimes," he said as he followed me across the clearing.

He came behind me along the game path down through the woods and the walk down through the rock garden to the house. I stuck the Mason jar in its crevice between two rocks with a third over it, unloaded the shotgun, and we went up on the porch. Two battered leather valises and a forest-green duffle bag were on the porch just outside the door.

"What's this for?" I asked. "I'm only visiting here myself."

"What kind of friends are they if a friend of yours isn't a friend of theirs? Anyhow I'll only be here a couple of days. You know I can't stand you much longer than that."

"Nothing doing. I'm trying to get a book started."

"That's what I wanted to talk to you about." He put a big hand on my back and urged me towards the door. "I can talk all right out here, but you need to be sitting down with a drink in your hand."

I took him into the house, put the shotgun and folding chair in a corner of the hallway, and poured him a drink. When he looked inquiringly at me, I said, "I haven't had any of it in three years."

He sloshed his whiskey and soda around the way people do when they wish to hear the ice tinkle. "It's probably just as well," he said. "I don't remember that you carried your liquor so good."

I laughed and waved him towards a dark-red armchair. We were in the living room, a large brown, red, green and white room with a nice Vuillard over the television set. "That's not the kind of thing that annoys ex-drunks. It's being told they never did drink so awful much anyway."

"Well, as a matter of fact, you—"

"Cut it out. Sit down and let me tell you why you're going back to town after dinner. I've got a book started and—"

"That's not what you told me out there," he said.

"Huh?"

"You said you were trying to get a book started. That's what I want to talk to you about. It's silly of you—it's always been very silly of you, Pop—not to see that I—"

"Look, Tulip—if you still insist that's your name—I'm not going to write a word about you ever if I can help it. You're a dull and foolish man who goes around doing dull and foolish things he thinks someday somebody will want to write about. Anything anybody did would be dull and foolish if it was done for that reason. And where in the name of God do you get the notion that writers go around hunting for things to write about? Organizing material is the problem, not getting it. Most of the writers I know have far too many things on tap; they're snowed under with stuff they'll never get around to."

"Words," he said. "If you've got so much stuff to write about, how come you haven't done any writing for so long?"

"How do you know how much writing I've done?"

"It can't be much. Magazines used to be lousy with you. All I ever see now is reprints of your early stuff, and less and less of that."

"I don't exist just to write. I—"

"You're changing the subject," he said. "We're talking about your writing. I don't care if you want to waste some of your time playing games with little animals out there or making yourself out a hero by going to jail, but— Look, Pop, you didn't go to jail just for the experience, did you? Because I could have saved you a lot of time and bother by telling you all you'd really have to know."

I said, "I'll bet you."

He shrugged, drank, wiped his lips with a thick forefinger and said, "That's just like a lot of other things you say, it doesn't mean a damned thing. You just say it. You writers have got more words that—" He looked around the room and seemed to like what he saw. "This is a pretty good layout. Who does it belong to?"

"Some people named Irongate."

"Friends of yours?"

"No, I never heard of them."

"Okay, that's funny," he said. "Are they around?"

"So far as I know they're still in Florida."

"That makes it sillier than ever saying I couldn't stay here for a couple of days. What are they like?"

"People."

"You may be an interesting writer, but you don't talk it. What kind of people are they like? Young people? Old people? Left-handed people?"

"Paulie's probably in her early thirties, Gus is a few years older."

"Just the two of them? No children?"

"Why don't you write these answers down so we won't have to go over the whole thing again when the census man comes? Three children, ranging in age from about sixteen to maybe twelve."

His grayish eyes brightened. "Sixteen, huh? And she's only in the early thirties? A shotgun wedding?"

"How do I know? I've only known them since I got out of the Army."

"What an army that was!" He stood up with his empty glass. "Don't bother. I'll fix it myself. You forgot whatever little you knew about pouring drinks since you stopped using them yourself. We fought one hell of a war in the

Aleutians, didn't we? Let's see, didn't you leave before I did?"

"I came back in September, '45."

"Then it's nearly seven years since I've seen you." He brought his drink back to the red armchair and sat down again.

"It's longer than that. The last time I saw you was on Kiska, and I haven't been there since '44."

"'44? '45? What the hell difference does it make? What are you, a lousy historian going through life with a calendar in your hand? Tell me more about these Irongates. Have they got money?"

"Oh, so you don't like being reminded of Kiska? I guess they have. I don't know how much."

"What does he do?"

"Paints pictures, but he doesn't make a living out of that. I think his old man left him some dough."

"His old man sounds like a nice guy."

"But anyway you're not to give them the business."

He stared at me, his thick-featured face all surprised honesty under his short-clipped thick sandy hair. "What business?"

"Any business. No angles, Tulip."

"Well, I'll be good and damned," he said. "You know, that's the hell of the prison system. It throws a man in contact with the lowest criminal elements and first thing you know he's seeing evil and skulduggery everywhere, not that you ever made much of a habit of seeing the best in your fellow man, but—"

"Besides," I said, "the FBI probably still keeps some kind of an eye on me and—"

"That's different," he said. "Why didn't you say so?"

"I didn't want to scare you away."

"Scare me? A fat chance! As a matter of fact, I'm pretty well fixed right now, sweating against silk, as the boys used to say, only that isn't exactly what they said."

"Where'd you get the potatoes?"

"Remember that crazy major that wanted us to go in

for cattle-raising in the Aleutians after the war, said he could fix it with Maury Maverick to rent us one of the islands cheap?"

"For God's sake, you didn't do that? With transportation costs the—"

"No, I just happened to think about it. What was the major's name?"

"You just happened to think about it to slide around my question about where you got the dough you claim you have."

"Oh, that! I got that down Oklahoma-Texas way."

"Oil-money widow?"

He laughed. "You're a character, Pop."

"Jailhouse experience. There were some guys waiting trial for that in West Street last summer."

Tulip seemed surprised. "Jesus, how does a guy go about breaking laws to get money from women?"

"There must be some way."

I went out to the kitchen where Donald was peeling vegetables at the sink while his wife, Linda, adjusted the radio so a song called "Cry" wouldn't be so noisy and told them, "Mr. Tulip, or Colonel Tulip, if he still calls himself that—he was a lieutenant colonel in the Army—will be staying overnight, or maybe for a day or two. Will you fix him up?"

"You want him in the room next to you?" Donald asked. "Or in that yellow room down the hall?"

"Give him the yellow room. Thanks."

Tulip got up when I returned to the living room and said, "You know, I've been thinking, Pop. I ought to phone a girl I know over in Everest, and she's got a kind of cute sister, so why don't I ask them if—"

"Oh, sure, and you must have some relations in the neighborhood, too. I can dig up some names and between us we ought to be able to get twenty or thirty people over here easily."

"It was just an idea," he said, and went over to the corner table to fix himself another drink. "Anyway, I'd rather talk to you about your writing. That's what I came for."

"You didn't. You came here to talk to me about you."

"Well, it's the same thing in a way." He went back to his chair, sat down, crossed his knees and looked me up and down. "Pop, do you want me to tell you why it is you always start to sulk as soon as anybody says anything about your writing?"

"No, I don't," I said honestly. "Get to the point. What have you been doing now that you think is so damned fascinating?"

"It's not like that." There was a touch of what could have been embarrassment in his always-husky voice. "Sometimes I don't think you understand me all the time. Did you ever run into Lee Branch down on Shemya?"

"Not that I remember. Why?"

"He was in the XIIth, a flier. No reason, I was just thinking. He was a kind of nice guy. I went down and visited him awhile after I got out."

Tulip told me about his visit, but he gave Branch a sister called Paulie—I had mentioned Paulie Irongate—he made their place sound a little like the Irongate's place, though he set it in another state, and there were shotguns in his story as there had been in my hands when he met me up in the clearing where I had been watching the fox.

Tulip was usually longwinded—especially when he thought it necessary to back into one of his tales—but the guts of what he told me, not in his language and without any of the thoughts he said he had at the time, was that Lee Branch said, "The flag is waving," and lowered his head a little to peer up under his dun hat brim through cattail tips.

Five ducks came in black against a dull pearl November sky, showing white underwings when they swept over the decoys and turned into the wind.

Tulip said, "Hit it, little man." The 20-gauge Fox was a dainty weapon in his big hands. He fired without rising from where he sat on the ground under the dying willow, first the left barrel and then the right as the lead duck hung momentarily motionless at the foot of too sharply rising an angle. Both birds hit the water together. One was dead. The other swam three-quarters of a small circle and died.

Lee Branch, up on his feet, swung his heavier gun to the right, fired, swung on and fired again. Both birds fell. One of them lost a good deal of feathers. Lee grinned down at Tulip, who was reloading. "I guess we've got our stuff with us today, Swede."

Tulip looked complacently at the dead ducks on the dry weeds beside him and at the four on the lake. "Uh-huh." He felt in a pocket for cigarettes. "But you bazookaed the bejesus out of that first one."

"I should've waited longer. I like a gun that jumps in my hand. I think I'll get me a 10-gauge." Lee reloaded the Belgian duck gun and laid it down tenderly. "Whose turn to fetch?"

Tulip jerked a thumb at Lee and lay back on the weeds. Lee Branch was twenty-eight, with smooth dark hair parted in the middle, and of course hidden just now by his dun hat, and bright dark eyes. He was not small, but his nimble trimness—even in horse-hide clothes pushing his way through briars to the other side of the tiny island where they had hidden their boat—made him seem smaller than he was.

When he returned with the birds Tulip was lying on his back smoking with his eyes shut.

Lee said, "One of yours was another wood duck." He held it out.

"I know." Tulip opened one eye to squint through smoke at the duck. "They'd be too pretty to kill if a man wasn't always so hungry." He tossed his cigarette over the cattails into the water and stretched his arms wide on the ground. "You weren't kidding, boysie. This has been everything you said."

Lee started to speak, then squatted on his heels, his

dark eyes alert. "What do you mean by has been?" he asked. "Is." A pause. "Will be." He seemed very young.

Tulip shut his eyes again. "I don't know, bub. How long have I been here?"

"A week. Ten days. I don't know. What difference does that make? When we used to talk about your coming here after the war we didn't—"

Tulip squirmed and frowned, but didn't open his eyes. "Okay, okay, but you don't think everybody ought to stick to all those post-war plans they make in the Army?"

"Of course not, but this is— This *is* different, isn't it, Swede?"

"This is by itself," Tulip said.

"Well, then?"

"Nobody's got all the answers."

"I'm not trying to tie you down, but— Listen, Swede, it's not because the place is Paulie's, is it?"

"No."

"Because she likes you and would like to have you stay."

"I'm glad she likes me," Tulip said, "because I like her plenty."

"And it's not that?"

"No."

Lee probably twisted a twig from the willow and split it with a thumb nail. "An old guy like you oughtn't to be roaming around just for the hell of it."

"I know. I don't like roaming, only things are always reminding me of something some place else." He opened his eyes and sat up, putting the Fox across his thighs. "You don't use this little gun. Want to sell it?"

"I'd give it to you, but it's Paulie's. Ask her."

Tulip shook his head. "She's bats as her brother. She'd give it to me."

"What are you? The last of the Confederates or something and don't take gifts from women?"

"I reckon you never knew many Confederates, suh. Was Paulie much in love with her husband?"

Lee looked at Tulip, who was looking out over the lake at the decoys. "I don't really know. He was a pretty good guy. You never ran into him, huh?"

"He was knocked off before I came down the Chain. They were still talking about him."

"They liked him." Lee threw the ruined willow twig away. "Why'd you ask that about Paulie?"

"I'm the nosey type, that's all."

"I didn't mean you shouldn't. Jesus, people are hard to talk to!"

Tulip shrugged his big shoulders. "You can talk to me about anything, only maybe there are some things you hadn't ought to."

"You mean things about you and Paulie?"

Tulip turned his head and looked carefully at the younger man. "Ah, the typical kid brother."

Lee reddened and laughed and said, "Go to hell." Then, after a little pause, "But that is what you mean, isn't it?"

Tulip shook his head. "I don't think there's much there you can't talk about."

Paulie Horris came around a tall whitewood tree at the far end of the lake, made a funnel of her hands and called, "Hey, murderers. The sun's down. You're ten minutes illegal."

They stood up to wave at her, picked up shotguns and dead ducks and went back through briars to the boat. Tulip stood in the stern of the boat and poled it out towards the decoys. Twice Lee Branch seemed about to say something, but he did not speak until he was leaning far over the side of the boat to pick up an artificial mallard. Then he asked, "You're not just being a dope, are you?"

Tulip, bending to retrieve two decoys as the boat crept past them, said, "Stop mumbling."

Lee straightened up and said clearly, "Her husband being a war hero and that kind of stuff. You're not letting it throw you, are you?"

Tulip said, "Tch, tch, tch, and I thought I'd heard everything."

Lee's face reddened again. He laughed and said, "There was never any use talking to you," and they picked up the rest of the decoys.

As Tulip poled the boat towards the bathhouse Paulie Horris came around a sumac thicket from the far end of the lake and walked down to the stone dock to meet them. She was a tall dark-haired, dark-eyed woman of thirty in a gray whipcord skirt and yellowish three-quarter-length leather coat.

"You're a mighty pretty-walking woman, Mrs. Horris," Tulip called to her.

She curtsied. "Thank you kindly, sir."

Lee stowed the decoys in the bathhouse while Tulip tied up the boat so it couldn't bang against the dock if wind blew. Then, each carrying some of the ducks, they walked abreast, with the girl in the middle, up the road towards the house.

When they had walked perhaps a hundred yards, Lee Branch told his sister, "Swede's leaving."

His tone made her look sharply at him and she asked, "Well?"

Lee said, "I'm a fool, I guess, but I thought we— Well, anyhow, he's talking about leaving." He kicked a small mound of gravel apart as he walked.

She stood still and the two men stopped with her. She turned her face to Tulip and it was quite pale now. "Did he," she began, and hesitated, "did he try to buy you with me?"

Tulip said, "That's a dopey way to look at it, Paulie."

She looked down at their feet and in a very low voice said, "Yes, I guess it is," and began to walk again as before.

They came back to the house and, after he had carried his share of the ducks to the kitchen, Tulip went upstairs to his room and began writing a letter to a girl in Atlanta.

Dear Judy:

You will probably be surprised to hear from me after all these years, but for some reason I have been thinking about you a lot this past week or ten days and I have to come down to Atlanta pretty soon anyhow, so I thought . . .

Donald had come into the living room to tell us dinner was ready while Tulip was telling his version of this tale. We had gone into the dining room and Tulip had talked through most of the meal, finishing as we were starting on the dessert, black-walnut tarts. He had never gone to Atlanta, of course, though he said he had meant to. On his way down there he had stopped over in Washington and got himself lengthily involved in something to do with a veterans' organization—or a potential veterans' organization—and by that time he was not so sure that Judy would still be in Atlanta after all these years even if he had remembered her address correctly, and of course Paulie wasn't around now to remind him of Judy.

"That's all right," I said when he had finished, "but it hasn't got much to do with you. You're just a cipher in it, unless, of course, you want to admit that as soon as things or people threaten to involve you, you make up a fantasy you call the memory of something some place else to drag you away from any sort of responsibility."

Tulip lowered his forkful of tart and said, "I don't know why I waste time talking to you. Look, I told you how I felt about Paulie, and about the girl in Atlanta. I—"

"What you tell me about what went on in your head at the time has got nothing to do with anything. I'm disregarding all that."

He shook his head. "You're a pip. No wonder writing hasn't got much to do with life if that's the way writers do."

"Go on and eat," I said. "It's your thoughts on life that haven't got much to do with life. Why do you suppose you turned your back on Paulie?"

He said through the bite of tart he was chewing, "Well, I've always been a love-'em-where-you-find-'em-and-leave-'em-where-you-love-'em guy and I—"

"That's what I mean; and you expect me to call that thinking?"

He took another bite of tart and shook his head again. "You're a pip."

"Do you suppose she was right in thinking her brother had done the same thing with Horris?"

"I never did any wondering about that. Look, Pop, whatever homo there is in Lee I don't think he ever knew about. He's not a bad kid."

"The chief trouble with people like you is not that your own thoughts are so childish, but that you keep people from thinking around you."

"I know. I haven't got the right kind of oohs and ahs for the half-baked pieces of Freudism that you misunderstood in a book somewhere to bring out the best in you. Girls are better at that, aren't they?"

"Not the ones I know. I guess I'm unlucky."

"Well, when I get rested a little I'll see if I can dig you up some numbers. I never was nuts about the kind of dames you ran around with except maybe that—"

"I'd hate to think I ran around with the kind of dames you're nuts about. Want coffee here or in the living room?"

We went back to the living room and Donald brought us coffee there. Donald Poynton was a trim medium-sized Negro of thirty-five with a handsome very dark face. I liked him. He had a pretty good sense of humor that he didn't use very much unless he knew you. He said, "The dogs are out in the kitchen if you want them."

"There's no hurry," I said. "Shoo 'em in when you're through, unless they're in your way."

"The trouble with you," Tulip began when Donald had gone out, and then corrected himself. "One of the troubles with you is you're always too sure you understand me."

"I don't think I understand you very often. Where we differ is that I don't think there's very much there worth understanding."

I crossed the room to get cigars while he was saying, "Oh, so you don't think everybody's worth understanding?"

"Theoretically, yes. But there's a time element involved and I can't count on living more than fifty or sixty years more." I brought the glass jar of cigars back to him and he took one.

"Yours? Or do they go with the house?" he asked.

"Mine."

"Good. Your cigars are probably the only thing about you that I've always liked, or did you think it was your hair? If you hadn't been so sure you understood me that time in Baltimore we wouldn't've had all that trouble."

"Oh, that? That wasn't really trouble."

He bit off the end of his cigar and stared glumly at me. "You're a tough man to talk to sometimes, Pop. No wonder they sent you to jail."

"You worry too much about that time in Baltimore, about getting off on the wrong foot with me. I'd've forgotten it years ago if you didn't keep bringing it up. Why don't you give it a skip?"

He said, "You patronizing son of a bitch," but laughed when I laughed. "It really gripes you to think you're only human."

"I don't like that word *only*, unless you mean of course Everest is *only* 29,000 feet high or the blue whale is *only* the largest animal or—"

"What are you trying to do?" he asked disgustedly. "Show off to me? Or if you're getting ready to launch into one of those dull speeches about the future of the human race and mankind's unused possibilities and potentialities I'm going to bed. Maybe you're not too old to talk that way, but I'm too old to listen to it." He burst out laughing. "Hey," he said, still laughing, "I finally read something you wrote. A fellow gave it to me in San Francisco. It's a pip."

"What is it?"

"It's in my bag, I'll show it to you tomorrow. I don't

want to spoil it by telling you about it. Is it a honey! I always knew you were bats, but—" He shook his head.

"Can I get you a drink? Maybe a shot of brandy. You get yourself all upset when you think about back in Baltimore, just as you did when I mentioned Kiska. I guess you must have a lot of things in your back life to upset you when you happen to think about them."

"That's the second time tonight you've mentioned Kiska," he said, "and that certainly wouldn't be one of them. What'd you expect me to do? You know I never pulled rank much, but just the same I was a lieutenant-colonel and you were a lousy non-com who tried to—"

"There weren't any Japanese officers' overcoats left on the island then, if there'd ever been any."

"I saw 'em myself. Don't tell me that."

"A couple of guys who had been tailors in civilian life were cutting up those good Japanese blankets and sewing them up into officers' overcoats with fake tabs and stuff and the boys were peddling them to the boats for a hundred and twenty-five bucks apiece, or its equivalent in liquor, which wasn't very much liquor in those days."

"Do you mean that?"

"I mean that. And you bitched up the whole thing hunting for an overcoat cache that was never there. We had plenty of the blankets, but you knew that."

He said, "You're lying. Just for that I'm going to get that piece you wrote. Where are my bags?"

"In the yellow room. Turn right at the head of the stairs and all the way down to the end of the hall."

He went out, climbed the stairs and presently I heard his feet overhead. When he came back he had a yellowing sheet of paper in his hand. "Here," he said, "and if you can read that without laughing you're a better deadpan comic than I am."

The sheet had been cut from a weekly that had gone out of existence in the depression days of the early '30s.

"It's a book review," I said.

"It's a pip," he said.
I read:

Out of that extraordinary chaos of guesses, ambiguities, mountebankery, and vagueness which is Rosicrucian history, Arthur Edward Waite, in *The Brotherhood of the Rosy Cross* (William Rider and Son, London, 1924), has essayed to bring orderly arrangement and evaluation of data. Painstakingly thorough, broadly experienced in mystical research, he has been successful in clearing the shelves of a vast amount of rubbish accumulated by students who in their enthusiasm have seen in each alchemist, each cabalist, each miscellaneous magician, an authentic Brother of the Rosy Cross.

Waite's facts seem always to be facts, although his reading of their implication is not always convincing. Thus, though he shows clearly that there is no actual evidence of the existence of the Rosicrucian order before the appearance, in 1614 and 1615 respectively, of the anonymous *Fama Fraternitatis R ∴ C ∴* and *Confessio Fraternitatis R ∴ C ∴*, and in 1616, of Johann Valentin Andreæ's *Chemical Marriage,* he denies that Andreæ could have been in any way a founder of the order. Supporting this denial, he quotes *Vita ab Ipso Conscripta,* in which Andreæ, listing the *Chemical Marriage* among his writing of the years 1602–1603, characterizes it as a youthful jest that proved prolific of other ridiculous monsters: "a playful delusion, which you may wonder by some was esteemed truthful, and interpreted with much erudition, foolishly enough, and to show the emptiness of the learned."

Waite suggests that the text of the *Chemical Marriage* was interpolated with its Rosicrucian symbolism after its author had read the *Fama* and *Confessio.* He overlooks a more probable alternative that the unknown author or authors of those two manifestoes got their symbolism from the *Chemical Marriage*. That they should have seen it during the fourteen years that elapsed between its composition and the first printing of which we have record is not at all unlikely. In that event, of course, the prevalent theory that Andreæ was the father of Rosicrucianism would be correct, even though his parenthood were the result of a jest. In this connection, there is no reason for thinking that the *Fama* and *Confessio* were excluded from, if not especially included in, the "other ridiculous monsters" of which Andreæ said his pamphlet was prolific.

Notwithstanding his own contrary belief, there is nothing in Waite's arrangement of the evidence to show that a corporate order of Rosicrucians whose members were not consciously imposters existed before the eighteenth century, when the order seems to have grown up side by side—if not more intimately mingled—with Speculative Masonry. In *Clavis Philosophiae et Alchymiae Fluddanae*, 1633, Robert Fludd, who was informed on his subject if anyone was, seems to have summed up the result of seventeen or more years of inquiry in the sentence: "I affirm that every *Theologus* of the Church Mystical is a real Brother of the Rosy Cross, wheresoever he may be and under what obedience soever of the Churches politic." This certainly does not indicate Fludd's acquaintance with any legitimate corporate body.

The Order of the Rosy and Golden Cross organized, or reorganized, by Sigmund Richter in Germany in 1710, undoubtedly became to the best of its members' belief an authentic Rosicrucian order. Thence to the present (Waite gives a chapter to American Rosicrucians) there is evidence of more or less sporadic groups of men who have employed the name and symbols of the Rosy Cross to mean whatever they liked, to further whatever purposes they happened to have, whether alchemical, medical, theosophical, or what not. Of connection between groups, even among contemporaries, of any lineage worthy of the name, there are few traces. The Stone and the Word have meant anything to any man, as he liked.

Waite chooses to discover some continuous thread of mystic purpose running from the inception of Rosicrucianism to the present day. Fortunately he does not tamper with the evidence to support any of his theories. He has cleared away fictions wherever he recognized them, regardless of their import, achieving by this means a scholarly— and as nearly authoritative as is possible in so confused a field—history of a symbol that has fascinated minds of theosophical or occult bent since early in the seventeenth century.

When I finished reading and looked up Tulip said, "You kept your face straight. Don't tell me you liked it."

"Who likes anything they've written in the past? But with the exception of a couple of points . . . Oh, well, I was an erudite fellow back in '24, wasn't I?"

"M-m-m. And you sure-God had your finger right in the hot life-pulse of daily doings too, didn't you? The man in the street must've had a hell of a time trying to figure out which way to jump till that piece came out to put him straight."

"And you figure this evens us up for your dopiness in Kiska?" I asked.

"Well, if you want to play it that way it's all right, of course, but I figured it put me a little ahead."

"Can I have a copy of this? I'd forgotten it."

"You can have that. I don't blame you for wanting to burn it."

"You said you got it from a fellow in San Francisco?"

"A guy named Henkle or something. You know him? He said he used to run around with you."

"I probably know him but don't remember his name. I started to write in San Francisco."

"So he said. He had some stories about you that were pretty good, especially one about you being tied up with a couple of racketeers down in Chinatown and—"

"I remember him now, a fellow named Henley or something that I used to see around the Radio Club. I suppose the racketeers were Bill and Paddy, unless that's just a touch you added."

"I don't add any touches. I just tell you what the man said."

"That's as unlikely a statement as I've ever heard, but all right. That was back in the days when if you ran a joint you had a bodyguard whether you needed one or not, just to rate. Bill had a roly-poly middle-aged Chinese pansy whom he offered to lend me if I had anybody I wanted pushed around—like a leg broken or something—but told me not to spoil him by giving him any money. 'Five or ten dollars is all right as a tip,' he said, 'but don't spoil him by giving him any money.' I wrote the Chinese into a picture in the '30s in Hollywood, but we had a he-man director who wouldn't shoot fags, so we had to change him around."

Tulip nodded. "This Hembry, or whatever his name was, told me about the fairy gunman. He also told me you had a girl named Maggie Dobbs who was engaged to a fellow in Tokyo and—"

"He liked to talk, didn't he?"

"Yes. He had something the matter with his voice and people with something the matter with their voices always like to talk. I guess he was a kind of admirer of yours."

The dogs came in from the kitchen with Donald. The Irongates had two brown poodles and a black one. One of the browns, Jummy, was enormous for a poodle. They came over to play with me awhile and then went back to see how much petting they could get out of Tulip. Donald said good night and took the coffee things away.

Tulip, scratching one of the dog's heads, looked after Donald and said, "He walks good." I remembered that was one of the things Tulip always noticed about people. He himself was a man of only medium height but carried himself so erect he seemed taller in spite of his massive chest and shoulders, walking with a conscious sort of forward thrust as if determined never to be pushed back or caught off balance. Somebody—I think it was his friend Dr. Mawhorter—once said he could have gone anywhere if he had had a compass.

"He used to be a pretty good welter-weight fifteen or sixteen years ago, fought out of Philly under the name of Donny Brown."

"Never heard of him."

"He was pretty good just the same; but he says he didn't have the hands for it and it's a hard way for a Negro to make a living unless he thinks he's going to the top pretty soon or can't do anything else."

"It's a hard way to make a living in Philly no matter what your color is. That's a hard town to get a taxi in, too, isn't it? You have to walk out to the curb and wave your arms at 'em to attract their attention."

The dogs decided they'd got all the attention out of Tulip they were going to get for the moment and left him, Jummy going to lie down in his usual place behind the sofa and Meg settling herself for the night on the floor at the end of the sofa. Cinq, the black, still had some puppy in him, so he started moving from room to room hunting for the ideal spot to lie down, favoring places where he would be in the draft from under a door.

"You've really got troubles," I told Tulip. "Why don't you—" I broke off as a car-horn honked out in the driveway.

Tony Irongate came in lugging a couple of canvas bags. He dropped them in the doorway when the dogs converged on him. He was a smallish wiry boy of fourteen with brown eyes in a bright pale face. "Hi," he said, "what do you hear from Paulie and Gus?"

"They should be home late tomorrow or sometime Wednesday," I said and introduced him to Tulip.

Tony waded through dogs to shake hands with Tulip, then told me, "I got a new crossbow from Mingey Baker. It's got a lot of power but the bolts slip when I aim it down. Can we fix that?"

"It ought to be easy enough."

"Swell. Shall we do it tomorrow? I don't suppose Sexo and Lola have showed up yet."

"Not yet."

"Well, I'm going to get some milk and go to bed. Want anything from the kitchen?"

I said, "No, thanks," and he said, "See you in the morning," to both of us, picked up the canvas bags and went out followed by the dogs.

Tulip asked, "What's this Sexo stuff?"

"That's his nickname for his older sister this month. She's at the age when she wants to know about things and she's been asking questions."

"And you've been answering them. Oh, boy, I can just see you licking your lips and snowing her under with answers. Is she a good lay? Some kids are."

"Now, now, it's nothing like that. This hasn't got anything to do with yes or no. It's on a level you probably wouldn't understand."

"If it's nothing like that, it's a cinch I wouldn't understand it," he agreed. "I'm a yes or no man myself."

"I know," I said, "you're a dominant personality, so you go around thinking you're getting a great deal of variety but really, when you look at it for what it is, it's only masturbating in one way or another, except for a couple of times when you were outsmarted."

He laughed. "I'll have to think that over, which is more than I can say for most of the things you tell me. Do you guess that's why it's dull sometimes, not really dull, but duller than it ought to be?"

"With your mind and your way of operating it ought to be always dull."

"You don't use your mind in that kind of operation, Pop, not if you've got anything else. That's only for writers. Look, while we're on the subject, you once told me a piece of advice you said your mother gave you. Remember?"

"She never gave me but two pieces of advice and they were both good. 'Never go out in a boat without oars, son,' she said, 'even if it's the Queen Mary; and don't waste your time on women who can't cook because they're not likely to be much fun in the other rooms either.'"

"You know your mother was dead and in her grave years before they even thought of building the Queen Mary."

"She was part Scot," I said, "and some of those people can see ahead."

"All right, but it was the other one we were talking about. There's more truth in it than I thought at first, but it's not always right."

"There aren't many things that are always right."

He got up and went over to the corner table. "I'm going to fix up my nightcap now so I can make a quick break for bed if you keep on talking like that. You're a dull bunny when you get philosophical, Pop. Why don't we just keep on talking about poontang?" He came back with his drink and sat down.

"Tulip," I said, "you look to me like a man who wants to tell me about a little girl he met in Boston and—"

"Well, it was actually in Memphis that I first ran into her, but—"

"And I hope I look to you like a man who's not going to listen, but who's about to go up to bed and read awhile before he falls asleep."

"Okay," he said good-naturedly. "I'm in no hurry to get anything off my chest, though this baby I ran across in Memphis couldn't cook worth a damn, just garlic in everything."

"You used to like garlic."

"Sure, I like it, but there's a lot of lousy cooks in this world who think you can make anything good by just slapping enough garlic in it, and then if you kick about it they grin at you like they'd caught you picking a pocket and say, 'Oh, so you don't really like garlic?' What time do you get up in the morning?"

"Around eight this time of the year, but you don't—"

"Call me when you get up. I'll have breakfast with you. Any particular reason for not telling me these Irongates were on their way home?"

"No, just my usual deviousness."

He finished his drink while I put out the lights and we went upstairs together. I went through the motions of looking into his room and bath to see that everything was all right, then said good night and went back to my own room at the other end of the hall. Cinq, the young black poodle, had made himself comfortable near the foot of my bed and after I'd undressed came over for his good-night head-scratch and pat. Then I got into bed and read Samuel's *Essay in Physics* with Einstein's polite letter declining to find anything in the Two-State Ether for a physicist to chew on.

I had meant to think about Tulip afterwards, but I got to thinking about the notion of an expanding universe being only an attempt to bootleg infinity again, and of what rearrangements would be necessary in mathematics if one, the unit, the single item, were not considered a number at all, except perhaps as a convenience in calculating. And presently I was pretty sleepy and put out the light and went to sleep.

Tony was in the dining room when I came down for breakfast, eating kippers and reading one of the newspapers. We said good morning and I sat down with another of the papers. Donald brought me orange juice and then kippers and toast. I was about halfway through my meal when Tulip joined us, and we left him to finish alone while the boy and I went out on the porch to look at the new crossbow he had asked me about the night before.

"It's brutal," Tony said as he handed it to me. "Of

course all of 'em are brutal, but this is really brutal." It was a sort of cross between an arbalest and the thing those fellows in western Pennsylvania used to make out of automobile springs. "It's got all the power in the world, but—see?—the bolt slides down if you tilt it." His dark eyes were very bright. He liked weapons.

"We can fix that with a dingus here to hold the bolt back till you pull the trigger, but I don't know that I'd bother with it. You're not going to shoot down a lot. Why don't you just dab a little piece of Scotch tape across the bolt when you need to hold it there? You can't make any speed loading and cocking these things anyhow and with a little piece of tape I doubt if you'll lose anything in force or accuracy."

"Well, if you really think so," he said slowly, "but—"

I looked down at him. "But maybe I'm just trying to get out of some work? Stop talking like Tulip."

He laughed and said, "Your friend Tulip's a character, isn't he?"

"In a way, but you've got to figure that he and I play games together and you'll probably come out closer to the facts by not believing either of us too exactly. Mostly he tries to make himself out a little worse than he is and I try to make myself out a little better. Old men cutting up old touches do a good deal of that, and a lot of male nonsense anyhow is only to impress women and children when it's not just to impress one another, or maybe themselves."

"You've told me that before," he said.

"That doesn't keep it from having some truth in it somewhere," I said. "Come on, let's take this thing over behind the garage and try it out." We went down off the porch—the screens were not up yet—and across the lawn that had the scrunchiness of early spring underfoot to the gravel road past the garage where the maples looked still a month from flowering. "They're some nice things about Tulip. One of 'em I always liked was about his education. He's a Harvard man, you know."

Tony, walking beside me carrying the crossbow and

the leather bag that went with it, said, "No kidding?" in a tone that I could not quite understand. I did not always understand Tony.

"Yes. I don't know anything about Tulip's family or where he came from—he's told me things I didn't choose to believe—but anyhow he went to Harvard for four years and when they graduated him he took for granted that he was an educated man till he ran into a fellow named Eubanks down in Jacksonville the next year who explained to him that there was more to being an educated man than just going through a university, though that might be a necessary first step. Tulip had never thought of that before, but he believed it when Eubanks explained it to him and said to hell with it and stopped being an educated man."

Tony said, "Hey, I like that too," and we began to zero in the crossbow against a tree stump we had used as target for various weapons before: the ground rose steeply behind it to the hill above the old orchard. This was really a murderous weapon: it hurled its three-inch steel bolts with force and—once we had got the hang of it—accuracy. Tony grinned up at me. "It's okay, isn't it?"

I nodded. "M-m-m."

His grin widened. "And it would be just silly to complain that it's no good for anything at all except this, wouldn't it?"

"It would for us."

He sighed and nodded.

When we got back to the house Tulip was reading a morning newspaper over a cup of coffee in the puce and white ground-floor room that for some reason was called the study, a nice many-windowed booky room that opened on the long end of the lawn that ran out of sight among trees.

He looked up from his newspaper to the crossbow. "Aren't you people backing up on time a little?" he asked. "I read about ray guns and blasters and disintegrators and—"

"Phases," I said, "that defeat themselves in the end, like gunpowder. Want to walk down to the pond?"

"Sure." He finished his coffee and stood up.

I found a mackinaw for him—it was still chilly—and the three of us cut across the lawn to the pond path. Some of the juncos that hadn't yet gone back up north were scratching the ground under a bird-feeder, one of the nuthatches that lived in the black walnut tree was waddling swiftly down its trunk, a chickadee sang out and three of them flew tentatively at us.

"They're looking for sunflower seeds," Tony told Tulip. "He feeds them out of his hand."

"It's the St. Francis streak in him," Tulip said. "He's a doddering old man who's read too much, and he always has been."

The boy laughed up at him: he was walking between us. "Have you ever seen him do his fly-petting act? It's sharp."

"I can imagine," Tulip said. "Pop's really a cute kid in a lot of ways. I wish I could tell you about once in a town out near Spokane—"

"Tony's one of the people we can talk in front of," I said. We were walking along the muddy path then. It was wide enough for us to go abreast. Some of the dogwood looked almost ready to start popping open; it always hangs on the verge for weeks and weeks before anything happens.

"You mean I can tell him about that time out in the Couer d'Alenes?" Tulip asked.

"I don't know what's on your mind, but you can tell him. About the flies, there's nothing much to it. You've seen how they like to scratch their wings. Well, if you're careful not to scare 'em with the shadow of your hand when you start, and you scratch them gently on the wings they like it and will stick around. That's all there is to it."

"Okay," Tulip said. "That's why you think they like it. Now why do you think you like it?"

"In case there's anything to the theory that the insects

will eventually take over the world it might be just as well to have friends among 'em."

"Isn't he a disgusting old fossil?" he asked the boy. He shook his head. "I can remember back when he had hair on it."

Tony said, "You've known each other a long time, haven't you?"

"Long enough, but you don't have to think we're such good friends. It's just that every once in a while he shows up wherever I am and hangs around for a few days. It's never very long."

Tulip said somewhat truculently over the boy's head, "You know when I show up and why I don't stay long."

When I didn't say anything Tony asked, "Do you?"

"He's nuts," I said. "I know, all right, but he's nuts just the same."

"That's easy enough to say," Tulip said indifferently.

"Hey," Tony said, "you said just now I was one of the people you could talk in front of. You're not talking in front of me; wherever you're talking it's certainly not in front of me."

Tulip poked Tony's shoulder with an elbow. "A juvenile wise guy, huh? You punks!" He scowled over the boy's head at me. "Shall we put the whole thing up to the boy and see what he says about it?"

"If you want," I said, "but you ought to know I'm making up my own mind for myself no matter who says what."

"I know that. You're an enemy of democracy."

"Not an enemy, though I don't trust its value much in small groups. Don't go around saying I'm an enemy of democracy, they'll put me in jail again."

"That's something to worry about on gloomy mornings before you've had your coffee. Look, Pop, why don't we approach this thing realistically? I—"

"Realistic is one of those words when it comes into a discussion sensible people pick up their hats and go home," I told Tony. "How'd you make out with that lamp you were going to try?"

He had had an idea—partly out of childish let's-try-and-seeness, partly out of a book on dynamic symmetry his father had around the place, partly out of knowing nobody had too much faith in the currently accepted theories of light—that a sheet of reflecting metal curled at both ends into a sort of right-angle spiral might make an economically valid lampshade. He was ignoring some heat factors, of course, or hoping to take care of them accidentally, but then what theory of lighting doesn't?

"Oh that? I never got around to it."

The dogs caught up to us as we reached the fork in the path—the left running over a hill to the McConnells' new bird sanctuary, the right going down to the pond—made their great momentary fuss over us, and went on scampering ahead, down towards where parts of the pond—all the ice had been gone for a few weeks now—were visible through still-bare trees: most of the evergreens were on the other side. It was an eight- or ten-acre spring-fed pond with a couple of small islands in it—not more than twelve feet deep at its deepest—and some large-mouthed bass, pickerel, sunfish, snakes, frogs and snapping turtles in season. I had never tried eating water snakes, the bass were a little too muddy tasting—from the bottom—for me, but the other things made good eating. The water got too warm in the summer for trout; there's not enough oxygen in warm water for them. I thought again of the likeness of the pond to Tulip's description of the Horris woman's lake, though he had given that a stone dock while this had only a ten-foot canvas-covered wooden pier.

"Heavy paper with aluminum foil pasted on it would be as good as shiny metal," I said. "The main thing's the base and top with spiral grooves in them to guide it. Paper might be better in a way, easier to cut off or paste together when you start finding out what length gives you most light."

"You think I ought to go ahead with it, then? I thought maybe I didn't know enough about what I was doing. I'd kind of like to try it, though, if you think it's all right."

"I think it's worth trying," I said. "Knowing what you're doing is only part of good work. It's using what you know—and not only what you know about the business at hand—to find out things you don't know yet that makes good work. Almost is pretty good as a result: it's only when you get what's known as common sense and start accepting it as a goal that you're in trouble. That's the difference between a carpenter and a man who's really making something."

"My father was a carpenter," Tulip said. "I don't know that I ought to let you talk like that."

"Your father was either a pickpocket or a pimp." We had left the path and were walking over towards the little pier on the edge of the pond. I was looking at Tulip, but couldn't decide whether he looked like a man who had seen this pond before.

"But he wasn't good enough at 'em to make a full-time living that way. Most of the time he had to do carpenter work." He nodded at the pond, looking sidewise at me almost as if he knew what I was thinking. "That lake of Loe's I was telling you about looked kind of like this, except it had a stone dock and the hut was down at the water instead of back aways like this one, and their lake's bigger."

What he called the hut used to be down on the edge of the pond till the Irongates had it moved back on dryer ground, and things were always bigger in Tulip's stories. That left the stone dock.

The dogs were wading in and out of the water in their usual examination of the shore-line. Twenty feet off the end of one island a pair of early-northing Canada geese or brant—I couldn't tell which at that distance—were watching us or the dogs: at this time of the year wild geese had more curiosity than timidity.

"What bothers me most," Tony said, "is the beginning of the spiral's going to be too close to the lightbulb unless the whole thing's too big."

"You're figuring on a lot of spiral," I said, "and you

might need a lot less than you think. Anyhow your light meter will tell you what length's best. If you want something to bother about, maybe your answer's in a three-dimensional spiral and not in the two we're fooling with."

The boy shut his dark eyes, then opened them to ask, "But how do you get light out of your three-dimensional spiral? It traps it, or most of it, doesn't it? And I'm not exactly sure how you hold this spiral—the way you mean it—down to three dimensions."

My mathematics wasn't good enough to answer any of his questions and I said so, adding, "Of course we might not be up against a mathematical problem at all. Folks call topology a branch of mathematics, but I think they're nuts, and we might be headed for topology. I don't mean only us; I mean anybody fooling with light problems."

Tony gave a little gurgle of delight when I said topology, as if I had mentioned an old friend. He used to listen one winter while Gus and I gave dimensions back to the sculptors and spent hours talking about painting having to do with the relationship in space of the surfaces of objects and nothing else. I liked topology: a few years before that I had written a story on a Möbius band, designed to be read from any point in it on around to that point again, and to be a complete and sensible story regardless of where you started. It had worked out pretty well—I don't mean perfectly; what story ever does that? But pretty well.

Tulip was throwing a stick out in the water for Cinq to swim for. The dogs used to swim a good deal till Jummy had to have some growths in his ears cut and water seemed to bother them so he stopped swimming very much and the other two didn't do things he didn't do. Cinq swam out for the stick now—head high out of the water, the way poodles swim even when not clipped for it. Jummy and Meg were wading in and out of the water around a bend in the pond shore.

Tony said to Tulip, slyly, I think, "We had an idea for a lamp, and—"

Tulip, watching the swimming black head, said, "If Pop's in on it it may be interesting in a way but it's impractical, or if it isn't impractical now it will be before he gets through with it. He's a talkative old fellow with theories and'll waste a lot of your time if you let him." He moved off to one side towards where Cinq was coming back with the stick.

"He's sulking," I told the boy.

"Well, you did dodge whatever it was he wanted to talk about when we started out. You kept saying it was all right to talk about, but you dodged it just the same."

"I hoped everybody would notice it," I said.

"It's for your own good," Tulip said, coming back to us. We were sitting on the little pier now and I was lighting a cigarette. "It's nothing to me, or not very much."

"By rights I should get up and run," I told Tony. "That's what the rules tell you to do when anybody says anything's for your own good."

Tulip groaned and sat down beside us, reaching for my cigarettes. "Don't you think anything ever gets tiresome?" he asked. "Scram," he told Cinq who arrived wet with a wet stick in his mouth. The black dog was a nice dog if still mostly puppy and went off a little distance to shake himself and lie down on the grass and chew at the stick. Tulip lit his cigarette from mine and looked over it at me. "All this fal-de-ral is getting us nowhere. It's leaving you just where you were before."

"Is that bad?"

"That's bad," he said with calm certainty, "and you can kid around all you want, but you know it is."

Tony sat crosslegged on the pier and watched us with bright dark eyes that pretended they weren't watching us. He didn't know what he was in the middle of, but he knew he was in the middle and he liked it. He was a nice boy. I suppose most of my talking was done to him and I think Tulip knew it and played it that way. I had always beaten Tulip by not talking, or, at least, by not talking about the things he wished to talk about.

"This time he thinks he's got me cold," I told Tony. "I'm just out of jail. The last of my radio shows went off the air while I was doing my time, and the state and federal people slapped heavy income tax liens on me. Hollywood's out during this red scare. So he figures I'll have to do another book—which doesn't take much figuring—and shows up dragging his lousy dull life behind him for me to write about."

"You'd never get it all in one book," Tulip said simply.

"I'll never get much of it in any book if I can help it," I said not so simply, because I liked Tulip most when he said things like that. "Look," I was talking to Tony again, or perhaps through him to Tulip, "I've been in a couple of wars—or at least in the Army while they were going on—and in federal prisons and I had t.b. for seven years and have been married as often as I chose and have had children and grandchildren and except for one fairly nice but pointless brief story about a lunger going to Tijuana for an afternoon and evening holiday from his hospital near San Diego I've never written a word about any of these things. Why? All I can say is they're not for me. Maybe not yet, maybe not ever. I used to try now and then—and I suppose I tried hard, the way I tried a lot of things—but they never came out meaning very much to me."

"I can see you wouldn't be so good to write about," Tulip said, "but that in a way is what I've been saying right along."

"Well, if I'm not," I asked, "why are you?"

"My God," he said earnestly, "I'm more interesting!"

"I don't think you are, but that's not an arguable point and anyhow hasn't anything to do with what I'm talking about."

Tulip said glumly, "I'm glad one of us knows what you're talking about," and asked Tony, "Do you know what he's talking about?"

The boy shook his head. "But he's getting at something."

Tulip said, "You're young. You've got time to wait

around while he gets at things," and then to me, because he had been thinking about what I said, "What's this about grandchildren? That's new since I saw you last, isn't it?"

"Uh-huh, a girl a couple of years ago and a boy in January—since I got out of the clink. I haven't seen him yet."

"Good stuff, good stuff. They out in California?" and when I had nodded, "The daughter you liked so much?"

"I liked both of my children."

Tulip raised his thick sandy eyebrows at Tony. "A stuffy old fellow sometimes, isn't he?" He turned back to me. "I'm an illiterate; you'll have to explain to me why being a more interesting character doesn't make me better to write about. You don't have to explain it, but you'll have to if you want me to understand you."

"Let's try it this way," I said to or through the boy. "I'm in a lung hospital in 1920, out in a converted Indian school on Puyallup Road in the fringes of Tacoma, Washington. Most of us were what came to be known as disabled veterans of World War I, but the Veterans Administration hadn't any hospitals of its own in those days—maybe hadn't even been organized under that name—so the United States Public Health Service took care of us in its hospitals. In this one about half of us were lungers; the other half what was then called shell shock victims, segregated as far as sleeping quarters and eating were concerned because I suppose some sort of control was kept over them—we didn't have much—and because they might catch t.b. from us. It was a nice sloppily run hospital and I think most of us who took it easy beat the disease—it's the lungers I'm talking about; I don't know how the shell shocks (goofs in our language) made out—while the more conscientious ones, those who chased the cure, died of it. The major in charge of the hospital was reputed to be a lush, but I don't remember any evidence of that. I remember, though, that he was afraid of the newly formed American Legion and we used that to beat him over the

head with whenever he tried to get strict, though I think
most of us belonged to another organization called the
Disabled Veterans. Our standard defense against any and
all attempts to impose anything approaching control over
us was the statement—made sulkily or triumphantly,
mumbled or shouted, depending on who made it and what
the circumstances were—*We're not in the Army now!* Our
doctors and nurses—most of them freshly out of the Army
themselves—got pretty tired of hearing it, but it was a
long long time before we got tired of saying it. We got
either eighty or sixty dollars a month compensation from
the government—I can't remember the exact figure—
though I suppose it must have varied with our degree of
sickness, since thermometers were called compensation
sticks; enough free cigarettes to help out, though not
enough to keep a reasonably heavy smoker fully supplied;
free room and board, of course; and we didn't need many
clothes. It wasn't a bad life. All liquor was bootleg then—
except for the occasional snort you could wheedle out of a
nurse or doctor—and the stuff we bought was pretty bad
but it was strong; lights were put out at probably ten
o'clock, but the room I shared with a kid from Snohomish
had been a matron's room in the old Indian-school days
and was on the same electric light circuit as the toilet, so
we had only to hang a blanket over the window to play
poker as late as we wished; as I remember it we came into
and went out of the hospital as we liked, needing a pass
only for overnight trips to Seattle and such, though there
may have been certain times we were supposed to be on
hand. Anyhow most of us found it a lot better than working for a living. Sometimes we were broke: I remember
Whitey Kaiser—a powerfully built squat blond Alaskan
with most of the diseases known to man; he could hit like
a pile driver, but his knucklebones would crumble like
soda crackers—borrowing a blackjack from me—I had
come to the hospital from working for a detective agency
in Spokane and you're always picking up things like that
when you're young—and giving it back to me the next
morning with ten bucks. When I read in an afternoon

paper about a man being slugged and robbed of a hundred and eighty dollars on the Puyallup Road—it ran from Tacoma to Seattle—the night before, I showed it to Whitey, who said people who were robbed always exaggerated the amounts. Sometimes we were flush: there was a lean hatchet-faced dark boy named Gladstone who finally got his bonus from the Army—a sizable sum, though I don't remember the amount any more—and spent it all for two used cars and the collected works of James Gibbons Huneker because he wanted culture and I'd told him Huneker had it. Most of the time we were bored. I suppose we bored pretty easily. I don't mean we were badly bored—though we may have been sometimes —but just bored. The weather out there's pretty good, you know. It rains at least once every day from September to May, but seldom very hard, and it doesn't get very cold, so you don't have to bother with an overcoat, but just automatically take a raincoat along when you go out and—"

The three dogs from three different places began barking and racing for the path along which we had come, vanishing noisily around a bend.

I said, "Visitors," while Tony was saying, "Do and Lola, I guess," and Tulip threw his cigarette end out on the water to hiss and dissolve.

Presently the three poodles came scampering back around the path's bend with the two Irongate girls walking behind them. Do was a lean blondish girl of sixteen, Lola a dark-eyed dark-haired pink-cheeked very pretty plump girl of twelve. Lola looked like her father and Tony, Do didn't look like anybody I'd seen though I'd been told—everybody has to take after somebody in most families—she resembled one of her aunts. They exchanged "Hi's" with Tony, kissed me and shook hands with Tulip.

Lola said, "Those people will be home this evening." She was excited.

Do said, "They'd never think of telling us whether they mean for dinner or afterwards." She was excited.

Tony said, "Now it's dinner we've got to worry about." He was excited.

I said it was fine, which it was because I hadn't seen the senior Irongates since I got out of prison: they had simply sent me word that the house and any money I needed was mine and they would be back from Florida as soon as Gus finished his painting chores there.

Tulip caught my eye, mutely asking if he would be in the way. I started to shake my head no, thought better—or anyhow differently: why should I make him think I wanted him to stay?—of it and shrugged.

Lola sat down on the pier close to me and asked hopefully, "Are we butting in on anything?" She wore darkblue ski pants and a short scarlet coat.

I said, "No."

Tulip, sitting down again, said, "I guess Pop was telling the story of his life; I don't know."

Do said, "Pop?" and then to me, "Oh, you," and laughed. She had a nice firm-lipped smile. "I like that," she told Tulip.

Lola leaned against me and said, "I want to hear the story of your life, Pop."

"You won't hear it from me, honey."

"You call everybody honey."

"I used to call everybody darling," I said, "but now I think honey's more refined."

Do said, "We are interrupting, aren't we?" She still stood, looking taller and leaner than she was in a long brown polo coat a couple of sizes too large for her. "Aren't we, Tony?"

Her brother, glancing first at me, said, "Well, yes."

"You're not doing anything," Tulip said. "If Pop wants to go ahead with what he was saying he'll go ahead. If he doesn't he'll pretend you interrupted him. Sit down and leave it up to him."

Do sat down.

Tony said, "You were at the part where you were bored and it was raining."

"Well the rain didn't mean very much," I said. "It wasn't that kind of rain. And I don't suppose the boredom

meant a lot either. None of us had been out of the Army
very long and we must have been used to it. This," I
explained to Lola and Do, "was a lung hospital out in
Tacoma right after the First World War. The last time I
saw Pavlova dance was that time in Tacoma, though that
hasn't anything to do with anything. About the boredom,
I'm not even sure I remember it. Maybe I just know that
we must've been. Somebody told the citizens of Tacoma
they were neglecting us and for two or three Sundays we
had visitors. Atrocity stories were popular then—especially
the ones that had to do with soldiers' tongues being cut
out—and we used to persuade hospital orderlies to sit in
wheel chairs and let us push them up to gullible visitors to
curdle their blood—or make them happy, which was often
the same thing—with the most fantastic horrors we could
think of.

"An ex-Marine named Bizzarri and I were pretty good
friends. There's a gag that for God knows how many years
or decades or centuries has been banging around lumber
and construction camps—any place men have to work and
live together and get tired of it—where two men build up
a fake animosity leading to a climactic fist fight—or gun
fight or knife fight, depending on where it is—and then
instead of fighting laugh at the assembled audience and go
off arm in arm. Well, this Bizzarri and I built up one of
those things, nursing it along carefully until we had most
of the hospital intensely interested, some taking one side,
some the other, in this thing that had happened to two
once-close friends; and we went out for our final violent
showdown and took a couple of pokes at each other that
were on the borderline between fake and real, but were
both too intelligent to pass up our laugh by going at it in
earnest, so we stopped in time to get our laugh, but were
never very good friends after that.

"A Filipino whose name I've forgotten was studying to
be a crooked gambler—in civilian life he seems to have
lost his wages each Saturday night in a Chinese gambling
joint—and had a deck of marked cards that we used to let

him sneak into the poker game once in a while, since most of us knew the markings better than he did. He got into a fight once—crooked gamblers have to be very touchy on points of honor—and his opponent had to wait while the Filipino went to his room for a pair of kid gloves, to protect his skin, I suppose, since they weren't weighted in the palms, had no stitching to amount to anything and were a little too tight to let him close his hands into effective fists. We liked things of those sorts, so I guess we were bored."

I was floundering a little now. Talking through Tony had seemed to make things easier for me, as Tulip had probably known, but I hadn't been able to find the key to this new combination. I don't mean that Do and Lola were likely to be an unsympathetic audience. They weren't. They liked me, and jail had even given me glamor, but what I was talking about—or trying to talk about—hadn't anything to do with that. A better talker would probably have gone on as before, ignoring them, but I had—or thought I had—to find some way of including them. I could have broken off, of course, waiting to go on when I had Tony and Tulip to myself again, but I suppose I felt like talking. So I went on, doing the best I could to tie them in along the way.

"Then the government opened, or reopened, a hospital down near San Diego—the old Army hospital in what had been Camp Kearney—and fourteen of us were transferred down there, mostly the undesirable cut-ups, I reckon. We went down in a private sleeping car, picking up a few more members at Portland. We had a couple among us who thought, or said, they were hopheads, a one-legged chap named Austen—they thought he had a tubercular infection of the bone and kept whittling pieces off his leg—and an ugly redhead named Quade with tubercular intestines. Whitey and I were broke, but among his diseases he had something wrong with his kidneys and the doctor at Tacoma had given him some white powders to take, folded up in bundles just like dope, so we peddled them to

Austen and Quade throughout the trip and they sniffed
them and got—or thought they got—a good bang out of
them all the way to San Diego. In the Camp Kearney
hospital we ran into our enemy—regulations. We got there
late at night and were awakened at an early hour by a
night orderly who wanted urine specimens before he went
off duty. That was easy, of course: we told him where to
go for his urine specimens and went back to sleep and he
went off-duty without the specimens. Then we found out
that not only would we have to have passes to leave the
hospital—Tijuana, wide open just across the border, had
been a major reason for our willingness to come here:
Agua Caliente hadn't been opened yet—but they were
issued only stingily, and, on top of that, we as newcomers
would have to spend two weeks in a quarantine ward
before we were eligible for anything, even for permission
to wander around the hospital. So we revolted happily and
announced that we were leaving the hospital for San
Diego. The management had us over for a conference, cut
the quarantine period to ten days, as I now remember it,
but stuck to the other rules, and we went outside for our
own conference, by this time most of us cheerfully looking
forward to San Diego and Tijuana with the local Red
Cross to throw ourselves on when we were broke. And
then up the duckwalk past us came one of the hospital's
civilian employees, a pretty little girl in a striped shirtwaist
and dark skirt with nice legs in silk stockings that had a run
up the back of one, and our revolt went blooey: we decided maybe the hospital wouldn't be so bad after all—
and we could always leave when we wanted to—and sent
Whitey, who had become our spokesman by now, in to tell
the commanding officer we were staying. (None of us ever
got anywhere with the pretty little girl; I'm not sure any of
us tried very hard.) One of us—I've forgotten which—had
by this time got himself sincerely convinced there was
some principle involved in our revolt and vanished San
Diegoward. The rest of us settled down to the new routine
of a new hospital. Whitey wasn't with us long; after a few

weeks he and another chap came back from the city pretty tight one night and he slugged a doctor—I think because the doctor had given Whitey's companion a shot of apomorphine for his drunkenness—and got thrown out. There was some talk about our leaving with him, but nothing came of it and he went on his way.

"The hospital was on the edge of a desert, so there were horned toads to make pets of, and battles between rattlesnakes and Gila monsters to stage in an empty boxcar on a nearby unused railroad track—the Gila monsters always won, but most of the sucker money backed the rattlers at first, and when there was no rattler money to be had we stopped staging the fights—and there was Tijuana to hit every couple of weeks. I still don't remember much about San Diego except that it was nice to look at riding downhill towards it between pink and pale-blue stucco houses, the U.S. Grant Hotel and the tonic stores where in those Prohibition days you bought and drank from a great variety of high-alcohol-content patent medicines. I suppose I read a good deal in the hospital, but I can't remember a single thing I read there. I know I had a good time in Camp Kearney, but when the races closed at Tijuana—in May, I think—I asked for a discharge from the hospital and they gave it to me. They couldn't say I was an arrested case—I didn't finally lick my t.b. until five or six years later—so they wrote *maximum improvement reached* and let me go."

When I stopped talking to light a cigarette Lola asked, "Where'd you go?"

Tony said, "Sh-h-h," to her.

"Back to Spokane, because they gave me a railroad ticket there and I wanted to see some people, then over to Seattle for a week or two—it was a noisy city but I liked it then—and down to San Francisco for what I meant to be at most a two-month stay before going home to Baltimore. But I stayed in San Francisco seven or eight years, and never did get back to Baltimore except on short visits. But what I'm getting at is," I was talking to Tony and Tulip again, "that out of all this I got only one brief and fairly

pointless story about a quiet lunger going to Tijuana for a
placid day's outing. And that's more writing material than
I got out of wars and prisons. And you"—to Tulip—"can
only bring me that kind of stuff: in one way or another
your whole lousy life's been like that, which may be fine
and dandy but it's not for me. I don't know what to do
with it."

"As a matter of fact," Tulip said, "I've never had t.b.
and the three guys I remember called Whitey were different from yours, though one of them managed a semi-pro
ball team I played third base on one summer and gypped
us out of our share. But I can see why none of the things
that happened to you were any good. They were happening to the wrong guy. You've got to think everything
comes through the mind, and of course things get dull
when you reason the bejesus out of 'em that way." He
looked at Tony. "Isn't that right, kid?"

Tony looked at Tulip and at me and didn't say anything.

"You and your immature emotions that can't bear the
weight of sense," I said somewhat didactically because I
was tired of this accusation. "No feeling can be very strong
if it has to be shielded from reason. Drunken wife-beaters
crying over a lame bird."

Lola asked, "What about this Whitey that managed
the baseball team?"

Tony sh-h-hed her again.

Tulip said, "I don't always know what you're talking
about, Pop. But couldn't you just write things down the
way they happen and let your reader get what he wants
out of 'em?"

"Sure, that's one way of writing, and if you're careful
enough in not committing yourself you can persuade
different readers to see all sorts of different meanings in
what you've written, since in the end almost anything can
be symbolic of anything else, and I've read a lot of stuff of
that sort and liked it, but it's not my way of writing and
there's no use pretending it is."

"You whittle everything down to too sharp a point,"

Tulip said. "I didn't say you ought to let your reader run hog-wild on you like that, though I can't see any objections to letting them do your work for you if they want to, but—"

"Not enough want to to make it profitable," I said, "though you're likely to get nice reviews."

"Money, money," Tulip said, which would have been funny from him except that we were arguing and in arguments you are inclined to say things that will help your side win.

"Sure, money," I said. "When you write you want fame, fortune and personal satisfaction. You want to write what you want to write and to feel that it's good and to sell millions of copies of it and have everybody whose opinion you value think it's good, and you want this to go on for hundreds of years. You're not likely to ever get all these things, and you're not likely to give up writing or commit suicide if you don't, but that is—and should be—your goal. Anything less is kind of piddling."

Do, who was seriously preparing herself for approaching womanhood and thought that women tried to keep men from quarreling, said, "I told Donald we'd have an early lunch. Is that all right?" while Tony scowled at her.

I said, "It's all right with me," and looked at my wristwatch: 11:54. "Want to go back to the house now?"

Tulip said, "Pop, did I ever tell you there were certain points on which I don't see exactly eye to eye with you?" as we stood up.

The dogs had disappeared into the woods beyond the pond. We went back up the path with Tulip and Do ahead, Lola, Tony and I walking abreast behind them. When we were past the old stone pumphouse—now a smokehouse—and cutting across the back lawn towards the house, Tony said, "You didn't finish what you were getting at, did you?"

"No, I'm not sure I got at it at all. I think I got myself sidetracked. Roughly speaking, there are two kinds of thinking in the world: that you use to try to make points, win arguments with, and that you use to find out things. We'll try it again sometime."

Lola asked, "Can I listen?"

I said, "Sure," with Tony giving me a quick smile because he thought I didn't mean it.

I got to thinking then about the first time I had ever seen Tulip, at Mary Mawhorter's house in Baltimore in 1930. I had gone down to Baltimore for a week on my way from New York to my first job in Hollywood—my father was still alive then and my sister lived in Baltimore too— and had of course looked up Mary, who was now a pediatrician, and Tulip was one of the people at her house the night I went over there. He was bossing a gang of Negro stevedores, I think, on the Sparrow's Point piers of the Pennsylvania Railroad, and the way I remember it is that he had been a third baseman in the Yankee farm system but had quit because there was no future in that line of work as long as Red Rolfe held on. However, Red Rolfe didn't come up to the Yankees till later and must have still been playing shortstop at Dartmouth when I first met Tulip, so the chances are I'm getting Tulip mixed up with an Army sergeant I ran into on the rifle range at Sea Girt in 1942. I drank a lot in those days, partly because I was still confused by the fact that people's feelings and talk and actions didn't have much to do with one another, and a great many of my memories are hazy. The Red Rolfe pattern fits Tulip, though, even if the dates let him out.

He liked Mary—she was a tall white-skinned brunette and very attractive and nice—but, out of male vanity or his kind of humor, was trying to get to her the hard way and not at that time making much progress. She was a good-humored girl but she took her profession very seriously and he didn't. He said he needed a physical examination and wanted to come to her as a patient and she said she didn't treat grown-ups and anyhow he only wanted to "play doctor" with her and that was kid stuff, and they made this their principal bone of bantering contention at the moment. She talked about him a good deal when I went back to her place later after the others had gone. She always talked a good deal and never used a three-syllable word if she could find a four-syllable one to take its place—that professional jargon you get a lot of from doctors and from others who think there is something esoteric about their line of work—but she was nice and didn't mind if you just lay there and smoked a cigarette and said, "Uh-huh," once in a while and let her babble on. She was a nice girl. She seemed to like Tulip.

He was then in his late twenties—just a couple of years older than Mary—and already had the idea that his life had been interesting and somebody ought to write about it. I didn't mind that so much because I had been writing for eight years and was used to people telling me stories and plots and things, to which I would pretend to listen politely while thinking of something else, but I suppose I was still a little touchy about the common notion that all writers had to be pallid bookkeeperish folk sitting at desks doing paper work, and it seemed to me that this husky youngster was putting it on pretty thick and rubbing it in, so we didn't get along very well. It wasn't so much that I was quarrelsome when I drank as that I forgot not to be. I don't know whether he was drunk, too; people have to be pretty drunk for me to notice it, even now that I don't drink.

This is how I remember the significant part of what was done and said that night, though it was a long time ago and I don't know how much I may have changed things around to make me look better or to prove my case. Anyhow, there were perhaps a dozen people there and after I got through the introductory bows and handshakes and words Mary left in a corner with Tulip while she went to get us something to drink, and he said, "So this is your home town, huh?"

"Yes. I grew up here except for a little while in Philadelphia, though I was born down in the southern part of the state."

"Been away long?"

"Ten or eleven years, I guess."

"You'll find it a pretty dull town now."

"It was then."

"But it's uglier now," he said and I asked, "What town isn't?" and he said, "But that isn't what I want to talk to you about," so I knew he wanted to talk to me about something.

Mary came back with our drinks then and a little brown-eyed girl from Catonsville who said she wanted me to look up a friend of hers in Pasadena but kept talking to me for Tulip's benefit. She finally wandered away and he said, "Look. You write and I don't, but you come pretty close to being my kind of writer and I'd like to talk to you."

That was all right. I liked Tulip and still like him, though not as much as he supposes.

"I get around a lot more than you do," he said, "and I see a lot of things."

It stopped being all right. In the first place I didn't think he got around much more than I did, and in the second place even then I didn't think that was the answer unless you wanted to write railroad time-tables from actual experience. Everybody has twenty-four hours a day, no more and seldom less, and one way of putting in the time seems as filling to me as another, depending of course on your own nature, so I said, "Yes?" and began to look around the room.

"Look," he insisted, "I don't mean you just know libraries and colleges and things. I wouldn't be picking on you if you were that kind of a writer. But I've got a lot of stuff in here," and he actually thumped his chest.

I thumped my head. "Then find a writer with a lot of stuff in here," I advised him, "and you'll make a good pair."

He said, "Oh, for God's sake," disgustedly and Mary, who could see we were not making out together very well, came over to see how we were making out. "Your friend is kind of touchy," he told her.

"Your friend is kind of touching," I told her.

Mary laughed and put a long white arm around each of us. "Want to tell me?"

I said, "No," and Tulip said, "No," and then he said to me, "Let me give you an example, tell you one of these things so you'll see what I mean."

"If it's not too gruesome why don't you let him tell you?" Mary said, and I knew she was being very earnest about something because she hadn't used any word with more than two syllables in it and only one of those, and that wasn't her natural way of talking. "Here, I'll get you something to drink," and she took our glasses and went away.

I said, "All right, then," and he told me the first of the many stories he told me or tried to tell me from then on.

This one was about some poor people in Providence who all seemed to have the right kind of feelings about everything that happened to them or around them, and a lot happened, but they kept having the proper feelings so none of it meant very much to me. Mary came back with our drinks and stood listening to the last two-thirds of the story. Tulip didn't say anything when he had finished telling it and neither did she.

"It's nice," I said, "but isn't it kind of literary?"

Tulip's face reddened a little, it seemed to me, under the deep sunburn he had got working on the docks, and he said, "I guess I did dress it up a little, maybe too much," and then when I didn't say anything, "But it really did happen, you know," and then when I still didn't say anything, "How do I know how much to dress things up?"

Mary said to me, "It's not necessary to be so insufferable," which was closer to her normal way of talking and made me think she had been anxious for me to listen to Tulip, but didn't care much one way or the other what I thought about him.

"What do you want?" I asked them.

Mary laughed and said, "You know what I want. Hand it down," while Tulip scowled at me and ran a big thick-fingered hand back through his hair. "How long are you going to be in town?" he asked.

"Three or four days more. Maybe a day or two after that, though I'd like to get out to Santa Monica to see my kids."

"How many have you got?" he asked.

"Two. A boy of eight and the girl must be about four now. A lot of people stop when they've got one of each."

The Catonsville girl came over and said, "You're two such nice men and here you've been hiding in this corner all evening just talking to each other." She said it mostly to me and mostly for Tulip, so I let him have her presently, moving away with Mary.

Tulip called after us, "I can get hold of you through the doctor, can't I?"

Mary and I nodded yes, and I asked her, "What's eating him?"

She shook her head. "It's difficult to conceive of anything eating him. I should imagine that what engaged him back there was his preoccupation with congruity. He devotes considerable attention to the various theories that a somewhat consecutive—though not necessarily chronological—course of events—no matter how dissimilar they may seem—gives life—or any life, for that matter, including perhaps most importantly his own—a—or it may be the—form. But nothing's exactly eating him."

"Oh," I said, "and he wants me to sort out the beads and string them for him?"

"You or somebody."

"What does he suppose people try to do with their own lives?"

"Surely you're not naïve enough to expect people to have any conception of what occupies other people or even to possess any awareness that other people have any interior occupations," she said, and she was pretty enough and I'd had enough to drink to make what she said seem sensible to me, so I changed the subject and we began to talk about us, and that was nice, and then some other people joined us or we joined them, and that was nice too. Everything was nice at that time.

Later Tulip found me in a small sort of sitting-room

affair in the back second-story—Mary had an old three-story house just off Cathedral Street—with a small semi-blonde girl named Mrs. Hatcher or something of the sort, and after she had gone away he said, "I wanted to talk to you, but I didn't mean to bust up anything."

"To tell you the truth, I don't know whether you did or you didn't."

"Oh, all right, then," he said and sat down, and started to offer me a cigarette and saw I had one, and I refilled the semi-blonde's glass and gave it to him. This was the Prohibition era, of course, and Baltimore seemed to be drinking more Scotch and less rye than I remembered. "We don't get along, do we?" he said after he had taken a drink, "and it's a shame because I think we could do each other a lot of good."

I must have shrugged then—I always liked to shrug—and said something about one of the nice things about being a man was that mankind could survive anything.

"Sure, sure," he said. "I'm not saying it's important. I'm just saying it's a shame, not even a big shame if that bothers you, but a little one like only having brown shoes to wear with blue pants."

I didn't believe him—or I don't now, and it's now that I'm trying to remember what went on at that time—so I kept quiet except for whatever noises I made breathing or smoking. I don't mean that I didn't believe what he said, but I didn't believe that he felt it, and even back then, the first time I met him, and full of alcohol as I was, I had a wary feeling that he might come to represent a side of me. His being a side of me was all right, of course, since everybody is in some degree an aspect of everybody else or how would anybody ever hope to understand anything about anybody else? But representations seemed to me—at least they seem now, and I suppose I must have had some inkling of the same opinion then, devices of the old and tired, or older and more tired—to ease up, like conscious symbolism, or graven images. If you are tired you ought to rest, I think, and not try to fool yourself and your customers with colored bubbles.

[Tulip was never completed and the manuscript ends here. But Hammett evidently wrote the very end of the book, and this is it, *L.H.*]

Two or three months later I heard Tulip was in a Minneapolis hospital, where he had had a leg amputated. I went out to see him and showed him this.

"It's all right, I guess," he said when he had read it, "but you seem to have missed the point."

People nearly always think that.

"But I'll read it again if you want me to," he added. "I hurried through it this first time, but I'll read it again kind of carefully if you want me to."

THE BIG KNOCKOVER

I found Paddy the Mex in Jean Larrouy's dive.

Paddy—an amiable conman who looked like the King of Spain—showed me his big white teeth in a smile, pushed a chair out for me with one foot, and told the girl who shared his table, "Nellie, meet the biggest-hearted dick in San Francisco. This little fat guy will do anything for anybody, if only he can send 'em over for life in the end." He turned to me, waving his cigar at the girl: "Nellie Wade, and you can't get anything on her. She don't have to work—her old man's a bootlegger."

She was a slim girl in blue—white skin, long green eyes, short chestnut hair. Her sullen face livened into beauty when she put a hand across the table to me, and we both laughed at Paddy.

"Five years?" she asked.

"Six." I corrected.

"Damn!" said Paddy, grinning and hailing a waiter. "Some day I'm going to fool a sleuth."

So far he had fooled all of them—he had never slept in a hoosegow.

I looked at the girl again. Six years before, this Angel Grace Cardigan had buncoed half a dozen Philadelphia boys out of plenty. Dan Morey and I had nailed her, but none of her victims would go to bat against her, so she had been turned loose. She was a kid of nineteen then, but already a smooth grifter.

In the middle of the floor one of Larrouy's girls began to sing "Tell Me What You Want and I'll Tell You What You Get." Paddy the Mex tipped a gin bottle over the glasses of ginger ale the waiter had brought. We drank and I gave Paddy a piece of paper with a name and address penciled on it.

"Itchy Maker asked me to slip you that," I explained. "I saw him in the Folsom big house yesterday. It's his mother, he says, and he wants you to look her up and see if she wants anything. What he means, I suppose, is that you're to give her his cut from the last trick you and he turned."

"You hurt my feelings," Paddy said, pocketing the paper and bringing out the gin again.

I downed the second gin-ginger ale and gathered in my feet, preparing to rise and trot along home. At that moment four of Larrouy's clients came in from the street. Recognition of one of them kept me in my chair. He was tall and slender and all dolled up in what the well-dressed man should wear. Sharp-eyed, sharp-faced, with lips thin as knife-edges under a small pointed mustache—Bluepoint Vance. I wondered what he was doing three thousand miles away from his New York hunting-grounds.

While I wondered I put the back of my head to him, pretending interest in the singer, who was now giving the customers "I Want to Be a Bum." Beyond her, back in a corner, I spotted another familiar face that belonged in another city—Happy Jim Hacker, round and rosy Detroit gunman twice sentenced to death and twice pardoned.

When I faced front again, Bluepoint Vance and his three companions had come to rest two tables away. His back was to us. I sized up his playmates.

Facing Vance sat a wide-shouldered young giant with red hair, blue eyes and a ruddy face that was good-looking in a tough, savage way. On his left was a shifty-eyed dark girl in a floppy hat. She was talking to Vance. The red-haired giant's attention was all taken by the fourth member of the party, on his right. She deserved it.

She was neither tall nor short, thin nor plump. She wore a black Russian tunic affair, green-trimmed and hung with silver dinguses. A black fur coat was spread over the chair behind her. She was probably twenty. Her eyes were blue, her mouth red, her teeth white, the hair-ends showing under her black-green-and-silver turban were brown, and she had a nose. Without getting steamed up over the details, she was nice. I said so. Paddy the Mex agreed with a "That's what," and Angel Grace suggested that I go over and tell Red O'Leary I thought her nice

"Red O'Leary the big bird?" I asked, sliding down in my seat so I could stretch a foot under the table between Paddy and Angel Grace. "Who's his nice girl friend?"

"Nancy Regan, and the other one's Sylvia Yount."

"And the slicker with his back to us?" I probed.

Paddy's foot, hunting the girl's under the table, bumped mine.

"Don't kick me, Paddy," I pleaded. "I'll be good. Anyway, I'm not going to stay here to be bruised. I'm going home."

I swapped so-longs with them and moved toward the street, keeping my back to Bluepoint Vance.

At the door I had to step aside to let two men come in. Both knew me, but neither gave me a tumble—Sheeny Holmes (not the old-timer who staged the Moose Jaw looting back in the buggy-riding days) and Denny Burke,

Baltimore's King of Frog Island. A good pair—neither of them would think of taking a life unless assured of profit and political protection.

Outside, I turned down toward Kearny Street, strolling along, thinking that Larrouy's joint had been full of crooks this one night, and that there seemed to be more than a sprinkling of prominent visitors in our midst. A shadow in a doorway interrupted my brainwork.

The shadow said, "Ps-s-s-s!"

Stopping, I examined the shadow until I saw it was Beno, a hophead newsie who had given me a tip now and then in the past—some good, some phony.

"I'm sleepy," I growled as I joined Beno and his arm-load of newspapers in the doorway, "and I've heard the story about the Mormon who stuttered, so if that's what's on your mind, say so, and I'll keep going."

"I don't know nothin' about no Mormons," he protested, "but I know somethin' else."

"Well?"

"'S all right for you to say 'Well,' but what I want to know is, what am I gonna get out of it?"

"Flop in the nice doorway and go shut-eye," I advised him, moving toward the street again. "You'll be all right when you wake up."

"Hey! Listen, I got somethin' for you. Hones' to Gawd!"

"Well?"

"Listen!" He came close, whispering. "There's a caper rigged for the Seaman's National. I don't know what's the racket, but it's real . . . Hones' to Gawd! I ain't stringin' you. I can't give you no monickers. You know I would if I knowed 'em. Hones' to Gawd. Gimme ten bucks. It's worth that to you, ain't it? This is straight dope—hones' to Gawd!"

"Yeah, straight from the nose-candy!"

"No! Hones' to Gawd! I—"

"What *is* the caper, then?"

"I don't know. All I got was that the Seaman's is gonna be nicked. Hones' to—"

"Where'd you get it?"

Beno shook his head. I put a silver dollar in his hand.

"Get another shot and think up the rest of it," I told him, "and if it's amusing enough I'll give you the other nine bucks."

I walked on down to the corner, screwing up my forehead over Beno's tale. By itself, it sounded like what it probably was—a yarn designed to get a dollar out of a trusting gumshoe. But it wasn't altogether by itself. Larrouy's—just one drum in a city that had a number—had been heavy with grifters who were threats against life and property. It was worth a look-see, especially since the insurance company covering the Seaman's National Bank was a Continental Detective Agency client.

Around the corner, twenty feet or so along Kearny Street, I stopped.

From the street I had just quit came two bangs—the reports of a heavy pistol. I went back the way I had come. As I rounded the corner I saw men gathering in a group up the street. A young Armenian—a dapper boy of nineteen or twenty—passed me, going the other way, sauntering along, hands in pockets, softly whistling "Brokenhearted Sue."

I joined the group—now becoming a crowd—around Beno. Beno was dead, blood from two holes in his chest staining the crumpled newspapers under him.

I went up to Larrouy's and looked in. Red O'Leary, Bluepoint Vance, Nancy Regan, Sylvia Yount, Paddy the Mex, Angel Grace, Denny Burke, Sheeny Holmes, Happy Jim Hacker—not one of them was there.

Returning to Beno's vicinity, I loitered with my back to a wall while the police arrived, asked questions, learned nothing, found no witnesses, and departed, taking what was left of the newsie with them.

I went home and to bed.

* * *

In the morning I spent one hour in the Agency file room, digging through the gallery and records. We didn't have anything on Red O'Leary, Denny Burke, Nancy Regan, Sylvia Yount, and only some guesses on Paddy the Mex. Nor were there any open jobs definitely chalked against Angel Grace, Bluepoint Vance, Sheeny Holmes and Happy Jim Hacker, but their photos were there. At ten o'clock—bank opening time—I set out for the Seaman's National, carrying these photos and Beno's tip.

The Continental Detective Agency's San Francisco office is located in a Market Street office building. The Seaman's National Bank occupies the ground floor of a tall gray building in Montgomery Street, San Francisco's financial center. Ordinarily, since I don't like even seven blocks of unnecessary walking, I would have taken a streetcar. But there was some sort of traffic jam on Market Street, so I set out afoot, turning off along Grand Avenue.

A few blocks of walking, and I began to see that something was wrong with the part of town I was heading for. Noises for one thing—roaring, rattling, explosive noises. At Sutter Street a man passed me, holding his face with both hands and groaning as he tried to push a dislocated jaw back in place. His cheek was scraped red.

I went down Sutter Street. Traffic was in a tangle that reached to Montgomery Street. Excited, bare-headed men were running around. The explosive noises were clearer. An automobile full of policemen when down past me, going as fast as traffic would let it. An ambulance came up the street, clanging its gong, taking to the sidewalks where the traffic was worst.

I crossed Kearny Street on the trot. Down the other side of the street two patrolmen were running. One had his gun out. The explosive noises were a drumming chorus ahead.

Rounding into Montgomery Street, I found few sight-seers ahead of me. The middle of the street was filled with trucks, touring cars, taxis—deserted there. Up in the next block—between Bush and Pine Streets—hell was on a holiday.

The holiday spirit was gayest in the middle of the block, where the Seaman's National Bank and the Golden Gate Trust Company faced each other across the street.

For the next six hours I was busier than a flea on a fat woman.

Late that afternoon I took a recess from bloodhounding and went up to the office for a powwow with the Old Man. He was leaning back in his chair, staring out the window, tapping on his desk with the customary long yellow pencil.

A tall, plump man in his seventies, this boss of mine, with a white-mustached, baby-pink, grandfatherly face, mild blue eyes behind rimless spectacles, and no more warmth in him than a hangman's rope. Fifty years of crook-hunting for the Continental had emptied him of everything except brains and a soft-spoken, gently smiling shell of politeness that was the same whether things went good or bad—and meant as little at one time as another. We who worked under him were proud of his cold-bloodedness. We used to boast that he could spit icicles in July, and we called him Pontius Pilate among ourselves, because he smiled politely when he sent us out to be crucified on suicidal jobs.

He turned from the window as I came in, nodded me to a chair, and smoothed his mustache with the pencil. On his desk the afternoon papers screamed the news of the Seaman's National Bank and Golden Gate Trust Company double-looting in five colors.

"What is the situation?" he asked, as one would ask about the weather.

"The situation is a pip," I told him. "There were a hundred and fifty crooks in the push if there was one. I saw a hundred myself—or think I did—and there were slews of them that I didn't see—planted where they could jump out and bite when fresh teeth were needed. They bit, too. They bushwacked the police and made a merry wreck out of 'em—going and coming. They hit the two banks at ten sharp—took over the whole block—chased away the reasonable people—dropped the others. The actual looting was duck soup to a mob of that size. Twenty or thirty of 'em to each of the banks while the others held the street. Nothing to it but wrap up the spoils and take 'em home.

"There's a highly indignant businessmen's meeting down there now—wild-eyed stockholders up on their hind legs yelling for the chief of police's heart's blood. The police didn't do any miracles, that's a cinch, but no police department is equipped to handle a trick of that size—no matter how well they think they are. The whole thing lasted less than twenty minutes. There were, say, a hundred and fifty thugs in on it, loaded for bear, every play mapped to the inch. How are you going to get enough coppers down there, size up the racket, plan your battle, and put it over in that little time? It's easy enough to say the police should look ahead—should have a dose for every emergency—but these same birds who are yelling, 'Rotten,' down there now would be the first to squawk, 'Robbery,' if their taxes were boosted a couple of cents to buy more policemen and equipment.

"But the police fell down—there's no question about that—and there will be a lot of beefy necks that feel the ax. The armored cars were no good, the grenading was about fifty-fifty, since the bandits knew how to play that game, too. But the real disgrace of the party was the police machine guns. The bankers and brokers are saying they were fixed. Whether they were deliberately tampered with or were only carelessly taken care of, is anybody's guess, but only one of the damned things would shoot, and it not very well.

"The getaway was north on Montgomery to Columbus. Along Columbus the parade melted, a few cars at a time, into side streets. The police ran into an ambush between Washington and Jackson, and by the time they had shot their way through it the bandit cars had scattered all over the city. A lot of 'em have been picked up since then— empty.

"All the returns aren't in yet, but right now the score stands something like this: The haul will run God only knows how far into the millions—easily the richest pickings ever got with civilian guns. Sixteen coppers were knocked off, and three times that many wounded. Twelve innocent spectators, bank clerks and the like, were killed and about as many banged around. There are two bandits and five shot-ups who might be either thugs or spectators that got too close. The bandits lost seven dead that we know of and thirty-one prisoners, most of them bleeding somewhere.

"One of the dead was Fat Boy Clarke. Remember him? He shot his way out of a Des Moines courtroom three or four years ago. Well, in his pocket we found a piece of paper, a map of Montgomery Street between Pine and Bush, the block of the looting. On the back of the map were typed instructions, telling him exactly what to do and when to do it. An X on the map showed him where he was to park the car in which he arrived with his seven men, and there was a circle where he was to stand with them, keeping an eye on things in general and on the windows and roofs of the buildings across the street in particular. Figures 1, 2, 3, 4, 5, 6, 7, 8 on the map marked doorways, steps, a deep window, and so on, that were to be used for shelter if shots had to be traded with those windows and roofs. Clarke was to pay no attention to the Bush Street end of the block, but if the police charged the Pine Street end he was to move his men up there, distributing them among points marked a, b, c, d, e, f, g, and h. (His body was found on the spot marked a.) Every five minutes during the looting he was to send a man to an automobile standing in the street at a point marked on the map with a star, to see if there were any new instructions. He was to tell his men that if he were shot down one of them must report to the car, and a new leader would be given them. When the signal for the getaway was given, he was to send one of his men to the car in which he had come. If it was still in commission, this man was to drive it, not passing the car ahead of him. If it was out of whack, the man was to report to the star-marked car for instructions how to get a new one. I suppose they counted on finding enough parked cars to take care of this end. While Clarke waited for his car he and his men were to throw as much lead as possible at every target in their district, and none of them was to board the car until it came abreast of them. Then they were to drive out Montgomery to Columbus to—blank.

"Get that?" I asked. "Here are a hundred and fifty gunmen, split into groups under group-leaders, with maps and schedules showing what each man is to do, showing the fire-plug he's to kneel behind, the brick he's to stand on, where he's to spit—everything but the name and address of the policeman he's to shoot! It's just as well Beno couldn't give me the details—I'd have written it off as a hophead's dream!"

"Very interesting," the Old Man said, smiling blandly.

"The Fat Boy's was the only timetable we found," I went on with my history. "I saw a few friends among the killed and caught, and the police are still identifying others. Some are local talent, but most of 'em seem to be imported stock. Detroit, Chicago, New York, St. Louis, Denver, Portland, L.A., Philly, Baltimore—all seem to have sent delegates. As soon as the police get through identifying them I'll make out a list.

"Of those who weren't caught, Bluepoint Vance seems to be the main squeeze. He was in the car that directed operations. I don't know who else was there with him. The Shivering Kid was in on the festivities, and I think Alphabet Shorty McCoy, though I didn't get a good look at him. Sergeant Bender told me he spotted Toots Salda and Darby M'Laughlin in the push, and Morgan saw the Dis-and-Dat Kid. That's a good cross-section of the lay-out—gunmen, swindlers, hijackers from all over Rand-McNally.

"The Hall of Justice has been a slaughter house all afternoon. The police haven't killed any of their guests—

none that I know of—but they're sure-God making be-lievers out of them. Newspaper writers who like to sob over what they call the third degree should be down there now. After being knocked around a bit, some of the guests have talked. But the hell of it is they don't know a whole lot. They know some names—Denny Burke, Toby the Lugs, Old Pete Best, Fat Boy Clarke and Paddy the Mex were named—and that helps some, but all the smacking power in the police force arm can't bring out anything else.

"The racket seems to have been organized like this: Denny Burke, for instance, is known as a shifty worker in Baltimore. Well, Denny talks to eight or ten likely boys, one at a time. 'How'd you like to pick up a piece of change out on the Coast?' he asks them. 'Doing what?' the candidate wants to know. 'Doing what you're told,' the King of Frog Island says. 'You know me. I'm telling you this is the fastest picking ever rigged, a kick in the pants to go through—air-tight. Everybody in on it will come home lousy with cash—and they'll all come home if they don't dog it. That's all I'm spilling. If you don't like it—forget it.'

"And these birds did know Denny, and if he said the job was good that was enough for them. So they put in with him. He told them nothing. He saw that they had guns, gave 'em each a ticket to San Francisco and twenty bucks, and told them where to meet him here. Last night he collected them and told them they went to work this morning. By that time they had moved around the town enough to see that it was bubbling over with visiting talent, including such moguls as Toots Salda, Bluepoint Vance and the Shivering Kid. So this morning they went forth eagerly with the King of Frog Island at their head to do their stuff.

"The other talkers tell varieties of the same tale. The police found room in their crowded jail to stick in a few stool-pigeons. Since few of the bandits knew very many of the others, the stools had an easy time of it, but the only thing they could add to what we've got is that the prisoners are looking for a wholesale delivery tonight. They seem to think their mob will crash the prison and turn 'em loose. That's probably a lot of chewing gum, but anyway this time the police will be ready.

"That's the situation as it stands now. The police are sweeping the streets, picking up everybody who needs a shave or can't show a certificate of attendance signed by his parson, with special attention to outward-bound trains, boats and automobiles. I sent Jack Counihan and Dick Foley down North Beach way to play the joints and see if they can pick up anything."

"Do you think Bluepoint Vance was the actual directing intelligence in this robbery?" the Old Man asked.

"I hope so—we know him."

The Old Man turned his chair so his mild eyes could stare out the window again, and he tapped his desk reflectively with the pencil.

"I'm afraid not," he said in a gently apologetic tone. "Vance is a shrewd, resourceful and determined criminal, but his weakness is one common to his type. His abilities are all for present action and not for planning ahead. He has executed some large operations, but I've always thought I saw in them some other mind at work behind him."

I couldn't quarrel with that. If the Old Man said something was so, then it probably was, because he was one of these cautious babies who'll look out of the window at a cloudburst and say, "It seems to be raining," on the off-chance that somebody's pouring water off the roof.

"And who is this arch-*gonif?*" I asked.

"You'll probably know that before I do," he said, smiling benignantly.

I went back to the Hall and helped boil more prisoners in oil until around eight o'clock, when my appetite reminded me I hadn't eaten since breakfast. I attended to that, and then turned down toward Larrouy's, ambling along leisurely, so the exercise wouldn't interfere with my digestion. I spent three-quarters of an hour in Larrouy's, and didn't see anybody who interested me especially. A few gents I know were present, but they weren't anxious to associate with me—it's not always healthy in criminal circles to be seen wagging your chin with a sleuth right after a job has been turned.

Not getting anything there, I moved up the street to Wop Healy's—another hole. My reception was the same here—I was given a table and let alone. Healy's orchestra was giving "Don't You Cheat" all they had while those customers who felt athletic were roughing it out on the dance-floor. One of the dancers was Jack Counihan, his arms full of a big olive-skinned girl with a pleasant, thick-featured stupid face.

Jack was a tall, slender lad of twenty-three or four who had drifted into the Continental's employ a few months before. It was the first job he'd ever had and he wouldn't have had it if his father hadn't insisted that if sonny wanted to keep his fingers in the family till, he'd have to get over the notion that squeezing through a college graduation was enough work for one lifetime. So Jack came to the Agency. He thought gumshoeing would be fun. In spite of the fact that he'd rather catch the wrong man than wear the wrong necktie, he was a promising young thief-catcher. A likable youngster, well-muscled for all his slimness, smooth-haired, with a gentleman's face and a gentleman's manner, nervy, quick with head and hands, full of the don't-give-a-damn gaiety that belonged to his youthfulness. He was jingle-brained, of course, and needed holding, but I would rather work with him than with a lot of old-timers I knew.

Half an hour passed with nothing to interest me.

Then a boy came into Healy's from the street—a small kid, gaudily dressed, very pressed in the pants-legs, very shiny in the shoes, with an impudent sallow face of pronounced cast. This was the boy I had seen sauntering down Broadway a moment after Beno had been rubbed out.

Leaning back in my chair so that a woman's widehatted head was between us, I watched the young Armenian wind between tables to one in a far corner, where three men sat. He spoke to them—offhand perhaps a dozen words—and moved away to another table where a snub-nosed, black-haired man sat alone. The boy dropped into the chair facing snub-nose, spoke a few words, sneered at snub-nose's questions, and ordered a drink. When his glass was empty he crossed the room to speak to a lean buzzard-faced man, and then went out of Healy's.

I followed him out, passing the table where Jack sat with the girl, catching his eye. Outside, I saw the young Armenian half a block away. Jack Counihan caught up with me, passed me. With a Fatima in my mouth I called to him, "Got a match, brother?"

While I lighted my cigarette with a match from the box he gave me I spoke to him behind my hands, "The goose in the glad rags—tail him. I'll string behind you. I don't know him, but if he blipped Beno off for talking to me last night, he knows me. On his heels!"

Jack pocketed his matches and went after the boy. I gave Jack a lead and then followed him. And then an interesting thing happened.

The street was fairly well-filled with people, mostly men, some walking, some loafing on corners and in front of soft-drink parlors. As the young Armenian reached the corner of an alley where there was a light, two men came up and spoke to him, moving a little apart so that he was between them. The boy would have kept walking, apparently paying no attention to them, but one checked him by stretching an arm out in front of him. The other man took his right hand out of his pocket and flourished it in the boy's face so that the nickel-plated knuckles on it twinkled in the light. The boy ducked swiftly under the threatening hand and outstretched arm, and went on across the alley, walking, and not even looking over his shoulder at the two men who were now closing on his back.

Just before they reached him another reached them—a

broad-backed, long-armed, ape-built man I had not seen
before. Each arm caught a man. By the napes of their
necks he yanked them away from the boy's back, shook
them till their hats fell off, smacked their skulls together
with a crack that was like a broom-handle breaking, and
dragged their rag-limp bodies out of sight up the alley.
While this was happening the boy walked jauntily down
the street, without a backward glance.

When the skull-cracker came out of the alley I saw his
face in the light—a dark-skinned heavily lined face, broad
and flat, with jaw-muscles bulging like abscesses under his
ears. He spit, hitched his pants, and swaggered down the
street after the boy.

The boy went into Larrouy's. The skull-cracker followed him in. The boy came out, and in his rear—perhaps
twenty feet behind—the skull-cracker rolled. Jack had
tailed them into Larrouy's while I had held up the outside.

"Still carrying messages?" I asked.

"Yes. He spoke to five men in there. He's got plenty of
bodyguard, hasn't he?"

"Yeah," I agreed. "And you be damned careful you
don't get between them. If they split, I'll shadow the skull-
cracker, you keep the goose."

We separated and moved after our game. They took us
to all the hangouts in San Francisco, to cabarets, grease-
joints, pool-rooms, saloons, flophouses, hockshops, gambling joints and what have you. Everywhere the kid found
men to speak his dozen words to, and between calls, he
found them on street-corners.

I would have liked to get behind some of these birds,
but I didn't want to leave Jack alone with the boy and his
bodyguard—they seemed to mean too much. And I
couldn't stick Jack on one of the others, because it wasn't
safe for me to hang too close to the Armenian boy. So we
played the game as we had started it, shadowing our pair
from hole to hole, while night got on toward morning.

It was a few minutes past midnight when they came
out of a small hotel up on Kearny Street, and for the first

time since we had seen them they walked together, side by side, up to Green Street, where they turned east along the side of Telegraph Hill. Half a block of this, and they climbed the front steps of a ramshackle furnished-room house and disappeared inside. I joined Jack Counihan on the corner where he had stopped.

"The greetings have all been delivered," I guessed, "or he wouldn't have called in his bodyguard. If there's nothing stirring within the next half hour I'm going to beat it. You'll have to take a plant on the joint till morning."

Twenty minutes later the skull-cracker came out of the house and walked down the street.

"I'll take him," I said. "You stick to the other baby."

The skull-cracker took ten or twelve steps from the house and stopped. He looked back at the house, raising his face to look at the upper stories. Then Jack and I could hear what had stopped him. Up in the house a man was screaming. It wasn't much of a scream in volume. Even now, when it had increased in strength, it barely reached our ears. But in it—in that one wailing voice—everything that fears death seemed to cry out its fear. I heard Jack's teeth click. I've got horny skin all over what's left of my soul, but just the same my forehead twitched. The scream was so damned weak for what it said.

The skull-cracker moved. Five gliding strides carried him back to the house. He didn't touch one of the six or seven front steps. He went from pavement to vestibule in a spring no monkey could have beaten for swiftness, ease or silence. One minute, two minutes, three minutes, and the screaming stopped. Three more minutes and the skull-cracker was leaving the house again. He paused on the sidewalk to spit and hitch his pants. Then he swaggered off down the street.

"He's your meat, Jack," I said. "I'm going to call on the boy. He won't recognize me now."

The street door of the rooming-house was not only unlocked but wide open. I went through it into a hallway, where a dim light burning upstairs outlined a flight of steps. I climbed them and turned toward the front of the house. The scream had come from the front—either this floor or the third. There was a fair likelihood of the skull-cracker having left the room door unlocked, just as he had not paused to close the street door.

I had no luck on the second floor, but the third knob I cautiously tried on the third floor turned in my hand and let its door edge back from the frame. In front of this crack I waited a moment, listening to nothing but a throbbing snore somewhere far down the hallway. I put a palm against the door and eased it open another foot. No sound. The room was black as an honest politician's prospects. I slid my hand across the frame, across a few inches of wallpaper, found a light button, pressed it. Two globes in the center of the room threw their weak yellow light on the shabby room and on the young American who lay dead across the bed.

I went into the room, closed the door and stepped over to the bed. The boy's eyes were wide and bulging. One of his temples was bruised. His throat gaped with a red slit that ran actually from ear to ear. Around the slit, in the few spots not washed red, his thin neck showed dark bruises. The skull-cracker had dropped the boy with a poke in the temple and had choked him until he thought him dead. But the kid had revived enough to scream—not enough to keep from screaming. The skull-cracker had returned to finish the job with a knife. Three streaks on the bed-clothes showed where the knife had been cleaned.

The lining of the boy's pockets stuck out. The skull-cracker had turned them out. I went through his clothes, but with no better luck than I expected—the killer had taken everything. The room gave me nothing—a few clothes, but not a thing out of which information could be squeezed.

My prying done, I stood in the center of the floor scratching my chin and considering. In the hall a floor-board creaked. Three backward steps on my rubber heels put me in the musty closet, dragging the door all but half an inch shut behind me.

Knuckles rattled on the room door as I slid my gun off

my hip. The knuckles rattled again and a feminine voice said, "Kid, oh, Kid!" Neither knuckles nor voice was loud. The lock clicked as the knob turned. The door opened and framed the shifty-eyed girl who had been called Sylvia Yount by Angel Grace.

Her eyes lost their shiftiness for surprise when they settled on the boy.

"Holy hell!" she gasped, and was gone.

I was half out of the closet when I heard her tiptoeing back. In my hole again, I waited, my eye to the crack. She came in swiftly, closed the door silently, and went to lean over the dead boy. Her hands moved over him, exploring the pockets whose linings I had put back in place.

"Damn such luck!" she said aloud when the unprofitable frisking was over, and went out of the house.

I gave her time to reach the sidewalk. She was headed toward Kearny Street when I left the house. I shadowed her down Kearny to Broadway, up Broadway to Larrouy's. Larrouy's was busy, especially near the door, with customers going and coming. I was within five feet of the girl when she stopped a waiter and asked, in a whisper that was excited enough to carry, "Is Red here?"

The waiter shook his head. "Ain't been in tonight."

The girl went out of the dive, hurrying along on clicking heels to a hotel in Stockton Street.

While I looked through the glass front, she went to the desk and spoke to the clerk. He shook his head. She spoke again and he gave her paper and envelope, on which she scribbled with the pen beside the register. Before I had to leave for a safer position from which to cover her exit, I saw which pigeonhole the note went into.

From the hotel the girl went by streetcar to Market and Powell Streets, and then walked up Powell to O'Farrel, where a fat-faced young man in gray overcoat and gray hat left the curb to link arms with her and lead her to a taxi stand up O'Farrell Street. I let them go, making a note of the taxi number—the fat-faced man looked more like a customer than a pal.

It was a little shy of two in the morning when I turned back into Market Street and went up to the office. Fiske, who holds down the Agency at night, said Jack Counihan had not reported; nothing else had come in. I told him to rouse me an operative, and in ten or fifteen minutes he succeeded in getting Mickey Linehan out of bed and on the wire.

"Listen, Mickey," I said, "I've got the nicest corner picked out for you to stand on the rest of the night. So pin on your diapers and toddle down there, will you?"

In between his grumbling and cursing I gave him the name and number of the Stockton Street hotel, described Red O'Leary, and told him which pigeonhole the note had been put in.

"It mightn't be Red's home, but the chance is worth covering," I wound up. "If you pick him up, try not to lose him before I can get somebody down there to take him off your hands." I hung up during the outburst of profanity this insult brought.

The Hall of Justice was busy when I reached it, though nobody had tried to shake the upstairs prison loose yet. Fresh lots of suspicious characters were being brought in every few minutes. Policemen in and out of uniform were everywhere. The detective bureau was a beehive.

Trading information with the police detectives, I told them about the Armenian boy. We were making up a party to visit the remains when the captain's door opened and Lieutenant Duff came into the assembly room.

"*Allez! Oop!*" he said, pointing a thick finger at O'Gar, Tully, Reecher, Hunt and me. "There's a thing worth looking at in Fillmore."

We followed him out to an automobile.

A gray frame house in Fillmore Street was our destination. A lot of people stood in the street looking at the house. A police-wagon stood in front of it, and police uniforms were indoors and out.

A red-mustached corporal saluted Duff and led us into

the house, explaining as we went, " 'Twas the neighbors give us the rumble, complaining of the fighting, and when we got here, faith, there weren't no fight left in nobody."

All the house held was fourteen dead men.

Eleven of them had been poisoned—overdoses of knockout drops in their booze, the doctor said. The other three had been shot, at intervals along the hall. From the looks of the remains, they had drunk a toast—a loaded one—and those who hadn't drunk, whether because of temperance or suspicious natures, had been gunned as they tried to get away.

The identity of the bodies gave us an idea of what their toast had been. They were all thieves—they had drunk their poison to the day's looting.

We didn't know all the dead men then, but all of us knew some of them, and the records told us who the others were later. The completed list read like *Who's Who in Crookdom.*

There was the Dis-and-Dat Kid, who had crushed out of Leavenworth only two months before; Sheeny Holmes; Snohomish Shitey, supposed to have died a hero in France in 1919; L. A. Slim, from Denver, sockless and underwearless as usual, with a thousand-dollar bill sewed in each shoulder of his coat; Spider Girrucci wearing a steel-mesh vest under his shirt and a scar from crown to chin where his brother had carved him years ago; Old Pete Best, once a congressman; Nigger Vojan, who once won $175,000 in a Chicago crapgame—*Abracadabra* tattooed on him in three places; Alphabet Shorty McCoy; Tom Brooks, Alphabet Shorty's brother-in-law, who invented the Richmond razzle-dazzle and bought three hotels with the profits; Red Cudahy, who stuck up a Union Pacific train in 1924; Denny Burke; Bull McGonickle, still pale from fifteen years in Joliet; Toby the Lugs, Bull's running-mate, who used to brag about picking President Wilson's pocket in a Washington vaudeville theatre; and Paddy the Mex.

Duff looked them over and whistled.

"A few more tricks like this," he said, "and we'll all be

out of jobs. There won't be any grifters left to protect the taxpayers from."

"I'm glad you like it," I told him. "Me—I'd hate like hell to be a San Francisco copper the next few days."

"Why especially?"

"Look at this—one grand piece of double-crossing. This village of ours is full of mean lads who are waiting right now for these stiffs to bring 'em their cut of the stick-up. What do you think's going to happen when the word gets out that there's not going to be any gravy for the mob? There are going to be a hundred and more stranded thugs busy raising getaway dough. There'll be three burglaries to a block and a stick-up to every corner until the carfare's raised. God bless you, my son, you're going to sweat for your wages!"

Duff shrugged his thick shoulders and stepped over bodies to get to the telephone. When he was through I called the Agency.

"Jack Counihan called a couple of minutes ago," Fiske told me, and gave me an Army Street address. "He says he put his men in there, with company."

I phoned for a taxi, and then told Duff, "I'm going to run out for a while. I'll give you a ring here if there's anything to the angle, or if there isn't. You'll wait?"

"If you're not too long."

I got rid of my taxicab two blocks from the address Fiske had given me, and walked down Army Street to find Jack Counihan planted on a dark corner.

"I got a bad break," was what he welcomed me with. "While I was phoning from the lunchroom up the street some of my people ran out on me."

"Yeah? What's the dope?"

"Well, after that apey chap left the Green Street house he trolleyed to a house in Fillmore Street, and—"

"What number?"

The number Jack gave was that of the death-house I had just left.

"In the next ten or fifteen minutes just about that many

other chaps went into the same house. Most of them came afoot, singly or in pairs. Then two cars came up together, with nine men in them—I counted them. They went into the house, leaving their machines in front. A taxi came past a little later, and I stopped it, in case my chap should motor away.

"Nothing happened for at least half an hour after the nine chaps went in. Then everybody in the house seemed to become demonstrative—there was a quantity of yelling and shooting. It lasted long enough to awaken the whole neighborhood. When it stopped, ten men—I counted them —ran out of the house, got into the two cars and drove away. My man was one of them.

"My faithful taxi and I cried *Yoicks* after them, and they brought us here, going into that house down the street in front of which one of their motors still stands. After half an hour or so I thought I'd better report, so, leaving my taxi around the corner—where it's still running up expenses—I went up to Fiske. And when I came back, one of the cars was gone—and I, woe is me!—don't know who went with it. Am I rotten?"

"Sure! You should have taken their cars along to the phone with you. Watch the one that's left while I collect a strong-arm squad."

I went up to the lunchroom and phoned Duff, telling him where I was, and, "If you bring your gang along maybe there'll be profit in it. A couple of carloads of folks who were in Fillmore Street and didn't stay there came here, and part of 'em may still be here, if you make it sudden."

Duff brought his four detectives and a dozen uniformed men with him. We hit the house front and back. No time was wasted ringing the bell. We simply tore down the doors and went in. Everything inside was black until flashlights lit it up. There was no resistance. Ordinarily the six men we found in there would have damned near ruined us in spite of our outnumbering them. But they were too dead for that.

We looked at one another sort of open-mouthed.

"This is getting monotonous," Duff complained, biting off a hunk of tobacco. "Everybody's work is pretty much the same thing over and over, but I'm tired of walking into roomfuls of butchered crooks."

The catalogue here had fewer names than the other, but they were bigger names. The Shivering Kid was here—nobody would collect all the reward money piled up on him now; Darby M'Laughlin, his horn-rimmed glasses crooked on his nose, ten thousand dollars' worth of diamonds on fingers and tie; Happy Jim Hacker; Donkey Marr, the last of the bow-legged Marrs, killers all, father and five sons; Toots Salda, the strongest man in crookdom, who had once picked up and run away with two Savannah coppers to whom he was handcuffed; and Rumdum Smith, who killed Lefty Read in Chi in 1916—a rosary wrapped around his left wrist.

No gentlemanly poisoning here—these boys had been mowed down with a .30-30 rifle fitted with a clumsy but effective homemade silencer. The rifle lay on the kitchen table. A door connected the kitchen with the dining room. Directly opposite the door, double doors—wide open—opened into the room in which the dead thieves lay. They were all close to the front wall, lying as if they had been lined up against the wall to be knocked off.

The gray-papered wall was spattered with blood, punctured with holes where a couple of bullets had gone all the way through. Jack Counihan's young eyes picked out a stain on the paper that wasn't accidental. It was close to the floor, beside the Shivering Kid, and the Kid's right hand was stained with blood. He had written on the wall before he died—with fingers dipped in his own and Toots Salda's blood. The letters in the words showed breaks and gaps where his fingers had run dry, and the letters were crooked and straggly, because he must have written them in the dark.

By filling in the gaps, allowing for the kinks, and guessing where there weren't any indications to guide us, we got two words: *Big Flora.*

"They don't mean anything to me," Duff said, "but it's

a name and most of the names we have belong to dead men now, so it's time we were adding to our list."

"What do you make of it?" asked bullet-headed O'Gar, detective-sergeant in the Homicide Detail, looking at the bodies. "Their pals got the drop on them, lined them against the wall, and the sharp-shooter in the kitchen shot 'em down—bing-bing-bing-bing-bing-bing?"

"It reads that way," the rest of us agreed.

"Ten of 'em came here from Fillmore Street," I said. "Six stayed here. Four went to another house—where part of 'em are not cutting down the other part. All that's necessary is to trail the corpses from house to house until there's only one man left—and he's bound to play it through by croaking himself, leaving the loot to be recovered in the original packages. I hope you folks don't have to stay up all night to find the remains of that last thug. Come on, Jack, let's go home for some sleep."

It was exactly 5 A.M. when I separated the sheets and crawled into my bed. I was asleep before the last draw of smoke from my good-night Fatima was out of my lungs. The telephone woke me at 5:15.

Fiske was talking, "Mickey Linehan just phoned that your Red O'Leary came home to roost half an hour ago."

"Have him booked," I said, and was asleep again by 5:17.

With the help of the alarm clock I rolled out of bed at nine, breakfasted, and went down to the detective bureau to see how the police had made out with the redhead. Not so good.

"He's got us stopped," the captain told me. "He's got alibis for the time of the looting and for last night's doings. And we can't even vag the son-of-a-gun. He's got means of support. He's salesman for Humperdickel's Universal Encyclopaediac Dictionary of Useful and Valuable Knowledge, or something like it. He started peddling these pamphlets the day before the knockover, and at the time it was happening he was ringing doorbells and asking folks to buy his durned books. Anyway, he's got three witnesses that say so. Last night he was in a hotel from eleven to four-thirty this morning, playing cards, and he's got witnesses. We didn't find a durned thing on him or in his room."

I borrowed the captain's phone to call Jack Counihan's house.

"Could you identify any of the men you saw in the cars last night?" I asked when he had been stirred out of bed.

"No. It was dark and they moved too fast. I could barely make sure of my chap."

"Can't, huh?" the captain said. "Well, I can hold him twenty-four hours without laying charges, and I'll do that, but I'll have to spring him unless you can dig up something."

"Suppose you turn him loose now," I suggested after thinking through my cigarette for a few minutes. "He's got himself all alibied up, so there's no reason why he should hide out on us. We'll let him alone all day—give him time to make sure he isn't being tailed—and then we'll get behind him tonight and stay behind him. Any dope on Big Flora?"

"No. That kid that was killed in Green Street was Bernie Bernheimer, alias the Motsa Kid. I guess he was a dip—he ran with dips—but he wasn't very—"

The buzz of the phone interrupted him. He said, "Hello, yes," and "Just a minute," into the instrument, and slid it across the desk to me.

A feminine voice: "This is Grace Cardigan. I called your agency and they told me where to get you. I've got to see you. Can you meet me now?"

"Where are you?"

"In the telephone station on Powell Street."

"I'll be there in fifteen minutes," I said.

Calling the Agency, I got hold of Dick Foley and asked him to meet me at Ellis and Market right away. Then I gave the captain back his phone, said "See you later," and went uptown to keep my dates.

Dick Foley was on his corner when I got there. He was a swarthy little Canadian who stood nearly five feet in his high-heeled shoes, weighed a hundred pounds minus, talked like a Scotchman's telegram, and could have shadowed a drop of salt water from Golden Gate to Hongkong without ever losing sight of it.

"You know Angel Grace Cardigan?" I asked him.

He saved a word by shaking his head, no.

"I'm going to meet her in the telephone station. When I'm through, stay behind her. She's smart, and she'll be looking for you, so it won't be duck soup, but do what you can."

Dick's mouth went down at the corners and one of his rare long-winded streaks hit him. "Harder they look, easier they are," he said.

He trailed along behind me while I went up to the station. Angel Grace was standing in the doorway. Her face was more sullen than I had ever seen it, and therefore less beautiful—except her green eyes, which held too much fire for sullenness. A rolled newspaper was in one of her hands. She neither spoke, smiled nor nodded.

"We'll go to Charley's, where we can talk," I said, guiding her down past Dick Foley.

Not a murmur did I get out of her until we were seated cross-table in the restaurant booth, and the waiter had gone off with our orders. Then she spread the newspaper out on the table with shaking hands.

"Is this on the level?" she demanded.

I looked at the story her shaking finger tapped—an account of the Fillmore and Army Street findings, but a cagey account. A glance showed that no names had been given, that the police had censored the story quite a bit. While I pretended to read I wondered whether it would be to my advantage to tell the girl the story was a fake. But I couldn't see any clear profit in that, so I saved my soul a lie.

"Practically straight," I admitted.

"You were there?" She had pushed the paper aside to the floor and was leaning over the table.

"With the police."

"Was—" Her voice broke huskily. Her white fingers wadded the tablecloth in two little bunches halfway between us. She cleared her throat. "Who was—?" was as far as she got this time.

A pause. I waited. Her eyes went down, but not before I had seen water dulling the fire in them. During the pause the waiter came in, put our food down, went away.

"You know what I want to ask," she said presently, her voice low, choked. "Was he? Was he? For God's sake tell me!"

I weighed them—truth against lie, lie against truth. Once more truth triumphed.

"Paddy the Mex was shot—killed—in the Fillmore Street house," I said.

The pupils of her eyes shrank to pin-points—spread again until they almost covered the green irises. She made no sound. Her face was empty. She picked up a fork and lifted a forkful of salad to her mouth—another. Reaching across the table, I took the fork out of her hand.

"You're only spilling it on your clothes," I growled. "You can't eat without opening your mouth to put the food in."

She put her hands across the table, reaching for mine, trembling, holding my hand with fingers that twitched so that the nails scratched me.

"You're not lying to me?" she half sobbed, half chattered. "You're on the square! You were white to me that time in Philly! Paddy always said you were one white dick! You're not tricking me?"

"Straight up," I assured her. "Paddy meant a lot to you?"

She nodded dully, pulling herself together, sinking back in a sort of stupor.

"The way's open to even up for him," I suggested.

"You mean—?"

"Talk."

She stared at me blankly for a long while, as if she was trying to get some meaning out of what I had said. I read the answer in her eyes before she put it in words.

"I wish to God I could! But I'm Paperbox-John Cardigan's daughter. It isn't in me to turn anybody up. You're on the wrong side. I can't go over. I wish I could. But there's too much Cardigan in me. I'll be hoping every minute that you nail them, and nail them dead right, but—"

"Your sentiments are noble, or words to that effect," I sneered at her. "Who do you think you are—Joan of Arc? Would your brother Frank be in stir now if his partner, Johnny the Plumber, hadn't put the finger on him for the Great Falls bulls? Come to life, dearie! You're a thief among thieves, and those who don't double-cross get crossed. Who rubbed your Paddy the Mex out? Pals! But you mustn't slap back at 'em because it wouldn't be clubby. My God!"

My speech only thickened the sullenness in her face.

"I'm going to slap back," she said, "but I can't, can't split. I can't tell you. If you were a gun, I'd—anyway, what help I get will be on my side of the game. Let it go at that, won't you? I know how you feel about it, but—will you tell me who besides—who else was—was found in those houses?"

"Oh, sure!" I snarled. "I'll tell you everything. I'll let you pump me dry. But you mustn't give me any hints, because it might not be in keeping with the ethics of your highly honorable profession!"

Being a woman, she ignored all this, repeating, "Who else?"

"Nothing stirring. But I will do this—I'll tell you a couple who weren't there—Big Flora and Red O'Leary."

Her dopiness was gone. She studied my face with green eyes that were dark and savage.

"Was Bluepoint Vance?" she demanded.

"What do you guess?" I replied.

She studied my face for a moment longer and then stood up.

"Thanks for what you've told me," she said, "and for meeting me like this. I do hope you win."

She went out to be shadowed by Dick Foley. I ate my lunch.

At four o'clock that afternoon Jack Counihan and I brought our hired automobile to rest within sight of the front door of the Stockton hotel.

"He cleared himself with the police, so there's no reason why he should have moved, maybe," I told Jack, "and I'd rather not monkey with the hotel people, not knowing them. If he doesn't show by late we'll have to go up against them then."

We settled down to cigarettes, guesses on who'd be the next heavyweight champion and where to get good gin and what to do with it, the injustice of the new Agency ruling that for purposes of expense accounts Oakland was not to be considered out of town, and similar exciting topics, which carried us from four o'clock to ten minutes past nine.

At 9:10 Red O'Leary came out of the hotel.

"God is good," said Jack as he jumped out of the machine to do the footwork while I stirred the motor.

The fire-topped giant didn't take us far. Larrouy's front door gobbled him. By the time I had parked the car and gone into the dive, both O'Leary and Jack had found seats. Jack's table was on the edge of the dance floor. O'Leary's was on the other side of the establishment against the wall, near a corner. A fat blond couple were leaving the table back in that corner when I came in, so I persuaded the waiter who was guiding me to a table to make it that one.

O'Leary's face was three-quarters turned away from me. He was watching the front door, watching it with an earnestness that turned suddenly to happiness when a girl appeared there. She was the girl Angel Grace had called

Nancy Regan. I have already said she was nice. Well, she was. And the cocky little blue hat that hid all her hair didn't handicap her niceness any tonight.

The redhead scrambled to his feet and pushed a waiter and a couple of customers out of his way as he went to meet her. As reward for his eagerness he got some profanity that he didn't seem to hear and a blue-eyed, white-toothed smile that was—well—nice. He brought her back to his table and put her in a chair facing me, while he sat very much facing her.

His voice was a baritone rumble out of which my snooping ears could pick no words. He seemed to be telling her a lot, and she listened as if she liked it.

"But, Reddy, dear, you shouldn't," she said once. Her voice—I know other words, but we'll stick to this one—was nice. Outside of the musk in it, it had quality. Whoever this gunman's moll was, she either had had a good start in life or had learned her stuff well. Now and then, when the orchestra came up for air, I would catch a few words, but they didn't tell me anything except that neither she nor her rowdy playmate had anything against the other.

The joint had been nearly empty when she came in. By ten o'clock it was fairly crowded, and ten o'clock is early for Larrouy's customers. I began to pay less attention to Red's girl—even if she was nice—and more to my other neighbors. It struck me that there weren't many women in sight. Checking up on that, I found damned few women in proportion to the men. Men—rat-faced men, hatchet-faced men, square-jawed men, slack-chinned men, pale men, scrawny men, funny-looking men, tough-looking men, ordinary men—sitting two to a table, four to a table, more coming in—and damned few women.

These men talked to one another as if they weren't much interested in what they were saying. They looked casually around the joint with eyes that were blankest when they came to O'Leary. And always those casual, bored glances did rest on O'Leary for a second or two.

I returned my attention to O'Leary and Nancy Regan.

He was sitting a little more erect in his chair than he had been, but it was an easy, supple erectness and though his shoulders had hunched   t, there was no stiffness in them. She said somethi   im. He laughed, turning his face toward the ce   room, so that he seemed to be laughing not only   said, but also at these men who sat around him,   . It was a hearty laugh, young and careless.

The girl looked surprised for a moment, as if something in the laugh puzzled her; then she went on with whatever she was telling him. She didn't know she was sitting on dynamite, I decided. O'Leary knew. Every inch of him, every gesture, said, "I'm big, strong, young, tough and red-headed. When you boys want to do your stuff I'll be here."

Time slid by. Few couples danced. Jean Larrouy went around with dark worry in his round face. His joint was full of customers, but he would rather have had it empty.

By eleven o'clock I stood up and beckoned to Jack Counihan. He came over, we shook hands, exchanged *How's everything* and *Getting muches,* and he sat at my table.

"What is happening?" he asked under cover of the orchestra's din. "I can't see anything, but there is something in the air. Or am I being hysterical?"

"You will be presently. The wolves are gathering, and Red O'Leary's the lamb. You could pick a tenderer one if you had a free hand, maybe. But these bimbos once helped pluck a bank, and when payday came there wasn't anything in their envelopes, not even any envelopes. The word got out that maybe Red knew how come. Hence this. They're waiting now—maybe for somebody—maybe till they get enough hooch in them."

"And we sit here because it's the nearest table to the target for all these fellows' bullets when the blooming lid blows off?" Jack inquired. "Let's move over to Red's table. It's still nearer, and I rather like the appearance of the girl with him."

"Don't be impatient, you'll have your fun," I promised

him. "There's no sense in having this O'Leary killed. If
they bargain with him in a gentlemanly way, we'll lay off.
But if they start heaving things at him, you and I are
going to pry him and his girl friend loose."

"Well spoken, my hearty!" He grinned, whitening
around the mouth. "Are there any details, or do we just
simply and unostentatiously pry 'em loose?"

"See the door behind me, to the right? When the pop-
off comes, I'm going back there and open it up. You hold
the line midway between. When I yelp, you give Red
whatever help he needs to get back there."

"Aye, aye!" He looked around the room at the assembled plug-uglies, moistened his lips, and looked at the
hand holding his cigarette, a quivering hand. "I hope you
won't think I'm in a funk," he said. "But I'm not an
antique murderer like you. I get a reaction out of this
prospective slaughtering."

"Reaction, my eye," I said. "You're scared stiff. But no
nonsense, mind! If you try to make a vaudeville act out of
it I'll ruin whatever those gorillas leave of you. You do
what you're told, and nothing else. If you get any bright
ideas, save 'em to tell me about afterward."

"Oh, my conduct will be most exemplary!" he assured
me.

It was nearly midnight when what the wolves waited
for came. The last pretense of indifference went out of
faces that had been gradually taking on tenseness. Chairs
and feet scraped as men pushed themselves back a little
from their tables. Muscles flexed bodies into readiness for
action. Tongues licked lips and eyes looked eagerly at the
front door.

Bluepoint Vance was coming into the room. He came
alone, nodding to acquaintances on this side and that,
carrying his tall body gracefully, easily, in its well-cut
clothing. His sharp-featured face was smilingly self-
confident. He came without haste and without delay to
Red O'Leary's table. I couldn't see Red's face, but muscles

thickened the back of his neck. The girl smiled cordially at Vance and gave him her hand. It was naturally done. She didn't know anything.

Vance turned his smile from Nancy Regan to the red-haired giant—a smile that was a trifle cat-to-mousey.

"How's everything, Red?" he asked.

"Everything suits me," bluntly.

The orchestra had stopped playing. Larrouy, standing by the street door, was mopping his forehead with a handkerchief. At the table to my right, a barrel-chested, broken-nosed bruiser in a widely striped suit was breathing heavily between his gold teeth, his watery gray eyes bulging at O'Leary, Vance and Nancy. He was in no way conspicuous—there were too many others holding the same pose.

Bluepoint Vance turned his head, called to a waiter, "Bring me a chair."

The chair was brought and put at the unoccupied side of the table, facing the wall. Vance sat down, slumping back in the chair, leaning indolently toward Red, his left arm hooked over the chair-back, his right hand holding a cigarette.

"Well, Red," he said when he was thus installed, "have you got any news for me?"

His voice was suave, but loud enough for those at nearby tables to hear.

"Not a word." O'Leary's voice made no pretense of friendliness, nor of caution.

"What, no spinach?" Vance's thin-lipped smile spread, and his dark eyes had a mirthful but not pleasant glitter. "Nobody gave you anything to give me?"

"No," said O'Leary, emphatically.

"My goodness!" said Vance, the smile in his eyes and mouth deepening, and getting still less pleasant. "That's ingratitude! Will you help me collect, Red?"

"No."

I was disgusted with this redhead—half-minded to let him go under when the storm broke. Why couldn't he have stalled his way out—fixed up a fancy tale that Bluepoint would have had to halfway accept? But no—this O'Leary boy was so damned childishly proud of his toughness that he had to make a show of it when he should have been using his bean. If it had been only his own carcass that was due for a beating, it would have been all right. But it wasn't all right that Jack and I should have to suffer. This big chump was too valuable to lose. We'd have to get ourselves all battered up saving him from the rewards of his own pig-headedness. There was no justice in it.

"I've a lot of money coming to me, Red," Vance spoke lazily, tauntingly. "And I need that money." He drew on his cigarette, casually blew the smoke into the redhead's face, and drawled. "Why, do you know the laundry charges twenty-six cents just for doing a pair of pajamas? I need money."

"Sleep in your underclothes," said O'Leary.

Vance laughed. Nancy Regan smiled, but in a bewildered way. She didn't seem to know what it was all about, but she couldn't help knowing that it was about something.

O'Leary leaned forward and spoke deliberately, loud enough for any to hear, "Bluepoint, I've got nothing to give you—now or ever. And that goes for anybody else that's interested. If you or them think I owe you something—try and get it. To hell with you, Bluepoint Vance! If you don't like it—you've got friends here. Call 'em on!"

What a prime young idiot! Nothing would suit him but an ambulance—and I must be dragged along with him.

Vance grinned evilly, his eyes glittering into O'Leary's face. "You'd like that, Red?"

O'Leary hunched his big shoulders and let them drop.

"I don't mind a fight," he said. "But I'd like to get Nancy out of it." He turned to her. "Better run along, honey, I'm going to be busy."

She started to say something, but Vance was talking to her. His words were lightly spoken, and he made no objection to her going. The substance of what he told her was that she was going to be lonely without Red. But he went intimately into the details of that loneliness.

Red O'Leary's right hand rested on the table. It went up to Vance's mouth. The hand was a fist when it got there. A wallop of that sort is awkward to deliver. The body can't give it much. It has to depend on the arm muscles, and not on the best of those. Yet Bluepoint Vance was driven out of his chair and across to the next table.

Larrouy's chairs went empty. The shindig was on.

"On your toes," I growled at Jack Counihan, and, doing my best to look like the nervous little fat man I was, I ran toward the back door, passing men who were moving not yet swiftly toward O'Leary. I must have looked the part of a scared trouble-dodger, because nobody stopped me, and I reached the door before the pack had closed on Red. The door was closed, but not locked. I wheeled with my back to it, blackjack in right hand, gun in left. Men were in front of me, but their backs were to me.

O'Leary was towering in front of his table, his tough red face full of bring-on-your-hell, his big body balanced on the balls of his feet. Between us, Jack Counihan stood, his face turned to me, his mouth twitching in a nervous grin, his eyes dancing with delight. Bluepoint Vance was on his feet again. Blood trickled from his thin lips, down his chin. His eyes were cool. They looked at Red O'Leary with the businesslike look of a logger sizing up the tree he's going to bring down. Vance's mob watched Vance.

"Red!" I bawled into the silence. "This way, Red!"

Faces spun to me—every face in the joint—millions of them.

"Come on, Red!" Jack Counihan yelped, taking a step forward, his gun out.

Bluepoint Vance's hand flashed to the V of his coat. Jack's gun snapped at him. Bluepoint had thrown himself down before the boy's trigger was yanked. The bullet went wide, but Vance's draw was gummed.

Red scooped the girl up with his left arm. A big automatic blossomed in his right fist. I didn't pay much attention to him after that. I was busy.

Larrouy's home was pregnant with weapons—guns, knives, saps, knucks, club-swung chairs and bottles, miscellaneous implements of destruction. Men brought their weapons over to mingle with me. The game was to nudge me away from my door. O'Leary would have liked it. But I was no fire-haired young rowdy. I was pushing forty, and I was twenty pounds overweight. I had the liking for ease that goes with that age and weight. Little ease I got.

A squint-eyed Portuguese slashed at my neck with a knife that spoiled my necktie. I caught him over the ear with the side of my gun before he could get away, saw the ear tear loose. A grinning kid of twenty went down for my legs—football stuff. I felt his teeth in the knee I pumped up, and felt them break. A pock-marked mulatto pushed a gun-barrel over the shoulder of the man in front of him. My blackjack crunched the arm of the man in front. He winced sidewise as the mulatto pulled the trigger—and had the side of his face blown away.

I fired twice—once when a gun was leveled within a foot of my middle, once when I discovered a man standing on a table not far off taking careful aim at my head. For the rest I trusted to my arms and legs, and saved bullets. The night was young and I had only a dozen pills—six in the gun, six in my pocket.

It was a swell bag of nails. Swing right, swing left, kick, swing right, swing left, kick. Don't hesitate, don't look for targets. God will see that there's always a mug there for your gun or blackjack to sock, a belly for your foot.

A bottle came through and found my forehead. My hat saved me some, but the crack didn't do me any good. I swayed and broke a nose where I should have smashed a skull. The room seemed stuffy, poorly ventilated. Somebody ought to tell Larrouy about it. How do you like that lead-and-leather pat on the temple, blondy? This rat on my left is getting too close. I'll draw him in by bending to the right to poke the mulatto, and then I'll lean back into him and let him have it. Not bad! But I can't keep this up all night. Where are Red and Jack? Standing off watching me?

Somebody socked me in the shoulder with something —a piano from the feel of it. I co⌐ ¹¹⌐'ᵗ ᵐⁱˢˢ it. Another thrown bottle took my hat and ⌐   ⌐ scalp. Red O'Leary and Jack Counihan sma⌐   ⌐ ⌐   ⌐ gh, dragging the girl between them.

While Jack put the girl through the door, Red and I cleared a little space in front of us. He was good at that. I didn't dog it on him, but I did let him get all the exercise he wanted.

"All right!" Jack called.

Red and I went through the door, slammed it shut. It wouldn't hold even if locked. O'Leary sent three slugs through it to give the boys something to think about, and our retreat got under way.

We were in a narrow passageway lighted by a fairly bright light. At the other end was a closed door. Halfway down, to the right, steps led up.

"Straight ahead?" asked Jack, who was in front.

O'Leary said, "Yes," and I said, "No. Vance will have that blocked by now if the bulls haven't. Upstairs—the roof."

We reached the stairs. The door behind us burst open. The light went out. The door at the other end of the passage slammed open. No light came through either door. Vance would want light. Larrouy must have pulled the switch, trying to keep his dump from being torn to toothpicks.

Tumult boiled in the dark passage as we climbed the stairs by the touch system. Whoever had come through the back door was mixing it with those who had followed us—mixing it with blows, curses and an occasional shot. More power to them! We climbed, Jack leading, the girl next, then me, and last of all, O'Leary.

Jack was gallantly reading road-signs to the girl, "Careful of the landing, half a turn to the left now, put your right hand on the wall and—"

"Shut up!" I growled at him. "It's better to have her falling down than to have everybody in the drum fall on us."

We reached the second floor. It was black as black. There were three stories to the building.

"I've mislaid the blooming stairs," Jack complained.

We poked around in the dark, hunting for the flight that should lead up toward the roof. We didn't find it. The riot downstairs was quieting. Vance's voice was telling his push that they were mixing it with each other, asking where we had gone. Nobody seemed to know. We didn't know, either.

"Come on," I grumbled, leading the way down the dark hall toward the back of the building. "We've got to go somewhere."

There was still noise downstairs, but no more fighting. Men were talking about getting lights. I stumbled into a door at the end of the hall, pushed it open. A room with two windows through which came a pale glow from the street lights. It seemed brilliant after the hall. My little flock followed me in and we closed the door.

Red O'Leary was across the room, his noodle to an open window.

"Back street," he whispered. "No way down unless we drop."

"Anybody in sight?" I asked.

"Don't see any."

I looked around the room—bed, couple of chairs, chest of drawers, and a table.

"The table will go through the window," I said. "We'll chuck it as far as we can and hope the racket will lead 'em out there before they decide to look up here."

Red and the girl were assuring each other that each was still all in one piece. He broke away from her to help me with the table. We balanced it, swung it, let it go. It did nicely, crashing into the wall of the building opposite, dropping down into a backyard to clang and clatter on a pile of tin, or a collection of garbage cans, or something beautifully noisy. You couldn't have heard it more than a block and a half away.

We got away from the window as men bubbled out of Larrouy's back door.

The girl, unable to find any wounds on O'Leary, had turned to Jack Counihan. He had a cut cheek. She was monkeying with it and a handkerchief.

"When you finish that," Jack was telling her, "I'm going out and get one on the other side."

"I'll never finish if you keep talking—you jiggle your cheek."

"That's a swell idea," he exclaimed. "San Francisco is the second largest city in California. Sacramento is the State capital. Do you like geography? Shall I tell you about Java? I've never been there, but I drink their coffee. If—"

"Silly!" she said, laughing. "If you don't hold still I'll stop now."

"Not so good," he said. "I'll be still."

She wasn't doing anything except wiping blood off his cheek, blood that had better been let dry there. When she finished this perfectly useless surgery, she took her hand away slowly, surveying the hardly noticeable results with pride. As her hand came on a level with his mouth, Jack jerked his head forward to kiss the tip of one passing finger.

"Silly!" she said again, snatching her hand away.

"Lay off that," said Red O'Leary, "or I'll knock you off."

"Pull in your neck," said Jack Counihan.

"Reddy!" the girl cried too late.

The O'Leary right looped out. Jack took the punch on the button, and went to sleep on the floor. The big redhead spun on the balls of his feet to loom over me.

"Got anything to say?" he asked.

I grinned down at Jack, up at Red.

"I'm ashamed of him," I said. "Letting himself be stopped by a palooka who leads with his right."

"You want to try it?"

"Reddy! Reddy!" the girl pleaded, but nobody was listening to her.

"If you'll lead with your right," I said.

"I will," he promised, and did.

I grandstanded, slipping my head out of the way, laying a forefinger on his chin.

"That could have been a knuckle," I said.

"Yes? This one is."

I managed to get under his left, taking the forearm across the back of my neck. But that about played out the acrobatics. It looked as if I would have to see what I could do to him, if anything. The girl grabbed his arm and hung on.

"Reddy, darling, haven't you had enough fighting for one night? Can't you be sensible, even if you are Irish?"

I was tempted to paste the big chew while his playmate had him tied up.

He laughed down at her, ducked his head to kiss her mouth, and grinned at me.

"There's always some other time," he said goodnaturedly.

"We'd better get out of here if we can," I said. "You've made too much rumpus for it to be safe."

"Don't get it up in your neck, little man," he told me. "Hold on to my coattails and I'll pull you out."

The big tramp. If it hadn't been for Jack and me he wouldn't have had any coattail by now.

We moved to the door, listened there, heard nothing.

"The stairs to the third floor must be up front," I whispered. "We'll try for them now."

We opened the door carefully. Enough light went past us into the hall to show a promise of emptiness. We crept down the hall, Red and I each holding one of the girl's hands. I hoped Jack would come out all right, but he had put himself to sleep, and I had troubles of my own.

I hadn't known that Larrouy's was large enough to have two miles of hallway. It did. It was an even mile in the darkness to the head of the stairs we had come up. We didn't pause there to listen to the voices below. At the end of the next mile O'Leary's foot found the bottom step of the flight leading up.

Just then a yell broke out at the head of the other flight. "All up—they're up here!"

A white light beamed up on the yeller, and a brogue addressed him from below, "Come on down, ye windbag."

"The police," Nancy Regan whispered, and we hustled up our new-found steps to the third floor.

More darkness, just like that we'd left. We stood still at the top of the stairs. We didn't seem to have any company.

"The roof," I said. "We'll risk matches."

Back in a corner our feeble match-light found us a ladder nailed to the wall, leading to a trap in the ceiling. As little later as possible we were on Larrouy's roof, the trap closed behind us.

"All silk so far," said O'Leary, "and if Vance's rats and the bulls will play a couple of seconds longer—bingavast."

I led the way across the roofs. We dropped ten feet to the next building, climbed a bit to the next, and found on the other side of it a fire-escape that ran down to a narrow court with an opening into the back street.

"This ought to do it," I said, and went down.

The girl came behind me, and then Red. The court into which we dropped was empty—a narrow cement passage between buildings. The bottom of the fire-escape creaked as it hinged down under my weight, but the noise didn't stir anything. It was dark in the court, but not black.

"When we hit the street, we split," O'Leary told me, without a word of gratitude for my help—the help he didn't seem to know he had needed. "You roll your hoop, we'll roll ours."

"Uh-huh," I agreed, chasing my brains around in my skull. "I'll scout the alley first."

Carefully I picked my way down to the end of the court and risked the top of my hatless head to peep into the back street. It was quiet, but at the corner, a quarter of a block above, two loafers seemed to be loafing attentively. They weren't coppers. I stepped out into the back street and beckoned them. They couldn't recognize me at that distance, in that light, and there was no reason why they shouldn't think me one of Vance's crew, if they belonged to him.

As they came toward me I stepped back into the court and hissed for Red. He wasn't a boy you had to call twice to a row. He got to me just as they arrived. I took one. He took the other.

Because I wanted a disturbance, I had to work like a mule to get it. These bimbos were a couple of lollipops for fair. There wouldn't have been an ounce of fight in a ton of them. The one I had didn't know what to make of my roughing him around. He had a gun, but he managed to drop it first thing, and in the wrestling it got kicked out of reach. He hung on while I sweated ink jockeying him around into position. The darkness helped, but even at that it was no cinch to pretend he was putting up a battle while I worked him around behind O'Leary, who wasn't having any trouble at all with his man.

Finally I made it. I was behind O'Leary, who had his man pinned against the wall with one hand, preparing to sock him again with the other. I clamped my left hand on my playmate's wrist, twisted him to his knees, got my gun out, and shot O'Leary in the back, just below the right shoulder.

Red swayed, jamming his man into the wall. I beaned mine with the gun-butt.

"Did he get you, Red?" I asked, steadying him with an arm, knocking his prisoner across the noodle.

"Yeah."

"Nancy," I called.

She ran to us.

"Take his other side," I told her. "Keep on your feet, Red, and we'll make the sneak O.K."

The bullet was too freshly in him to slow him up yet, though his right arm was out of commission. We ran down the back street to the corner. We had pursuers before we made it. Curious faces looked at us in the street. A policeman a block away began to move our way. The girl helping O'Leary on one side, me on the other, we ran half a block away from the copper, to where I had left the automobile Jack and I had used. The street was active by the time I got the machinery grinding and the girl had Red stowed safely in the back seat. The copper sent a yell and a high bullet after us. We left the neighborhood.

I didn't have any special destination yet, so after the necessary first burst of speed I slowed up a little, went around lots of corners, and brought the bus to rest in a dark street beyond Van Ness Avenue.

Red was drooping in one corner of the back, the girl holding him up, when I screwed around in my seat to look at them.

"Where to?" I asked.

"A hospital, a doctor, something!" the girl cried. "He's dying!"

I didn't believe that. If he was, it was his own fault. If he had had enough gratitude to take me along with him as a friend I wouldn't have had to shoot him so I could go along as nurse. "Where to, Red?" I asked him, prodding his knee with a finger.

He spoke thickly, giving me the address of the Stockton Street hotel.

"That's no good," I objected. "Everybody in town knows you bunk there, and if you go back, it's lights out for yours. Where to?"

"Hotel," he repeated.

I got up, knelt on the seat, and leaned back to work on him. He was weak. He couldn't have much resistance left. Bulldozing a man who might after all be dying wasn't gentlemanly, but I had invested a lot of trouble in this egg, trying to get him to lead me to his friends, and I wasn't going to quit in the stretch. For a while it looked as if he wasn't weak enough yet, as if I'd have to shoot him again. But the girl sided with me, and between us we finally convinced him that his only safe bet was to go somewhere where he could hide while he got the right kind of care. We didn't actually convince him—we wore him out and he gave in because he was too weak to argue longer. He gave me an address out by Holly Park.

Hoping for the best, I pointed the machine thither.

The house was a small one in a row of small houses. We took the big boy out of the car and between us to the door. He could just about make it with our help. The street was dark. No light showed from the house. I rang the bell.

Nothing happened. I rang again, and then once more.

"Who is it?" a harsh voice demanded from the inside.

"Red's been hurt," I said.

Silence for a while. Then the door opened half a foot. Through the opening a light came from the interior, enough light to show the flat face and bulging jaw-muscles of the skull-cracker who had been the Motsa Kid's guardian and executioner.

"What the hell?" he asked.

"Red was jumped. They got him," I explained, pushing the limp giant forward.

We didn't crash the gate that way. The skull-cracker held the door as it was.

"You'll wait," he said, and shut the door in our faces. His voice sounded from within, "Flora." That was all right—Red had brought us to the right place.

When he opened the door again he opened it all the way, and Nancy Regan and I took our burden into the hall. Beside the skull-cracker stood a woman in a low-cut black silk gown—Big Flora, I supposed.

She stood at least five feet ten in her high-heeled slippers. They were small slippers, and I noticed that her ringless hands were small. The rest of her wasn't. She was broad-shouldered, deep-bosomed, thick-armed, with a pink throat which for all its smoothness was muscled like a wrestler's. She was about my age—close to forty—with very curly and very yellow bobbed hair, very pink skin, and a handsome, brutal face. Her deep-set eyes were gray, her thick lips were well-shaped, her nose was just broad enough and curved enough to give her a look of strength, and she had chin enough to support it. From forehead to throat her pink skin was underlaid with smooth, thick, strong muscles.

This Big Flora was no toy. She had the look and the poise of a woman who could have managed the looting and the double-crossing afterward. Unless her face and body lied, she had all the strength of physique, mind and will that would be needed, and some to spare. She was made of stronger stuff than either the ape-built bruiser at her side or the red-haired giant I was holding.

"Well?" she asked, when the door had been closed behind us. Her voice was deep but not masculine—a voice that went well with her looks.

"Vance ganged him in Larrouy's. He took one in the back," I said.

"Who are you?"

"Get him to bed," I stalled. "We've got all night to talk."

She turned, snapping her fingers. A shabby little old man darted out of a door toward the rear. His brown eyes were very scary. "Get to hell upstairs," she ordered. "Fix the bed, get hot water and towels."

The little old man scrambled up the stairs like a rheumatic rabbit.

The skull-cracker took the girl's side of Red, and he and I carried the giant up to a room where the little man was scurrying around with basins and cloth. Flora and Nancy Regan followed us. We spread the wounded man face-down on the bed and stripped him. Blood still ran from the bullet hole. He was unconscious.

Nancy Regan went to pieces.

"He's dying! Get a doctor! Oh, Reddy, dearest—"

"Shut up!" said Big Flora. "The damned fool ought to

croak—going to Larrouy's tonight!" She caught the little man by the shoulder and threw him at the door. "Zonite and more water," she called after him. "Give me your knife, Pogy."

The ape-built man took from his pocket a springknife with a long blade that had been sharpened until it was narrow and thin. This is the knife, I thought, that cut the Motsa Kid's throat.

With it, Big Flora cut the bullet out of Red O'Leary's back.

The ape-built Pogy kept Nancy Regan over in a corner of the room while the operating was done. The little scared man knelt beside the bed, handing the woman what she asked for, mopping up Red's blood as it ran from the wound.

I stood beside Flora, smoking cigarettes from the pack she had given me. When she raised her head, I would transfer the cigarette from my mouth to hers. She would fill her lungs with a draw that ate half the cigarette and nod. I would take the cigarette from her mouth. She would blow out the smoke and bend to her work again. I would light another cigarette from what was left of that one, and be ready for her next smoke.

Her bare arms were blood to the elbows. Her face was damp with sweat. It was a gory mess, and it took time. But when she straightened up for the last smoke, the bullet was out of Red, the bleeding had stopped, and he was bandaged.

"Thank God that's over," I said, lighting one of my own cigarettes. "Those pills you smoke are terrible."

The little scared man was cleaning up. Nancy Regan had fainted in a chair across the room, and nobody was paying any attention to her.

"Keep your eye on this gent, Pogy," Big Flora told the skull-cracker, nodding at me, "while I wash up."

I went over to the girl, rubbed her hands, put some water on her face, and got her awake.

"The bullet's out. Red's sleeping. He'll be picking fights again within a week," I told her.

She jumped up and ran over to the bed.

Flora came in. She had washed and changed her blood-stained black gown for a green kimono affair, which gaped here and there to show a lot of orchid-colored underthings.

"Talk," she commanded, standing in front of me. "Who, what and why?"

"I'm Percy Maguire," I said, as if this name, which I had just thought up, explained everything.

"That's the who," she said, as if my phony alias explained nothing. "Now what's the what and why?"

The ape-built Pogy, standing on one side, looked me up and down. I'm short and lumpy. My face doesn't scare children, but it's a more or less truthful witness to a life that hasn't been over-burdened with refinement and gentility. The evening's entertainment had decorated me with bruises and scratches, and had done things to what was left of my clothes.

"Percy," he echoed, showing wide-spaced yellow teeth in a grin. "My Gawd, brother, your folks must of been color-blind!"

"That's the what and why," I insisted to the woman, paying no attention to the wheeze from the zoo. "I'm Percy Maguire, and I want my hundred and fifty thousand dollars."

The muscles in her brows came down over her eyes.

"You've got a hundred and fifty thousand dollars, have you?"

I nodded up into her handsome brutal face.

"Yeah," I said. "That's what I came for."

"Oh, you haven't got them? You want them?"

"Listen, sister, I want my dough." I had to get tough if this play was to go over. "This swapping *Oh-have-yous* and *Yes-I-haves* don't get me anything but a thirst. We were in the big knockover, see? And after that, when we find the pay-off's a bust, I said to the kid I was training with, 'Never mind, Kid, we'll get our whack. Just follow Percy.' And then Bluepoint comes to me to throw in with him, and I said, 'Sure' and me and the kid throw in with him until we all come across Red in the dump tonight.

Then I told the kid, 'These coffee-and-doughnut guns are going to rub Red out, and that won't get us anything. We'll take him away from 'em and make him steer us to where Big Flora's sitting on the jack. We ought to be good for a hundred and fifty grand apiece, now that there's damned few in on it. After we get that, if we want to bump Red off, all right. But business before pleasure, and a hundred and fifty thou is business.' So we did. We opened an out for the big boy when he didn't have any. The kid got mushy with the broad along the road and got knocked for a loop. That was all right with me. If she was worth a hundred and fifty grand to him—fair enough. I came on with Red. I pulled the big tramp out after he stopped the slug. By rights I ought to collect the kid's dib, too—making three hundred thou for me—but give me the hundred and fifty I started out for and we'll call it even-steven."

I thought this hocus ought to stick. Of course I wasn't counting on her ever giving me any money, but if the rank and file of the mob hadn't known these people, why should these people know everybody in the mob?

Flora spoke to Pogy, "Get that damned heap away from the front door."

I felt better when he went out. She wouldn't have sent him out to move the car if she had meant to do anything to me right away.

"Got any food in the joint?" I asked, making myself at home.

She went to the head of the steps and yelled down, "Get something for us to eat."

Red was still unconscious. Nancy Regan sat beside him, holding one of his hands. Her face was drained white. Big Flora came into the room again, looked at the invalid, put a hand on his forehead, felt his pulse.

"Come on downstairs," she said.

"I—I'd rather stay here, if I may," Nancy Regan said. Voice and eyes showed utter terror of Flora.

The big woman, saying nothing, went downstairs. I

followed her to the kitchen, where the little man was working on ham and eggs at the range. The window and back door, I saw, were reinforced with heavy planking and braced with timbers nailed to the floor. The clock over the sink said 2:50 A.M.

Flora brought out a quart of liquor and poured drinks for herself and me. We sat at the table and while we waited for our food she cursed Red O'Leary and Nancy Regan, because he had got himself disabled keeping a date with her at a time when Flora needed his strength most. She cursed them individually, as a pair, and was making it a racial matter by cursing all the Irish when the little man gave us our ham and eggs.

We had finished the solids and were stirring hooch in our second cups of coffee when Pogy came back. He had news.

"There's a couple of mugs hanging around the corner that I don't much like."

"Bulls or—?" Flora asked.

"Or," he said.

Flora began to curse Red and Nancy again. But she had pretty well played that line out already. She turned to me.

"What the hell did you bring them here for?" she demanded. "Leaving a mile-wide trail behind you! Why didn't you let the lousy bum die where he got his dose?"

"I brought him here for my hundred and fifty grand. Slip it to me and I'll be on my way. You don't owe me anything else. I don't owe you anything. Give me my rhino instead of lip and I'll pull my freight."

"Like hell you will," said Pogy.

The woman looked at me under lowered brows and drank her coffee.

Fifteen minutes later the shabby little old man came running into the kitchen, saying he had heard feet on the roof. His faded brown eyes were dull as an ox's with fright, and his withered lips writhed under his straggly yellow-white mustache.

Flora profanely called him a this-and-that kind of old one-thing-and-another and chased him upstairs again. She got up from the table and pulled the green kimono tight around her big body.

"You're here," she told me, "and you'll put in with us. There's no other way. Got a rod?"

I admitted I had a gun but shook my head at the rest of it.

"This is not my wake—yet," I said. "It'll take one hundred and fifty thousand berries, spot cash, paid in the hand, to buy Percy in on it."

I wanted to know if the loot was on the premises.

Nancy Regan's tearful voice came from the stairs, "No, no, darling! Please, please, go back to bed! You'll kill yourself, Reddy, dear!"

Red O'Leary strode into the kitchen. He was naked except for a pair of gray pants and his bandage. His eyes were feverish and happy. His dry lips were stretched in a grin. He had a gun in his left hand. His right arm hung useless. Behind him trotted Nancy. She stopped pleading and shrank behind him when she saw Big Flora.

"Ring the gong, and let's go," the half-naked redhead laughed. "Vance is in our street."

Flora went over to him, put her fingers on his wrist, held them there a couple of seconds, and nodded.

"You crazy son-of-a-gun," she said in a tone that was more like maternal pride than anything else. "You're good for a fight right now. And a damned good thing, too, because you're going to get it."

Red laughed—a triumphant laugh that boasted of his toughness—then his eyes turned to me. Laughter went out of them and a puzzled look drew them narrow.

"Hello," he said. "I dreamed about you, but I can't remember what it was. It was— Wait. I'll get it in a minute. It was— By God! I dreamed it was you that plugged me!"

Flora smiled at me, the first time I had seen her smile, and she spoke quickly, "Take him, Pogy!"

I twisted obliquely out of my chair.

Pogy's fist took me in the temple. Staggering across the room, struggling to keep my feet, I thought of the bruise on the dead Motsa Kid's temple.

Pogy was on me when the wall bumped me upright.

I put a fist—spat!—in his flat nose. Blood squirted, but his hairy paws gripped me. I tucked my chin in, ground the top of my head into his face. The scent Big Flora used came strong to me. Her silk clothes brushed against me. With both hands full of my hair she pulled my head back, stretching my neck for Pogy. He took hold of it with his paws. I quit. He didn't throttle me any more than was necessary, but it was bad enough.

Flora frisked me for gun and blackjack.

".38 special," she named the caliber of the gun. "I dug a .38 special bullet out of you, Red." The words came faintly to me through the roaring in my ears.

The little old man's voice was chattering in the kitchen. I couldn't make out anything he said. Pogy's hands went away from me. I put my own hands to my throat. It was hell not to have any pressure at all there. The blackness went slowly away from my eyes, leaving a lot of little purple clouds that floated around and around. Presently I could sit up on the floor. I knew by that I had been lying down on it.

The purple clouds shrank until I could see past them enough to know there were only three of us in the room now. Cringing in a chair, back in a corner, was Nancy Regan. On another chair, beside the door, a black pistol in his hand, sat the scared little old man. His eyes were desperately frightened. Gun and hand shook at me. I tried to ask him to either stop shaking or move his gun away from me, but I couldn't get any words out yet.

Upstairs, guns boomed, their reports exaggerated by the smallness of the house.

The little man winced.

"Let me get out," he whispered with unexpected abruptness, "and I will give you everything. I will! Everything—if you will let me get out of this house!"

This feeble ray of light where there hadn't been a dot gave me back the use of my vocal apparatus. "Talk turkey," I managed to say.

"I will give you those upstairs—that she-devil. I will give you the money, I will give you all—if you will let me go out. I am old. I am sick. I cannot live in prison. What have I to do with robberies? Nothing. Is it my fault that she-devil—? You have seen it here. I am a slave—I who am near the end of my life. Abuse, cursings, beatings— and those are not enough. Now I must go to prison because that she-devil is a she-devil. I am an old man who cannot live in prisons. You let me go out. You do me that kindness. I will give you that she-devil—those other devils —the money they stole. That I will do!" Thus this panic-stricken little old man squirming and fidgeting on his chair.

"How can I get you out?" I asked, getting up from the floor, my eye on his gun. If I could get to him while we talked.

"How not? You are a friend of the police—that I know. The police are here now—waiting for daylight before they come into this house. I myself with my old eyes saw them take Bluepoint Vance. You can take me out past your friends, the police. You do what I ask, and I will give you those devils and their moneys."

"Sounds good," I said, taking a careless step toward him. "But can I just stroll out of here when I want to?"

"No! No!" he said, paying no attention to the second step I took toward him. "But first I will give you those three devils. I will give them to you alive but without power. And their money. That I will do, and then you will take me out—and this girl here." He nodded suddenly at Nancy, whose white face, still nice in spite of its terror, was mostly wide eyes just now. "She, too, has nothing to do with those devils' crimes. She must go with me."

I wondered what this old rabbit thought he could do. I frowned exceedingly thoughtful while I took still another step toward him.

"Make no mistake," he whispered earnestly. "When that she-devil comes back into this room you will die—she will kill you certainly."

Three more steps and I would be close enough to take hold of him and his gun.

Footsteps were in the hall. Too late for a jump.

"Yes?" he hissed desperately.

I nodded a split-second before Big Flora came through the door.

She was dressed for action in a pair of blue pants that were probably Pogy's, beaded moccasins, a silk waist. A ribbon held her curly yellow hair back from her face. She had a gun in one hand, one in each hip pocket.

The one in her hand swung up.

"You're done," she told me, quite matter-of-fact.

My newly acquired confederate whined, "Wait, wait, Flora! Not here like this, please! Let me take him into the cellar."

She scowled at him, shrugging her silken shoulders.

"Make it quick," she said. "It'll be light in another half-hour."

I felt too much like crying to laugh at them. Was I supposed to think this woman would let the rabbit change her plans? I suppose I must have put some value on the old gink's help, or I wouldn't have been so disappointed when this little comedy told me it was a frame-up. But any hold they worked me into couldn't be any worse than the one I was in.

So I went ahead of the old man into the hall, opened the door he indicated, switched on the basement light, and went down the rough steps.

Behind me he was whispering, "I'll first show you the moneys, and then I will give you those devils. And you will not forget your promise? I and that girl shall go out through the police?"

"Oh, yes," I assured the old joker.

He came up beside me, sticking a gun-butt in my hand.

"Hide it," he hissed, and, when I had pocketed that one, gave me another, producing them with his free hand from under his coat.

Then he actually showed me the loot. It was still in the boxes and bags in which it had been carried from the banks. He insisted on opening some of them to show me the money—green bundles belted with the bank's yellow wrappers. The boxes and bags were stacked in a small brick cell that was fitted with a padlocked door, to which he had the key.

He closed the door when we were through looking, but he did not lock it, and he led me back part of the way we had come.

"That, as you see, is the money," he said. "Now for those. You will stand here, hiding behind these boxes."

A partition divided the cellar in half. It was pierced by a doorway that had no door. The place the old man told me to hide was close beside this doorway, between the partition and four packing cases. Hiding there, I would be to the right of, and a little behind, anyone who came downstairs and walked through the cellar toward the cell that held the money. That is, I would be in that position when they went to go through the doorway in the partition.

The old man was fumbling beneath one of the boxes. He brought out an eighteen-inch length of lead pipe stuffed in a similar length of black garden hose. He gave this to me as he explained everything.

"They will come down here one at a time. When they are about to go through this door, you will know what to do with this. And then you will have them, and I will have your promise. Is it not so?"

"Oh, yes," I said, all up in the air. He went upstairs. I

crouched behind the boxes, examining the guns he had given me—and I'm damned if I could find anything wrong with them. They were loaded and they seemed to be in working order. That finishing touch completely balled me up. I didn't know whether I was in a cellar or a balloon.

When Red O'Leary, still naked except for pants and bandage, came into the cellar, I had to shake my head violently to clear it in time to bat him across the back of the noodle as his first bare foot stepped through the doorway. He sprawled down on his face.

The old man scurried down the steps, full of grins.

"Hurry! Hurry!" he panted, helping me drag the redhead back into the money cell. Then he produced two pieces of cord and tied the giant hand and foot.

"Hurry!" he panted again as he left me to run upstairs, while I went back to my hiding place and hefted the lead pipe, wondering if Flora had shot me and I was now enjoying the rewards of my virtue—in a heaven where I could enjoy myself forever and ever socking folks who had been rough with me down below.

The ape-built skull-cracker came down, reached the door. I cracked his skull. The little man came scurrying. We dragged Pogy to the cell, tied him up.

"Hurry!" panted the old gink, dancing up and down in his excitement. "That she-devil next—and strike hard!" He scrambled upstairs and I could hear his feet pattering overhead.

I got rid of some of my bewilderment, making room for a little intelligence in my skull. This foolishness we were up to wasn't so. It couldn't be happening. Nothing ever worked out just that way. You didn't stand in corners and knock down people one after the other like a machine, while a scrawny little bozo up at the other end fed them to you. It was too damned silly! I had enough!

I passed up my hiding place, put down the pipe and found another spot to crouch in, under some shelves, near the steps. I hunkered down here with a gun in each fist.

This game I was playing in was—it had to be gummy around the edges. I wasn't going to stay put any longer.

Flora came down the steps. Behind her trotted the little man.

Flora had a gun in each hand. Her gray eyes were everywhere. Her head was down like an animal's coming to a fight. Her nostrils quivered. Her body, coming down neither slowly nor swiftly, was balanced like a dancer's. If I live to a million I'll never forget the picture this handsome brutal woman made coming down those unplaned cellar stairs. She was a beautiful fight-bred animal going to a fight.

She saw me as I straightened.

"Drop 'em!" I said, but I knew she wouldn't.

The little man flicked a limp brown blackjack out of his sleeve and knocked her behind the ear just as she swung her left gun on me. I jumped over and caught her before she hit the cement.

"Now, you see!" the old man said gleefully. "You have the money and you have them. And now you will get me and that girl out."

"First we'll stow this with the others," I said.

After he had helped me do that I told him to lock the cell door. He did, and I took the key with one hand, his neck with the other. He squirmed like a snake while I ran my other hand over his clothes removing the blackjack and a gun, and finding a money-belt around his waist.

"Take it off," I ordered. "You don't carry anything out with you."

His fingers worked with the buckle, dragged the belt from under his clothes, let it fall on the floor. It was padded fat.

Still holding his neck, I took him upstairs, while the girl still sat frozen on the kitchen chair. It took a stiff hooker of whiskey and a lot of words to thaw her into understanding that she was going out with the old man and that she wasn't to say a word to anybody, especially not to the police.

"Where's Reddy?" she asked when color had come back into her face—which had even at the worst never lost its niceness—and thoughts to her head.

I told her he was all right, and promised her he would be in a hospital before the morning was over. She didn't ask anything else. I shooed her upstairs for her hat and coat, went with the old man while he got his hat, and then put the pair of them in the front ground-floor room.

"Stay here till I come for you," I said, and I locked the door and pocketed the key when I went out.

The front door and the front window on the ground floor had been planked and braced like the rear ones. I didn't like to risk opening them, even though it was fairly light by now. So I went upstairs, fashioned a flag of truce out of a pillow-slip and a bed-slat, hung it out a window, waited until a heavy voice said, "All right, speak your piece," and then I showed myself and told the police I'd let them in.

It took five minutes' work with a hatchet to pry the front door lo se. The chief of police, the captain of detectives, and half the force were waiting on the front steps and pavement when I got the door open. I took them to the cellar and turned Big Flora, Pogy and Red O'Leary over to them, with the money. Flora and Pogy were awake, but not talking.

While the dignitaries were crowded around the spoils I went upstairs. The house was full of police sleuths. I swapped greetings with them as I went through to the room where I had left Nancy Regan and the old gink. Lieutenant Duff was trying the locked door, while O'Gar and Hunt stood behind him.

I grinned at Duff and gave him the key.

He opened the door, looked at the old man and the girl—mostly at her—and then at me. They were standing in the center of the room. The old man's faded eyes were miserably worried, the girl's blue ones were darkly anxious. Anxiety didn't ruin her looks a bit.

"If that's yours I don't blame you for locking it up," O'Gar muttered in my ear.

"You can run along now," I told the two in the room. "Get all the sleep you need before you report for duty again."

They nodded and went out of the house.

"That's how your Agency evens up?" Duff said. "The she-employees make up in looks for the ugliness of the he's."

Dick Foley came into the hall.

"How's your end?" I asked.

"Finis. The Angel led me to Vance. He led here. I led the bulls here. They got him—got her."

Two shots crashed in the street.

We went to the door and saw excitement in a police car down the street. We went down there. Bluepoint Vance, handcuffs on his wrists, was writhing half on the seat, half on the floor.

"We were holding him here in the car, Houston and me," a hard-mouthed plain-clothes man explained to Duff. "He made a break, grabbed Houston's gat with both hands. I had to drill him—twice. The cap'll raise hell! He specially wanted him kept here to put up against the others. But God knows I wouldn't of shot him if it hadn't been him or Houston!"

Duff called the plain-clothes man a damned clumsy mick as they lifted Vance up on the seat. Bluepoint's tortured eyes focused on me.

"I—know—you?" he asked painfully. "Continental—New—York?"

"Yes," I said.

"Couldn't—place—you—Larrouy's—with—Red?"

"Yeah," I told him. "Got Red, Flora, Pogy and the cush."

"But—not—Papa—dop—oul—os."

"Papa does what?" I asked impatiently, a shiver along my spine.

He pulled himself up on the seat.

"Papadopoulos," he repeated, with an agonizing summoning of the little strength left in him. "I tried—shoot him—saw him—walk 'way—with girl—bull—too damn quick —wish . . ."

His words ran out. He shuddered. Death wasn't a sixteenth of an inch behind his eyes. A white-coated intern tried to get past me into the car. I pushed him out of the way and leaned in taking Vance by the shoulders. The back of my neck was ice. My stomach was empty.

"Listen, Bluepoint," I yelled in his face. "Papadopoulos? Little old man? Brains of the push?"

"Yes," Vance said, and the last live blood in him came out with the word.

I let him drop back on the seat and walked away.

Of course! How had I missed it? The little scoundrel— if he hadn't, for all his scaredness, been the works, how could he have so neatly turned the others over to me one at a time? They had been absolutely cornered. It was be killed fighting, or surrender and be hanged. They had no other way out. The police had Vance, who could and would tell them that the little buzzard was the headman— there wasn't even a chance for him beating the courts with his age, his weakness and his mask of being driven around by the others.

And there I had been—with no choice but to accept his offer. Otherwise lights out for me. I had been putty in his hands, his accomplices had been putty. He had slipped the cross-over on them as they had helped him slip it over on the others—and I had sent him safely away.

Now I could turn the city upside down for him—my promise had been only to get him out of the house— but . . .

What a life!

$106,000 BLOOD MONEY

"I'm Tom-Tom Carey," he said, drawling the words.

I nodded at the chair beside my desk and weighed him in while he moved to it. Tall, wide-shouldered, thick-chested, thin-bellied, he would add up to say a hundred and ninety pounds. His swarthy face was hard as a fist, but there was nothing ill-humored in it. It was the face of a man of forty-something who lived life raw and thrived on it. His blue clothes were good and he wore them well.

In the chair he twisted brown paper around a charge of Bull Durham and finished introducing himself, "I'm Paddy the Mex's brother."

I thought maybe he was telling the truth. Paddy had been like this fellow in coloring and manner.

"That would make your real name Carrera," I suggested.

"Yes." He was lighting a cigarette. "Alfredo Estanislao Cristobal Carrera, if you want all the details."

I asked him how to spell Estanislao, wrote the name down on a slip of paper, adding *alias Tom-Tom Carey*, rang for Tommy Howd, and told him to have the file clerk see if we had anything on it.

"While your people are opening graves I'll tell you why I'm here," the swarthy man drawled through smoke when Tommy had gone away with the paper.

"Tough, Paddy being knocked off like that," I said.

ex   He was too damned trusting to live long," his brother
     plained. "This is the kind of hombre he was—the last
time I saw him was four years ago, here in San Francisco.
I'd come in from an expedition down to—never mind
where. Anyway I was flat. Instead of pearls all I'd got out
of the trip was a bullet-crease over my hip. Paddy was
dirty with fifteen thousand or so he'd just nicked somebody
for. The afternoon I saw him he had a date that he was
leery of toting so much money. So he gives me the fifteen
thousand to hold for him till that night."

Tom-Tom Carey blew out smoke and smiled softly past
me at a memory.

"That's the kind of hombre he was," he went on. "He'd
trust even his own brother. I went to Sacramento that
afternoon and caught a train east. A girl in Pittsburgh
helped me spend the fifteen thousand. Her name was
Laurel. She liked rye whiskey with milk for a chaser. I
used to drink it with her till I was all curdled inside, and
I've never had any appetite for *schmierkäse* since. So
there's a hundred thousand dollars reward on this Papadopoulos, is there?"

"And six. The insurance companies put up a hundred
thousand, the bankers' association five, and the city a
thousand."

Tom-Tom Carey chucked the remains of his cigarette
in the cuspidor and began to assemble another one.

"Suppose I hand him to you?" he asked. "How many
ways will the money have to go?"

"None of it will stop here," I assured him. "The Continental Detective Agency doesn't touch reward money—
and won't let its hired men. If any of the police are in on
the pinch, they'll want a share."

"But if they aren't, it's all mine?"

"If you turn him in without help, or without any help
except ours."

"I'll do that." The words were casual. "So much for the
arrest. Now for the conviction part. If you get him, are you
sure you can nail him to the cross?"

"I ought to be, but he'll have to go up against a ju
and that means anything can happen."

The muscular brown hand holding the brown cigarette
made a careless gesture.

"Then maybe I'd better get a confession out of him
before I drag him in," he said offhand.

"It would be safer that way," I agreed. "You ought to
let that holster down an inch or two. It brings the gunbutt
too high. The bulge shows when you sit down."

"Uh-huh. You mean the one on the left shoulder. I took
it away from a fellow after I lost mine. Strap's too short.
I'll get another one this afternoon."

Tommy came in with a folder labeled, Carey, Tom-
Tom, 1361-C. It held some newspaper clippings, the
oldest dated ten years back, the youngest eight months. I
read them through, passing each one to the swarthy man
as I finished it. Tom-Tom Carey was written down in them
as soldier of fortune, gunrunner, seal poacher, smuggler,
and pirate. But it was all alleged, supposed and suspected.
He had been captured variously but never convicted of
anything.

"They don't treat me right," he complained placidly
when we were through reading. "For instance stealing that
Chinese gunboat wasn't my fault. I was forced to do it—I
was the one that was doublecrossed. After they'd got the
stuff aboard they wouldn't pay for it. I couldn't unload it. I
couldn't do anything but take gunboat and all. The insurance companies must want this Papadopoulos plenty to
hang a hundred thousand on him."

"Cheap enough if it lands him," I said. "Maybe he's
not all the newspapers picture him as, but he's more than a
handful. He gathered a whole damned army of strongarm
men here, took over a block in the center of the financial
district, looted the two biggest banks in the city, fought off
the whole police department, made his getaway, ditched
the army, used some of his lieutenants to bump off some
more of them—that's where your brother Paddy got his—
then with the help of Pogy Reeve, Big Flora Brace and Red

ary, wiped out the rest of his lieutenants. And remember, those lieutenants weren't schoolboys—they were slick grifters like Bluepoint Vance and the Shivering Kid and Darby M'Laughlin—birds who knew their what's what.

"Uh-huh." Carey was unimpressed. "But it was a bust just the same. You got all the loot back, and he just managed to get away himself."

"A bad break for him," I explained. "Red O'Leary broke out with a complication of love and vanity. You can't chalk that against Papadopoulos. Don't get the idea he's half-smart. He's dangerous, and I don't blame the insurance companies for thinking they'll sleep better if they're sure he's not out where he can frame some more tricks against their policy-holding banks."

"Don't know much about this Papadopoulos, do you?"

"No." I told the truth. "And nobody does. The hundred-thousand offer made rats out of half the crooks in the country. They're as hot after him as we—not only because of the reward but because of his wholesale double-crossing. And they know just as little about him as we do—that he's had his fingers in a dozen or more jobs, that he was the brains behind Bluepoint Vance's bond tricks, and that his enemies have a habit of dying young. But nobody knows where he came from, or where he lives when he's home. Don't think I'm touting him as a Napoleon or a Sunday supplement mastermind—but he's a shifty, tricky old boy. As you say, I don't know much about him—but there are lots of people I don't know much about."

Tom-Tom Carey nodded to show me he understood the last part and began making his third cigarette.

"I was in Nogales when Angel Grace Cardigan got word to me that Paddy had been done in," he said. "That was nearly a month ago. She seemed to think I'd romp up here pronto—but it was no skin off my face. I let it sleep. But last week I read in a newspaper about all this reward money being posted on the hombre she blamed for Paddy's

rub-out. That made it different—a hundred-thousand
lars different. So I shipped up here, talked to her, and th
came in to make sure there'll be nothing between me and
the blood money when I put the loop on this Papadoodle."

"Angel Grace sent you to me?" I inquired.

"Uh-huh—only she don't know it. She dragged you
into the story—said you were a friend of Paddy's, a good
guy for a sleuth and hungry as hell for this Papadoodle. So
I thought you'd be the gent f r me to see."

"When did you leave Nogales?"

"Tuesday—last week."

"That," I said, prodding my memory, "was the day
after Newhall was killed across the border."

The swarthy man nodded. Nothing changed in his
face.

"How far from Nogales was that?" I asked.

"He was gunned down near Ocuitoa—that's somewhere around sixty miles southwest of Nogales. You interested?"

"No—except I was wondering about your leaving the
place where he was killed the day after he was killed, and
coming up where he had lived. Did you know him?"

"He was pointed out to me in Nogales as a San
Francisco millionaire going with a party to look at some
mining property in Mexico. I was figuring on maybe
selling him something later, but the Mexican patriots got
him before I did."

"And so you came north?"

"Uh-huh. The hubbub kind of spoiled things for me. I
had a nice little business in—call it supplies—to and fro
across the line. This Newhall killing turned the spotlight
on that part of the country. So I thought I'd come up and
collect that hundred thousand and give things a chance to
settle down there. Honest, brother, I haven't killed a millionaire in weeks, if that's what's worrying you."

"That's good. Now as I get it, you're counting on
landing Papadopoulos. Angel Grace sent for you, thinking
you'd run him down just to even up for Paddy's killing,

s the money you want, so you figure on playing with
is well as the Angel. That right?"

"Check."

"You know what'll happen if she learns you're stringing
along with me?"

"Uh-huh. She'll chuck a convulsion—kind of balmy on
the subject of keeping clear of the police, isn't she?"

"She is—somebody told her something about honor
among thieves once and she's never got over it. Her
brother's doing a hitch up north now—Johnny the
Plumber sold him out. Her man Paddy was mowed down
by his pals. Did either of those things wake her up? Not a
chance. She'd rather have Papadopoulos go free than join
forces with us."

"That's all right," Tom-Tom Carey assured me. "She
thinks I'm the loyal brother—Paddy couldn't have told her
much about me—and I'll handle her. You having her
shadowed?"

I said, "Yes—ever since she was turned loose. She was
picked up the same day Flora and Pogy and Red were
grabbed, but we hadn't anything on her except that she
had been Paddy's ladylove, so I had her sprung. How
much dope did you get out of her?"

"Descriptions of Papadoodle and Nancy Regan, and
that's all. She don't know any more about them than I do.
Where does this Regan girl fit in?"

"Hardly any, except that she might lead us to Papadopoulos. She was Red's girl. It was keeping a date with
her that upset the game. When Papadopoulos wriggled out
he took the girl with him. I don't know why. She wasn't in
on the stick-ups."

Tom-Tom Carey finished making and lighting his
fourth cigarette and stood up.

"Are we teamed?" he asked as he picked up his hat.

"If you turn in Papadopoulos I'll see that you get every
nickel you're entitled to," I replied. "And I'll give you a
clear field—I won't handicap you with too much of an
attempt to keep my eyes on your actions."

He said that was fair enough, told me he was st~~~~
at a hotel in Ellis Street. ~~~ went away.

Calling ~~~~~~~~~~ whall's office on the phone, I
was told th~ ~~~~~~~~~ nformation about his affairs
I should try hi~ ~~~~~ e, some miles south of San
Francisco. I trie~ ~~~~~~ ial voice that said it be-
longed to the but~~~~~ ~~~~ hat Newhall's attorney,
Franklin Ellert, was the *hardly have* ~~~~ ould see. I went over to
Ellert's office.

He was a nervous, irritable old man with a lisp and
eyes that stuck out with blood pressure.

"Is there any reason," I asked pointblank, "for supposing that Newhall's murder was anything more than a
Mexican bandit outburst? Is it likely that he was killed
purposely, and not resisting capture?"

Lawyers don't like to be questioned. This one sputtered and made faces at me and let his eyes stick out still
further and, of course, didn't give me an answer.

"How? How?" he snapped disagreeably. "Exthplain
your meaning, thir!"

He glared at me and then at the desk, pushing papers
around with excited hands, as if he were hunting for a
police whistle. I told my story—told him about Tom-Tom
Carey.

Ellert sputtered some more, demanded, "What the
devil do you mean?" and made a complete jumble of the
papers on his desk.

"I don't mean anything," I growled back. "I'm just
telling you what was said."

"Yeth! Yeth! I know!" He stopped glaring at me and
his voice was less peevish. "But there ith abtholutely no
reathon for thuthpecting anything of the thort. None at all,
thir, none at all!"

"Maybe you're right." I turned to the door. "But I'll
poke into it a little anyway."

"Wait! Wait!" He scrambled out of his chair and ran
around the desk to me. "I think you are mithtaken, but if

e going to invethtigate it I would like to know what dithcover. Perhapth you'd better charge me with your gular fee for whatever ith done, and keep me informed of your progreth. Thatithfactory?"

I said it was, came back to his desk and began to question him. There was, as the lawyer had said, nothing in Newhall's affairs to stir us up. The dead man was several times a millionaire, with most of his money in mines. He had inherited nearly half his money. There was no shady practice, no claim-jumping, no trickery in his past, no enemies. He was a widower with one daughter. She had everything she wanted while he lived, and she and her father had been very fond of one another. He had gone to Mexico with a party of mining men from New York who expected to sell him some property there. They had been attacked by bandits, had driven them off, but Newhall and a geologist named Parker had been killed during the fight.

Back in the office I wrote a telegram to our Los Angeles branch, asking that an operative be sent to Nogales to pry into Newhall's killing and Tom-Tom Carey's affairs. The clerk to whom I gave it to be coded and sent told me the Old Man wanted to see me. I went into his office and was introduced to a short, roly-poly man named Hook.

"Mr. Hook," the Old Man said, "is the proprietor of a restaurant in Sausalito. Last Monday he employed a waitress named Nelly Riley. She told him she had come from Los Angeles. Her description, as Mr. Hook gives it, is quite similar to the description you and Counihan have given of Nancy Regan. Isn't it?" he asked the fat man.

"Absolutely. It's exactly what I read in the papers. She's five feet five inches tall, about, and medium in size, and she's got blue eyes and brown hair, and she's around twenty-one or two, and she's got looks, and the thing that counts most is she's high-hat as the devil—she don't think nothin's good enough for her. Why, when I tried to be a little sociable she told me to keep my 'dirty paws' to

myself. And then I found out she didn't know
nothing about Los Angeles, though she claimed to |
lived there two or three years. I bet you she's the girl, |
right," and he went on talking about how much reward
money he ought to get.

"Are you going back there now?" I asked him.

"Pretty soon. I got to stop and see about some dishes.
Then I'm going back."

"This girl will be working?"

"Yes."

"Then, we'll send a man over with you—one who
knows Nancy Regan."

I called Jack Counihan in from the operatives' room
and introduced him to Hook. They arranged to meet in
half an hour at the ferry and Hook waddled out.

"This Nelly Riley won't be Nancy Regan," I said. "But
we can't afford to pass up even a hundred-to-one chance."

I told Jack and the Old Man about Tom-Tom Carey
and my visit to Ellert's office. The Old Man listened with
his usual polite attentiveness. Young Counihan—only four
months in the man-hunting business—listened with wide
eyes.

"You'd better run along now and meet Hook," I said
when I had finished, leaving the Old Man's office with
Jack. "And if she should be Nancy Regan—grab her and
hang on." We were out of the Old Man's hearing, so I
added, "And for God's sake don't let your youthful gal-
lantry lead you to a poke in the jaw this time. Pretend
you're grown up."

The boy blushed, said, "Go to hell!" adjusted his
necktie, and set off to meet Hook.

I had some reports to write. After I had finished them I
put my feet on my desk, made cavities in a package of
Fatimas and thought about Tom-Tom Carey until six
o'clock. Then I went down to the States for my abalone
chowder and minute steak and home to change clothes
before going out Sea Cliff way to sit in a poker game.

The telephone interrupted my dressing. Jack Counihan
was on the other end.

m in Sausalito. The girl wasn't Nancy, but I've got
of something else. I'm not sure how to handle it. Can
u come over?"

"Is it important enough to cut a poker game for?"

"Yes, it's—I think it's big." He was excited. "I wish
you would come over. I really think it's a lead."

"Where are you?"

"At the ferry there. Not the Golden Gate, the other."

"All right. I'll catch the first boat."

An hour later I walked off the boat in Sausalito. Jack
Counihan pushed through the crowd and began talking,
"Coming down here on my way back—"

"Hold it till we get out of the mob," I advised him. "It
must be tremendous—the eastern point of your collar is
bent."

He mechanically repaired this defect in his otherwise
immaculate costuming while we walked to the street, but
he was too intent on whatever was on his mind to smile.

"Up this way," he said, guiding me around a corner.
"Hook's lunchroom is on the corner. You can take a look at
the girl if you like. She's of the same size and complexion
as Nancy Regan, but that is all. She's a tough little job
who probably was fired for dropping her chewing gum in
the soup the last place she worked."

"All right. That lets her out. Now what's on your
mind?"

"After I saw her I started back to the ferry. A boat came
in while I was still a couple of blocks away. Two men who
must have come in on it came up the street. They were
Greeks, rather young, tough, though ordinarily I shouldn't
have paid much attention to them. But, since Papadopoulos is a Greek, we have been interested in them, of course,
so I looked at these chaps. They were arguing about something as they walked, not talking loud, but scowling at one
another. As they passed me the chap on the gutter side
said to the other, 'I tell him it's been twenty-nine days.'

"Twenty-nine days. I counted back and it's just twenty-
nine days since we started hunting for Papadopoulos. He

is a Greek and these chaps were Greeks. When I fin
counting I turned around and began to follow them. I
took me all the way through the town and up a hill on the
fringe. They went to a little cottage—it couldn't have
more than three rooms—set back in a clearing in the
woods by itself. There was a 'For Sale' sign on it, and no
curtains in the windows, no sign of occupancy—but on the
ground behind the back door there was a wet place, as if a
bucket or pan of water had been thrown out.

"I stayed in the bushes until it got a little darker. Then
I went closer. I could hear people inside, but I couldn't see
anything through the windows. They're boarded up. After
a while the two chaps I had followed came out, saying
something in a language I couldn't understand to whoever
was in the cottage. The cottage door stayed open until the
two men had gone out of sight down the path—so I
couldn't have followed them without being seen by whoever was at the door.

"Then the door was closed and I could hear people
moving around inside—or perhaps only one person—and
could smell cooking, and some smoke came out of the
chimney. I waited and waited and nothing more happened
and I thought I had better get in touch with you."

"Sounds interesting," I agreed.

We were passing under a street light. Jack stopped me
with a hand on my arm and fished something out of his
overcoat pocket.

"Look!" He held it out to me. A charred piece of blue
cloth. It could have been the remains of a woman's hat
that had been three-quarters burned. I looked at it under
the street light and then used my flashlight to examine it
more closely.

"I picked it up behind the cottage while I was nosing
around," Jack said, "and—"

"And Nancy Regan wore a hat of that shade the night
she and Papadopoulos vanished," I finished for him. "On
to the cottage."

We left the street lights behind, climbed the hill,

down into a little valley, turned into a winding
dy path, left that to cut across sod between trees to a
dirt road, trod half a mile of that, and then Jack led the
way along a narrow path that wound through a black
tangle of bushes and small trees. I hoped he knew where
he was going.

"Almost there," he whispered to me.

A man jumped out of the bushes and took me by the
neck.

My hands were in my overcoat pockets—one holding
the flashlight, the other my gun.

I pushed the muzzle of the pocketed gun toward the
man—pulled the trigger.

The shot ruined seventy-five dollars' worth of overcoat
for me. But it took the man away from my neck.

That was lucky. Another man was on my back.

I tried to twist away from him—didn't altogether make
it—felt the edge of a knife along my spine.

That wasn't so lucky—but it was better than getting
the point.

I butted back at his face—missed—kept twisting and
squirming while I brought my hands out of my pockets
and clawed at him.

The blade of his knife came flat against my cheek. I
caught the hand that held it and let myself go down
backward—him under.

He said, "Uh!"

I rolled over, got hands and knees on the ground, was
grazed by a fist, scrambled up.

Fingers dragged at my ankle.

My behavior was ungentlemanly. I kicked the fingers
away—found the man's body—kicked it twice—hard.

Jack's voice whispered my name. I couldn't see him in
the blackness, nor could I see the man I had shot.

"All right here," I told Jack. "How did you come out?"

"Top-hole. Is that all of it?"

"Don't know, but I'm going to risk a peek at what I've
got."

Tilting my flashlight down at the man under my [...]
snapped it on. A thin blond man, his face bloodsmear[...]
his pink-rimmed eyes jerking as he tried to play 'possum i[...]
the glare.

"Come out of it!" I ordered.

A heavy gun went off back in the bush—another,
lighter one. The bullets ripped through the foliage.

I switched off the light, bent to the man on the ground,
knocked him on the top of the head with my gun.

"Crouch down low," I whispered to Jack.

The smaller gun snapped again, twice. It was ahead,
to the left.

I put my mouth to Jack's ear. "We're going to that
damned cottage whether anybody likes it or no. Keep low
and don't do any shooting unless you see what you're
shooting at. Go ahead."

Bending as close to the ground as I could, I followed
Jack up the path. The position stretched the slash in my
back—a scalding pain from between my shoulders almost
to my waist. I could feel blood trickling down over my
hips—or thought I could.

The going was too dark for stealthiness. Things
crackled under our feet, rustled against our shoulders. Our
friends in the bush used their guns. Luckily the sound of
twigs breaking and leaves rustling in pitch blackness isn't
the best of targets. Bullets zipped here and there, but we
didn't stop any of them. Neither did we shoot back. We
halted where the end of the bush left the night a weaker
gray.

"That's it," Jack said about a square shape ahead.

"On the jump," I grunted and lit out for the dark
cottage.

Jack's long slim legs kept him easily at my side as we
raced across the clearing.

A man-shape oozed from behind the blot of the building and his gun began to blink at us. The shots came so
close together that they sounded like one long stuttering
bang.

ulling the youngster with me I flopped, flat to the
ound except where a ragged-edged empty tin-can held
my face up.

From the other side of the building another gun
coughed. From a tree-stem to the right, a third. Jack and I
began to burn powder back at them.

A bullet kicked my mouth full of dirt and pebbles. I
spit mud and cautioned Jack, "You're shooting too high.
Hold it low and pull easy."

A hump showed in the house's dark profile. I sent a
bullet at it.

A man's voice yelled, "Ow-ooh!" and then, lower but
very bitter, "Oh, damn you—damn you!"

For a warm couple of seconds bullets spattered all
around us. Then there was not a sound to spoil the night's
quietness.

When the silence had lasted five minutes, I got myself
up on hands and knees and began to move forward, Jack
following. The ground wasn't made for that sort of work.
Ten foot of it was enough. We stood up and walked the
rest of the way to the building.

"Wait," I whispered, and leaving Jack at one corner of
the building, I circled it, seeing nobody, hearing nothing
but the sounds I made.

We tried the front door. It was locked but rickety.
Bumping it open with my shoulder, I went indoors—flashlight and gun in my fists.

The shack was empty.

Nobody—no furnishings—no traces of either in the
two bare rooms—nothing but bare wooden walls, bare
floor, bare ceiling with a stove-pipe connected to nothing
through it.

Jack and I stood in the middle of the floor, looked at
the emptiness, and cursed the dump from back door to
front for being empty. We hadn't quite finished when feet
sounded outside, a white light beamed on the open doorway, and a cracked voice said, "Hey! You can come out
one at a time—kind of easy-like!"

"Who says so?" I asked, snapping off the flash, moving over close to a side wall.

"A whole goldurned flock of deputy sheriffs," the voice answered.

"Couldn't you push one of 'em in and let us get a look at him?" I asked. "I've been choked and carved and shot at tonight until I haven't got much faith left in anybody's word."

A lanky knock-kneed man with a thin leathery face appeared in the doorway. He showed me a buzzer, I fished out my credentials, and the other deputies came in. There were three of them in all.

"We were driving down the road bound for a little job near the point when we heard the shooting," the lanky one explained. "What's up?"

I told him.

"This shack's been empty a long while," he said when I had finished. "Anybody could have camped in it easy enough. Think it was that Papadopoulos, huh? We'll kind of look around for him and his friends—especially since there's that nice reward money."

We searched the woods and found nobody. The man I had knocked down and the man I shot were both gone.

Jack and I rode back to Sausalito with the deputies. I hunted up a doctor there and had my back bandaged. He said the cut was long but shallow. Then we returned to San Francisco and separated in the direction of our homes.

And thus ended the day's doings.

Here is something that happened next morning. I didn't see it. I heard about it a little before noon and read about it in the papers that afternoon. I didn't know then that I had personal interest in it, but later I did—so I'll put it in here where it happened.

At ten o'clock that morning, into busy Market Street staggered a man who was naked from the top of his battered head to the soles of his blood-stained feet. From

are chest and sides and back, little ribbons of flesh
ng down, dripping blood. His left arm was broken in
two places. The left side of his bald head was smashed in.
An hour later he died in the emergency hospital—without
having said a word to anyone, with the same vacant,
distant look in his eyes.

The police easily ran back the trail of blood drops.
They ended with a red smear in an alley beside a small
hotel just off Market Street. In the hotel the police found
the room from which the man had jumped, fallen or been
thrown. The bed was soggy with blood. On it were torn
and twisted sheets that had been knotted and used for rope.
There was also a towel that had been used as a gag.

The evidence read that the naked man had been
gagged, trussed up and worked on with a knife. The doctors said the ribbons of flesh had been cut loose, not torn
or clawed. After the knife-user had gone away, the naked
man had worked free of his bonds and, probably crazed by
pain, had either jumped or fallen out of the window. The
fall had crushed his skull and broken his arm, but he had
managed to walk a block and a half.

The hotel management said the man had been there
two days. He was registered as H. F. Barrows, City. He
had a black Gladstone bag in which, besides clothes,
shaving implements and so on, the police found a box of
.38 cartridges, a black handkerchief with eyeholes cut in
it, four skeleton keys, a small jimmy and a quantity of
morphine, with a needle and the rest of the kit. Elsewhere
in the room they found the rest of his clothes, a .38 revolver and two quarts of liquor. They didn't find a cent.

The supposition was that Barrows had been a burglar,
and that he had been tied up, tortured and robbed,
probably by pals, between eight and nine that morning.
Nobody knew anything about him. Nobody had seen his
visitor or visitors. The room next to his on the left was
unoccupied. The occupant of the room on the other side
had left for his work in a furniture factory before seven
o'clock.

While this was happening I was at the office, forward in my chair to spare my back, reading reports, of which told how operatives attached to various Continental Detective Agency branches had continued to fail to turn up any indications of the past, present or future whereabouts of Papadopoulos and Nancy Regan. There was nothing novel about these reports—I had been reading similar ones for three weeks.

The Old Man and I went out to luncheon together, and I told him about the previous night's adventures in Sausalito while we ate. His grandfatherly face was as attentive as always, and his smile as politely interested, but when I was half through my story he turned his mild blue eyes from my face to his salad, and he stared at his salad until I had finished talking. Then, still not looking up, he said he was sorry I had been cut. I thanked him and we ate a while.

Finally he looked at me. The mildness and courtesy he habitually wore over his cold-bloodedness were in his face and eyes and voice as he said, "This first indication that Papadopoulos is still alive came immediately after Tom-Tom Carey's arrival."

It was my turn to shift my eyes.

I looked at the roll I was breaking while I said, "Yes."

That afternoon a phone call came in from a woman out in the Mission who had seen some highly mysterious happenings and was sure they had something to do with the well-advertised bank robberies. So I went out to see her and spent most of the afternoon learning that half of her happenings were imaginary and the other half were the efforts of a jealous wife to get the low-down on her husband.

It was nearly six o'clock when I returned to the Agency. A few minutes later Dick Foley called me on the phone. His teeth were chattering so I could hardly get the words. C-c-anyoug-g-get-t-townt-t-tooth-ar-r-rbr-r-spit-tle?"

"What?" I asked, and he said the same thing again, or

se. But by this time I had guessed that he was asking
e if I could get down to the Harbor Hospital.

I told him I could in ten minutes, and with the help of
a taxi I did.

The little Canadian operative met me at the hospital
door. His clothes and hair were dripping wet, but he had
had a shot of whiskey and his teeth had stopped
chattering.

"Damned fool jumped in bay!" he barked as if it were
my fault.

"Angel Grace?"

"Who else was I shadowing? Got on Oakland ferry.
Moved off by self by rail. Thought she was going to throw
something over. Kept eye on her. Bingo! She jumps." Dick
sneezed. "I was goofy enough to jump after her. Held her
up. Were fished out. In there," nodding his wet head
toward the interior of the hospital.

"What happened before she took the ferry?"

"Nothing. Been in joint all day. Straight out to ferry."

"How about yesterday?"

"Apartment all day. Out at night with man. Roadhouse. Home at four. Bad break. Couldn't tail him off."

"What did he look like?"

The man Dick described was Tom-Tom Carey.

"Good," I said. "You'd better beat it home for a hot
bath and some dry rags." I went in to see the near-suicide.

She was lying on her back on a cot, staring at the
ceiling. Her face was pale, but it always was, and her
green eyes were no more sullen than usual. Except that her
short hair was dark with dampness she didn't look as if
anything out of the ordinary had happened.

"You think of the funniest things to do," I said when I
was beside the bed.

She jumped and her face jerked around to me, startled.
Then she recognized me and smiled—a smile that brought
into her face the attractiveness that habitual sullenness

kept out. "You have to keep in practice—sneaking up people?" she asked. "Who told you I was here?"

"Everybody knows it. Your pictures are all over the front pages of the newspapers, with your life history and what you said to the Prince of Wales."

She stopped smiling and looked steadily at me. "I got it!" she exclaimed after a few seconds. "That runt who came in after me was one of your ops—tailing me. Wasn't he?"

"I didn't know anybody had to go in after you," I answered. "I thought you came ashore after you had finished your swim. Didn't you want to land?"

She wouldn't smile. Her eyes began to look at something horrible. "Oh! Why didn't they let me alone?" she wailed, shuddering. "It's a rotten thing, living."

I sat down on a small chair beside the white bed and patted the lump her shoulder made in the sheets. "What was it?" I was surprised at the fatherly tone I achieved. "What did you want to die for, Angel?"

Words that wanted to be said were shiny in her eyes, tugged at muscles in her face, shaped her lips—but that was all. The words she said came out listlessly, but with a reluctant sort of finality. They were, "No. You're law, I'm thief. I'm staying on my side of the fence. Nobody can say—"

"All right! All right!" I surrendered. "But for God's sake don't make me listen to another of those ethical arguments. Is there anything I can do for you?"

"Thanks, no."

"There's nothing you want to tell me?"

She shook her head.

"You're all right now?"

"Yes. I was being shadowed, wasn't I? Or you wouldn't have known about it so soon."

"I'm a detective—I know everything. Be a good girl."

From the hospital I went up to the Hall of Justice, to the police detective bureau. Lieutenant Duff was holding

, the captain's desk. I told him about the Angel's
.

"Got any idea what she was up to?" he wanted to
know when I had finished.

"She's too far off center to figure. I want her vagged."

"Yeah? I thought you wanted her loose so you could
catch her."

"That's about played out now. I'd like to try throwing
her in the can for thirty days. Big Flora is in waiting trial.
The Angel knows Flora was one of the troupe that rubbed
out her Paddy. Maybe Flora don't know the Angel. Let's
see what will come of mixing the two babies for a month."

"Can do," Duff agreed. "This Angel's got no visible
means of support and it's a cinch she's got no business
running around jumping in people's bays. I'll put the word
through."

From the Hall of Justice I went up to the Ellis Street
hotel at which Tom-Tom Carey had told me he was
registered. He was out. I left word that I would be back in
an hour and used that hour to eat. When I returned to the
hotel the tall swarthy man was sitting in the lobby. He
took me up to his room and set out gin, orange juice and
cigars.

"Seen Angel Grace?" I asked.

"Yes, last night. We did the dumps."

"Seen her today?"

"No."

"She jumped in the bay this afternoon."

"The hell she did." He seemed moderately surprised.

"She was fished out. She's O.K."

The shadow in his eyes could have been some slight
disappointment.

"She's a funny sort of kid," he remarked. "I wouldn't
say Paddy didn't show good taste when he picked her, but
she's a queer one!"

"How's the Papadopoulos hunt progressing?"

"It is. But you oughtn't have split on your word. You
halfway promised you wouldn't have me shadowed."

"I'm not the big boss," I apologized. "Sometimes
I want don't fit in with what the headman wants. T
shouldn't bother you much—you can shake him, can
you?"

"Uh-huh. That's what I've been doing. But it's a
damned nuisance jumping in and out of taxis and back
doors."

We talked and drank a few minutes longer, and then I
left Carey's room and hotel, and went to a drug store
telephone booth, where I called Dick Foley's home, and
gave Dick the swarthy man's description and address. "I
don't want you to tail Carey, Dick. I want you to find out
who is trying to tail him—and that shadower is the bird
you're to stick to. The morning will be time enough to
start—get yourself dried out."

And that was the end of that day.

I woke to a disagreeable rainy morning. Maybe it was
the weather; maybe I'd been too frisky the day before;
anyway the slit in my back was like a foot-long boil. I
phoned Dr. Canova, who lived on the floor below me, and
had him look at the cut before he left for his downtown
office. He rebandaged it and told me to take life easy for a
couple of days. It felt better after he had fooled with it,
but I phoned the Agency and told the Old Man that unless
something exciting broke I was going to stay on sick-call
all day.

I spent the day propped up in front of the gas-log,
reading and smoking cigarettes that wouldn't burn right
on account of the weather. That night I used the phone to
organize a poker game, in which I got very little action
one way or the other. In the end I was fifteen dollars
ahead, which was just about five dollars less than enough
to pay for the booze my guests had drunk on me.

My back was better the following day, and so was the
day. I went down to the Agency. There was a memo-
randum on my desk saying Duff had phoned that Angel
Grace Cardigan had been vagged—thirty days in the city
prison. There was a familiar pile of reports from various

...nes on their operatives' inability to pick up anything ...Papadopoulos and Nancy Regan. I was running ...rough these when Dick Foley came in.

"Made him," he reported. "Thirty or thirty-two. Five, six. Hundred, thirty. Sandy hair, complexion. Blue eyes. Thin face, some skin off. Rat. Lives dump in Seventh Street."

"What did he do?"

"Tailed Carey one block. Carey shook him. Hunted for Carey till two in morning. Didn't find him. Went home. Take him again?"

"Go up to his flophouse and find out who he is."

The little Canadian was gone half an hour.

"Sam Arlie," he said when he returned. "Been there six months. Supposed to be barber—when he's working—if ever."

"I've got two guesses about this Arlie," I told Dick. "The first is that he's the gink who carved me in Sausalito the other night. The second is that something's going to happen to him."

It was against Dick's rules to waste words, so he said nothing.

I called Tom-Tom Carey's hotel and got the swarthy man on the wire. "Come over," I invited him. "I've got some news for you."

"As soon as I'm dressed and breakfasted," he promised.

"When Carey leaves here you're to go along behind him," I told Dick after I had hung up. "If Arlie connects with him now, maybe there'll be something doing. Try to see it."

Then I phoned the detective bureau and made a date with Sergeant Hunt to visit Angel Grace Cardigan's apartment. After that I busied myself with paper work until Tommy came in to announce the swarthy man from Nogales.

"The jobbie who's tailing you," I informed him when he had sat down and begun work on a cigarette, "is a barber named Arlie," and I told him where Arlie lived.

"Yes. A slim-faced, sandy lad?"

I gave him the description Dick had given me.

"That's the hombre," Tom-Tom Carey said. "Kₙ anything else about him?"

"No."

"You had Angel Grace vagged."

It was neither an accusation nor a question, so I didn't answer it.

"It's just as well," the tall man went on. "I'd have had to send her away. She was bound to gum things with her foolishness when I got ready to swing the loop."

"That'll be soon?"

"That all depends on how it happens." He stood up, yawned and shook his wide shoulders. "But nobody would starve to death if they decided not to eat any more till I'd got him. I oughtn't have accused you of having me shadowed."

"It didn't spoil my day."

Tom-Tom Carey said, "So long," and sauntered out.

I rode down to the Hall of Justice, picked up Hunt, and we went to the Bush Street apartment house in which Angel Grace Cardigan had lived. The manager—a highly scented fat woman with a hard mouth and soft eyes—already knew her tenant was in the cooler. She willingly took us up to the girl's room.

The Angel wasn't a good housekeeper. Things were clean enough, but upset. The kitchen sink was full of dirty dishes. The folding bed was worse than loosely made up. Clothes and odds and ends of feminine equipment hung over everything from bathroom to kitchen.

We got rid of the landlady and raked the place over thoroughly. We came away knowing all there was to know about the girl's wardrobe, and a lot about her personal habits. But we didn't find anything pointing Papadopoulos-ward.

No report came in on the Carey-Arlie combination that afternoon or evening, though I expected to hear from Dick every minute.

At three o'clock in the morning my bedside phone took

...ar out of the pillows. The voice that came over the
...e was the Canadian op's.

"Exit Arlie," he said.

"R.I.P.?"

"Yep."

"How?"

"Lead."

"Our lad's?"

"Yep."

"Keep till morning?"

"Yep."

"See you at the office," and I went back to sleep.

When I arrived at the Agency at nine o'clock, one of
the clerks had just finished decoding a night letter from
the Los Angeles operative who had been sent over to
Nogales. It was a long telegram, and meaty.

It said that Tom-Tom Carey was well known along the
border. For some six months he had been engaged in over-
the-line traffic—guns going south, booze and probably
dope and immigrants coming north. Just before leaving
there the previous week he had made inquiries concerning
one Hank Barrows. This Hank Barrows' description fit the
H. F. Barrows who had been cut into ribbons, who had
fallen out of the hotel window and died.

The Los Angeles operative hadn't been able to get
much of a line on Barrows, except that he hailed from San
Francisco, had been on the border only a few days and
had apparently returned to San Francisco. The operative
had turned up nothing new on the Newhall killing—the
signs still read that he had been killed resisting capture by
Mexican patriots.

Dick Foley came into my office while I was reading the
news. When I had finished he gave me his contribution to
the history of Tom-Tom Carey.

"Tailed him out of here. To hotel. Arlie on corner.
Eight o'clock, Carey out. Garage. Hire car without driver.
Back hotel. Checked out. Two bags. Out through park.

Arlie after him in flivver. My boat after Arlie.
boulevard. Off crossroad. Dark. Lonely. Arlie steps on
Closes in. Bang! Carey stops. Two guns going. Exit Arlie.
Carey back to city. Hotel Marquis. Registers George F.
Danby, San Diego. Room 622."

"Did Tom-Tom frisk Arlie after he dropped him?"

"No. Didn't touch him."

"So? Take Mickey Linehan with you. Don't let Carey
get out of your sight. I'll get somebody up to relieve you
and Mickey late tonight, if I can, but he's got to be
shadowed twenty-four hours a day until—" I didn't know
what came after that so I stopped talking.

I took Dick's story into the Old Man's office and told it
to him, winding up, "Arlie shot first, according to Foley, so
Carey gets a self-defense on it, but we're getting action at
last and I don't want to do anything to slow it up. So I'd
like to keep what we know about this shooting quiet for a
couple of days. It won't increase our friendship any with
the county sheriff if he finds out what we're doing, but I
think it's worth it."

"If you wish," the Old Man agreed, reaching for his
ringing phone.

He spoke into the instrument and passed it on to me.
Detective-sergeant Hunt was talking, "Flora Brace and
Grace Cardigan crushed out just before daylight. The
chances are they—"

I wasn't in a humor for details. "A clean sneak?" I
asked.

"Not a lead on 'em so far, but—"

"I'll get the details when I see you. Thanks," and I
hung up. "Angel Grace and Big Flora have escaped from
the city prison," I passed the news on to the Old Man.

He smiled courteously, as if at something that didn't
especially concern him. "You were congratulating yourself
on getting action," he murmured.

I turned my scowl to a grin, mumbled, "Well, maybe,"
went back to my office and telephoned Franklin Ellert.
The lisping attorney said he would be glad to see me, so I
went over to his office.

And now, what progreth have you made?" he asked eerly when I was seated beside his desk.

"Some. A man named Barrows was also in Nogales when Newhall was killed, and also came to San Francisco right after. Carey followed Barrows up here. Did you read about the man found walking the streets naked, all cut up?"

"Yeth."

"That was Barrows. Then another man comes into the game—a barber named Arlie. He was spying on Carey. Last night, in a lonely road south of here, Arlie shot at Carey. Carey killed him."

The old lawyer's eyes came out another inch. "What road?" he gasped.

"You want the exact location?"

"Yeth!"

I pulled his phone over, called the Agency, had Dick's report read to me, gave the attorney the information he wanted.

It had an effect on him. He hopped out of his chair. Sweat was shining along the ridges wrinkles made in his face. "Mith Newhall ith down there alone! That path ith only half a mile from her houth!"

I frowned and beat my brains together, but I couldn't make anything out of it. "Suppose I put a man down there to look after her?" I suggested.

"Exthellent!" His worried face cleared until there weren't more than fifty or sixty wrinkles in it. "She would prefer to thtay there during her firth grief over her fatherth death. You will thend a capable man?"

"The Rock of Gibraltar is a leaf in the breeze beside him. Give me a note for him to take down. Andrew MacElroy is his name."

While the lawyer scribbled the note I used his phone again to call the Agency, to tell the operator to get hold of Andy and tell him I wanted him. I ate lunch before I returned to the Agency. Andy was waiting when I got there.

Andy MacElroy was a big boulder of a man—not very

tall, but thick and hard of head and body. A glum, man with no more imagination than an adding machi. I'm not even sure he could read. But I was sure that when Andy was told to do something, he did it and nothing else. He didn't know enough not to.

I gave him the lawyer's note to Miss Newhall, told him where to go and what to do, and Miss Newhall's troubles were off my mind.

Three times that afternoon I heard from Dick Foley and Mickey Linehan. Tom-Tom Carey wasn't doing anything very exciting, though he had bought two boxes of .44 cartridges in a Market Street sporting goods establishment.

The afternoon papers carried photographs of Big Flora Brace and Angel Grace Cardigan, with a story of their escape. The story was as far from the probable facts as newspaper stories generally are. On another page was an account of the discovery of the dead barber in the lonely road. He had been shot in the head and in the chest, four times in all. The county officials' opinion was that he had been killed resisting a stick-up and that the bandits had fled without robbing him.

At five o'clock Tommy Howd came to my door. "That guy Carey wants to see you again," the freckle-faced boy said.

"Shoot him in."

The swarthy man sauntered in, said "Howdy," sat down, and made a brown cigarette. "Got anything special on for tonight?" he asked when he was smoking.

"Nothing I can't put aside for something better. Giving a party?"

"Uh-huh. I had thought of it. A kind of surprise party for Papadoodle. Want to go along?"

It was my turn to say, "Uh-huh."

"I'll pick you up at eleven—Van Ness and Geary," he drawled. "But this has got to be a kind of tight party—just you and me—and him."

"No. There's one more who'll have to be in on it. I'll bring him along."

don't like that." Tom-Tom Carey shook his head
wly, frowning amiably over his cigarette. "You sleuths
oughtn't outnumber me. It ought to be one and one."

"You won't be outnumbered," I explained. "This jobbie
I'm bringing won't be on my side more than yours. And
it'll pay you to keep as sharp an eye on him as I do—and
to see he don't get behind either of us if we can help it."

"Then what do you want to lug him along for?"

"Wheels within wheels," I grinned.

The swarthy man frowned again, less amiably now.
"The hundred and six thousand reward money—I'm not
figuring on sharing that with anybody."

"Right enough," I agreed. "Nobody I bring along will
declare themselves in on it."

"I'll take your word for it." He stood up. "And we've
got to watch this hombre, huh?"

"If we want everything to go all right."

"Suppose he gets in the way—cuts up on us. Can we
put it to him, or do we just say, 'Naughty! Naughty!'"

"He'll have to take his own chances."

"Fair enough." His hard face was good-natured again
as he moved toward the door. "Eleven o'clock at Van Ness
and Geary."

I went back into the operatives' room, where Jack
Counihan was slumped down in a chair reading a
magazine.

"I hope you've thought up something for me to do," he
greeted me. "I'm getting bedsores from sitting around."

"Patience, son, patience—that's what you've got to
learn if you're ever going to be a detective. Why, when I
was a child your age, just starting in with the Agency, I
was lucky—"

"Don't start that," he begged. Then his good-looking
young face got earnest. "I don't see why you keep me
cooped up here. I'm the only one besides you who really
got a good look at Nancy Regan. I should think you would
have me out hunting for her."

"I told the Old Man the same thing," I sympathized.

"But he is afraid to risk something happening to yu says in all his fifty years of gumshoeing he's never s. such a handsome op, besides being a fashion plate and a social butterfly and the heir to millions. His idea is we ought to keep you as a sort of show piece and not let you—"

"Go to hell!" Jack said, all red in the face.

"But I persuaded him to let me take the cotton packing off you tonight," I continued. "So meet me at Van Ness and Geary before eleven o'clock."

"Action?" He was all eagerness.

"Maybe."

"What are we going to do?"

"Bring your little pop-gun along." An idea came into my head and I worded it. "You'd better be all dressed up—evening duds."

"Dinner coat?"

"No—the limit—everything but the high hat. Now for your behavior: you're not supposed to be an op. I'm not sure just what you're supposed to be, but it doesn't make any difference. Tom-Tom Carey will be along. You act as if you were neither my friend nor his—as if you didn't trust either of us. We'll be cagey with you. If anything is asked that you don't know the answer to you fall back on hostility. But don't crowd Carey too far. Got it?"

"I—I think so." He spoke slowly, screwing up his forehead. "I'm to act as if I was going along on the same business as you, but that outside of that we weren't friends. As if I wasn't willing to trust you. That it?"

"Very much. Watch yourself. You'll be swimming in nitroglycerine all the way."

"What is up? Be a good chap and give me some idea."

I grinned up at him. He was a lot taller than I.

"I could," I admitted, "but I'm afraid it would scare you off. So I'd better tell you nothing. Be happy while you can. Eat a good dinner. Lots of condemned folks seem to eat hearty breakfasts of ham and eggs just before they parade out to the rope. Maybe you wouldn't want 'em for dinner, but—"

t five minutes to eleven that night, Tom-Tom Carey ought a black touring car to the corner where Jack and I stood waiting in a fog that was like a damp fur coat.

"Climb in," he ordered as we came to the curb.

I opened the front door and motioned Jack in. He rang up the curtain on his little act, looking coldly at me and opening the rear door.

"I'm going to sit back here," he said bluntly.

"Not a bad idea," and I climbed in beside him.

Carey twisted around in his seat and he and Jack stared at each other for a while. I said nothing, did not introduce them. When the swarthy man had finished sizing the youngster up, he looked from the boy's collar and tie—all of his evening clothes not hidden by his overcoat—to me, grinned, and drawled, "Your friend's a waiter, huh?"

I laughed, because the indignation that darkened the boy's face and popped his mouth open was natural, not part of his acting. I pushed my foot against his. He closed his mouth, said nothing, looked at Tom-Tom Carey and me as if we were specimens of some lower form of animal life.

I grinned back at Carey and asked, "Are we waiting for anything?"

He said we weren't, left off staring at Jack, and put the machine in motion. He drove us out through the park, down the boulevard. Traffic going our way and the other loomed out of and faded into the fog-thick night. Presently we left the city behind and ran out of the fog into clear moonlight. I didn't look at any of the machines running behind us, but I knew that in one of them Dick Foley and Mickey Linehan should be riding.

Tom-Tom Carey swung our car off the boulevard into a road that was smooth and well made, but not much traveled.

"Wasn't a man killed down along here somewhere last night?" I asked.

Carey nodded his head without turning it and, when we had gone another quarter-mile, said, "Right here."

We rode a little slower now, and Carey turned ⌐ lights. In the road that was half moon-silver, half shado⌐ gray, the machine barely crept along for perhaps a mile. We stopped in the shade of tall shrubs that darkened a spot of the road.

"All ashore that's going ashore," Tom-Tom Carey said, and got out of the car.

Jack and I followed him. Carey took off his overcoat and threw it into the machine.

"The place is just around the bend, back from the road," he told us. "Damn this moon! I was counting on fog."

I said nothing, nor did Jack. The boy's face was white and excited.

"We'll beeline it," Carey said, leading the way across the road to a high wire fence.

He went over the fence first, then Jack, then—the sound of someone coming along the road from ahead stopped me. Signalling silence to the two men on the other side of the fence, I made myself small beside a bush. The coming steps were light, quick, feminine.

A girl came into the moonlight just ahead. She was a girl of twenty-something, neither tall nor short, thin nor plump. She was short-skirted, bare-haired, sweatered. Terror was in her white face, in the carriage of her hurrying figure—but something else was there too—more beauty than a middle-aged sleuth was used to seeing.

When she saw Carey's automobile bulking in the shadow, she stopped abruptly, with a gasp that was almost a cry.

I walked forward, saying, "Hello, Nancy Regan."

This time the gasp was a cry. "Oh! Oh!" Then, unless the moonlight was playing tricks, she recognized me and terror began to go away from her. She put both hands out to me, with relief in the gesture.

"Well?" A bearish grumble came from the big boulder of a man who had appeared out of the darkness behind her. "What's all this?"

"Hello, Andy," I greeted the boulder.

"Hullo," MacElroy echoed and stood still.

Andy always did what he was told to do. He had been told to take care of Miss Newhall. I looked at the girl and then at him again.

"Is this Miss Newhall?" I asked.

"Yeah," he rumbled. "I came down like you said, but she told me she didn't want me—wouldn't let me in the house. But you hadn't said anything about coming back. So I just camped outside, moseying around, keeping my eyes on things. And when I seen her shinnying out a window a little while ago, I just went on along behind her to take care of her, like you said I was to do."

Tom-Tom Carey and Jack Counihan came back into the road, crossed it to us. The swarthy man had an automatic in one hand. The girl's eyes were glued on mine. She paid no attention to the others.

"What is it all about?" I asked her.

"I don't know," she babbled, her hands holding on to mine, her face close to mine. "Yes, I'm Ann Newhall. I didn't know. I thought it was fun. And then when I found out it wasn't, I couldn't get out of it."

Tom-Tom Carey grunted and stirred impatiently. Jack Counihan was staring down the road. Andy MacElroy stood stolid in the road, waiting to be told what to do next. The girl never once looked from me to any of these others.

"How did you get in with them?" I demanded. "Talk fast."

I had told the girl to talk fast. She did. For twenty minutes she stood there and turned out words in a chattering stream that had no breaks except where I cut in to keep her from straying from the path I wanted her to follow. It was jumbled, almost incoherent in spots, and not always plausible, but the notion stayed with me throughout that she was trying to tell the truth—most of the time.

And not for a fraction of a second did she turn her gaze from my eyes. It was as if she was afraid to look anywhere else.

This millionaire's daughter had, two months before,

been one of a party of four young people returning late [at] night from some sort of social affair down the coast. Somebody suggested that they stop at a roadhouse along their way—a particularly tough joint. Its toughness was its attraction, of course—toughness was more or less of a novelty to them. They got a first-hand view of it that night, for, nobody knew just how, they found themselves taking part in a row before they had been ten minutes in the dump.

The girl's escort had shamed her by showing an unreasonable amount of cowardice. He had let Red O'Leary turn him over his knee and spank him—and had done nothing about it afterward. The other youth in the party had been not much braver. The girl, insulted by this meekness, had walked across to the red-haired giant who had wrecked her escort, and she had spoken to him loud enough for everybody to hear, "Will you please take me home?"

Red O'Leary was glad to do it. She left him a block or two from her city house. She told him her name was Nancy Regan. He probably doubted it, but he never asked her any questions, pried into her affairs. In spite of the difference in their worlds, a genuine companionship had grown up between them. She liked him. He was so gloriously a roughneck that she saw him as a romantic figure. He was in love with her, knew she was miles above him, and so she had no trouble making him behave so far as she was concerned.

They met often. He took her to all the rowdy holes in the bay district, introduced her to yeggs, gunmen, swindlers, told her wild tales of criminal adventuring. She knew he was a crook, knew he was tied up in the Seamen's National and Golden Gate Trust jobs when they broke. But she saw it all as a sort of theatrical spectacle. She didn't see it as it was.

She woke up the night they were in Larrouy's and were jumped by the crooks that Red had helped Papadopoulos and the others double-cross. But it was too late

ı for her to wriggle clear. She was blown along with
ᵈ to Papadopoulos' hangout after I had shot the big lad.
She saw then what her romantic figures really were—what
she had mixed herself with.

When Papadopoulos escaped, taking her with him, she
was wide awake, cured, through forever with her dangerous trifling with outlaws. So she thought. She thought
Papadopoulos was the little, scary old man he seemed to
be—Flora's slave, a harmless old duffer too near the grave
to have any evil in him. He had been whining and terri-
fied. He begged her not to forsake him, pleaded with her
while tears ran down his withered cheeks, begging her to
hide him from Flora. She took him to her country house
and let him fool around in the garden, safe from prying
eyes. She had no idea that he had known who she was all
along, had guided her into suggesting this arrangement.

Even when the newspapers said he had been the
commander-in-chief of the thug army, when the hundred-
and-six-thousand-dollar reward was offered for his arrest,
she believed in his innocence. He convinced her that Flora
and Red had simply put the blame for the whole thing on
him so they could get off with lighter sentences. He was
such a frightened old gink—who wouldn't have believed
him?

Then her father's death in Mexico had come and grief
had occupied her mind to the exclusion of most other
things until this day, when Big Flora and another girl—
probably Angel Grace Cardigan—had come to the house.
She had been deathly afraid of Big Flora when she had
seen her before. She was more afraid now. And she soon
learned that Papadopoulos was not Flora's slave but her
master. She saw the old buzzard as he really was. But that
wasn't the end of her awakening.

Angel Grace had suddenly tried to kill Papadopoulos.
Flora had overpowered her. Grace, defiant, had told them
she was Paddy's girl. Then she had screamed at Ann
Newhall, "And you, you damned fool, don't you know they
killed your father? Don't you know—?"

Big Flora's fingers, around Angel Grace's th. stopped her words. Flora tied up the Angel and turned the Newhall girl.

"You're in it," she said brusquely. "You're in it up to your neck. You'll play along with us, or else. Here's how it stands, dearie. The old man and I are both due to step off if we're caught. And you'll do the dance with us. I'll see to that. Do what you're told and we'll all come through all right. Get funny and I'll beat holy hell out of you."

The girl didn't remember much after that. She had a dim recollection of going to the door and telling Andy she didn't want his services. She did this mechanically, not even needing to be prompted by the big blonde woman who stood close behind her. Later, in the same fearful daze, she had gone out her bedroom window, down the vine-covered side of the porch, and away from the house, running along the road, not going anywhere, just escaping.

That was what I learned from the girl. She didn't tell me all of it. She told me very little of it in those words. But that is the story I got by combining her words, her manner of telling them, her facial expressions, with what I already knew and what I could guess.

And not once while she talked had her eyes turned from mine. Not once had she shown that she knew there were other men standing in the road with us. She stared into my face with a desperate fixity, as if she was afraid not to, and her hands held mine as if she might sink through the ground if she let go.

"How about your servants?" I asked.

"There aren't any there now."

"Papadopoulos persuaded you to get rid of them?"

"Yes—several days ago."

"Then Papadopoulos, Flora and Angel Grace are alone in the house now?"

"Yes."

"They know you ducked?"

"I don't know. I don't think they do. I had been in my room some time. I don't think they suspected I'd dare do anything but what they told me."

It annoyed me to find I was staring into the girl's eyes as fixedly as she into mine, and that when I wanted to take my gaze away it wasn't easily done. I jerked my eyes away from her, took my hands away.

"The rest of it you can tell me later," I growled, and turned to give Andy MacElroy his orders. "You stay here with Miss Newhall until we get back from the house. Make yourselves comfortable in the car."

The girl put a hand on my arm. "Am I—? Are you—?"

"We're going to turn you over to the police, yes," I assured her.

"No! No!"

"Don't be childish," I begged. "You can't run around with a mob of cutthroats, get yourself tied up in a flock of crimes, and then when you're tripped say, 'Excuse it, please,' and go free. If you tell the whole story in court— including the parts you haven't told me—the chances are you'll get off. But there's no way in God's world for you to escape arrest. Come on," I told Jack and Tom-Tom Carey. "We've got to shake it up if we want to find our folks at home."

Looking back as I climbed the fence, I saw that Andy had put the girl in the car and was getting in himself. "Just a moment," I called to Jack and Carey, who were already starting across the field.

"Thought of something else to kill time," the swarthy man complained.

I went back across the road to the car and spoke quickly and softly to Andy, "Dick Foley and Mickey Linehan should be hanging around the neighborhood. As soon as we're out of sight, hunt 'em up. Turn Miss Newhall over to Dick. Tell him to take her with him and beat it for a phone—rouse the sheriff. Tell Dick he's to turn the girl over to the sheriff, to hold for the San Francisco police. Tell him he's not to give her up to anybody else—not even to me. Got it?"

"Got it."

"All right. After you've told him that and have given him the girl, then you bring Mickey Linehan to the Newhall house as fast as you can make it. We'll likely need the help we can get as soon as we can get it."

"Got you," Andy said.

"What are you up to?" Tom-Tom Carey asked suspiciously when I rejoined Jack and him.

"Detective business."

"I ought to have come down and turned the trick all by myself," he grumbled. "You haven't done a damned thing but waste time since we started."

"I'm not the one that's wasting it now."

He snorted and set out across the field again, Jack and I following him. At the end of the field there was another fence to be climbed. Then we came over a little wooded ridge and the Newhall house lay before us—a large white house, glistening in the moonlight, with yellow rectangles where blinds were down over the windows of lighted rooms. The lighted rooms were on the ground floor. The upper floor was dark. Everything was quiet.

"Damn the moonlight!" Tom-Tom Carey repeated, bringing another automatic out of his clothes so that he now had one in each hand.

Jack started to take his gun out, looked at me, saw I was letting mine rest, let his slide back in his pocket.

Tom-Tom Carey's face was a dark stone mask—slits for eyes, slit for mouth—the grim mask of a manhunter, a mankiller. He was breathing softly, his big chest moving gently. Beside him Jack Counihan looked like an excited schoolboy. His face was ghastly, his eyes all stretched out of shape, and he was breathing like a tirepump. But his grin was genuine, for all the nervousness in it.

"We'll cross to the house on this side," I whispered. "Then one of us can take the front, one the back, and the other can wait till he sees where he's needed most. Right?"

"Right," the swarthy one agreed.

"Wait!" Jack exclaimed. "The girl came down the vines from an upper window. What's the matter with my going up that way? I'm lighter than either of you. If they haven't

...ed her, the window would still be open. Give me ten ...inutes to find the window, get through it, and get myself placed. Then when you attack I'll be there behind them. How's that?" he demanded applause.

"And what if they grab you as soon as you light?" I objected.

"Suppose they do. I can make enough racket for you to hear. You can gallop to the attack while they're busy with me. That'll be just as good."

"Blue hell!" Tom-Tom Carey barked. "What good's all that? The other way's best. One of us at the front door, one at the back, kick 'em in and go in shooting."

"If this new one works, it'll be better," I gave my opinion. "If you want to jump in the furnace, Jack, I won't stop you. I won't cheat you out of your heroics."

"No!" the swarthy man snarled. "Nothing doing!"

"Yes," I contradicted him. "We'll try it. Better take twenty minutes, Jack. That won't give you any time to waste."

He looked at his watch and I at mine, and he turned toward the house.

Tom-Tom Carey, scowling darkly, stood in his way. I cursed and got between the swarthy man and the boy. Jack went around my back and hurried away across the too-bright space between us and the house.

"Keep your feet on the ground," I told Carey. "There are a lot of things to this game you don't know anything about."

"Too damned many!" he snarled, but he let the boy go.

There was no open second-story window on our side of the building. Jack rounded the rear of the house and went out of sight.

A faint rustling sounded behind us. Carey and I spun together. His guns went up. I stretched out an arm across them, pushing them down.

"Don't have a hemorrhage," I cautioned him. "This is just another of the things you don't know about."

The rustling had stopped.

"All right," I called softly.

Mickey Linehan and Andy MacElroy came out of the tree-shadows.

Tom-Tom Carey stuck his face so close to mine that I'd have been scratched if he had forgotten to shave that day.

"You double-crossing—"

"Behave! Behave! A man of your age!" I admonished him. "None of these boys want any of your blood money."

"I don't like this gang stuff," he snarled. "We—"

"We're going to need all the help we can get," I interrupted, looking at my watch. I told the two operatives: "We're going to close in on the house now. Four of us ought to be able to wrap it up snug. You know Papadopoulos, Big Flora and Angel Grace by description. They're in there. Don't take any chances with them—Flora and Papadopoulos are dynamite. Jack Counihan is trying to ease inside now. You two look after the back of the joint. Carey and I will take the front. We'll make the play. You see that nobody leaks out on us. Forward march!"

The swarthy man and I headed for the front porch—a wide porch, grown over with vines on the side, yellowly illuminated now by the light that came through four curtained French windows.

We hadn't taken our first steps across the porch when one of these tall windows moved—opened.

The first thing I saw was Jack Counihan's back.

He was pushing the casement open with a hand and foot, not turning his head.

Beyond the boy—facing him across the brightly lighted room—stood a man and a woman. The man was old, small, scrawny, wrinkled, pitifully frightened—Papadopoulos. I saw he had shaved off his straggly white mustache. The woman was tall, full-bodied, pink-fleshed and yellow-haired—a she-athlete of forty with clear gray eyes set deep in a handsome brutal face—Big Flora Brace. They stood very still, side by side, watching the muzzle of Jack Counihan's gun.

...ile I stood in front of the window looking at this , Tom-Tom Carey, his two guns up, stepped past me, ...g through the tall window to the boy's side. I did not follow him into the room.

Papadopoulos' scary brown eyes darted to the swarthy man's face. Flora's gray ones moved there deliberately, and then looked past him to me.

"Hold it, everybody!" I ordered, and moved away from the window, to the side of the porch where the vines were thinnest.

Leaning out between the vines, so my face was clear in the moonlight, I looked down the side of the building. A shadow in the shadow of the garage could have been a man. I put an arm out in the moonlight and beckoned. The shadow came toward me—Mickey Linehan. Andy MacElroy's head peeped around the back of the house. I beckoned again and he followed Mickey.

I returned to the open window.

Papadopoulos and Flora—a rabbit and a lioness—stood looking at the guns of Carey and Jack. They looked again at me when I appeared, and a smile began to curve the woman's full lips.

Mickey and Andy came up and stood beside me. The woman's smile died grimly.

"Carey," I said, "you and Jack stay as is. Mickey, Andy, go in and take hold of our gifts from God."

When the two operatives stepped through the window—things happened.

Papadopoulos screamed.

Big Flora lunged against him, knocking him at the back door. "Go! Go!" she roared.

Stumbling, staggering, he scrambled across the room.

Flora had a pair of guns—sprung suddenly in her hands. Her big body seemed to fill the room, as if by willpower she had become a giantess. She charged—straight at the guns Jack and Carey held—blotting the back door and the fleeing man from their fire.

A blur to one side was Andy MacElroy moving.

I had a hand on Jack's gun arm.

"Don't shoot," I muttered in his ear.

Flora's guns thundered together. But she was bling. Andy had crashed into her. Had thrown himseu . her legs as a man would throw a boulder.

When Flora tumbled, Tom-Tom Carey stopped waiting.

His first bullet was sent so close past her that it clipped her curled yellow hair. But it went past—caught Papa-dopoulos just as he went through the door. The bullet took him low in the back—smeared him out on the floor.

Carey fired again—again—again—into the prone body.

"It's no use," I growled. "You can't make him any deader."

He chuckled and lowered his guns.

"Four into a hundred and six." All his ill-humor, his grimness was gone. "That's twenty-six thousand, five hundred dollars each of those slugs was worth to me."

Andy and Mickey had wrestled Flora into submission and were hauling her up off the floor.

I looked from them back to the swarthy man, muttering, "It's not all over yet."

"No?" He seemed surprised. "What next?"

"Stay awake and let your conscience guide you," I replied, and turned to the Counihan youngster. "Come along, Jack."

I led the way out through the window and across the porch, where I leaned against the railing. Jack followed and stood in front of me, his gun still in his hand, his face white and tired from nervous tension. Looking over his shoulder, I could see the room we had just quit. Andy and Mickey and Flora sitting between them on a sofa. Carey stood a little to one side, looking curiously at Jack and me. We were in the middle of the band of light that came through the open window. We could see inside—except that Jack's back was that way—and could be seen from there, but our talk couldn't be overheard unless we made it loud.

that was as I wanted it.

Now tell me about it," I ordered Jack.

"Well, I found the open window," the boy began.

"I know all that part," I cut in. "You came in and told your friends—Papadopoulos and Flora—about the girl's escape, and that Carey and I were coming. You advised them to make out you had captured them single-handed. That would draw Carey and me in. With you unsuspected behind us, it would be easy for the three of you to grab the two of us. After that you could stroll down the road and tell Andy I had sent you for the girl. That was a good scheme—except that you didn't know I had Dick and Mickey up my sleeve, didn't know I wouldn't let you get behind me. But all that isn't what I want to know. I want to know why you sold us out—and what you think you're going to do now."

"Are you crazy?" His young face was bewildered, his young eyes horrified. "Or is this some—?"

"Sure, I'm crazy," I confessed. "Wasn't I crazy enough to let you lead me into that trap in Sausalito? But I wasn't too crazy to figure it out afterward. I wasn't too crazy to see that Ann Newhall was afraid to look at you. I'm not crazy enough to think you could have captured Papadopoulos and Flora unless they wanted you to. I'm crazy—but in moderation."

Jack laughed—a reckless young laugh, but too shrill. His eyes didn't laugh with mouth and voice. While he was laughing his eyes looked from me to the gun in his hand and back to me.

"Talk, Jack," I pleaded huskily, putting a hand on his shoulder. "For God's sake why did you do it?"

The boy shut his eyes, gulped, and his shoulders twitched. When his eyes opened they were hard and glittering and full of merry hell. "The worst part of it," he said harshly, moving his shoulder from under my hand, "is that I wasn't a very good crook, was I? I didn't succeed in deluding you."

I said nothing.

"I suppose you've earned your right to the story," went on after a little pause. His voice was conscious, monotonous, as if he was deliberately keeping out of it every tone or accent that might seem to express emotion. He was too young to talk naturally. "I met Ann Newhall three weeks ago, in my own home. She had gone to school with my sisters, though I had never met her before. We knew each other at once, of course—I knew she was Nancy Regan, she knew I was a Continental operative.

"So we went off by ourselves and talked things over. Then she took me to see Papadopoulos. I liked the old boy and he liked me. He showed me how we together could accumulate unheard-of piles of wealth. So there you are. The prospect of all that money completely devastated my morals. I told him about Carey as soon as I had heard from you, and I led you into that trap, as you say. He thought it would be better if you stopped bothering us before you found the connection between Newhall and Papadopoulos.

"After that failure, he wanted me to try again, but I refused to have a hand in any more fiascos. There's nothing sillier than a murder that doesn't come off. Ann Newhall is quite innocent of everything except folly. I don't think she has the slightest suspicion that I have had any part in the dirty work beyond refraining from having everybody arrested. That, my dear Sherlock, about concludes the confession."

I had listened to the boy's story with a great show of sympathetic attentiveness. Now I scowled at him and spoke accusingly, but still not without friendliness.

"Stop spoofing! The money Papadopoulos showed you didn't buy you. You met the girl and were too soft to turn her in. But your vanity—your pride in looking at yourself as a pretty cold proposition—wouldn't let you admit it even to yourself. You had to have a hard-boiled front. So you were meat to Papadopoulos' grinder. He gave you a part you could play to yourself—a super-gentleman-crook, a mastermind, a desperate suave villain, and all that kind mantic garbage. That's the way you went, my son. ou went as far as possible beyond what was needed to save the girl from the hoosegow—just to show the world, but chiefly yourself, that you were not acting through sentimentality, but according to your own reckless desires. There you are. Look at yourself."

Whatever he saw in himself—what I had seen or something else—his face slowly reddened, and he wouldn't look at me. He looked past me at the distant road.

I looked into the lighted room beyond him. Tom-Tom Carey had advanced to the center of the floor, where he stood watching us. I jerked a corner of my mouth at him— a warning.

"Well," the boy began again, but he didn't know what to say after that. He shuffled his feet and kept his eyes from my face.

I stood up straight and got rid of the last trace of my hypocritical sympathy.

"Give me your gun, you lousy rat!" I snarled at him.

He jumped back as if I had hit him. Craziness writhed in his face. He jerked his gun chest-high.

Tom-Tom Carey saw the gun go up. The swarthy man fired twice. Jack Counihan was dead at my feet.

Mickey Linehan fired once. Carey was down on the floor, bleeding from the temple.

I stepped over Jack's body, went into the room, knelt beside the swarthy man. He squirmed, tried to say something, died before he could get it out. I waited until my face was straight before I stood up.

Big Flora was studying me with narrowed gray eyes. I stared back at her.

"I don't get it all yet," she said slowly, "but if you—"

"Where's Angel Grace?" I interrupted.

"Tied to the kitchen table," she informed me, and went on with her thinking aloud. "You've dealt a hand that—"

"Yeah," I said sourly, "I'm another Papadopoulos."

Her big body suddenly quivered. Pain clouded her

handsome brutal face. Two tears came out of her eyelids.

I'm damned if she hadn't loved the old scoundrel!

It was after eight in the morning when I got back to the city. I ate breakfast and then went up to the Agency, where I found the Old Man going through his morning mail.

"It's all over," I told him. "Papadopoulos knew Nancy Regan was Taylor Newhall's heiress. When he needed a hiding place after the bank jobs flopped, he got her to take him down to the Newhall country place. He had two holds on her. She pitied him as a misused old duffer, and she was—even if innocently—an accomplice after the fact in the stick-ups.

"Pretty soon Papa Newhall had to go to Mexico on business. Papadopoulos saw a chance to make something. If Newhall was knocked off, the girl would have millions— and the old thief knew he could take them away from her. He sent Barrows down to the border to buy the murder from some Mexican bandits. Barrows put it over, but talked too much. He told a girl in Nogales that he had to go back 'to Frisco to collect plenty from an old Greek,' and then he'd return and buy her the world. The girl passed the news on to Tom-Tom Carey. Carey put a lot of twos together and got at least a dozen for an answer. He followed Barrows up here.

"Angel Grace was with him the morning he called on Barrows here—to find out if his 'old Greek' really was Papadopoulos, and where he could be found. Barrows was too full of morphine to listen to reason. He was so dope-deadened that even after the dark man began to reason with a knife-blade he had to whittle Barrows all up before he began to feel hurt. The carving sickened Angel Grace. She left, after vainly trying to stop Carey. And when she read in the afternoon papers what a finished job he had made of it, she tried to commit suicide, to stop the images from crawling around in her head.

"Carey got all the information Barrows had, but Bar-

..vs didn't know where Papadopoulos was hiding. Papadopoulos learned of Carey's arrival—you know how he learned. He sent Arlie to stop Carey. Carey wouldn't give the barber a chance—until the swarthy man began to suspect Papadopoulos might be at the Newhall place. He drove down there, letting Arlie follow. As soon as Arlie discovered his destination, Arlie closed in, hell-bent on stopping Carey at any cost. That was what Carey wanted. He gunned Arlie, came back to town, got hold of me, and took me down to help wind things up.

"Meanwhile, Angel Grace, in the cooler, had made friends with Big Flora. She knew Flora but Flora didn't know her. Papadopoulos had arranged a crush-out for Flora. It's always easier for two to escape than one. Flora took the Angel along, took her to Papadopoulos. The Angel went for him, but Flora knocked her for a loop.

"Flora, Angel Grace and Ann Newhall, alias Nancy Regan, are in the county jail," I wound up. "Papadopoulos, Tom-Tom Carey and Jack Counihan are dead."

I stopped talking and lighted a cigarette, taking my time, watching cigarette and match carefully throughout the operation. The Old Man picked up a letter, put it down without reading it, picked up another.

"They were killed in course of making arrests?" His mild voice held nothing but its usual unfathomable politeness.

"Yes. Carey killed Papadopoulos. A little later he shot Jack. Mickey—not knowing—not knowing anything except that the dark man was shooting at Jack and me—we were standing apart talking—shot and killed Carey." The words twisted around my tongue, wouldn't come out straight. "Neither Mickey nor Andy know that Jack— Nobody but you and I know exactly what the thing—exactly what Jack was doing. Flora Brace and Ann Newhall did know, but if we say he was acting on orders all the time, nobody can deny it."

The Old Man nodded his grandfatherly face and smiled, but for the first time in the years I had known him

I knew what he was thinking. He was thinking that if J⸱ had come through alive we would have had the nasty choice between letting him go free or giving the Agency a black eye by advertising the fact that one of our operatives was a crook.

I threw away my cigarette and stood up. The Old Man stood also, and held out a hand to me.

"Thank you," he said.

I took his hand, and I understood him, but I didn't have anything I wanted to confess—even by silence.

"It happened that way," I said deliberately. "I played the cards so we would get the benefit of the breaks—but it just happened that way."

He nodded, smiling benignantly.

"I'm going to take a couple of weeks off," I said from the door. I felt tired, washed out.

DASHIELL HAMMETT was born in St. Mary's County, Maryland, in 1894. He grew up in Philadelphia and Baltimore. He left school at fourteen and held all kinds of jobs thereafter—messenger boy, newsboy, clerk, timekeeper, yardman, machine operator, and stevedore. He finally became an operative for Pinkerton's Detective Agency.

World War I, in which he served as a sergeant, interrupted his sleuthing and injured his health. When he was finally discharged from the last of several hospitals, he resumed detective work. Subsequently he turned to writing, and in the late 1920's he became the unquestioned master of detective-story fiction in America. During World War II, Mr. Hammett again served as a sergeant in the Army, this time for over two years, most of which was spent in the Aleutians. He died in 1961.

VINTAGE HISTORY—WORLD

VINTAGE POLITICAL SCIENCE
AND SOCIAL CRITICISM

VINTAGE POLITICAL SCIENCE
AND SOCIAL CRITICISM